RAGE
OF
SWORDS

DAVID GILMAN

MASTER OF WAR IX

RAGE
OF
SWORDS

HEAD
ZEUS

An Aries Book

First published in the UK in 2025 by Head of Zeus,
part of Bloomsbury Publishing Plc

9 7 5 3 1 2 4 6 8

A catalogue record for this book is available from the British Library.

ISBN (HB): 9781035911752
ISBN (ePub): 9781035911721

Cover design: Simon Michele | Head of Zeus
Map design: Vanessa Periam

Typeset by Siliconchips Services Ltd UK

Printed and bound in Great Britain by Clays Ltd, Elcograf S.p.A.

MIX
Paper | Supporting
responsible forestry
FSC
www.fsc.org   FSC® C018072

Bloomsbury Publishing Plc
50 Bedford Square, London, WC1B 3DP, UK
Bloomsbury Publishing Ireland Limited,
29 Earlsfort Terrace, Dublin 2, D02 AY28, Ireland

HEAD OF ZEUS LTD
5–8 Hardwick Street
London, EC1R 4RG

To find out more about our authors and books
visit www.headofzeus.com
For product safety related questions contact productsafety@bloomsbury.com

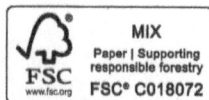

For Suzy

DERBY CITY COUNCIL	
51446478 1	
PETERS	18-Nov-2025
	22.00
	CHADDESDEN

PART ONE
BROTHER TO THE WOLF
5

PART TWO
ROAD OF DEATH
43

PART THREE
DEATH IN THE MONASTERY
133

PART FOUR
A FEAST OF THE DEAD
167

PART FIVE
ILLUMINATRIX
245

PART SIX
ASSASSINATION
295

PART SEVEN
THE TRIAL, THE DUEL & FIRST BLOOD
351

PART EIGHT
La Battaglia del Dosso dell'Aquila
THE BATTLE AT EAGLE'S RIDGE
451

CHARACTER LIST

*SIR THOMAS BLACKSTONE

THOMAS BLACKSTONE'S MEN
*Henry Blackstone
*Hugh Gifford: man-at-arms
*Sir Gilbert Killbere
*Meulon: Norman captain
*John Jacob: Blackstone's squire
*Renfred: German man-at-arms and captain
*Will Longdon: veteran archer and centenar
*Jack Halfpenny: archer and ventenar
*Aicart: Gascon captain
*William Ashford: man-at-arms and captain
*Bullard: man-at-arms
*Walter Mallin: man-at-arms and horsemaster
*John Terrel: man-at-arms
*Arnald Bezián: Gascon man-at-arms
*Girald: Gascon man-at-arms
*Eckehart Brun: German man-at-arms
*Becker: Renfred's scout

ENGLISH MERCENARIES:
*Richard Bell

ENGLISH ROYALTY AND NOBILITY:
Prince Lionel of Antwerp, Duke of Clarence
Lord Edward Despenser, Knight of the Garter

FRENCH ROYALTY:
Charles V: King of France

FRENCH OFFICIALS, NOBILITY AND OTHERS
Simon Bucy: counsellor to the French King
Duke of Berry
Duke of Burgundy
Amadeus VI, Count of Savoy
Countess Bonne of Bourbon: Amadeus's wife
*Onfroi: Norman mercenary
*Guichard: goatherder
*Melisende: Guichard's wife
*Abbot Jean
*Brother Baptiste
*Brother Gabriel

ITALIAN NOBILITY, OFFICIALS AND OTHERS
Galeazzo Visconti: ruler of Milan
Bianca of Savoy: Galeazzo's wife
Violante Visconti: Galeazzo's daughter
Isabelle de Valois: Galeazzo's daughter-in-law
Bernabò Visconti: ruler of Milan
Beatrice Regina della Scala: Bernabò's wife
Cansignorio della Scala: Lord of Verona
John II, Marquis de Montferrat
Secondotto: Montferrat's son
*Messer Salvarini
*Donna Elena Salvarini
*Cardinal Guido Alberti da Viterbo: papal legate
*Maestro Bernini: Veronese lawyer
*Signor Corrado: podestà of Piacenza

*Stefano: servant
*Morena: servant woman
*Salvatore: Milan gate commander
*Mattia Marchesi: man-at-arms and captain
*Mastino Gambetti: man-at-arms
*Abbess Lucia

*Indicates fictional characters

1368

NORTHERN ITALY

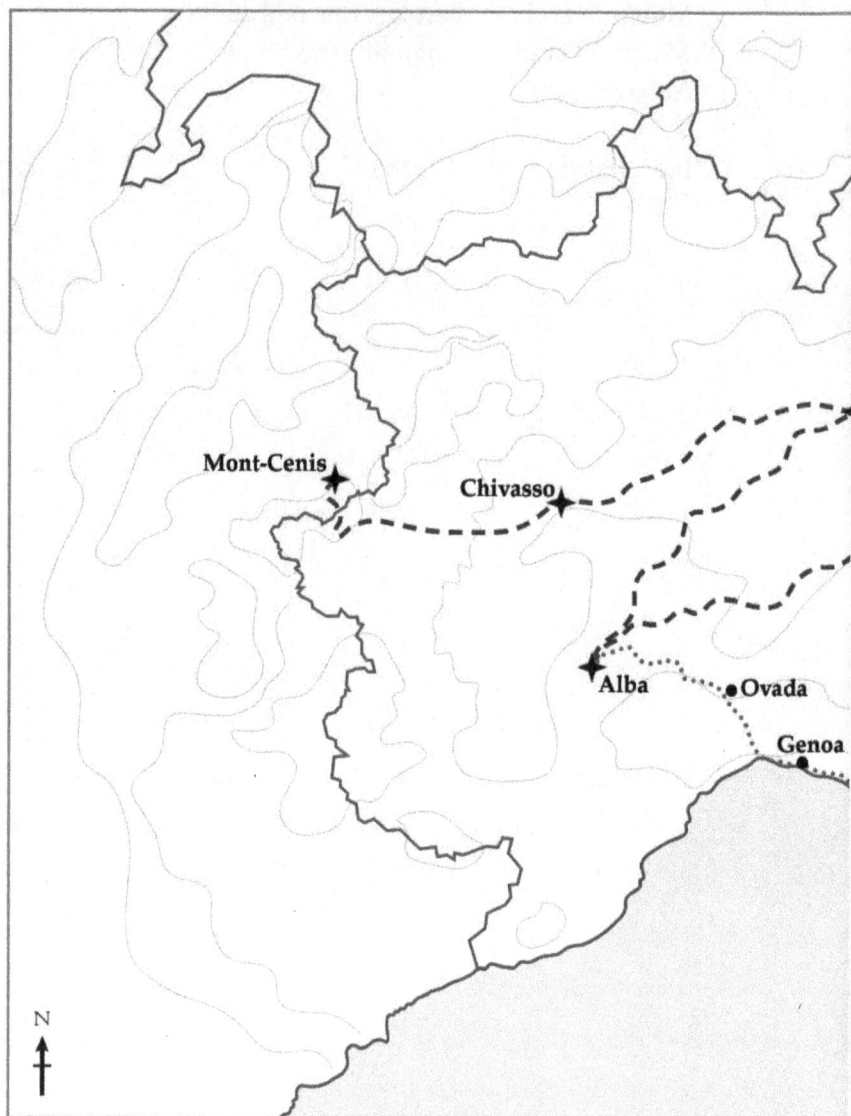

Milan

Verona

Piacenza

La Battaglia del
Dosso dell'Aquila
*(The Battle at
Eagle's Ridge)*

Rapallo

La Spezia

Viareggio

Lucca

Florence

BLACKSTONE AND HENRY'S ROUTE ▬ ▬ ▬

WILLIAM ASHFORD'S ROUTE TO LUCCA ⋯⋯⋯

What is this rage of swords? What is this lust for blood?

Petrarch, *Epistolae familiares (Letters to Friends)*

PROLOGUE

Prince Lionel, Duke of Clarence, the English King's second son, rode into Paris via the Porte Saint-Denis. The twenty-nine-year-old English Prince was on his way to Milan at the head of several hundred men. The lavish hospitality offered in Paris by the French King Charles V would give him a place to rest before continuing onward into Italy, where his father had arranged a marriage between Lionel and Violante, the daughter of Milan's ruler, Galeazzo Visconti.

The French King's valued adviser, Simon Bucy, gazed from his vantage point in the old Palais de la Cité towards the right bank of the River Seine and his monarch's private residence at the Hôtel Saint-Pol. The sound of distant cheering occasionally usurped the babble of voices from the narrow streets below him. The raucous welcome grew ever closer. The commoners did not know why they were cheering for an English prince, but raise their voices they did because it was a pageant and the men and women of Paris liked nothing more than a spectacle.

Bucy admired the political canniness of the Visconti lord. Several years earlier Galeazzo's son had married Isabelle de Valois, the French King's sister. The more-than-generous dowry that the Milanese ruler had paid had helped discharge the extortionate ransom demanded by the English for Jean le Bon, the King's father, after his capture at Poitiers. And now, with this imminent marriage, the Visconti would have a foothold in both kingdoms – and the English would gain a powerful alliance. Bucy tugged his cloak tighter against the cold air sweeping up from the River Seine below the window. The river twisted through the city, reminding him of the Visconti's blazon of a serpent entwining a man and devouring him. Prince Lionel's arrival signalled a fragile peace between the English and the French. Bucy knew it to be a momentary one. The winds of good fortune were finally blowing more than the pungent stench of human waste, fish and meat stalls across the city. They heralded a victory over the English – if his plans came to fruition.

But Bucy knew he had another enemy that could not be defeated. His age. While his mind and instincts were as sharply honed as any assassin's dagger, he knew that the grim reaper's distant horseman was fast approaching, and he would be lucky to have another year left. Two, if the horse went lame. Now was the time to set in place the final act to defeat the old enemy. Nothing mattered more than delivering France from the English.

Fighting them on the ground had proved disastrous for the King's father, but with Bucy's skilful advice the thirty-year-old Charles's slow, determined policy of ridding France of its transgressors was finally bearing fruit. He and Bucy had devised a plan the previous year to send the plague of foreign mercenaries who blighted France into Spain to fight alongside Henry of Trastámara, the bastard half-brother who had seized the crown from Castile's King, Pedro I. Don Pedro had escaped to Aquitaine with the help of that other suppurating wound in France's side, Thomas Blackstone.

The English Prince of Wales and Aquitaine needed Don Pedro as an ally on the southern side of the Pyrenees. Had Blackstone not led an army against Trastámara, who made the cardinal mistake of facing the Master of War on the field of battle, the bastard usurper would still be in power. All had seemed lost once Don Pedro was back on the throne, until he reneged on his agreement to pay the cost of the war. After several months of waiting in Spain, the Prince of Wales had limped home to Bordeaux. Sick and with his coffers empty, he had had to raise taxes, which had driven Gascon lords over to the French King's side. That was the first sign of change in France's favour.

Bucy beckoned a servant to refill his wine glass as he gazed across the city roofs, dabbing a tear from the cold April wind and mentally unfolding the plan he and the King had been secretly working on. A month after the Prince of Wales had left Castile, French arms and money had secretly funded Trastámara's return. Within a year, Trastámara would seize back the Castilian crown, after which he would cross the Pyrenees and forge into Aquitaine while the Castilian fleet attacked Bordeaux. Then Charles would unleash the French army. Another year. No more. And France would crush the sickly Prince of Wales who would have no money in his treasury to fight a war.

But before then, Bucy needed to take one final risk. An act his pious King would not countenance. Stop Prince Lionel's marriage; destroy the strategic accord between England and Milan; deny the Prince of Wales the dowry being paid by the Visconti to his younger brother – two hundred thousand gold florins that could sustain the English in Aquitaine long enough to thwart French plans. Bucy had already sent word to the only man in Italy who could commit such a deed and whose murderous actions in killing the Prince would deflect any blame for French involvement. Bucy was a past master of forward planning. Only when those he marked for death thought themselves safe would the final blow be delivered.

He stepped back into the room from the balcony and closed the window. As he gripped the locking handle, his knuckles whitened. He had set in motion the beginnings of the next war with England and the means to defeat them. What could stop it? Where was the weakness in his plan?

Bucy sighed.

Where was Thomas Blackstone?

PART ONE

BROTHER TO THE WOLF

CHAPTER ONE

Mont Cenis Pass
Savoy
May 1368

The mountain wolf pack ran silently through the night. Moonlight silvered their fur. The alpha male's unerring instinct was guiding him to where the pack would feast. The scent of blood was on the wind.

Thomas Blackstone's eyes flared in the light from the burning huts, a devil incarnate to those he attacked. His gore-streaked face and bared teeth turned his enemies' blood cold, such was the ferocity of the violence he inflicted on them.

Killbere snorted and spat. Lungs heaving, he and the others had run at Blackstone's heels through the darkness to a goatherders' hamlet which had been attacked by an unknown enemy. The settlement was burning. Cracking timbers hurled sparks high into the heavens, guiding the souls of the dead who lay slaughtered along the high plateau. Some of the mercenaries responsible for the killing had escaped Blackstone's onslaught out of the darkness, but a pocket of survivors remained, backed against boulders at the edge of the settlement. As Blackstone stepped closer to the beleaguered routiers, a group of his men went among the dead checking for survivors. The hamlet's inhabitants – man, woman, child and dog – had been brutally assaulted and butchered, some bodies left among rock clefts, others, charred, twisted corpses, in their burnt-out huts. The mercenaries' bestial attack on the hamlet had showed no compassion.

One of the goatherds, Guichard, had run from these routiers when they had first attacked and, by good fortune, had stumbled into Blackstone's camp hours away. Fear-riven, dried blood from a head wound matted into his beard, he had fallen to his knees, thinking Blackstone's men were brigands, and begged not to be slain. John Jacob took him to Blackstone.

Guichard had run ahead of the mounted scar-faced Englishman and his men back to where his hamlet nestled in the high pass. After three hours Blackstone and his troop pulled up, hobbled their horses and ran the last mile with the goatherd, guided by the distant huts' burning thatch. The routiers were readying to leave the destroyed hamlet before first light when Blackstone swooped out of the night.

And now the goatherd had come across the bodies of his children. He bellowed, an animal howl of pain soaring into the wind. Snatching a rock he plunged through Blackstone's men, desiring nothing more than to kill the routiers with his bare hands. Had the biggest man in the ranks not sidestepped and grabbed him, he would have died on the point of a routier's blade. Meulon was strong enough to restrain the man's impulse. Spent, Guichard sank sobbing to his knees.

Blackstone addressed the routier he took to be the leader, whose face snarled in the moonlight. The man uttered a curse in French. He was ready to die. The others with him looked more fearful.

'There are a dozen of you left standing. Some of you are wounded. Surrender and we'll offer you a swift death,' said Blackstone, speaking to the man in his own language.

'English?' he said.

'What difference does it make who kills you?' said Blackstone. 'Were you sent to ambush us? Sixty of you against my hundred was no bargain, if that's what you were paid to do.'

The mercenary shook his head. 'Why would Englishmen come across the mountains into Italy if not to fight for one of the Italian lords? If that's your plan, then join us. I don't care who you are. Thirty of my men escaped. We need others to make up our numbers. Your men will be worth good money.'

The man's answer made it clear that they had not been sent to ambush Blackstone. They were one of the bands of brigands that plagued town, village and hamlet. These were French routiers.

'You sell your sword to the Visconti?' said Killbere.

'If he paid enough.'

'There's someone who pays more?' said Blackstone.

'Stand with us and you'll be welcomed. These Italian lords fight like rats in a sack.' The man grinned. The men he faced were obviously killers. They could be bought. If tempted, they and the survivors could join those who had escaped and have an even stronger company of men whose skills would fetch a better price.

He licked his lips. Give too much information and the man wearing the open bascinet, whose scarred face was etched by the bleak moonlight, might still kill them, take that information and replace him. He had a contract waiting. How far to go with this unsmiling fighter who stared so hard that his gaze sapped courage? 'Della Scala, Lord of Verona. He offers a contract. He means to claim back lost towns that the Visconti seized and the taxes they bring.'

Killbere grunted. 'The Scaligeri are contracting men?' He blew snot from his nose, his sword dangling from its blood knot. 'More murderous bastards on the loose. God's tears, Thomas, we're going back into a hornet's nest.'

The mercenary's confidence ebbed. There were legends about an Englishman who fought in France and Italy. Thomas Blackstone. He swallowed hard. For the first time he stared at Blackstone's shield. The blazon of a gauntleted fist clutching a sword's narrowing blade beneath its crossguard and pommel was faded but still visible. Beneath the gauntlet were words he couldn't make out, so scarred was the shield.

Killbere saw the man trying to read it.

'*Défiant à la Mort*,' said Killbere. 'That's Sir Thomas Blackstone's blazon. Given by the Prince of Wales at the behest of the English King. There'll be no mercy this night. Scum like you have no right to life.' Killbere gripped his sword again.

The routier's courage wavered between helpless resignation and his own belligerent defiance. 'We are all scum, Sir Thomas. Even so, we would wish to be shriven before we die. There's a monastery not five leagues hence.'

'No,' said Blackstone. 'I hang rapists and killers of women and children, but there are no trees here. Yield and we give you a choice of death. A blade or'—he gestured beyond the plateau—'the cliff.'

'Who knows, you might even survive going over the edge,' said Killbere.

'We fight,' said one man, taking a crouched step forward, his eyes wide at the thought of plunging thousands of feet.

Anticipation rippled through Blackstone's ranks.

Somewhere beyond them, wolves howled.

'No!' said their leader, primal fear getting the better of him. He threw down his sword. 'I'll not bleed to death and be torn apart by wolves.'

The others wavered. The eerie cry of the night hunters swept down on the wind. Even Blackstone's men looked uneasily over their shoulder. Wolves were demonic creatures living on the edge between this world and the next whose fangs ripped flesh to devour a man's heart and with it his soul. Every child was warned about them. Pray to God that a wolf never seized them. Pray to God that you die shriven. Or pray to the man holding the blade at your throat to kill you fast and bury you beneath stone.

The leader stared at Blackstone. 'You're no better than those ravening wolves.' He glanced again to where the pack waited. 'No wolf will take my soul,' he said. 'I'll take the plunge.'

The pack howled, each lending its voice, each announcing its intent. The routiers followed their leader's example and threw down their swords.

Blackstone's men seized the mercenaries' weapons. Knife, axe, sword and mace. They kicked their shields aside and dragged them clear of the boulders.

'Your name?' said Blackstone to their leader as he forced him to his knees as Will Longdon and his archers quickly tied the men's wrists behind them.

'Onfroi.'

'You're Norman,' said Blackstone, recognizing the name's origin.

'I am. And a better man than the scum who ride with me.'

'Ah, a better class of scum,' said Killbere. 'We shall give you the respect you need, noble scum.'

The archers hauled the men towards the cliff edge. Some dug their heels in, but the archers' strength in back and arm drove them forward. Some stumbled; others whimpered for mercy. Blackstone pushed Onfroi behind his men and then kicked his legs from under him.

'Let's watch your scum die.'

Blackstone's men needed no signal to push the routiers from the ridge into the darkness below. The clouds briefly smothered the moon but not their screams. The sound of bone hitting rocky outcrops echoed. Blackstone's men peered down as the moonlight reappeared. Broken bodies littered the void.

'Vulture bait,' said Will Longdon with a grin. 'Though they'll probably choke on them.'

Blackstone grabbed a handful of Onfroi's hair, twisting him around, his back to the death ridge and marched him back into the ruined hamlet.

'We will bury the dead villagers and cover them with rock and stones. You commanded men and gave them free rein to butcher and rape. A man must pay dearly for such actions.'

Onfroi struggled but Blackstone's grip easily held him.

'Guichard!' he called.

Meulon helped the distraught goatherd to his feet, who took a few faltering steps forward. Blackstone nodded to Meulon, who slid his throat-cutting knife from his belt and pressed it into the man's hand.

The routier struggled violently but Killbere cuffed him. Onfroi raised his head. 'You offered me a good death,' he accused Blackstone. 'You are no better than any other whoreson of an Englishman.' He snarled, spat and squirmed but to no avail. John Jacob pressed his foot down on the man's bent leg, and Blackstone's grip was that of the stonemason and archer he once was.

'This man will pay for the death of your children. Don't kill him quickly.'

The goatherd had recovered his composure. Killing the man who knelt in front of him was all he could do to avenge his wife and children. He smeared a tear across his cheek.

'How... how should I kill him?' he said falteringly, his hesitation caused by an impediment in his speech.

'Hamstring him and feed him to the wolves,' said Killbere.

Onfroi screamed and begged for mercy. It did him no good. He bellowed as the goatherd severed his tendons. They dragged him to the edge of the hamlet, weeping in pain and terror.

A hundred yards away, the silver-backed wolves sat behind their pack leader. Each wolf knew his place in the order of things. Knew who would be the first to kill and eat.

Onfroi sobbed, pleaded with an unhearing Christ and then tried to squirm in the dirt.

Blackstone and his men turned back to bury the villagers.

Onfroi's screams ended abruptly, leaving only the sound of snuffling and ravenous wolves as they tore into him.

A soul seized by demons.

Killbere spat. 'Our road is paved with the dead.'

'It always will be,' said Blackstone.

CHAPTER TWO

With Blackstone's promise that they would track the surviving routiers and find the women they had seized, Guichard the goatherd ran at an unwavering pace across the scree ahead of Blackstone's men, while they followed on the track that would lead them into Italy. With his children dead and his livelihood destroyed by the mercenaries, he had begged to guide Blackstone through the higher pass in the hope of finding his wife. Once the hamlet's bodies had been laid out and buried beneath rock and stone, four women were found to be missing. His wife one of them. The route was already familiar to Blackstone and Killbere, but they couldn't refuse the man's sincere desire to show his gratitude. And should there be hidden danger ahead, who better to warn them than a man born and bred in the high mountains? Any other man would struggle with the physical exertion, but a man like Guichard could run at altitude through a day and into the night with the stamina of a demon wolf.

'He dances across ground that could turn a man's ankle,' said Killbere as he watched the scrawny man move surefootedly towards the huddle of distant buildings. 'That monastery wasn't here when we went into Italy all those years ago. Unless we took another route.'

As they crested the track, they had a clearer view of the beckoning monastery nestled in the lee of the rockface. 'When I was a boy and a stonemason before you took me to war,' said Blackstone, 'I could cut stone and build a wall ten feet high and a hundred yards long in a month. In eight years, Gilbert, with enough willing hands a man can build a castle. The monks will have been helped by either Amadeus or Montferrat.'

Amadeus VI, the Count of Savoy, controlled this territory until responsibility passed to the Marquis de Montferrat on the other side of the Alps, whose domain extended south of the Po River and east of Turin. It served both men to keep the route open for trade.

'And I'll be damned if they didn't build it on gruel and a crust and lie without blankets on a bare board cot. If you're thinking about food and shelter,' said Killbere, 'that's what they'll offer us. Not a morsel of meat or lard spread on a piece of bread.'

Blackstone glanced over his shoulder. The column of horsemen snaked behind him. Storm clouds gave chase. The wind already carried droplets of rain.

'It makes no sense enduring that storm, Gilbert. Cold, soaked men are slow to react in a fight. And if there are more skinners ahead, then we need to be sharp.'

'I swear, Thomas, you'll make the men as soft as a fat whore's breasts. Are we to coddle them at the teat like mewling infants?' Killbere snorted and swigged from his wineskin.

'Is it not enough to be served thin gruel? No need to turn our men into monks, Gilbert.'

'The devil himself wouldn't take them, let alone a religious order.'

Blackstone gathered his reins as Killbere raised the wineskin again. 'I share your concern, Gilbert. And I know you'll want to set an example for the men. You sleep in the open. I'll make sure the gruel is cold and the crust mouldy for you. The men and I will bed down in the stable with the horses. I would not wish you to be coddled.'

Blackstone spurred the bastard horse into its ungainly canter before Killbere could splutter a reply.

Guichard squatted, waiting patiently at the monastery gate as Blackstone and John Jacob reined in.

'John, have Renfred take his men around the walls. See if there are signs of any other visitors.'

John Jacob wheeled away. Blackstone addressed the goatherd. 'Will you knock, Master Guichard, and rouse the monks from their duties? Tell them Sir Thomas Blackstone and his men seek shelter for the night.'

Guichard grinned. To be asked to announce an English knight was an honour, one likely never to be repeated. He picked up a rock and pounded on the iron-studded gate. He shouted so that a gatekeeper could not fail to hear his words.

Blackstone let his eye follow the line of the building. It had been constructed with thought. Unless belligerent men had scaling ladders twenty feet long, they would not breach the walls by direct assault. The iron-studded gate was wide enough for a cart to pass through. There was no sign of a latrine dribbling human waste through the wall. Such a gap could allow men to cut away the mortar and widen it to force an entry. The monks would have built a latrine pit and used their waste on whatever vegetables they grew. He had little doubt there would be cisterns inside to collect rain and run-off from the high peaks when the melt came. Everything suggested that a fighting man had assisted the monks in constructing their modest yet formidable place, where they practised the Rule of Saint Benedict: obedience, self-sufficiency and hard labour. And, he reasoned, a place where fighting men could support the monks if the Mont Cenis Pass needed to be held against an enemy.

A secondary door behind the iron-studded gate creaked.

An inspection hatch opened. A face appeared, pressing into the gap. The monk had not scraped the whiskers from his face for a few days. His eyes darted nervously from the goatherd to the men on horseback.

'We have nothing,' said the monk. 'We are a poor house of God. Be gone before the Lord brings down the heavens and smites you for the evil you are!'

'We seek only the comfort of shelter for the night,' said Blackstone.

'The only comfort you'll get is when you bend over and offer your arse to the devil.' With that, the monk slammed closed the hatch.

The goatherd looked abashed, as if he had been the one to cause offence. He looked at Blackstone.

'Foul-mouthed monks need to feel a flagellant's lash or the toe of my boot,' said Will Longdon.

'They sound like brothel-keepers not monks,' said Meulon.

'And how would you know the difference?' Longdon replied. 'Your name is etched on every whore's bedchamber wall but your knees have never smoothed a church's stone floor.'

'Again,' said Blackstone to the goatherd.

Guichard slammed the stone against the door in a furious summons. No response came. By this time, Killbere had brought his horse alongside Blackstone. 'Are they not opening the gate?'

'They don't want us inside,' said John Jacob.

'Damned monks. Do they have enough coin to deny travellers shelter? You would think their hospitality came out of their own purse,' he fumed. 'Curse them, Thomas, let's move on and find what shelter we can.'

Blackstone was about to nudge the bastard horse away when Renfred returned.

'There are tracks on the far side. Mostly washed away by the storms. Thirty horses, perhaps more. Looks as though they had left through a postern gate in the far corner. The tracks lead away from us.' Renfred pinched a drip of cold snot from the end of his nose. 'But I'm not so sure.' He grinned. 'You walk horses in backwards and you fool anyone who's looking for you.'

'It's near enough noon, Sir Thomas,' said John Jacob. 'Three hours ago, I think we would have heard the terce bell ring carry across the pass, even with the wind behind us. There's no sound in the mountains except for the wind, and now there's no bell calling them to midday prayer. Monks always lay down their tools when the sext bell chimes. Silent prayer is one thing, but they would never silence the bell.'

Blackstone heeled the bastard horse away from the gate. 'We'll turn our backs. They'll have someone watching from a spy hole.' He beckoned the goatherd. 'Guichard. Take us beyond those rocks. Find a place for us to shelter from that storm.'

Guichard glanced at the darkening sky in the distance. With the knowledge of a man born and raised in the high peaks, he darted off at an angle away from where Blackstone had pointed.

'Do you think the slaughter has turned his mind?' said Killbere, watching the light-footed goatherd run in the wrong direction.

'He couldn't be blamed if it had,' Blackstone said, spurring his horse to follow the survivor. 'But he knows the mountains. We'll follow him.'

'At least he's downwind,' said Killbere. 'A man who shared his hut with goats does not have the fragrance of a spring flower.'

'And we hardly bathe in rose petals,' said Will Longdon.

The horses cantered after Blackstone. 'And an archer's nose is too close to his armpit,' said Killbere over his shoulder.

Guichard led them on a circuitous route to reach a jagged outcrop of boulders a mile beyond the monastery. He waited as the horsemen crested the track and then eased their mounts down into a perfect shelter against the approaching storm. If they had followed Blackstone's original plan, they would have approached down a steep scree-covered slope that would have made horses lose their footing. Guichard stood expectantly as he offered his refuge against the squall: an amphitheatre set into the mountainside. For want of a deeper gouge into the rock face, it would have been a vast cave. The overhang was high, the sides of the rocks giving depth on either side of a flat area large enough to embrace Blackstone's hundred men and horses.

'Guichard, you've done well.'

The goatherd grinned and pointed beyond the shelter. 'The wind will... will turn the rain and strike the back of the overhang. We'll be dry here. I can help... with... with the horses.'

Blackstone nodded and pointed at the men who were dismounting and settling their horses, nudging them into some kind of order as each mount was hobbled.

'Walter?' he called.

One of the older men raised his head. Walter Mallin had ridden across France with Henry Blackstone when he was searching for his father the year before. Like the four other men-at-arms who had survived that journey, he had been a mercenary in his time, abandoned by a king's army when no longer needed to fight. His age might slow him in battle, but his natural skill with horses gave him value to Blackstone.

'Use this man with the horses,' Blackstone told him. Mallin raised a hand in acknowledgement. Blackstone turned to Guichard. 'Go to that man. He'll put you to use. You have already served me well.'

'What else could I do, lord? You avenged my family. I am... am in your debt.'

The goatherd scurried off towards Walter Mallin.

'Another mouth to feed, Thomas,' said Killbere.

'We have enough. He's a humble man who wants nothing more than a distraction from his grief and the companionship of the men who struck down his enemy.'

'Then we see out the storm and find a way to breach the monastery tonight?'

Blackstone pushed his shoulder against the bastard horse, keeping a tight hold on the opposite rein to stop its yellow teeth snapping at him. As he held the beast against the rock face John Jacob hobbled its legs.

'There'll be nothing to see tonight. We need daylight to see what's over the walls. A rope, a hook, a man on top. Whoever's in there will be sheltering from the storm and have their heads down from the rain. We'll use it to our advantage. I'll take Renfred, John, Meulon and a man to climb. Who?'

'Henry, if he were here.'

Blackstone faltered for a second. 'Well, he isn't. Jack?'

Killbere didn't pursue discussing Henry's whereabouts. 'Aye, I'd have Halfpenny on the rope but you'll put Will Longdon's nose out of joint if you do. Will can clamber up a wall as good as any man. And those scab-arsed Welsh archers among his men will see it for what it is. The man who commands them taking the biggest risk. They're high walls. You need an archer's strength to haul yourself up them.'

'All right. If, as I suspect, there are skinners inside – those that escaped from Guichard's village – they'll have the monks imprisoned along with their hostages. If there's no sign of lookouts and we can find a way in, I'll send Will back. Be ready. Captains can choose their own men, but keep the archers back. Their bows are no good in this weather and I'll not risk them in a close-quarter fight.'

Blackstone grinned and laid a hand on his friend's shoulder. 'You might still get your wish to be cold and wet.'

CHAPTER THREE

Blackstone led the way back across the undulating ground towards the monastery. Guichard had begged Blackstone to let him accompany the men in case they discovered his wife inside the walls. Blackstone had assured him that if routiers had seized the monastery, the goatherd would be part of the assault to rescue her. Not that Blackstone knew how they would launch an attack on such a formidable place when he gave that assurance.

John Jacob, Meulon and Renfred stood with Blackstone, their necks craned as Will Longdon coiled the rope. He stepped back from the wall and swung the scaling hook in ever-lengthening arcs, and then hurled it. It clattered ten feet from the top of the wall and fell back, forcing the men to avoid its clattering descent.

'We could always knock on the gate again and tell them we are trying to scale the walls,' said Meulon. 'If they didn't hear that, they are drunk or deaf.'

Longdon rewound the rope. The storm was reaching them. Hard rain stung their face and hands.

'Why don't you throw and I climb?' said the archer.

'You just need to get a bigger swing,' Meulon told him. 'Stand back another yard and then throw.'

Will Longdon looked from the disapproving Meulon to Blackstone and John Jacob. Blackstone shrugged and nodded. Longdon sighed, stepped back another yard, craned his neck and began swinging the rope through his hand and then hurled the scaling hook upward. The iron claw gripped the top of the wall. Longdon's look challenged Meulon, who nodded. He grinned. 'Now you can climb. I'll take the slack.'

'It's a long climb, Meulon. Why don't I stand on your shoulders, then I'd be halfway there, you lumbering oaf.'

'Why don't I just kick your arse over the wall?'

Blackstone hunched against the biting rain. 'Get on with it, Will.'

Longdon gripped the rope and began to haul himself up, the soles of his boots slipping on the wet stone as Meulon took the strain of the rope so that his friend had the best chance of purchase. There was no doubt it was a hard climb.

John Jacob wiped a hand across his face. 'Let's hope there are no crossbowmen on night watch. Will's going to be an easy target when he straddles the wall.'

'There's no reason for them to have a night watch,' said Renfred. 'Those skinners will be heavy with wine and having sport with the women they seized. Which plays into our hands.'

'That's if they're inside and those tracks didn't mean that they had already left.'

Blackstone kept his eyes on Will Longdon as he neared the top of the wall. 'Those who escaped our attack will seek shelter. I think Renfred is right. The bastards are inside.'

Meulon's strength had kept the rope taut allowing Longdon to haul himself onto the top stonework. 'He's there, Sir Thomas.'

'All right. Renfred, send a couple of men to check the back wall and keep watch. I don't want anyone coming outside for any reason. If the walls had walkways along the ramparts, I wager they'd have someone up there. John, keep your eyes on the front corner.'

*

Will Longdon lay flat across the top of the wall. Peering down into the interior of the monastery, he could see the vast space of the courtyard. Gloom blanketed the buildings, deepened by the hard rain cast down from the mountaintops by the wind behind him. He shielded his eyes and let them adjust to the dull light of the yard below. He could make out raised beds where seasonable vegetables would be grown, and the dark shapes of horses in the open-fronted stables to his left along the opposite wall. Beyond the well in the middle of the courtyard, timber and stone-built cloisters ran the length of the barely visible wall. The monks' cells were likely behind the arched walkway. Between the stables and the cloisters stood what he took to be a small chapel, its stumpy belfry housing the chapel bell. The following wind moaned across the walls and he could hear the faintest sound of the clapper nudging the bell. The courtyard, as far as he could see, was empty. If there were any guards, they were under the cloisters out of the downpour that was becoming ever harder as storm clouds got closer.

Longdon wiped rain from his face and, half crawling, half straddling the wall, moved another ten feet to his left to seek out the postern gate. If it was unguarded, then it gave Blackstone the way in: it being more easily opened than the huge main gate. The breadth of the wall allowed him to stand. He balanced, arms outstretched for a moment against the buffeting wind, and then stepped more confidently along its top.

'What is he doing?' said Meulon.

'He's pointing at something,' said Blackstone.

'He's showing us where the postern gate is,' said Renfred.

'He's a damned fool,' Meulon added. 'We know where the gate is.'

'Aye, but he's showing us that he can get close to it and open it,' Blackstone said. 'Renfred, get back to Sir Gilbert, bring up the men. If there were guards inside, then Will wouldn't be showing himself.'

Blackstone unstrapped Wolf Sword and slung its belt across his shoulders. He grasped the rope with one hand. 'Even from here, I can see where the wall takes the brunt of the weather. There'll be loose mortar between the stones. If he slips, he's a dead man and we can forget any attack. Take the slack, Meulon. John, be ready in case the alarm is raised. If the skinners dare to come out from behind their walls, Sir Gilbert will deal with them.'

'And if they don't, and you're standing up there in plain sight?'

Blackstone reached above his head with his other hand and took his weight on the rope. 'It will be time to learn to fly.'

CHAPTER FOUR

As Blackstone heaved himself upward he felt the old injury in his leg protest from the effort. After the Battle of Nájera the previous year he had fought a master swordsman in order to save his son's life. Will Longdon's surgical skills, crude as they were, had stopped him bleeding to death from the deep wound, but the damaged muscle complained when Blackstone made demands of it and he knew it could prove to be a weakness.

He clawed himself over the top of the wall, stared down into the mist-laden courtyard. He tested his leg and then clambered onto his feet, crouching against the buffeting storm. He saw Will Longdon half turn and point to where the postern gate was undefended. Blackstone peered down to Meulon and John Jacob and signalled them to go around the walls. Steadying himself, he half knelt and began hauling up the rope. As he gathered the loops over his arm he squinted into the rain to try and make out if Killbere had left the shelter of the overhanging rocks. If he and Longdon were going to climb down and open the postern gate the men needed to be in place.

Will Longdon had watched and waited until Blackstone was ready to join him. Blackstone coiled the rope over his arm and grabbed the iron hook, then he raised a hand, meaning for

Longdon to wait, but Longdon mistook the gesture to mean he should carry on along the wall.

Blackstone cursed under his breath. It was becoming difficult for a man his size to keep his balance against the swirling storm but he had to reach Longdon before the bowman got to the place where the wall was at its weakest. Casting caution aside, he stood, braced his weak leg and took long strides along the top of the wall, fighting the clawing wind and rain.

Longdon was half crouched, trying not to be blown off; he faltered, found his balance, edged forward. Blackstone's voice carried on the wind. He gripped the wall, half turned, saw Blackstone striding behind him, swaying left and right in his attempt to stay upright. What was he saying? The wall? Something about the wall. Longdon peered through the rain. There was no obstacle that he could see. He would wait. Blackstone was closer now; Longdon twisted to face him. His left foot pressed into the stonework; it wobbled, mortar crumbling; Longdon twisted sideways, arms flailing, knowing in that moment he was going to fall into the courtyard. He had the presence of mind not to cry out. He saw Blackstone throwing himself harshly forward onto the stonework, reaching out to snatch at his centenar. Longdon managed to grab the top of the crumbling wall as Blackstone's fist curled over his forearm. Blackstone grimaced as Longdon's weight pulled his face into the stone. Both men stared hard at each other. Longdon shook his head. The wall was crumbling under their combined weight. Blackstone saw rather than heard him say, *Let me go.*

Blackstone shook his head. He fought the weight, hunched his back, got one knee beneath him and tugged on Longdon's arm, soaking wet, slipping from his grasp. Longdon's fingertips still gripped the top of the wall. Blackstone shrugged the rope off his other shoulder. The bitterly cold rain and wind froze his hand, his back muscles felt as though they were being torn and he was losing his grip on Longdon. Blackstone twisted and managed to shake free the rope which snaked into the space between the two men.

Blackstone's right hand still gripped Longdon's left arm and there was only one way for Longdon to reach the rope. Blackstone would have to release him and let his archer make a wild and desperate grab for the rope. And if he succeeded he would plunge down the face of the wall until Blackstone could seize the rope and take his weight. And doing that could rip the flesh from Blackstone's hands. The two men locked gazes. Longdon nodded. He understood. Blackstone saw Longdon's fingers lose their grip as the mortar gave way beneath the piece of stone. He gave the final muscle-straining heave and let go of Longdon's arm. The archer scrambled wildly for a few seconds before his fingers caught the rope. He plummeted downwards. The rope hissed against the stonework. Blackstone threw his weight onto the rope, snatched at the iron hook and threw it onto the outside of the wall. Iron and stone fought. The hook caught. Longdon jerked to a halt five feet from the ground. He dropped down, crouched against the courtyard's inner wall, bruised from his rapid descent but otherwise uninjured. He stared up. Blackstone's actions had saved him.

Blackstone squinted into the storm. Distant grey shapes bent against the rain and uneven ground were making their way towards the monastery. Blackstone gripped the rope, tested that the hook had caught in the uneven stonework, then got to his feet, bent his body and pushed his back away from the wall using his legs to brace against the stonework. Yet again the old wound deep in his thigh muscle complained. Gripping the soaking rope he fed it through his hands as he walked slowly down the wall. The five-foot drop was because the iron hook had used that length to embed itself into the outside wall. Blackstone released his grip and jumped. Ignoring the burning pain in his leg, he gripped Longdon's shoulder, checked he was all right. The archer nodded. No words were needed as Blackstone edged along the length of the wall towards the postern gate. They failed to notice the canvas lean-to that sat in the shadows of the wall: a hastily constructed shelter for one of the killers ordered to keep watch. But what need was there when the weather was so foul and the walls so high? A wineskin offered comfort until his night-watch replacement came.

Blackstone and Longdon stopped where they were as a man staggered out, his cowl pulled up against the storm. Eyes down he fumbled for the wall, pressed the palm of his hand against it, and loosened his hose. Steam plumed from his piss. He snorted and spat. Blackstone and Longdon were ten paces away. If he finished and turned to his left he would see them. Blackstone and Longdon didn't move. They watched him go through the process of re-dressing himself. The man shrugged, spat again, squared his shoulders from the relief of emptying his bladder and, turning left, saw two men facing the wall, each with one hand extended to steady themselves as if they too were relieving themselves. The routier grunted, his words lost in the swirling rain. Were these his replacements? Neither man he saw responded. He wiped a grubby hand across his face and approached them. If they were taking a piss they were taking a long time about it. He stood next to the bigger of the two men and laid a hand on his shoulder. Blackstone turned. The routier frowned. He didn't know this man. The second he saw the dangling rope – too late for him to cry out a warning – fierce pain ripped into his throat. A blinding light seared into his brain. He was dead before his knees sagged and he fell against Blackstone, who pulled free his archer's knife from the corpse.

Longdon was already two strides beyond the dead man. Knife in hand, he pulled back the canvas flap. It was empty. Blackstone hauled the man's body and threw it back under the canvas.

'If he was a guard, then they might not miss him for a while.'

The postern gate was fifty yards away and the way ahead was clear. By the time they threw the bolts on the postern gate, Meulon and John Jacob would be there to lead Killbere and the men inside and then the killing would begin.

Blackstone ran at Longdon's side.

Thirty yards from the gate.

A thunderclap shook the ground beneath their feet. It felt as though the Almighty had deemed their efforts unworthy and decided to test them further. Time stopped. Horses broke loose and men were suddenly spilling into the yard. Sword or mace in hand they bawled their displeasure at the two intruders.

'The gate! I'll hold them!' Blackstone knew he couldn't run as fast as the stocky bowman. He had to buy Longdon time enough to open the gate and pray that Killbere had covered the ground in time.

The routiers had spilled out from various doors and were scattered across the yard. So far there were at least twenty. Three were close to Blackstone. One lurched ahead of him towards Longdon as his two companions closed in. The first made a wild undisciplined slash of his sword that was easily sidestepped. Blackstone put the man between him and the other. The slashing motion took the man off balance, exposing his right side. Blackstone rammed Wolf Sword below the man's rib cage into his liver. His scream was choked by another crack of lightning piercing the clouds and striking the mountains. A horse whinnied, eyes wide in terror, making the second attacker falter. An easy kill. Blackstone parried his strike, twisted Wolf Sword's honed blade and struck down with sufficient force to cleave apart the man's shoulder and neck muscle. His sword dropped. He staggered. Blackstone rammed his sword's pommel into the man's face. He went down. Several others had now gained ground and blocked Blackstone's path. He snatched the dead man's sword. A blade in each hand, he took five paces rapidly backwards, felt the wall against his back. Now they had to come at him front on. He parried a chained mace, let it wrap around the spare sword. The man yanked it free. Blackstone spun on his right foot. Changed angle. Cut through the man's arm as he tried to shake free the sword from the mace's chain. He staggered into the man next to him: a fat-bellied brute who looked as though he could crush a tree with his bare hands. Food stained his beard: sated with food, he was too slow. Blackstone eviscerated him, letting him drop to his knees screaming as he tried to hold in his intestines.

Blackstone knew he would soon be overwhelmed. He dared a glance at Longdon who had just killed the man that had bypassed Blackstone. Another swung an axe. Longdon ducked, rammed his knife into the man's groin, ignored his howl of pain and turned back to the postern gate's bolt.

A terrified horse barged into two of the men encircling Blackstone. It broke their attack. Blackstone went forward, taking the fight to them. One of them was the man who had pretended to be a monk at the gate. They fell back. Slipped in the mud. Died where they fell. Routiers dodged wheeling horses as they tried to find space to attack Blackstone, who pressed on, sidestepping a panicked horse, crouched and scythed another man's legs from beneath him. Just then a bellowing roar, louder than rolling thunder, distracted the routiers. Blackstone glanced at the postern gate. Meulon's huge frame stormed into the fray, John Jacob at his heels.

War dogs had been unleashed. The two fighting men and the stocky archer at their side stabbed, cut and thrust, leaving bodies to be trampled by horses. That one man had been able to stem the routiers' attack sent a shock wave through the surviving skinners. The six men left standing backed into the cloisters as the scar-faced man and the three equally ferocious killers strode towards them.

A horse bolted through the postern gate; the others, still panicked, followed. The courtyard was empty except for twenty-two dead men. Soaked, standing in bloodied puddles and mud, the routiers stared hollow-eyed at the four merciless swordsmen who had killed so many of their comrades. They knew surrender was not an option.

One man lunged desperately forward. It triggered the others to go with him. Six against four.

They died quickly.

CHAPTER FIVE

Meulon, John Jacob and Will Longdon pushed their shoulders against the doors leading inside the monastery to search for any of those taken at the goatherders' hamlet.

Killbere, sword in hand, led forty of Blackstone's men through the postern gate. They spread quickly across the courtyard, ready for any assault. It was apparent as they stepped over the fallen dead that Blackstone and the others had needed no help to subdue the routiers who had taken over the monastery.

Killbere sheathed his sword and trudged through the mud to where Blackstone stood under the cloisters.

'You bring me across broken ground, slick with rain, enough to twist a man's legs from beneath him, to a place of the dead. Was there any need to send Renfred to drag us into the storm?' said Killbere, spitting the phlegm from his breathless lungs.

'You took so long to get here, I thought you were walking. I couldn't wait. Besides, you wanted to get wet and cold and I had no wish to deprive you.'

Killbere grunted. He pointed to the top of Blackstone's arm. 'You're bleeding.'

'It's nothing. A skinner's lucky cut when he went down.'

Killbere took in the killing ground. 'Where are the monks?'

'Will and Meulon are inside with John looking for them. They'll be alive, locked up somewhere. These bastards weren't likely to feed themselves. They'll have used the monks for that.'

Guichard stepped around the dead, uncertain whether his wife might be among them. He looked to where Killbere stood with Blackstone and the women being ushered into the cloisters by John Jacob. Guichard cried out.

'Melisende!'

One woman looked up sharply. She was older than the goatherd but in small communities men and women often had little choice whom they married. Blackstone and Killbere watched as the woman uncertainly stepped forward, away from the others. She stopped at the edge of the cloisters. It seemed a reunion with her husband did not warrant her going out into the mud and rain. Guichard stood in front of her, extending his arms.

'Don't touch me!' she hissed.

The rebuke was as good as a slap in the face. Guichard looked stunned.

Before he could utter a reply, tears sprang into her eyes, her face an echo of pain. 'You ran! Our children are dead. You abandoned us.'

Guichard looked in disbelief. 'No, no. I was... struck down. By the time I came to, they had already seized you. I couldn't find the children. So I ran, hope... hoping our Lord Amadeus's men might be patrolling the pass. This is Sir Thomas Blackstone. He killed those who raided us. I only learnt of our children's fate when I returned. Forgive me, Melisende. I beg you... to... to forgive me. I did what I could to find you.'

Blackstone's men stood silently watching Guichard's humiliation. It was a pitiful sight. He sank to his knees in the mud, face raised to the rain, hands outstretched imploringly.

Melisende stared down at him with contempt. 'Now I am too old to bear children. Everything I lived for has been taken from me.'

Blackstone touched the woman's arm and turned her to face him. 'You falsely accuse your husband of cowardice. He ran to save you and your children. He took his revenge on the man responsible for the attack. Were it not for his bravery in taking us across the mountains in search of you and the others'—Blackstone raised his eyes to include the other dishevelled women—'you would either be dead or sold into slavery when the routiers took you into Italy. You should ask forgiveness for doubting him. Embrace him, woman. He has courage. More than that, he clearly loves you.'

Her face crumpled, her mind and heart in conflict. Her anger was compounded by her treatment at the hands of the killers. She and the other women had been raped. Need she confess this? Was it obvious? What man would want to take back a woman used by other men? She looked at the women huddled behind her. They understood. One shook her head, then cast her eyes down.

Melisende looked at her husband. She dragged her forearm across her face, wiping away tears and snot. Heaving a sigh, she nodded, but turned back inside.

'Go to her, Guichard,' said Blackstone. 'Be careful what you say. Words can hurt. And take your time. The words will come more easily.'

Guichard stood and wiped his hands across his goatskin tunic. He stepped after her, but faltered at Blackstone's side. His voice dropped to barely a whisper. 'My thanks, lord, for your kindness.' He nodded. 'I know what happened to her. Nothing will be said of it.'

The women parted, letting him follow his wife.

'John, send a couple of men inside to find blankets for these women.'

As John Jacob picked two of the men, Longdon and Meulon ushered out two dozen monks. Some bore the signs of a beating.

'Who leads you?' Blackstone said.

A short, gaunt-looking figure, bent with age or pain, raised his hand. 'I am Brother Jean.'

Like the other monks, he wore a dark habit with a cowl resting on his shoulders. The wool was grubby from their rough treatment at the hands of the skinners. His emblems of office and authority, a ring and a cross that would have hung on a cord around his chest, were missing.

'Brother Jean,' said Blackstone, 'have any in your community been killed?'

'We have not. We have been beaten and robbed of what little we had, but our lives were spared.'

'You have food?'

'Yes.' He stared at the dead lying in the mud. 'They brought and slaughtered some goats.'

'Then have your brothers in the kitchen prepare food for these women and my men.'

The abbot's chin lifted as if Blackstone had pushed a dagger under his chin. 'Women cannot be served in the refectory.'

'They can today, Brother Abbot. And have your infirmarian set out his lotions and bandages for any of them who are wounded.'

'That is a request too far. A monk will not attend to a woman in such a way.'

'It's not a request,' said Blackstone.

The abbot's jaw opened and closed, his hands clenched. Before he replied to Blackstone's demands, one of the women spoke out.

'Lord, if we are given what we need, we will attend to ourselves.'

Blackstone considered her intervention as the abbot raised his eyes, head nodding.

'That is acceptable.'

'Very well,' said Blackstone. 'I have another sixty men who need shelter and food. We will take the stables. The women will take your dormitory. They will eat where they choose.'

It was the abbot's turn for his words to falter. 'But... but... where are the brothers to sleep?'

Killbere pointed at the abbot. 'Brother Jean, you will have no time for sleep. Food and medicine are needed and then a night's prayers thanking the Almighty for Sir Thomas Blackstone saving your wrinkled skin.'

It was a meagre price to pay. The abbot nodded and turned back to usher his fellow brothers back inside.

Blackstone addressed the women. 'Choose the place to attend to yourselves. Then eat and rest. Tomorrow you can go back and try to salvage what you can of your lives.'

The women bowed their heads and shuffled away.

'God's tears, Thomas. Now I know why I never married or took to the cloistered life.'

'Neither marriage nor the Church would have you, Gilbert.'

'Then I have the hand of good fortune on my shoulder.' He kicked free some mud from his boots on the edge of the cloister. 'Thank God it's not Friday. At least we get to eat meat.'

CHAPTER SIX

Killbere's stomach growled.

The rich smell of cooked meat and gravy clung to the air like the steam from the monastery kitchen. Blackstone and his captains had taken over the refectory, each captain ensuring his men received enough food before they themselves got their meal. Longdon and Halfpenny's archers sat with their backs against the walls; men-at-arms squatted where they could. The room was crowded. Half of Blackstone's men ate in the stables. Benches at the monks' usual table were kept for the captured women. Blackstone and Killbere shared their table with John Jacob.

As the light faded after the storm, the monks insisted on praying for the dead mercenaries' souls – their mutterings joined by Killbere's scorn for the souls of murdering whoresons.

Walter Mallin, hunched into his cloak, approached Blackstone and Killbere.

'Sir Thomas?'

'Walter. The men have food and wine?'

'They do. Horses are secure. Half in the stables – there's only room enough for fifty mounts. The rest are hobbled and in the lee of the walls. They'll be dry enough should rain come in. Your horse is where you put him in the corner of the stables. Away from the others. I got a feed bag on him.'

The three men at the table exchanged glances.

'You still have fingers on your hand?' said Killbere.

'Aye. You have to be quick with him, mind. He's a bugger with them teeth. I reckon I'll get him on my side in time.'

'Then when that day comes, Walter, I'll make sure you are found a softer bed.'

'I'm slow, Sir Thomas, I know that, but I'm not a damned woman fearful of sleeping with the beasts. It's where I find my comfort, thank you.'

Admonished, Blackstone raised a hand in apology. Mallin's skill with horses was a welcome addition to the fighting men. 'Then what is it?'

'You killed twenty-eight men but they had thirty horses in the stables before they all bolted.'

'What's this, Walter, you have a divining stick now?' said Killbere.

'No, Sir Gilbert, I've eyes in my head. There are thirty piles of horseshit where their beasts were tethered. Don't take a bloody scholar to see what's there to see.'

The older man had put the veteran knight in his place. Killbere stiffened at the affront and the horsemaster quickly apologized.

'Begging your pardon, Sir Gilbert.'

'None needed, Walter,' said Blackstone with a glance at Killbere in case the veteran knight was in an unforgiving mood. 'Go and make sure you get your share of supper.'

'Aye, already arranged by Renfred and his lads.' He turned away, heading back to the stables.

'If there are two men loose then they'll be hard-pressed to get very far. They must have got behind us when we were fighting in the yard and escaped through the gate,' said John Jacob.

Killbere pierced a piece of goat meat. 'Perhaps we should have Walter keeping count when you do the killing, Thomas,' he said, dribbling gravy into his beard.

'We were busy and you were slow to arrive,' Blackstone said.

'True enough. But you could have waited. Foolish to take on those odds without the rest of the lads.'

'We were sharpening our appetite,' said John Jacob.

Killbere grunted and concentrated on his food. 'Did the monks clean your wound or should Longdon take out his needle and thread?' said Killbere, pointing his knife at Blackstone's arm.

The day's fighting had left some with minor wounds needing treatment in the monastery's infirmary. Blackstone had waited until the others had been attended to before offering his own slashed arm to be cleaned, packed with herbal potion and bound. The grizzled old monk remained silent, barely raising his eyes. He knew his ministrations must have caused the Englishman discomfort, but the man who towered over him made no complaint.

Finally, the monk had nodded to indicate he was finished. And then, unexpectedly, he grasped Blackstone's hands in his own, bent his head and pressed his lips against them. He raised his face to Blackstone. Tears welled in his eyes. Then he had turned away and returned to his other duties.

Blackstone related what had happened to Killbere. For a moment, he told the veteran, he didn't understand the monk's gratitude. Religious orders condemned violence and despised those who inflicted it. Their cloistered life offered spiritual calm and sanctuary from men such as Blackstone.

'Aye, they're useless to any man in a fight,' said Killbere, 'but the monk knew when the hand of an angel had touched their shoulders. No harm in showing gratitude to men who inflict death to protect their way of life.' He wiped his plate clean, belched and stood, intending to get another helping. 'We have our uses, Thomas. Just as they have theirs. I swear I am more partial to goat meat than I thought possible.'

Blackstone's gaze followed Killbere's path to where a novice monk stood with an urn of stew and baked bread. He saw the goatherd Guichard sitting awkwardly with his back against the wall near the women and his wife, watching the women whisper among themselves. Blackstone caught his eye and beckoned him to the table. He crouched on one knee in front of Blackstone. John Jacob understood Blackstone's irritation at the subservient gesture. 'A man cannot be blamed for his birthright, Sir Thomas,' he said, knowing the goatherd would not understand.

'Guichard, get to your feet,' said Blackstone.

He stood, hands clasped in front of him.

Blackstone twisted on the bench to face him. 'We leave tomorrow and you must take your wife and those women back. You understand that, don't you?'

'I do, lord.'

'Is there a life there for you to salvage?'

'My children and the others are buried there. We can rebuild... our huts and... and there will still be goats grazing freely in the high pastures. Yes, lord, it is where we belong.'

Blackstone nodded towards the women at the far end of the refectory. 'And what about them? Will they find new husbands?'

Guichard looked at the women survivors. 'They are still young enough to bear children. There are other herdsmen scattered in the lower hills. They'll come and take up where these women lost their men.'

'The monks have laid out the dead in the courtyard. The weather promises to be clear and dry tomorrow. You and the women take what you want from them. Each man will have a purse and weapons. Strip those and what clothing you want from them. It's little recompense for your loss, but you can use and trade what you take.'

'Thank you, Sir Thomas.'

'Guichard, your wife, Melisende, she will mourn her children and that bitterness can poison relations between a man and a woman. Only you can decide how to deal with this, but I suggest you make sure that she and the others see you as a man they can turn to.' Blackstone felt the inadequacy of his words. 'What I'm saying, Guichard, is take control. Lead them. Do not be cowed by a woman's bitterness.'

The goatherd nodded. His look of consternation at the task at hand showed he understood what was expected of him.

'All men are vulnerable when they drop their guard. And love for a woman can make you do that.' Then Blackstone sighed. 'Ignore what I say, Guichard. I am no more knowledgeable about such matters than anyone else.' He nodded his dismissal.

Blackstone turned back to his food. A glance at John Jacob, who shrugged helplessly.

'Some things remain a mystery to us all, Sir Thomas.'

Killbere squeezed back onto the bench with a more meagre plate of food than he had expected. 'Did you offer the poor wretch booty from the killing?'

'I did.'

Killbere grunted. 'Well, his stolen goats have fed enough of us, so it's only right he gets some reward. Though it looks as though I got the remains of the scrawniest.' He slurped some gravy, wiped his mouth, and looked at Blackstone and his squire. 'We are too few to take on any force larger than those skinners, Thomas. If Verona plans to fight Milan then the men della Scala is recruiting will be gathering somewhere in their hundreds. And we must hope we are not caught between the Scaligeri and the Visconti. We must pick our fights carefully if we are to do what has been asked of us.'

Blackstone pushed his plate away. A few scraps of bread and meat remained. Killbere dragged the plate over. 'The pass can be threatened because while we were fighting in Spain, Amadeus took himself off on crusade against the Ottomans and his men stopped patrolling the pass. Now that he's returned, he is in Paris to escort Prince Lionel across into Italy. That is why we were tasked to go ahead and ensure the route is safe. Then, when our work is done, we wait beyond the walls of Milan and escort the Prince and the gold from the dowry home.'

'Sir Thomas,' said John Jacob, 'Prince Lionel has an entourage of hundreds. Would they not have a better chance of dealing with the skinners?'

Killbere finished scraping both plates. 'John's got a point, Thomas. If the Prince is being escorted by Amadeus and the men led by Edward Despenser, we should let them deal with any marauders.'

'Except most of those who ride with the Prince are courtiers. Despenser is a decent enough commander, otherwise the King would not have charged him with the Prince's safety. But I'll wager less than half of those with him would be any use in a fight.'

'Thomas,' said Killbere. 'Let's be realistic. The trouble lies less on the pass with whoreson skinners than in the Visconti territory. There is more enmity there than on any battlefield. And there are those who would benefit from the Prince not returning home with either his child bride or the two hundred thousand gold florins.'

'Sir Gilbert's right,' said John Jacob. 'Despenser knows how to fight a battle, but he has never had to deal with the Visconti. And even the King was uncertain if everyone in the Prince's entourage could be trusted. Given time and money, the Visconti could corrupt the Pope. Hard to know what safety could be guaranteed for the Prince.'

They fell silent. Blackstone looked uncertain; a guilty secret was written all over his face. Killbere understood.

He sighed. 'God's tears, Thomas, Henry?'

'Yes.'

'Then Henry did not travel to the university in Bologna as you made him promise.'

'He's with the Prince in Paris?' said John Jacob.

Killbere looked on in disbelief. 'Damned if you didn't let the boy have his way to do more than continue his studies.'

'That and the King's desire to have someone he trusts close to his son.'

'Then Henry rides at Lionel's side?' said John Jacob.

'At his back, more like. Only the Prince knows his true identity. He travels under his mother's name. I couldn't deny him. I still bear the guilt of duping him and taking his place in the fight.'

Killbere and Jacob knew very well that if Blackstone had not taken his son's place in the deadly challenge made by a master swordsman seeking revenge for Henry killing the man's father when they were in France after the Battle of Nájera, then Henry would be dead. Blackstone's wounds bore witness to the killer's skills with a blade.

'Thomas, no matter how close he is to the Prince, if he is recognized or even the name de Sainteny becomes known he could be taken. Or worse. Are you forgetting the King of France ordered him seized last year as a hostage to snare you?'

'I have not forgotten, but the truth is we know the French did not intend for Henry to be harmed.'

'But if discovered the lad could still be taken by the French,' said John Jacob.

'It's doubtful Henry will even be noticed. And he could have no greater protection than travelling as part of Prince Lionel's household,' Blackstone said, placating them.

Killbere and John Jacob fell silent.

'A gamble, Thomas,' said Killbere.

Blackstone spread his palms in a helpless gesture. 'He has to prove himself and reclaim his pride. He will be our eyes and ears in the Prince's camp. If we hear of danger to the Prince, then we act.'

Killbere swallowed the last of the wine in his flask. 'So once again we are to protect a prince of the realm.'

'I am the King's Master of War, Gilbert. We go where we are sent. We do our duty as the King sees fit.'

They pushed back the bench. It was time to rest before the journey into Italy and uncertainty.

'You know, Thomas, these monks owe you their lives,' said

Killbere. 'It would not be wrong to ask the abbot to hold a mass and pray for young Henry's safety. If he remains unscathed in Paris and during the journey to Milan, he's the one who will ride into the heart of the whore. The Visconti have a vendetta against any Blackstone. And if they discover Henry's identity, he faces a harsh death.' He laid a hand on Blackstone's shoulder. 'Even I will go down on my knees and pray for the lad's well-being.'

'Thank you, Gilbert, but I fear the Almighty will turn a deaf ear to the likes of us. Other than having Hugh Gifford with him, the boy's on his own.'

PART TWO

ROAD OF DEATH

CHAPTER SEVEN

Paris
April 1368

Church bells rang their greeting as Henry Blackstone rode with Hugh Gifford at his side as part of Prince Lionel's entourage, clattering through the streets buffeted by a cheering throng of Parisians. The city and the French King were hosting an honoured guest, yet the peace between England and France hung by a mere thread.

For the past three years the man-at-arms Gifford had been serving as Henry's bodyguard, placed by the King of England as a reward for Blackstone saving the Prince of Wales during a previous assassination attempt. Henry had been studying at Oxford University, using his mother's name de Sainteny for his own protection, but a year ago the lure of fighting at his father's side against the Spanish had proven too strong. Absconding from his studies, he had travelled across France to join his father and that recklessness had resulted in Thomas Blackstone being gravely wounded in a duel against a master swordsman who had been determined to kill Henry. That his father had taken his place in combat had damaged Henry's pride and honour.

But then came a chance for redemption. The English incursion into Spain that year had bled the Treasury dry. As his father slowly recovered from his wounds, Henry begged for the chance to redeem his reputation by being part of the King's plan to secure the dowry for his second son Lionel's marriage to the daughter of the wealthy Visconti. It was this gold – two hundred thousand florins – that Thomas Blackstone was to secure and return to the Treasury. A chance for the English to hold Aquitaine against France in a war that would surely come again.

The horses' hooves clattered along the cobbled road. Prince Lionel and his impressive cavalcade had been met by the French Dukes of Burgundy and Berry on the road at Saint-Denis. Henry grinned at Gifford.

'Is this not a sight, Hugh? There is no place like Paris,' he called, his voice raised against the clamour of cheering crowds, the rhythmic hooves and ringing bells.

Gifford had been struck mute once they entered the city's walls, leaving the tilled fields of the *faubourg* behind. Everywhere he looked, Paris assailed his senses. 'You know this place?'

Henry's sense of excitement was impossible to ignore. He nodded. 'I'll tell you later. Look!'

He pointed away from the main boulevard over the heads of the crowds to the labyrinth of narrow streets. Huge shop signs declared the shop-owner's wares. A swinging sign bore the image of a tooth.

'You can get your teeth pulled, Hugh, or buy a new tunic. Boots, hats, cloth, silk, women and drink. It's all here. It makes Oxford look little more than a jumble of ancient houses surrounded by fields.'

'It's a place for a nobleman with *livres* to spend. Not a common man-at-arms like me, Master Henry.' Gifford caught a whiff of human excrement that fouled the narrow streets. 'And shit stinks, no matter how grand a city.'

The deafening noise made it impossible to converse easily. Gifford fell silent and absorbed the sights around him. He knew Henry Blackstone had to deny his father's name for his own good on this journey: should his true identity be revealed, being a part of Prince Lionel's private household would be risky. Henry still had a recklessness in him. A compulsion to prove himself. Even though, in Hugh's mind and in those of Blackstone's men, there was no need. The lad did not lack courage. And his willingness to take needless risks sometimes caused admiration, but it also raised concerns for his safety. To protect Henry against anyone who wished him ill was one thing; to protect him from himself another.

Several horses ahead rode the unmistakable figure of Lionel, Duke of Clarence. The Prince was wearing his best armour and riding his favourite bay stallion. The animal was taller at the withers than most horses: the Prince's great height meant riding a smaller mount risked him looking foolish. Lionel's stature and flowing fair hair drew attention to his regal bearing. He was almost seven feet tall, which made the Prince even taller than Thomas Blackstone.

And the taller a man was, thought the short sturdy bodyguard, the further he had to fall. If anyone hoped to stop this marriage alliance between English royalty and the wealthy Visconti, the Prince made a fine target. Gifford watched the flaxen-haired man raise a gauntleted hand in greeting to the crowds. Pennons fluttered behind him. A royal bodyguard of knights led by Edward Despenser flanked him half a length back. Much good this would do him, Gifford thought, should the Prince become the target for an assassin. No, he corrected himself, a killer would not lunge from the crowd, they would come as someone familiar. A servant, a knight, a lover or companion. And come at night.

And that worried Gifford. Henry Blackstone's true identity was known only to the Prince, who had requested Henry remain close, to be his eyes and ears among the jostling servants and courtiers. And that meant there were times when Gifford could not be there to do his duty.

If anyone struck in the privacy of the Prince's quarters, it was likely the only person between him and an assassin would be Henry.

★

Simon Bucy waited at the Louvre with other courtiers as Prince Lionel and his retinue hove into sight. The column of horsemen with the tall Prince flanked by the Dukes of Burgundy and Berry was, he admitted to himself, a magnificent sight. The power and the glory of the English throne proclaimed itself as if King Edward in person rode through the city he once tried to conquer. An ambition he still held, of course. The English King had never relinquished his claim to the French throne and the Prince's shield, pennons and flags reflected as much. His blazon, with the first and fourth quarter displaying the fleur-de-lys of France against blue and the second and third quarters the golden English lions against a red field, seemed almost a taunt.

Ten paces in front of Bucy, the French King Charles V stood ready to receive his guest. As the Prince drew closer, the man Bucy had served so loyally half turned his thin frame and glanced towards his counsellor. In the weak April sunshine, Charles looked paler than usual, giving the impression of a sickly man, which was close to the truth. He had rid himself of the various ailments he endured when regent but remained plagued with a fistula and abscess on his left arm, and gout weakened his right arm. A frail man to look at, but the glance he gave Bucy was one of pure cunning. That was his strength. Guile. He used it to deflect doubt. To show the old enemy he bore no ill will. Hosting the Prince with such a lavish welcome and then to honour him with feasts and gifts for the next two days allayed any suspicion the English King might have that Charles was contemplating a resurgence of war. A long-term strategy to achieve this was already in place.

It warmed Bucy to know the look was meant for him, and only him. A shared conspiracy. But then Bucy felt his chest tighten. The warmth cooled. Had he misinterpreted that knowing glance? Had the French King discovered Bucy's own plan to thwart this marriage? The old lawyer reasoned it out.

Logically, he could not know. Bucy's dealings with the few involved in his plan was stringently bound with secrecy. No future scribe would ever have the facts of what really happened to this English Prince. But Bucy knew that no plan was ever perfect and if his plot were discovered, such intimacy with the King would end. Perhaps violently.

He watched his King greet the Prince, who dipped his head respectfully. He did not bend low or take the knee. An English prince would only acknowledge the French King's divine right to rule. Not to inherit the earth. Bucy swore he saw a glint of contempt flicker from the Prince's eyes. A trick of the light perhaps? Perhaps not. At least the knight who dismounted and stood three paces behind the Prince bowed more respectfully. The man's coat of arms was as glorious in its colours as those of the man he served. Two black bars cutting across his shield from the top quarter over red and silver fields declared the man's heritage. He was Edward Despenser, the Prince's deputy commander. And the others? Bucy's gaze swept across the blazons, some of which he recognized. What's more he knew that many of those who stared down from horseback would have fought the Kings of France on the bloody fields of Crécy and Poitiers. Thirty-one years of bloodshed and now his monarch who was not yet born when the war started welcomed them as guests in the very heart of France. It felt wrong. And it spurred his determination to see his plan through.

Several horses behind the Prince's escort a high-spirited mount fought its bit. Someone cursed and called out for the rider, named as Henry, to rein in the beast. The horse was expertly brought under control by a young man who bore arms Bucy did not recognize. But being so close to the Prince suggested he was part of Lionel's retinue. What was it about him that pricked at a memory? The name was common enough. The old lawyer could not place him but he had a sense that he had seen him before... and if he had, why was it that the man rode with the Prince?

CHAPTER EIGHT

Ostlers and stable hands guided the knights' horses into the vast stables in and around the Louvre and the Hôtel Saint-Pol. Only those in the Prince's immediate retinue would have their mounts cared for close to where the Prince was accommodated in the sumptuous rooms of the Louvre. The hundreds of other high-bred horses were taken to the many stables across that part of the city which had secured prodigious amounts of fodder beyond the usual demands made on a city that used animals for daily haulage.

Henry pressed a couple of deniers into a stable lad's hand. No one else in such an entitled entourage would consider paying a boy, little more than an urchin who slept in the stables, to ensure their horse received extra hay. Thomas Blackstone had taught his son well. Give a care and a coin to those who serve you and you will be well served.

Gifford strode after Henry, who left the stables heading towards the River Seine. 'You give a lad money from our own purse when we need it. Our stipend from the Prince is not the most generous.'

Henry grinned as he increased his pace. 'Our horses benefit, Hugh, as do we.'

'Are we racing for a reason? I'm hungry and my arse aches from today's ride. Food and drink is what I want – in the nearest tavern. It's some time yet until sundown and supper.'

They reached the banks of the river and Henry made for a bridge. 'You are blessed with seeing one of the great cities of the world and all you can think of is your stomach. Can't you feel the surge of the place? Look around you. How it bustles. Listen to these people. Listen to them shouting and cursing, cajoling and promising. They have goods to sell. Our stomachs can wait.'

'Then my stomach needs to be told when food and drink might pass my lips. It believes my throat has been cut.'

'Twenty minutes. No more. You can feast on bread and mutton and drink rough red wine to strip what sheen your belt buckle might once have had. I will be busy.'

Gifford spat out phlegm as he struggled to keep up with the younger man's boundless energy. 'Where are you going – and why does it have to be so fast?'

'Time is short, Hugh. I have to be with the Prince when he retires, which means I have just these few hours and what time I can steal tomorrow. And then we are back on the road.' He crossed the wooden bridge, stepping aside to let a man hauling a handcart pass. An impatient owner whipping his overladen donkey shouted ahead, cursing the less wealthy villein obliged to haul his own load. There was no polite society at street level. Graceful gestures and courtly behaviour, as false as they might be, resided elsewhere. Henry pointed vaguely towards an island in the Seine and the wooden tower of a cathedral on the far side. 'Notre-Dame. They'll be building it for ever.' He pressed back against the rail to let past some women bearing baskets on their backs: heavy loads requiring a strap around their forehead. 'It's the Île de la Cité. See that building, Hugh? That's where the King once lived. That's where I was presented to the Dauphin as he was then. This is the Paris my father brought me to eight years ago.'

'Dammit, Master Henry, you cannot just throw such

information at me. I know nothing of your life other than it seems to be continually in danger. Why would your father bring you here? Why would he be here himself? He's a wanted man.'

'Not far now, Hugh,' said Henry, ignoring the questions and turning into one of the malodorous streets, straddling the narrow gutter running along the middle to avoid piles of human shit. He pressed on until they found a street free of ordure, shops with awnings and wooden trestles loaded with books.

'Here's the feast that will satisfy my hunger.'

'Books?' said Gifford.

'Rue de la Parcheminerie. Books, manuscripts, stitched parchment sheets, maps, drawings, illustrated works.'

'Then when do we eat? I can smell food.'

Henry pointed to a street angling away from where they stood. 'Meat and bread from a street vendor. Give them two sous and they will give you enough to satisfy your hunger until supper.'

Gifford appeared torn. 'I'll not let you out of my sight, Master Henry. That's my duty.' He swallowed at the thought of sacrificing the food. 'Besides, two sous is a sou too much for barley bread and roasted mutton. For two sous I could be seated in a tavern drinking ale or wine with a plate of stew.'

Henry let him complain. When Gifford shifted his belt and tugged it a notch tighter it was a sign the bodyguard had made his decision.

'Then step inside this shop and I will show you wonders on the page.'

'I am not a man for words, you know that. I like my life plain and simple. I follow trumpet and drum. No words are needed when you go to battle.'

'Then either stand out here in the street and let your mouth water from the smell of cooked meat or come inside with me.'

'As if that is any kind of choice,' said Gifford, and followed Henry inside.

★

As Henry browsed, Gifford found a stool and, under the watchful eye of a wary bookseller, picked through the books stacked close to hand on the floor. The shop was brimming with copied works: cut sheets of text bound with a stiff board and cloth. It did not take long for Henry to find the book he had looked for both in England and Avignon but which had always eluded him. He should have known that the book of poetry given to him by his French mother all those years ago would be found in Paris. He smiled with anticipation at the thought of being reunited with the poems and with them a sense of closeness to his mother. He placed it on the counter. 'I'll take this,' he said.

The bookseller appeared impressed. 'An educated man, young sir,' he said, his voice honey sweet and fawning as he sought to patronize and at the same time overcharge. He eyed Henry up and down and named a price. Henry knew it was more than the volume was worth but the copyist had a good fist and the writing was clear with good spacing between the lines. Henry paid and tucked the book into his tunic and then returned to browsing. A bookshop like this would feed his soul as much a tavern would fill his stomach.

Henry's hand darted in and out of shelves. He tugged free a map tied with red ribbon. Unrolling the parchment he knelt next to Gifford. It was a fine ink drawing of the city.

Henry placed books on each side to stop it curling. 'Here, this is where we came into the city. We followed this route. And here is where we crossed the river and this street'—he pressed his finger into a labyrinth of narrow lines—'is where we are now.'

Gifford finally had something of interest to look at.

'These are the city walls?' he asked.

'They are.'

'Then I can see why we never seized the place. I fought in

Caen as a boy, and the street fighting made us bleed. To get inside these walls and fight these whoresons...'

Henry glanced towards the robed bookseller to see if he had heard the insult. He had not. The old man was bent over studying a large text.

'... would take too many of us.' Gifford sucked his teeth and bent closer. 'It is a city like no other I have ever seen.'

It pleased Henry to see the man-at-arms engage with what lay at his feet if only to see it through the eyes of a fighting man. 'It is always worth knowing what a city can offer by way of danger and possible escape.' He hovered his finger over certain areas. 'Tanners and butchers have their quarter here around the Châtelet. Where we are is near the university so the scribes, parchment- and ink-sellers are here. Over there fishmongers and bakers; there blacksmiths...' He paused and pressed his finger close to Les Halles. 'My father told me he once escaped with my mother across the wall into the faubourg just there.'

That fact seemed to impress Gifford. He could see it would be no mean feat to get out of such a maze of alleyways, with the river and high walls, being pursued by an enemy. It would take skill and courage.

'We have to get used to being confined behind city walls, Hugh, because, like Paris, Milan will cage us. And we must learn where to run if the need arises.'

'Then when we get there we will buy a map and see what a high-flying bird sees. I am happy to sit a while longer and study this if that suits you?'

Henry had found the one thing that would stave off Gifford's boredom. He meandered through the shelves, occasionally bending to pick up a book from those stacked on the floor. Expensive leather-bound books were stored in a glass cabinet, a lure to his enquiring mind. Henry eased one of the books free and carefully, almost tenderly, turned the first few pages. The rich hues of an illuminated manuscript stared back at him. What he held was a work of beauty. It was unlike anything he had seen before even when studying at the Oxford University library. Light shone from the page. He was transfixed. His heartbeat quickened. His hand hovered over the page, not daring to touch its mystery. He had fallen in love – or lust – a dozen times when he was a student and the sight of these drawings prompted no less a passion in him. The bookseller's admonishment broke the spell.

'Young master, it's best you do not handle any of those books,' he said. 'They are worth a great deal.' He turned on his assistant and shouted, 'That cabinet should be locked!'

The pale, stooped youth, a student perhaps, thought Henry, cringed under the bookseller's tongue-lashing.

'Of course,' said Henry. 'I apologize.' He took it to the counter. 'Is it a rare book? Do you know who the illuminator is?'

'Why else would a book like this be encased? Because it is rare,' said the bookseller, laying a proprietary hand across the volume. Henry felt a lecture looming. He interrupted the man's next breath.

'Because of the text or the illumination?'

'Both of course. The half-uncial is a beautiful script.'

'Of course. But the gilding and the colours. They are like nothing I have ever seen before.'

'And likely never to see again this side of the Alps,' said the bookseller with the unmistakable hint of smugness. 'You have heard of Don Silvestro dei Gherarducci?'

'I have not.'

'A Camaldolese monk and illuminator. He created and illustrated many fine books and paintings for the Church. The text is copied from St Jerome's fourth-century translation of the bible. Though, of course, only the first chapters.'

'Of course,' said Henry patiently. 'So this is Don Silvestro's work?'

The bookseller sighed. He cast a glance along the shelves as if anyone might be lurking within earshot even though the shop was empty except for Henry and Gifford and the cowed assistant. 'A young woman. Raised in a Benedictine monastery.

A child with God-given gifts. She was taught by the Master himself.'

'A girl?'

'No longer,' said the bookseller. 'This was done at least ten years ago. But I have it on good authority that she still undertakes commissions. She brings the Master's skill to the outside world. I'm told she resides in an abbey somewhere beyond Milan.'

Henry's heartbeat increased. If he could find this abbey when he reached the city with the Prince he could find her. 'And her name?'

'Unknown to the world, which makes her work all the more desirable.' For a moment even the bookseller seemed entranced. 'For a woman's hand and heart to do this... a rare beauty. A union with the Holy Spirit.'

'Will you accept a silver gros for it?'

The bookseller recoiled, releasing his hand from the book to clutch at his heart. 'A gros? This book is worth many gold écus. You would need a purseful, young master.'

Henry smiled. 'Then how is it that you have it in your possession? Could it be that it was taken from a church by a thief and sold to you for a few sous?'

The bookseller's face pinched. He swallowed hard. 'Who are you?' It had apparently struck him that the educated younger man and the ruffian who accompanied him might be official.

Henry saw it at once. 'It's all right,' he said. 'I have known brigands who would steal silver from a church altar. I doubt they would know the value of such a work as this.'

It placated the bookseller. Henry eased the book from the counter. 'I'll put it back where it belongs.'

He turned for the cabinet, glanced at Gifford. It was a look well-rehearsed over the years with a barely perceptible nod in response. Henry took another two strides and heard the map furl with a snap. Gifford cursed, reached for it and knocked over a pile of books, then he sprawled to the floor in a vain attempt to stop the minor catastrophe from getting worse. Bookseller and assistant stooped to save tumbling books.

Henry berated Gifford. 'Get out, you oaf!'

He approached the bookseller as Gifford scurried for the door. He bent and picked up some books. 'I offer my apologies,' he said.

The bookseller paused in his efforts and glanced beyond Henry. The book was where it should be. The cabinet door closed. His immediate suspicion of theft was allayed.

'There is no need, young master. My thanks for your purchase.'

Henry dipped his head in acknowledgement and left the shop.

Gifford fell in beside him. 'And that was for what?'

'Something I desired but could not afford to buy,' said Henry and slipped out the folded illuminated page he had torn from the book.

'What use is that? If you have become a thief you should steal a sheep instead of a lamb. The result if discovered is the same.'

'This is all I need.'

'For what?'

'To find her.'

'Find who?'

'I don't know her name but she must be a creature of great beauty in order to create such delicate and enticing illuminations.'

Gifford cursed under his breath. 'You're a damned fool. A woman whose name you do not know. Where is she?'

'I don't know that either. Somewhere in Italy. She will become a reason for me to stay – once my duty to my father is done – and delay riding on to Bologna and my studies.'

Gifford gripped his arm, momentarily halting Henry's stride. 'You are tasked by your father to stay close to the Prince and have your wits about you, not behave like a damned stable lad squeezing his cock as he gazes at a kitchen maid. Men with swords are a threat I can face down, but a man whose life is ruled by his lust is much more dangerous.'

Henry was unperturbed. 'This is more than lust. I can't explain, Hugh. We ride to Milan; perhaps someone there can help me seek her out. Trust me, I will not fail my father or you.'

Gifford grunted. 'Then I ask for the mercy of angels to protect us. You're determined to find trouble. Can we eat now?'

They headed for the river unaware of the cowled man who followed them.

CHAPTER NINE

Simon Bucy stared into the flames of his fireplace. Standing out in the open to welcome Prince Lionel had chilled him, and even with the warmth of the fire, he needed to pull his thick cloak tighter around him. The young man he'd had followed was none other than Henry de Sainteny. What was it that had triggered Bucy's curiosity in the first place? He was conflicted and cursed his lawyer's memory for detail. Had he not seen Blackstone's son eight years ago when he was brought to court and introduced to the Dauphin – as he was then – he would never have had the slightest inkling the man who rode with Prince Lionel was one and the same.

'You're certain?' he demanded of the man tasked with following the young Englishman.

'I followed them back to the quarters where he and others are billeted. It was easy enough to confirm his identity. Those I questioned knew little about him, but he began the journey in London with Prince Lionel. He bears the insignia of a dead knight, a Sir Robert Lownes.'

Bucy dismissed his servant. The turmoil of so many years of war with the constant threat of defeat whenever Thomas Blackstone fought against the French had been a disease afflicting the nation, as surely as the sickness that ate away inside of him. The physicians had assured him he would survive for another year, but who in their right mind believed those who practised such an inexact science? The previous year he had convinced the King to send routiers to capture Blackstone's son and that had been a terrible mistake, for Bucy had learnt the mercenaries planned to kill the young man instead of capturing him. His reputation with the King had faltered and it had taken months to re-establish the trust that had resulted in their new plan to ready the nation for war against England once again. And now the opportunity to seize Blackstone's son had once again, unbelievably, been placed in the palm of his hand. The irony did not escape him. Whatever had happened in the past, and for whatever reason, Henry Blackstone was part of the Prince's household; he was untouchable. To blatantly seize him would create a political tempest even he with his skills would be unable to calm. So close, so very close to hold the young man and to use his capture against his father. Dare he order it? One more slip with the King and he would be stripped of his properties and rank and condemned to die alone in a dank cell, forgotten by history.

Unless, of course, he could convince the King to make the bold decision.

The King was being dressed by his *maître de la garderobe* and his valets. 'Here?' said the King. 'In Paris?'

'Yes, highness. As part of the Prince's household. He wears the blazon of a dead knight to disguise his identity.'

The King looked bewildered. 'No, it cannot be. Your mind becomes feverish. We should never have allowed you to stand out in the cold wind. It was inconsiderate of us, Simon. We must pay more attention to your well-being.' The King grimaced as the wardrobe master had a valet fuss with his silk overshirt.

'Too tight, too tight. We are to dance and feast this evening – would you have us trussed like a cooked goose?'

The wardrobe master ushered the valet away and stepped in to personally deal with the King's dress.

'Why were you suspicious? Surely this is a figment of your imagination, Simon?' He cast a worried glance at his oldest and most trusted adviser as the wardrobe master extended the King's arm to check the length of shirtsleeve.

'Sire,' said Bucy, eager to keep the King's attention on the matter at hand and not on the immediate comfort of a long silk shirt that would soon be hidden by voluminous and more decorative robes. 'I caught a glance only, but it rekindled a memory from years ago. The young man has a certain look which brought his name back to me. I cannot explain it any more than I can explain the mystery of a recurring dream. The mind holds secrets locked away, only to be released when one least expects it.'

'And now you're talking like a philosopher, not our keen-minded counsellor. We would remind you, Simon, we have plans that are already being put into—Desist!' he snapped at the wardrobe master. 'Leave us!' A valet quickly put the King's cloak around his shoulders as the *maître de la garderobe* bowed, ushered the valets away, bowed again and scuttled backwards for the door.

Charles V, King of France, stood unmoving for a moment. His thoughts flitted here and there as his eyes settled on Bucy. Then he stepped towards the log-fire, gestured for a servant to pour wine. He did not offer a glass to Bucy. He sipped, nodded dismissal to the servant, and finally addressed Bucy.

'You will remember the unfortunate circumstances last year regarding young Blackstone, and at the time how our memory recalled that he and his father had been brought to our father's court when I was Dauphin.'

'I do, sire. It was that very moment, as brief as it was, that pricked my own recollection.'

'There can be no doubt it is him? That there is no other male sibling, or bastard son of Blackstone's or his wife? Just hearing a name called among ranks of horsemen is not proof of identity, Simon.'

Bucy scoured his memory for what he knew of Blackstone's family. Over the years, a dossier had been compiled on England's Master of War. That document had been closed once it had been brought up to date after the Battle of Nájera.

'Nothing suggests Blackstone has any bastard sons...' He hesitated. The King waited, glass hovering near his lips.

'There is something?' said the King.

'There is a child. A boy. The product of an assault on his wife. He was placed in an abbey. We don't know where, highness, but we do know he exists.'

'Could he be of age?'

'No, he would be no more than twelve years old. Sire, this man riding with Prince Lionel is, without doubt, Henry Blackstone and he is using his mother's name of de Sainteny.' Bucy took a moment longer before he continued. It was always a good ploy to let the young King watch him. To extend the silence. As if allowing the lawyer's mind to consider all options. For Bucy it was simple. 'Sire, he has been delivered into our hands. A gift. After everything you and your father tried over the years, now the means to halt Blackstone – wherever he is, whatever he plans – is here. We should thank God for His benevolence.'

The decision-making had been neatly passed back to the King. He looked at Bucy. 'You will point him out when the occasion arises. Fate is taunting us, Simon. Do you not see? Eight years ago, when our young sister, Isabelle, was travelling to Milan to marry, it was Thomas Blackstone who was her escort. It was he who got her there safely. And now his son rides with a prince who will also marry a Visconti.' He drained the wine. 'Truly, it is our blessed Lord Jesus who controls our destiny, and who pits us against ourselves in order to challenge our desires.' He put down the glass. 'It would serve us as well now to seize

Blackstone's son as it did when we planned to do so a year past. But we have a brief peace, while we plan for war. Nothing must jeopardize that. So you will remain silent. This matter is ended. He is protected.'

Bucy was dismissed.

He shuffled along the corridors to where his carriage waited. It was true, he thought. Fate laughs in our face, and the good Lord tests us. No matter: his secret plan to stop the Visconti gold reaching English hands remained in place. When the time of his own death came, that secret would die with him. But there would be an added satisfaction. Henry Blackstone was riding to Milan as close to Prince Lionel as any would be permitted. It would be there Bucy's plan would unfold, far away from Paris, beyond the knowledge of the French King, who would remain blameless for the terrible act that would be committed.

He must hurry. Irony had served him well. Messengers must be sent to Italy to those in his pay with the change of plan. Bucy smiled as he clambered into his carriage. The cold was less biting for he was warmed within. Fate embraced him. Like the temptress she was, she now paved the way to rid France of father and son.

Henry Blackstone could be the key to his father's destruction.

A sacrificial offering.

CHAPTER TEN

Count Amadeus VI of Savoy, returning from his crusade against the Ottoman Turks, had reached Paris in time to accompany Prince Lionel on his journey to Milan. Being the maternal uncle of the bride offered the possibility of advantageous economic and political ties with the English, even though he was allied to France. Amadeus had indulged himself in a shopping spree in the city. His extravagance had little to do with relief from any privation experienced while taking the cross. He was, by nature, a lover of show. Orders were placed for jewellery, clothing, boots, silks and table knives. When a husband returned from campaigning and then went to Paris to accompany an English prince, it was prudent to smooth his homecoming to a loyal and patient wife. His servants packed lengths of cloth woven in Rheims for her and a *jaquette* lined with 1,200 squirrel skins.

'What I don't know,' said Gifford as they approached Amadeus's castle at Chambéry, 'is how these noblemen manage to spend so much money in such a short time.'

'They're well practised,' Henry explained. 'They use ostentation and flamboyance to overshadow their peers. Pageantry gilds their fear of the pestilence, too. As a common man awakes and thinks only of his labour, noblemen greet the dawn with a pious prayer and then seek out comfort and indulgence.'

'You would know about that, would you? Being Sir Thomas's son, a man who has likely as not spent less than a month of his life on a straw mattress.'

'My father knows the likes of the Count. I've been here before, as well as Paris.'

'Master Henry, you appear to have travelled every road across France and Italy, whereas I'm nothing more than a fighting man who goes to war and then waits for the next call to arms.'

The entourage rode through the town, whose buildings carpeted the approach to the sheer walls of Amadeus's castle. Shopkeepers on the route closed their shutters as the townspeople gathered together with villeins from the field to welcome back their liege lord.

'Hugh, my father's life has been a journey of its own making. And at times I have shared it with him. I told you eight years ago we escorted the young Princess Isabelle to Milan, which was when I met the Dauphin. He gifted me a book of chivalry from his own library. That's why I stayed out of sight of him and his courtiers. It's unlikely they would recognize me after these years, but the Prince and I agreed that I keep my distance until celebrations eased. Now that we have put Paris behind us, there will be fewer sumptuous feasts and entertainment. From now on, I will be closer to him.'

'I'll wager they won't give you a bed as soft as the one in your room at Oxford once we leave this place. It will be a tent and a blanket and a rock for a pillow.'

Hooves clattered across the drawbridge. A gaggle of courtiers hovered at the entrance to the courtyard leading to the inner yards of Amadeus's castle. Across the heads of those in front, Henry saw a chamberlain bow as valets and pages were urged forward to take the guests' reins. Despenser was quick to dismount and the first to stand ready at the Prince's shoulder as Amadeus led them deeper into the castle. Everyone else was guided towards the stables. The acrid smell of a forge mingled with that of baked bread: cooks and blacksmiths shared a common yard. The bustling horsemen jostled to hand over their mounts.

'We had no such luxury when we travelled the length of France last year, Hugh. You still doubt I am unable to endure a soldier's life?'

They dismounted and joined others leading their horses towards the stables. Henry shouldered his mount aside as Gifford drew alongside him.

'Master Henry, you have proved yourself intelligent and courageous enough to cleave men to you. I have seen you face danger and not flinch, but beyond all of that, you are a scholar – the book of poetry you bought in Paris proves that. Gentle words scratched on paper in this harsh time. Your mind is sharp and your heart is strong, but you are drawn to plentiful wine, soft beds and willing girls. And here we are now. Being in the Prince's company will bring benefits. Women will fawn over you so that they might get closer to him. And I don't suppose you will turn down a soft bed so you might enjoy their favour.'

Gifford handed his mount's reins to a stable hand, slid his panniers free and draped them over his shoulder, then untied his bedroll and blanket from the saddle. 'And that is when you will be distracted. If I were your enemy, or the Prince's, that's the moment I would seize or kill you both.'

Henry ran a tender hand over his horse's muzzle and pulled his saddlebag free. The two men pushed through the crowded yard to where the chamberlain's men were shouting orders about where men would be quartered.

'Hugh, I am not the Prince's bodyguard. Those duties lie with Despenser and his men. Being in his company is more about sharing a love of poetry and books. It offers him respite from courtly duties. And it allows me to listen to idle gossip from his servants. Whispers of unrest and discontent slither like draughts through old castles.'

They were directed through a postern gate across another yard and into the keep. Men trudged this way and that, carrying their bedrolls and blankets. Some were already curling up on steps and lying on half-landings. Henry was only given what was little more than an alcove off a landing because he had been placed in the Prince's personal entourage.

'At least we can stretch out,' said Gifford. 'I'll take the inside against the wall because if you're going to be supping wine with the Prince you'll be coming back late and I've no desire to have you kicking me in the head as you climb over.'

'I wouldn't want to disturb your beauty sleep, Hugh.'

'And I wouldn't want to be startled and stick my knife in your ribs.'

Henry unrolled his bedding and blanket. Gifford's casual rejoinder served as a reminder that he, a veteran of many battles, had an ingrained instinct to kill. It was a sobering thought. He would never take Gifford for granted.

'Master de Sainteny?' said a laboured voice as a servant clambered up the stairs with a flickering lantern, stepping over sprawled legs, ignoring curses from the men on the crowded stairs.

'Here,' said Henry.

'Prince Lionel is asking for you. Leave any weapon you carry here.'

Henry tugged free the knife at his belt and handed it to Gifford. 'I am armed only with this,' he said, raising the book he held.

Moments after Henry picked his way down the steps, Gifford followed at a distance. He would stay well back, find a place in the darkness of the vast castle where he could observe his charge and then, when Henry made his way back to his bedroll, he would return ahead of him. There were times it was prudent not to let Blackstone's son know he was being protected, especially when he slipped away to gamble with servants. Gifford knew all the excuses Henry used to cover his occasional absences. There was no harm in letting him have such freedom but the man-at-arms was responsible for his safety by order of the King of England. That Henry's father had allowed his son to undertake the journey as a spy in the Prince's camp had placed an extra burden on the man who served as his protector.

Gifford found a place behind a thick stone column to wait until Henry departed the Prince's quarters. It would be a few cold hours yet before he returned to his bedroll. Once this journey was over, then his duty would be done. Henry would have regained his pride. There was no excuse for him to break his promise and not pursue his law studies at university in Bologna. Once there, Gifford would return to service with his Lord Warwick and let another take his place. Until then, he would watch over Henry Blackstone like a hawk guarding its young.

Henry followed the servant through narrow unlit passages that broadened into a hall where he saw two of Despenser's men guarding a door. They studied him for a moment, alert for any outsider trying to gain access to the Prince. The man nearest Henry recognized him as being part of the entourage. He nodded to his companion, who then stepped forward, knocked on the door, waited until a muted voice answered. The guard stood erect, facing the unseen man.

'Master de Sainteny, highness.'

The tall figure standing by the blazing fire wore an ermine-lined cloak. A small table bore plates of half-eaten food and a glass of red wine. The chair was low, cushioned, its crescent-shaped arms waiting to half encircle a sitter. Resting on the chair seat was a splayed book, its pages open.

The Prince's face glowed with colour. The fast ride from Paris had wind-burnt his face; the fire glow accentuated the fair hair falling to his shoulders; his beard touched his chest. He looked relaxed. He stooped to retrieve his wine glass with one hand, the book with the other and then sat.

Henry stood at a respectful distance and bowed.

Prince Lionel's smile suggested he was less burdened by his privilege compared to his older brother, who had the princely responsibility of holding Aquitaine. The twenty-nine-year-old Duke of Clarence had no such burden. Already widowed these five years past, he seemed in a hurry to reach Milan and his fourteen-year-old child-bride-to-be, Violante.

'Master de Sainteny, come forward.'

Henry took a couple of strides and then hesitated. A shadow moved in the corner of the room not ten feet behind the Prince. Edward Despenser stepped into view. His quilted gambeson bore his colours; his eyes rested on Henry.

'My Lord Despenser, this is the young man you have been asking about,' said the Prince without turning around, knowing that Despenser was there.

The Prince smiled at Henry. 'Lord Edward is most solicitous about our safety, Master Henry. He believes we are often too naive to choose who it is we wish to engage with. Not so, Edward?'

The sturdy knight dipped at the waist even though the Prince's back was to him. 'I am only responsible for your highness's safety until after the wedding. Then my duty is done, although I am here to serve at your will.'

The Prince beckoned Henry closer. 'Stand there, Master Henry, so that our guardian might see that you carry nothing more than a book.'

Henry opened his arms, exposing his belt.

'I would not disrespect a guest of yours, my lord. My men would not have permitted anyone to enter your presence were they armed.'

'Now, Sir Edward, we summoned Master Henry because he speaks and reads Latin and also the Tuscan vernacular: the language of the poets in the common tongue. We are content to have you stay with us. Even if you do not understand what is being said, the cadence will caress your soul. Poetry is a balm in a time of violence and vice, a solace – in addition to prayer – a man must find in this sordid world.'

'Your Grace, I will leave you to the poet's musings. I know they will be beyond my grasp.'

Henry dipped his head as Despenser passed him as he went to the door. The knight's contemptuous gaze conveyed a nobleman's disgust at such a lowly companion being honoured by the King's son.

It was not lost on the Prince. The door closed behind Despenser. 'Master Henry, I fear Edward harbours unwavering contempt for the art of poetry. Too soft. Too feminine. Outpourings from a feeble heart. Unlike us, he is not knowledgeable about courtly love and manners.'

'Then it is his loss, highness.'

'Quite so. Take the stool there by the fire. Now, what is the book?'

'Petrarch, lord. I found it in a bookshop in Paris. I have sought a copy for a long time. It is one of the first books of poetry with which my mother blessed me. It's a good copy by a well-formed hand.'

The Prince laid aside his own book. 'Then that shall take precedence over Boccaccio. But first...' His voice lowered. 'Master Blackstone...' He smiled, the subterfuge pleasing him. 'Let me hear what you have witnessed of your father's exploits from whenever you have been at his side. Our desire to share evenings of poetry is one thing. The exploits of a legend is another.'

CHAPTER ELEVEN

The Count of Savoy's hospitality at Chambéry, celebrating the Prince's journey, would have gone beyond the seven days the Prince had enjoyed, but Lionel, like any considerate guest, had expressed his wish not to outstay his welcome. This was a polite reason to press on across the Alps and into Piedmont and thence to Milan, for the month of May had arrived, offering favourable weather for a few days in which to cross the mountains. Lionel knew that the Visconti would stage more celebrations every day until the ceremony itself at the end of the month. The political significance of forging an alliance between Galeazzo and the House of Plantagenet was evident, but amidst the festivities, legal matters required attention as to what lands and towns would be ceded to the Prince.

It was the morning of his departure. The Prince had bathed, attended mass and bade farewell to Amadeus's wife, the Countess Bonne, a woman of innate beauty and charm whose intelligence Lionel appreciated. Despenser's captains marshalled his cavalcade, already mounted, waiting for Lionel to step onto the mounting block and lead them, with Amadeus at his side.

Prince Lionel settled in the saddle and looked at his entourage, ready to follow him, when he saw Henry several horses behind.

His lip was split, and a bruise discoloured his cheekbone. The Prince caught the ever-vigilant Despenser's eye.

'Highness?'

'Is there discord among us? Henry de Sainteny's appearance suggests as much.'

'I questioned him earlier, lord. He left your quarters late last night, I believe?'

'He did.'

'I fear he consumed too much of your generous helping of wine, sire. He tripped on the stairs and took a fall.'

'Do we need to send for a physician?'

'No. He's young enough to take a tumble and get back on his feet.'

Lionel nodded his acceptance. Urging his horse forward, he led the cavalcade out of the great courtyard towards the pass.

The truth of Henry's injury differed from the explanation given to Edward Despenser. Once the Prince and his companions departed the castle, there was no doubt in Gifford's mind that Amadeus's steward would soon uncover the injuries sustained by three of his men.

Gifford knew Henry had the common touch. Had the lad not spent time as a boy with Blackstone's men? And had Gifford not witnessed for himself Henry's ability when a student at Oxford to throw dice, play cards and drink until the early hours with tradesmen, men-at-arms and any other of low birth who shared his vices?

Gifford had waited in his usual place the previous night and followed Henry after he left the Prince. Henry had made his way into the yard and then the stables. At the end of the building was the blacksmith's forge, where a few yardmen and stable hands gathered to roll dice. The fire pit's cinders were kept alive for the night by the bellows boy. Cider and wine were supped and coins were bet as each man cast the dice. The doors were closed to the prying eyes of any wall sentries. Henry had visited on three of the seven nights they stayed at the castle, always shadowed by Gifford. And it was obvious when Henry returned to his bedroll that he had been a winner. The purse on his belt always looked heavier than before he entered the forge.

Gifford witnessed a knock, a pause, another knock and the forge door opening, allowing a warm yellow glow to seep into the night. But then, once the door closed, there was little sound. Gifford knew the gamblers would be gathering further back in a store room. Any sounds were muffled by thick stone walls.

Hazard was a common dice game across England and France. Gifford had played it often enough himself in inns and taverns and back rooms. Whoever threw the dice called out the number he wanted to win and he knew someone with a sharp mind like Henry could alternate the call and with luck get a consistent winning throw. This was not a game that could be won by cheating, but with a keen eye for odds, a successful call could be made.

It was Henry's luck and skill that night which caused the fight. Happy with his winnings and knowing the Prince was to leave next morning, he had left the game. But as he set off back to his quarters, the bull-necked blacksmith, his leather apron smeared with food grease, stood up. He was huge: his frame could fill a postern gate and he looked as strong as an iron-studded door. He pushed aside the bellows boy and furiously pumped air into the fire pit, which roared and cracked as the fire bed sucked in vital air, and he began to twist a length of flattened iron in the embers. Henry slowed his pace. The hulking man was unpopular, that had been plain to see, and during their gambling he'd communicated with grunts or by a threatening pointed finger at the others who played. Not Henry, though. He never gave Henry any cause for alarm besides a glare when he lost. But now, two other gamblers, clearly obedient to the blacksmith's unspoken demands from his place at the fire pit, blocked Henry's way to the door. They were stable hands. Wiry, but muscled. Shorter by several inches to Henry.

'You're in my way,' said Henry.

'You've taken a lot from us,' said one.

'I concentrate: that's how I win.'

'It's a game of chance,' called the blacksmith, easing the white-hot metal in the embers.

'That's true,' Henry answered. 'But the odds come around time and time again. All you have to do is pick the time you think your call on the dice is going to show. You're still in my way.'

Henry's hand moved to his belt where his knife should be. Despenser's security had robbed him of the only means of defending himself if the situation turned ugly. And the scowling men were not smiling. He glanced around, trying to find a weapon he could use. Only a few items were within his reach. A looped chain on a hook, heavy, but short enough to use like a mace; a pitchfork and a dozen lengths of iron ready to be forged and shaped at the blacksmith's hands. And one more potential weapon: a raking fork for the coals.

'We think you should give us back what we lost over the last few nights,' said the third man, who had forearms of twisted muscle from manhandling plough horses. He pulled out a short-bladed curved knife that would gut man or beast. 'No man can win so often if he isn't cheating.'

Henry splayed his hands. 'Be reasonable. You have shared wine with me and we have laughed and enjoyed the game. Let it go.'

'You can go, but the money stays.'

'You French are such poor losers. If you had half a brain between the three of you, you would be intelligent enough to know I could not cheat at throwing dice, but that I could weigh the odds. Now get out of my way before I cause you pain. Your masters will not be pleased when you cannot attend to your duties tomorrow. I don't want to hurt you but I will if my hand is forced.'

The knife-man sneered. 'You will hurt *us*?' He looked at his companions in disbelief. 'The night's work is not yet done. It is a simple trade. Hand over your purse. If not, there's a slurry pit in the back yard. In a year's time when it is drained your rotting carcass will be found.'

The blacksmith pulled the length of white-hot iron from the fire, holding it in front of his face as would a knight with his sword. 'You and your English Prince leave in the morning. If you want to ride on you should give us your purse.'

Henry had inched a step closer to his side of the fire pit, legs braced ready for their attack. His father had taught him to always seek the advantage in any confrontation. If Henry Blackstone was to survive the night and ride on to Milan, he needed to inflict swift violence. And the most dangerous of these men needed to be hurt first.

As the stable hand with the curved blade stepped away from the door and took a casual stride towards him, Henry grabbed the coal rake from the fire and thrust it at the blacksmith. It struck his hands and the searingly hot iron he held caught the side of his face. He staggered back, giving Henry the chance to wrap the hefty length of chain over the knife-man's wrist; he pulled the man close in, headbutted him and, as he hit the ground, booted him hard between the legs. The fallen man slowed his companion's advance. Henry lunged with the pitchfork, forced the man off balance and pushed him stumbling into the blacksmith, who was regaining his balance, recovering from his seared neck. As the man fell back Henry struck him with one of the iron rods. It caught the side of the man's head. He fell senseless.

There was no time to escape the raging bull of a blacksmith. Henry struck at the brute's neck. What there was of it. The muscle that connected his skull to his shoulders was indistinguishable and in the near darkness, Henry's blow struck the smith's shoulders. Stepping clear of the unconscious man at his feet, the bull of a man grabbed Henry's tunic in a grip that couldn't be broken. His fist swung. Henry didn't resist. He let his weight fall and the man almost dropped him. What would have been a killing blow from a mallet-sized fist to his head became nothing more than a bruising glance across his cheek and lip.

Henry was down, the man swinging his boot into Henry's side as he curled to protect himself. He had no chance to roll clear as his back came up against a cartwheel. The blacksmith snatched the pitchfork. Blood gorged his face. The burnt welt on his neck looked raw and painful. He raised the deadly spikes, ready to skewer the young Englishman.

Henry hoped the tines might only pierce his leg, then he would have a chance to grasp the haft and go for the blacksmith's eyes. He heard a dull, sickening thud and the clang of metal as the pitchfork fell from the blacksmith's hands. His eyes rolled back in his head and he slumped like a dropped sack of grain.

Gifford stood behind him. Then he tossed aside the shovel he had used on the big man's skull.

'Is he dead?' said Henry, scrambling to his feet.

'A man like that? No. He'll sleep it off.' He slapped his hand across the dirt on Henry's tunic. 'You're good at dice, but you need to weigh the odds regarding the men you gamble with, Master Henry. I won't always be here to save you.'

Henry pulled straw from his hair. He slapped a hand on Gifford's shoulder. 'Hugh, you are my shadow and I am ever grateful. Half of what I have in my purse is yours.'

'If I'd let him kill you, I'd have had the whole purse.'

'And enough money to get drunk for a month, but you'd have failed in your duty.'

'A man gets pissed long enough he stops caring about such matters. You'd better think up a story about that bruise and cut lip. The Prince will not tolerate fighting on this journey.'

'I shall make up a reasonable tale.'

'Aye, well, keep me out of it,' said Gifford, shepherding Henry into the night.

CHAPTER TWELVE

Blackstone's men waited outside the Mont Cenis monastery walls as he addressed the abbot.

'You will find the means to hang the dead on the outside walls. Wolves and crows can feast on them. You will place a sign telling those who travel this way that these brigands were killed by Sir Thomas Blackstone. Understood?'

The abbot looked unhappy. 'Sir Thomas, this is a place of peace and meditation. To desecrate the dead, even these vile men, is against our beliefs.'

'They will be fair warning to others and buy you the peace you pursue. You will do it because murdering scum need to be made an example of to their brethren. Men such as these are as dedicated to rape and murder as your own community is to preserving the values of your order. I will hear of it if you do not do as I say.'

Reluctantly the abbot nodded. 'We shall do it.'

'Leave them until they rot and enough flesh has been taken from their bones.'

'We shall pray for their souls.'

'Aye, pray more of their kind don't come your way again. Their souls are already hoisted on the devil's horns. There will be a column of men passing your gates in a couple of weeks. They are too many for you to accommodate, but if you are wise you'll bring your best wine from your barrel room and offer it to them, for they are led by the Lord of Savoy and an English prince. Offer prayers and blessings without your palm extended for payment. They will be generous enough without you seeking coin to hold a mass in their honour.'

'We are grateful to you and your men. It is for all of you that we will offer mass.' The abbot pointed at the silver medallion that nestled next to his dead wife's Christian cross around Blackstone's neck. 'You are conflicted, Sir Thomas? A talisman resting with the cross of Christ? Shall we entreat the Lord to cleave you to Him rather than a pagan symbol?'

'Arianrhod is the Goddess of the Silver Wheel beloved of my Welsh archers. It is she who protects me. The cross bears the love of a lost wife. They are what I believe in, Brother Jean. Have no fear for my soul; rather pray for yourselves.'

Blackstone heeled the bastard horse away from the gathered monks. 'And take care who you open your gate to. I will not be here to save you next time.'

Mounted archers and hobelars alike depended on a sturdy horse to travel far, and a good horsemaster was a valuable asset to fighting men. Walter Mallin brought up the rear of the column as Blackstone led them across the vast plateau, past a shimmering lake, aiming for a distant point on the horizon. The old man's skill in treating horse ailments brought him as much favour with the men as did Will Longdon's deft hand with needle and silk thread when stitching wounds. Mallin was grateful to be of use and content that the Master of War had given him his trust. He was of little worth otherwise. His age had threatened to be an encumbrance for his companions when he had journeyed through France the previous year with Henry Blackstone and the others and faced death with them. Perhaps back then it was the unwavering loyalty he had shown to a dying comrade that made those men put up with his slow progress when forced to travel on foot. Now, on horseback, he led the pack animals, ageing rounceys like himself, but still able to carry their burden.

'I'm in a shit pit and I can't get out of it,' moaned John Terrel, a fellow traveller of Mallin's the year before. 'I should have gone with Master Henry to Bologna.'

Terrel's loyalty could blow hot and cold depending on the risk to his own well-being. He was careful not to let Blackstone hear his whingeing complaints, however; he shared them only with those companions who had survived Henry Blackstone's journey with him.

'Do we know for certain that is where he went? Master Henry has ideas of his own, as we know. Besides, did he ask you to accompany him to Bologna?' said Mallin, knowing the man who had pulled up alongside him would need to vent his frustration over whatever it was that troubled him.

'He did not, but when we spent those months waiting for Sir Thomas's wounds to heal I made a great effort to make myself useful to him and that guard dog of his, Gifford. It was he who kept me at bay. I swear that otherwise Master Henry would have seen my value to him. Who else can scrounge like me?'

'Or complain,' said Mallin, easing the rope from the trailing horse in his aching hand.

'I have every right to complain. I held back when we killed those skinners because I could see these mad bastards loved to fight. Who plunges his hand into the cauldron without testing its heat first? I swear these men have a death wish.'

'You made a big mistake when Sir Thomas took us in. You saved Sir Gilbert's life in that skirmish.'

'A year back. And that was an accident. I flailed my sword because I was shit scared and by chance slew a skinner who was about to kill him. I didn't intend to save his life. Now look where it's got me. I'm a gravedigger and a thief. Nothing more. I haven't raised my blade in anger since and I have no desire to.'

'And now you are in a shit pit.'

'I am.'

'Why so?'

'Sir Gilbert seems to think I am valuable and I'm not. I'm to ride with Renfred and his scouts for the day. He's a man short.'

Mallin pointed towards the head of the column. 'You'd best get to it. I see Renfred's men on the move.'

'Merciful Christ, Walter, Renfred doesn't need me. I am not of their kind. Don't you have something to give me the palsy or the shits that will last an hour or so? Or any herbs that you use on the horses? Renfred and his men are Sir Thomas's sword point. If there's going to be an ambush then they will die first. I need something – anything that will help get me out of this duty without arousing suspicion.'

'Of your cowardice?'

'Mock me if you must, but Sir Thomas and Killbere are better served with me engaged elsewhere.'

Mallin reached for a flask tied to his pommel. 'I can give you one drink of this potion.'

'I am in your debt. What will it do? Be quick, Walter, I can see Renfred searching the ranks for me.'

Mallin uncorked the flask and handed it to Terrel, who raised it to his lips and took a deep swig. He spluttered and choked as Mallin retrieved the flask.

Gasping for breath, eyes watering, Terrel could barely speak. 'What... in... God's name...?'

'I found it in the monks' barrel room. It's a fiery concoction known for its properties.'

Terrel regained his breath with deep gasps. 'To do what?'

'I don't know. I daren't use it again after that last horse died,' Mallin said solemnly.

A dumbstruck Terrel gaped. And then Mallin grinned. 'It's a fruit brandy. If it doesn't kill you then at least it will let you face death with courage.'

Terrel cursed, eyes streaming from the astringent concoction.

'You old bastard. I hope a horse kicks you in the head.' He heeled his mount and cantered down the line to join Renfred and his scouting party, who had pulled away from the column.

Mallin sighed and took a sip. He grimaced. 'Then at least one of us will have some sense knocked into him,' he said to himself, 'because one thing is certain, these men are looking for a fight.'

CHAPTER THIRTEEN

Renfred's scouts crested an undulating fold in the ground, disturbing four vultures who were pecking at the dead two hundred yards away.

Renfred gestured his men to split and circle the area in case any brigands were still close by. Terrel stayed with the three men who rode behind the German scout. Terrel eased his horse forward; the scent of death had made it skittish at first until he tightened the rein and spurred it on. Renfred glanced back at him. A stone-cold stare that needed no words: *Keep your damned horse under control.*

Terrel looked nervously left and right. The scouts had disappeared from view and Renfred was leading the men into the belly between the folding land. If there were enemy hidden, there would be no escape. Terrel wanted to urge Renfred to stop until his men had returned, but instinct told him to remain silent. He bit his tongue.

They eased their mounts forward. Four men lay dead. Panniers and two wooden trunks stood opened on the ground, their contents – clothing – tossed aside. Hessian-wrapped goods had been split open, scattering what looked like herbs and spices across the fallen bodies. Straw-filled baskets lay lopsided, with a few remaining bottles of wine visible. A bolt of tanned soft leather had been abandoned, and another of fine silk, the breeze flapping a length of cloth like a forlorn banner of the fallen.

The men's boots had been stripped, so too their tunics. Blood seeped into their shirts; one man had a crushed skull; his companion had died from a knife or sword thrust.

Renfred looked at the tracks on the ground, unperturbed by the slain men. 'Merchants taking their goods into Savoy. At any other time, when the count's men were patrolling, they would have a safe passage.' He stood in the stirrups to gaze around him. 'Killers took their horses. Looks as though they're heading for Montferrat territory on the other side of the pass.'

One of the men who had drifted to one side, eyes down, checking for tracks pointed eastward. 'Pack horse or mule broke free at some point.'

'It'll be the two skinners who escaped Sir Thomas's blade at the monastery.' Renfred saw his men converge from ahead once they had reconnoitred the flanks. 'Long gone by the look of it. All right, we'll stay and cover the bodies as best we can. One of you ride back and tell Sir Thomas.'

Terrel said, 'I'll turn back!' and then realized he had spoken too eagerly and too quickly. He tried to recover what he could of his composure.

Renfred barely suppressed his look of disdain. A couple of his men smirked.

'You won't get lost, will you, Terrel?' one of them taunted.

'There are no graveyards up here to act as signposts,' said another.

Terrel was still light-headed from Mallin's heady brew. 'You will be glad of a gravedigger when your time comes. Speak no ill to the man who will put you in the ground when God calls your soul.'

'Aye, and I'll wager I'll go into the ground without my boots,' came the answer.

'Boots are of little use when you tread the devil's coals,' Terrel retorted.

Renfred nudged his horse around before tempers flared at the insults. 'Enough of this. Terrel: keep your eyes sharp. This land can confuse a man. One track looks like another. Get yourself straight to Sir Thomas. Tell him what we found and that half my lads will go on and check the way ahead.' Renfred looked at the storm clouds creeping across the distant peaks. 'You've no cloak with you, so make haste. These storms are as short as they are fierce. You'll feel their bite.'

Terrel stared for a moment at the faces turned towards him. They were glad to see him go. An outsider in a tightly knit band of fighters. Men who knew instinctively what the other would do when they faced an enemy. Of course he didn't belong with the likes of them. He yanked the reins and spurred his horse back the way they had come.

The wind had sharpened. After half a mile, Terrel drew up his mount. Had he followed the correct route when he'd tried to return to the well-worn track? If he remembered correctly, he should have nudged his horse left for a few hundred yards and then right between the two small hills that lay either side of the way back. In truth, he admitted to himself he had not paid sufficient attention, being more concerned with the possibility of an ambush. He stared at the blackening sky. Would the storm have approached Sir Thomas's rear or come at him from the flank? Flank, he decided. Was he certain? No, he told himself, but he would ride to the right and find higher ground to search for the column. And if he did not spur the horse too much but kept him at the trot, then he'd be able to spy out the land more easily without the cold air making his eyes weep. All would be well, he assured himself. No one could lose a column of a hundred men in such an empty land. Not a tree in sight. A desolate, godforsaken, bare-arsed mountain pass. The thought of making a run back to the French border was quickly dismissed. If he was uncertain where he was now any further attempt to find his way back with that approaching storm would surely have him frozen dead on the pass for the monks to find after the next snowfall.

He did not know for how long he rode. The storm was nearly upon him, and he cursed his stupidity for volunteering to go back to Blackstone. What had he been thinking? Trying to save his own skin, he told himself. The first splatter of wind-driven rain reached him ahead of the bruising storm. He cursed again. His horse veered gently away, turning its head from the stinging rain. Terrel had let the reins become too loose, and the beast took advantage. Terrel, face turned away like his mount, realized it had taken him off the course he had set. He yanked it around with rein and heel. Now he was directly facing the distant storm that would soon lash him. Before the clouds smothered the sky completely, he scanned the terrain. A cave, an overhang, anything for shelter. Two hundred yards away, a hunchback mound protruded from an undulating hillside, its black granite canopy peaking forward. It was the best shelter to be had in the shortest possible time.

Terrel urged his horse forward, wary of the approaching bend on the narrow track, aware that his horse could slip if they approached too quickly. Now the rain was splattering his gambeson, pricking his neck. He hunched. Eased the beast around the corner. He was fifty yards from the overhang. And he was not the only one seeking shelter. Two horses stood hobbled with their backs to him, as had the two men who sat hunched on the ground, cloaks wrapped against the wind.

With unerring failure, Terrel knew he had stumbled upon the two mercenary killers.

He yanked the reins. The horse dug its rear legs into the wet ground, slipped and, in trying to regain its balance, twisted its body. Terrel lurched in a helpless fall from the saddle. His back slammed into the bank and he winced in pain but his fist still gripped the rein as the bolting horse dragged him closer to the huddled men. His arm felt as though it was being torn from his shoulder. The horse ran on as if trying to join the routiers' mounts. A rumble of thunder and crack of lightning made it veer away. Terrel released his hand, rolled and sprawled. The hobbled mounts snorted and tried to break their bonds, alerted by his panicked horse. The routiers, one with a bottle in his hand, got unsteadily to their feet to calm them and turned, unsure what had spooked them. They saw a stricken Terrel scrambling to his feet.

The moment froze.

Terrel had nowhere to run.

Except forward. Driven by fear, he realized he had the men at a disadvantage. Wrapped in their cloaks, trying to soothe restless horses, slow from drink, they could not move quickly enough. Terrel bellowed, lungs bursting, his own terror forging strength into his legs and arms. He struck the first man as he tried to draw his sword, his body falling beneath a fatal blow from the rear hooves of a horse, his face slashed from Terrel's wild sword thrust. The man's companion reacted quicker. Knife in hand, he flipped his cloak, snared Terrel's blade, and lunged. Terrel's feet went from under him as he stepped on two empty wine bottles. He fell hard, snatched at the cloak to save himself and pulled the man down on top of him. Terrel raised his free hand to protect himself as the man's body and cloak smothered him. The sword twisted in Terrel's grip. The routier could not avoid the entangled blade; he made a strangled, choking sound as he impaled himself. He fell silent.

Terrel bellowed in pain, heaving the man off him, whose body rolled next to his dead companion, eyes staring blindly. Terrel squirmed away until his back rested against a sack of stolen goods taken from the slaughtered merchants. Wind-whipped rain clawed into his meagre shelter, stinging his face. He raised a hand to wipe it away and saw his hand covered in blood, thinned by the rain into rivulets running down his wrist into his gambeson. He had taken a knife thrust in his side. His hand pressed into the dirt to find purchase so he could stand. Instead, it found a bottle of unopened wine. He knocked the bottle's neck against a rock, broke it and poured the life-affirming liquid into his mouth.

Terrel looked out at the heavy clouds, so low he thought he could touch them. His horse was nowhere in sight. He glugged more wine. Rested his head back on the sack. If he was going to die he would die drunk. With a determined final swallow, he finished the bottle, sighed, belched, closed his eyes and slipped away into a darker place than the storm's enveloping clouds.

CHAPTER FOURTEEN

The rain had been swept away by the time Blackstone stood with Killbere and Renfred looking down at Terrel.

'His horse found its way back to us, so we knew he'd run into trouble,' said Blackstone's scout. 'I think he got lost on his way to you, Sir Thomas.' Renfred nodded to where the two dead routiers now lay in the open. 'We tracked his horse back here. I never thought much of the man, but he took the fight to them, so I owe him respect for that,' he said.

Blackstone acknowledged his German captain. 'Renfred, take the road ahead again. Let's make sure there are no more skinners hiding under rocks.'

Renfred rejoined his men.

'Well, what of it?' said Blackstone to his centenar, Will Longdon.

'If the whimpering bastard would stop fidgeting I could close the wound,' said Longdon.

'You cause more pain than the wound itself,' moaned Terrel as Longdon cleaned and stitched the gash.

'Be a man, Goddammit, and bite on that stick I gave you.'

'A stick that stinks and tastes of horse shit. Give me my belt to bite on if you must...' Terrel yelped as Longdon tied off his stitch.

'Think yourself fortunate you're already half pissed,' said Longdon, getting to his feet. 'It's little more than a damned scratch and you're whining like a three-legged dog trying to mount a bitch in season.'

'Can you ride?' said Blackstone to Terrel.

'Of course, Sir Thomas.'

'Then let's move on. We make camp by nightfall.'

'With your permission, Sir Thomas, I thought I might work with Walter Mallin until the wound heals,' Terrel said, gingerly arranging his torn short around the gash.

'Heal?' snorted Killbere. 'I once spent a day pinned to my saddle with an arrow through my leg and still fought a battle. Healing comes from ignoring the damned wound, man.'

Terrel looked past his accuser to where Walter Mallin stood holding the bastard horse's bridle. It was a begging look for help. Mallin spoke up. Even a malingering wretch like Terrel could make his life easier.

'Sir Thomas,' said Mallin, 'he would be of more use to me for a time than to any captain who needs a man with a sword in his hand.'

Blackstone nodded and took the reins. 'Very well,' he said. 'The wound will be assessed in a day or so. By then we'll be in Montferrat country and his barber surgeon will see to him.'

Killbere's look of disgust made Terrel turn his face away. 'Don't think killing the two bastards who escaped us brings you favour. It's what every man here would have done. So get off your arse and back in the saddle.'

Killbere mounted and gathered the reins. 'Mallin, make sure he cleans the shit out of every hoof.' He looked at Blackstone. 'You think me too harsh on the man?'

'He saved your life in France.'

'That is no reason to coddle him. He's seeking an easier life than any man here. And looking at those two skinners – one had a slash on his face and a crushed skull from a horse's hoof, and the other's carcass reeked of wine even in death. Killing drunks is sport for a night in a tavern.'

'Still, he did not run.'

'Thomas, every man here has to pull his weight. We took in those men who rode with Henry but they have not yet been sufficiently tested. Killing a few skinners is not enough to show a man's worth in a fight.'

'That day is not far off. If we get off this mountain without more trouble I'd be surprised. The route is not patrolled and already we have had a savage attack on peasants, a threat to a monastery and now the death of four merchants who, from the look of the markings on their satchels that Renfred found, are from Milan. It would be no great leap of imagination for the Visconti to lay the blame on us should they hear of their misfortune.'

The bastard horse yanked its head forward, jerking Blackstone, forcing him to tighten the reins.

'God's tears, Thomas, even that belligerent beast knows when we need to leave. We are as exposed up here as a boil on a whore's arse.'

'If we are seen by an enemy then we will see them too. They won't have a hiding place either. But we must ensure the way is clear for the Prince.'

John Jacob strode back from the dead routiers once Jack Halfpenny's archers had stripped what they wanted. 'Sir Thomas? These men?'

'Tie them onto their horses. We'll take them back to the road. Send men out to scour for wood to hang them at the roadside. We leave them as a warning as we did before.'

John Jacob instructed men to do as Blackstone had ordered.

'If skinners are joining the Scaligeri, word will soon reach him that you are depleting his call to arms,' said Killbere. 'Don't we have enough trouble waiting for us when the Visconti learn we are at their gates?'

'Cansignorio della Scala wanting to wage war is a distraction for the Visconti. And those bastards from Milan won't risk coming for us until after the wedding, by which time we will be making our way back to deliver the gold and will have Montferrat to cover our backs should they dare to cross into his domain. The Visconti and the della Scala will be at each other's throats.'

'Aye, but those whoresons are worse than Visconti's hunting hounds. They tear each other apart as soon as not. Cansignorio della Scala imprisoned one brother and assassinated another. There's little to choose between the Scaligeri and the Visconti. We could be caught in the middle of it all,' said Killbere. 'They could make common cause against us.'

'Then that is when you can test the value of the men we took in from Henry.'

Riding with the wind at their backs, Blackstone led his men across the vast plateau. The quicker they could begin their descent the sooner shelter would be found in the lee of the mountains. The high peaks still bore snow, and swirling storms gave chase, as if the mountain gods were keen to rid themselves of these killers who stained the high pastures with blood.

John Jacob oversaw the hanging of the two mercenaries, draping their spreadeagled bodies on what was nothing more than a frame of bound pieces of weathered timber. A poor man's cross so that passing travellers would know who these carrion-pecked men were and who had killed them. He thought on Killbere's words. It was true: the road they travelled was paved with the dead. Blackstone would never show mercy to the likes of these men, but John Jacob knew the fear Blackstone struck into the hearts of others also served as a challenge. There were surely many who would like to claim victory over the English King's Master of War and his small band of hobelars, archers and a veteran knight. Blackstone's force seldom numbered more than a hundred, so they were able to move quickly and strike when least expected. But a greater force could overwhelm them. There was little doubt that word of their journey from Chambéry in Savoy and their ascent into the pass would soon reach the French King. Now the French would know not only that Thomas Blackstone had surfaced after months of his whereabouts being unknown, but also where he was heading. The question that would soon be answered was whether they would risk the fragile truce between England and France and send French-backed routiers in force to pursue them into Italy.

Would they dare? Or would they strike a deal with the Visconti to do their killing? John Jacob cast a final glance at the dead men hanging forlornly on the makeshift hurdle. No, scum like these would not be sent. More likely the Vipers of Milan would use the Prince's wedding to find a way to snare Blackstone.

He turned his horse away from the sagging bodies. He had no doubt that the man he served knew the danger Henry would face if his true identity was discovered. Blackstone had risked his life by keeping him close to the Prince. To warn Blackstone of any threat. He had placed his duty to the King over the love of his own son.

John Jacob spurred his horse.

Italy beckoned, where their fate would unfold.

CHAPTER FIFTEEN

Blackstone led his men down into Italy where, after the bleak mountain pass, there was better grazing for the horses and fresh food to be bought from the villages for his men. Amadeus of Savoy still controlled the domain they entered, but there was still no sign of his troops who should have been protecting the pass. Blackstone rested the men on the outskirts of Susa before leaving for the Marquis de Montferrat's stronghold at Chivasso, sixty miles to the east.

'How far behind us do you think the Prince is?' said Killbere as he heaved free a boot, followed by the other, then dangled his feet in the cooling water of the mountain-fed river, shallow enough for a man to bathe and broad enough to keep unwelcome visitors in sight.

'You're keen to be invited to the wedding?' said a shirtless Blackstone, sluicing water across his chest and arms. He dunked his head and pulled his fingers through his hair.

Killbere sighed. 'Because we need to linger with Montferrat. My boots need repair, my sword needs sharpening, and I need a blacksmith for my holy-water sprinkler. A spiked mace is no good to a man if there's a damaged link in the chain. My pride would suffer if the damned thing whirled in the air like a woman's skirts and had as much effect.'

Blackstone dried himself. He glanced at the meadow behind him where his men were encamped. Decent pasture and warmer than the mountain pass. 'We should stay here for a day or two. Let the horses rest. We don't know what lies ahead. Amadeus's men have stayed in their beds at Chambéry, so who knows who's scavenging between here and Chivasso.'

John Jacob approached, carrying a cooking pot of food. 'Sir Thomas, a decent pottage. Plenty of vegetables but little meat to be had. That last village had only a milking cow and a couple of scrawny chickens. No eggs and no fresh bread.'

'Not even a trencher of stale bread?'

'No, Sir Gilbert, we near exhausted our supplies coming over the pass. Cold weather makes a man eat more. We have enough for a few days. But we'll find another village. We'll buy what we can.'

'Aye, but a hundred men devour in a day what a village would eat in a week,' said Killbere.

'Then we'll send Will and Jack out. Between them they'll find something to shoot,' said Blackstone, sitting cross-legged, his spoon dipping into the pottage.

'Knowing them, they'd put a broadhead arrow into an old nag and tell you it was prime venison.'

'It wouldn't be the first time we feasted on a dead horse,' said John Jacob. He settled down between the two men.

'Men can fast, but we need fodder for the horses,' said Blackstone. 'Montferrat will have grain.'

Killbere slurped the hot food. 'And if I remember the last time we were here, he was partial to roast duck.' He winced. 'John, where's the salt?'

'I shared what we had left among the men.'

Killbere grunted and spooned more food. He gazed out across the river. Willow, birch and oak lined the banks. The breeze rustled the willow and birch; the oaks were yet to burst open their leaves. 'A man could get used to a place of tranquillity like this,' he said.

Blackstone glanced at John Jacob as Killbere gazed across the river.

'Then you're ready to stop fighting,' said Blackstone.

'When the time comes, Thomas.'

Blackstone smiled. 'A time to sit on a wicker chair in the sun.'

'Aye, that kind of thing. Even if only for a short while.'

'With a woman in your bed, of course.'

'Of course.'

'The last time we rode through this countryside, you found a monastery.'

Killbere's chin lifted. 'I did?'

'And we lost you for three days because you were bedding that nun.'

'Was that here?' said Killbere with feigned innocence.

'You're damned right it is,' said Blackstone. 'So you won't be sitting in the sun this time and your nun will still be going to daily confession.'

'Ah,' said Killbere. 'Well, it was worth considering,' he said with a smile.

They fell into contented silence as they ate.

The twinkling light on the water and the shade from the willow evoked memories for Blackstone. Of times he and Christiana had roamed from Normandy into Aquitaine. How often the warmth of spring sun let them bathe in cold waters and then cleave, wet and hungry for each other as the breeze dried them, puckering skin and nipples. Blackstone could almost taste the lust he had for his wife. So young. So unaware of the fear and tragedy that awaited them.

Blackstone's spoon hovered at his lips. His eyes focused. Ever keen, his archer's eyes had seen something break the surface of the water as the river rippled across the shallows at its bend. It was a body. Floating feet first. Boots. Billowing surcoat. A soldier.

He dropped the spoon into the blackened pot.

He stood. Eyes searching the far bank. Movement at the bend. Shadows flitting further back in the trees. Killbere and John Jacob stood with him, their food abandoned. Then they too saw the body. And the others that followed. How many? A dozen? More. Twenty dead at least, tumbling across the shallows yet to reach them.

Blackstone raised his arm.

A hundred men knew without question that danger was close. They moved quickly and silently into battle positions.

'In the trees,' said Blackstone.

'Horsemen,' said Killbere.

John Jacob pointed. 'One of them lives.'

As the bodies got closer, they saw a man struggling to save himself from drowning. One hand clutched his shoulder while his head craned, trying to keep his mouth clear. The bodies swept past, water-soaked clothing dragging them lower, bodies bumping against the boulders beneath the surface.

Blackstone waded into the water. The current tugged at his thighs, but he had the strength to fight it. He heard John Jacob splash in behind him and Killbere call out for Will Longdon's archers. They would be in line, arrows nocked, eyes watching the far bank, ready for Killbere's command to loose if an enemy appeared.

Blackstone did his best to avoid the fast-moving dead but one collided with him, a crossbow quarrel embedded in his throat, eyes wide and mouth open in the shock and surprise of death. Blackstone pushed him away. Chest deep, he balanced himself, eyes searching for the floundering man. As the bodies swirled past, he saw they had vicious wounds. A recent fight. Upstream. How close? Ten miles? And if there were men in the trees, then why would they pursue the dead? No, one was alive. So he was important. He had rank. Or he had witnessed who had done the killing and perhaps those who followed had no desire for the slaughter to become known.

Blackstone braced against the current, John Jacob positioning himself two yards to his right and slightly behind him. If the bodies were moving this rapidly, it could take two to seize the injured man.

Blackstone pushed aside another dead man, squared himself, and then lunged as the grimacing man raised his bloodied hand away from his wound, offering it to the stranger's grasp. Blackstone grabbed him. The water twisted them both, almost taking Blackstone off his feet. John Jacob blocked the wounded man's passage downstream and caught his legs. Between the two of them, they fought the current and dragged the man ashore.

As they hauled him onto the river bank, horsemen on the opposite side nudged their horses into the shallows but stopped short from plunging onward. They wore black surcoats and the man who led them rode a destrier with a black caparison draped over its muscular frame. His blazoned shield bore no colour, only a white cross on a black shield. His helmet's visor was up, but his face was shadowed by the trees.

Killbere ignored Blackstone and his squire. His eyes fixed on the horsemen, his arm raised, ready to give the order to unleash a lethal arrow storm. He waited. It served no purpose to have Longdon's archers loose their shafts into men who had made no attempt to attack. The men in the water and the men on the far side were enemies. But was either one friend or foe?

Blackstone got to his feet, reached for Wolf Sword, lying in the grass where he had left it while he had bathed and eaten. He yanked it free of its scabbard and stood ready for the charge. Behind, his captains stood with their men, shields at the ready. Behind them, Longdon's archers. If a charge was in the horseman's mind, he would leave a lot of his men dead in the river and the meadow on that opposite bank. The man's horse pawed the shallows and fought the bit: it was as much a beast of war as Blackstone's own bastard horse. Its rider stood in the stirrups and gazed across the divide as if surveying the strength of the opposing men. Then he settled back into the saddle, shifted his weight so that his horse backed away from the water's edge and was soon swallowed by the shadows and trees. A fleeting shimmer of light and shade told Blackstone that the horsemen had retreated away from the river.

John Jacob cradled the wounded man, dribbling wine from his flask between the man's lips as Blackstone knelt beside him. Killbere instructed William Ashford to have his men double the picket lines and to bring the horses into the centre of their encampment.

Despite the man's gambeson being soaked, blood still seeped copiously. John Jacob said quietly: 'Shall I fetch Will?'

Blackstone shook his head. The man's pallor was already a death mask. He shivered, trembling from the cold water and the shock of losing too much blood.

'Who did the killing?' said Blackstone, speaking Italian.

The man's teeth clenched, whether from the blood loss or to try to slow his body's tremors. He tried to speak.

'Do you want more to drink?' said John Jacob.

The man nodded.

'Not too much,' said Blackstone. Then waited as the man nodded gratefully at the sweet wine. 'Who did the killing?' he asked again. 'Those riders show no blazon that I know. Are they Visconti men?'

The dying man shook his head and tapped his chest on his own stitched blazon of a stag's head encompassed by a shield.

Blackstone and John Jacob looked at each other, neither recognizing the blazon. It was not the Visconti device of a serpent devouring a man.

'Does he understand you?' said Killbere, looking down at the cradled man. 'There are different dialects here.'

'I don't know,' said Blackstone. He thumbed some mud from the man's cheek, his voice tender towards the dying man. 'Those men,' he said, indicating the river. He placed one forefinger across the other making the sign of the cross. 'Who are they? *Chi sono?*' he repeated, carefully pronouncing his question again.

The man's eyes flared, his brow furrowed.

'*Chi j'é,*' said Killbere, crouching down, trying the local dialect.

The man smiled at the attempt and nodded. His hand grabbed Killbere's wrist, as if he had found a friend. His head raised, eyes locked on the veteran knight.

'*La furia 'd Diò,*' he whispered, nodding his head as if to emphasize the words. His head lowered, his grip eased, his eyes half closed as he sank into death.

John Jacob laid the man's head down. He too had caught the dialect's meaning.

'God's fury,' he said.

CHAPTER SIXTEEN

Blackstone led the men north-east to where a bridge straddled a narrow point across the River Po and then turned down along the riverside to reach Montferrat's castle at Chivasso. Its octagonal towers, each capped with a supported roof, loomed a hundred feet above the city walls on the north bank of the river, its southern flank protected by the breadth of water.

Blackstone's unfurled banner was recognized and the city gates opened. The Marquis de Montferrat's steward hurriedly roused the household servants as the city gate's guard commander escorted Blackstone into the castle yard.

To Blackstone's eye, Montferrat's men were already on a war footing. The walls were manned and patrolled. Supplies bulged from the store rooms; sacks of grain were stacked in the stables. He knew that barrels of wine would choke the cellars and that the wells in the yards drew cistern water from the Po. Everything suggested that Montferrat was not prepared to go beyond the city and that, if trouble came, he would fight first at the city walls and then through the streets of Chivasso until the enemy reached the castle gates.

'He's readying himself for a siege,' said Killbere.

'And we'll soon find out who is causing him to make such

preparations,' Blackstone answered as they were escorted up the steps towards the great hall.

Montferrat was not a man who wasted time trying to impress others. His workmanlike approach to the difficulties he faced, sandwiched as he was between the Milanese Visconti and Amadeus of Savoy, meant he had to use what wealth he had to invest in men and equipment. He came from a lineage that dated back hundreds of years and he displayed sufficient adornment and comfort to proclaim his status once guests were brought into the great hall. Here banners and tapestries brought colour to the grey stone walls.

Raised voices echoed across the hall from another room. Montferrat's chamberlain showed no sign of unease as one voice in particular grew louder and more insistent, the words muffled by the distance from where the chamberlain beckoned Blackstone and Killbere to approach the fire and wait for their host.

The old man clutched his staff of office with one hand, snapping the fingers of the other for a servant to pour wine as the heated voice bellowed.

'My lord will be with us shortly, Sir Thomas.'

'Have we intruded at a difficult time?' said Blackstone.

The old man shook his head; a smile suggested what they were hearing was not an uncommon occurrence. 'No, no. It is a family matter. No connection to your unexpected arrival.'

Killbere glanced at Blackstone. *Unexpected arrival?* Perhaps it was exactly that which had caused the commotion. Blackstone shrugged.

John, Marquis de Montferrat, stormed into the hall, cloak billowing, his long hair flowing. Two hounds slunk in at a respectful distance behind him, wary of their master's temper. Teeth bared behind his beard: a smile to greet his guests.

'Thomas, Gilbert! You arrive as I castigate my wayward son. I have bred a turd. A vile stain on my name. If I did not know better, I'd swear he was sired by that cruel bastard Bernabò Visconti.'

A boy, no more than ten years old, peered around the far corner from where the Marquis had appeared. Montferrat caught Killbere's glance. He turned and pointed a threatening finger at the lad. 'Secondotto! You will be flogged and then you will spend the day in prayer. Get out!'

The child ducked out of sight.

Montferrat instructed his chamberlain: 'See his tutor flogs him and then turn him over to the priest. I don't want that evil slur on my name in my sight.'

The chamberlain bowed and scurried away.

'And have food brought. Here. We eat here. By the fire. Damned wind comes down the valley and creases a man's soul.' He shooed away one dog, eager for attention. 'That a child of mine takes pleasure in strangling cats and then tearing them limb from limb. For sport. For pleasure! Damned if I know where such vile behaviour comes from. Not from my seed.' He lowered his voice. 'Though I do not lay blame at my wife's door either,' he said. 'He is an aberration of nature and I shall have it beaten out of him.' He took a breath and calmed. 'Now, sit, for pity's sake. How long has it been? Nine, ten years since you were last here?'

'Ten, my lord,' said Blackstone.

'And during that time, I have fought and lost many a battle. No matter. You have succeeded more than most, Thomas. Your legend grows.'

'And I lose more blood along the way.'

'Your limp?' said Montferrat.

'A wound last year. The leg serves me well enough. If it complains, I ignore it. It strengthens every day.'

Servants came into the room, bearing trays of food. Others lifted a table and brought it closer. They threw a cloth over the scrubbed wooden surface and eating knives were placed at each setting. The servants placed platters of food on the table and poured wine. A bench was placed at the table and a chair for Montferrat. The chamberlain fussed and then shooed away the servants. Three other men appeared with bowls and cloths. Blackstone and Killbere washed their hands, the grime from their journey swirling as thick as broth. The hand cloth soon bore similar stains. Then, when his master was ready to eat, the chamberlain bowed and retreated to the far side of the hall.

Montferrat gestured for Blackstone and Killbere to take their places.

'My Lord Montferrat, with your permission, I would like to take care of my men. We rode hard these past few days.'

'Don't be anxious about your men, Thomas. I have already made arrangements for their needs. Wine and cold meats, bread and pottage from the kitchens. My chamberlain and I remember well your last visit. I know you care for man and horse before your own comforts.' He reached forward and began forking food onto a platter and then passed it to Killbere. 'Gilbert, here. You look like a man whose stomach thinks your throat has been cut. I take pleasure in serving it myself.'

Killbere salivated. His stomach growled. 'I'm honoured, my lord. Our last decent meal was goat stew in a monastery in the high pass.'

Montferrat, continuing to play the generous host, piled food onto Blackstone's platter. It was no common tin plate but embossed silver. That alone was a significant acknowledgment of his respect for his guests.

'I heard you killed some routiers,' he said. 'Don't look so surprised, Thomas. Whispers carry down those mountain passes, pushed along by the wind. Don't ask me how this information travels so quickly, but it does.'

'They were Scaligeri's men. It seems the Lord of Verona is gathering men to fight the Visconti.'

Montferrat chewed; picking a piece of stringy meat from his mouth he tossed it to the dogs. He nodded. 'He does. Della Scala has acted swiftly and with good timing.'

'And we found butchered men in the river at Susa,' said Killbere. 'But they were sworn men, not skinners.'

Blackstone proffered the stag's head blazon he had cut off the tunic of the man he'd dragged from the river. 'I don't know these colours.'

Montferrat put down his eating knife and held the patch between finger and thumb. 'D'Alessandro. He's a minor lord north of here. In Lombardy. He serves the Visconti. Susa, you say?'

'Yes. Those who killed him and his men wore black surcoats with a white cross. The man we saved called them *La furia 'd Diò*.'

'You got that close?'

'Across the other side of the river. They thought better of attacking us.'

'More likely they did not know who you were and were cautious of antagonizing those who might be allied to their cause.' He dropped his knife onto his plate, leaned back and drank his wine. He tossed more scraps to the dogs. 'Mostly Germans, with some Hungarians and English. They raid across Visconti territory. I'm surprised they ventured into Amadeus's domains, though. It is a difficult time, Thomas. While Galeazzo Visconti courts the great royal houses of France and England and marries his children into them and gains influence, his brother Bernabò declares war on the Pope, and the papal forces have been gathering along his border. Those men you saw are his. The Pope's and God's fury are directed at the excommunicated Bernabò.'

'Then that's why the Scaligeri have been recruiting,' said Killbere. 'If the Pope is fighting the Visconti, then what better time for della Scala to strike?'

'And you?' said Blackstone to Montferrat.

'I am an island surrounded by angry men. Papal forces want me to declare for them, but they don't see how quickly that would have me crushed from all sides. I bide my time. Amadeus of Savoy went on crusade last year. I believe he can be brought to be my ally. If that can be achieved then yes, I will fight Bernabò, but not before I have Savoy on my side.'

'And that's why you are preparing for a siege,' said Killbere. 'In case you cannot secure his goodwill.'

'If it comes to it, yes. Now, Thomas, you grace my table and you will always be welcome here, but look at how your presence might appear to these warring factions. The Pope denied your King's request to marry his youngest son to a princess of Flanders to stop your King's power spreading in Europe. Instead, he gave that dispensation to the French King's brother. That is insult enough and denied your King everything he planned. So, now he marries his son Lionel to a Visconti. There is an alliance in the making which suits the enmity between the Pope and your King. Yet here is the English King's Master of War visiting Montferrat, who does not yet declare for either side. For whom does your King declare? Clearly it is the Visconti, given his son's intended marriage.' He paused and studied Blackstone over the rim of his goblet, one hand draped lazily down, scratching a dog's ear. 'Everyone involved will ask whose side you are on, Thomas.'

'Visconti are my bitter enemies, you know that,' said Blackstone. 'Eight years ago I killed Bernabò's bastard son for planning my wife and child's murder.'

'Then does that mean you side with the Pope against your own King?'

'We are not involved with this conflict. We are here for Prince Lionel. Nothing more.'

Montferrat poured more wine for Blackstone. 'You think your mission simple? I am not the only one being squeezed by the Vipers of Milan and Amadeus of Savoy. You might lose your King's favour if you are caught up in this fight.'

'Then I had better tread carefully,' said Blackstone.

Montferrat leaned forward on the table. His voice laden with concern. 'You? Whenever have you done so? It's too late, Thomas.' He pushed a small folded bloodstained parchment across the table. The red wax seal was broken. 'You have stepped on a mantrap. The only question is how long before it snaps shut.'

Montferrat sat back as Blackstone unfolded the letter. 'A month before your Prince arrived in Paris, someone of importance there despatched a rider bearing that letter. The seal bears no warrant of office. Whoever sent it wanted to stay anonymous.'

Blackstone handed it to Killbere after reading the few cryptic words.

'"Beware of Thomas Blackstone. His whereabouts are unknown,"' Killbere read aloud.

'The rider?' said Blackstone.

'Dead. He tried to outrun my men. His horse fell. He was crushed. There is little doubt that the man who despatched that letter would have sent more than one rider and by different routes. It would be too important to leave to the luck and skill of one lone horseman.'

'And where did this happen?'

'South of here. I think he got lost.'

'A message to the Visconti?' said Killbere. 'The letter suggests a warning. Of what? There's no instruction in this letter to prepare a trap for us.'

Blackstone took it back from Killbere and refolded it. 'It's warning whoever this was intended for that our presence will cause a problem. That we may disrupt something already planned.' He tossed the letter onto the table. 'If he was riding south, and you thought him lost, then he could have been skirting your domain.'

Montferrat rubbed the wine stain on the table as his thoughts retraced the courier's journey. 'Thomas, I don't think so. Anyone coming over the pass would know to ride north and east of here to Milan. It's a well-worn route for traders and routiers. No, I think he was afraid of travelling through Visconti territory. So, he rides south, then swings east and that takes him where?' He raised his eyes to his two guests.

Blackstone saw the route in his mind's eye. 'Verona.'

Montferrat nodded and sipped his wine. 'Where else?'

Killbere grimaced. A huge conflict loomed and Blackstone and his men were being drawn into it. 'Verona against Milan. We know the Scaligeri family is bringing in skinners,' he said. 'We killed enough of them on the pass. Would the French side with Verona? And to what end? Their King's sister is married to Visconti's son. Damned if we didn't bring her across the mountains ourselves years back. It makes no sense.'

The three men fell silent.

'Whatever the French and della Scala are planning, it has to do with the Prince's wedding,' said Blackstone.

'Would Verona launch an attack during the ceremony?' said Montferrat. 'To open another flank aligned with the Pope's men? The Pope and your King hold no love for each other. And delaying this wedding alliance would strengthen the Pope's hand and hinder the English Throne's ambitions.'

Killbere drained his drink. He grunted, suppressing a belch. 'It's an ideal time to squeeze the Visconti who fight on their border with the Pope's army. They're vulnerable.'

'The bastard Visconti. I wish a plague on their house,' said Blackstone. 'But if we are to do what we were sent to do, then we must put ourselves between Verona and Milan.'

Montferrat eyed his guests. They had made no mention of their reason for being so far in advance of Prince Lionel's cavalcade. 'You have a specific reason for being here, Thomas?'

Blackstone showed no sign of subterfuge. He answered plainly, gazing directly at his host. There was to be no mention of the gold dowry. 'We are to ensure the Prince's marriage goes ahead unhindered by anyone.'

Montferrat dipped his finger into the droplet of wine left at the bottom of his goblet. He sucked its sweetness. Did he believe Blackstone? The English King's Master of War was no stranger to northern Italy. He knew the warring factions: families pitted against each other year in, year out; alliances changing as rapidly as the wind. If Blackstone chose the wrong side today, he could be outlawed tomorrow. What game was being played out here? It was beneficial for Montferrat to know how Blackstone's presence might affect his own status. At the moment his position was fragile. It was appropriate, he decided, that the English King would send his best commander to skirmish and throw a wide net of protection around his son, so Montferrat believed Blackstone had been tasked as he had answered. But any commander in the field of conflict was forced to make urgent decisions: it would be up to Blackstone alone whom he would fight for or against in order to protect the Prince. How great the risk was the question? At the stroke of a sword an even greater crevasse than already existed could tear asunder what diplomatic niceties remained between the English King and His Holiness the Pope.

'Even if it means aiding Bernabò Visconti?' said Montferrat.

'If we are to protect the Prince, then we have no choice but to side with the devil,' said Blackstone.

'Then you pit yourself against God's fury,' said the Marquis.

CHAPTER SEVENTEEN

Blackstone and Killbere made their way across the vast courtyard to where their men had settled for the night, their bedrolls laid out in the stables with their mounts.

'Thomas, you're putting us between the anvil and the hammer. Do we ride to Milan and declare ourselves for those whoresons?'

'Gilbert, I will not offer us up to those murdering bastards. But I have to get inside the gates of Milan somehow and meet up with the Prince.'

Killbere looked at him. He gave it a moment's thought. 'Ah, so you were never prepared to let Henry risk everything on his own.'

Blackstone smiled. 'That – and my duty.'

Killbere grunted. 'You court death, Thomas. You poke a wounded beast like Bernabò Visconti who wants nothing more than to kill you?'

'I won't start anything.'

'Thomas, tell me this is not a deliberate act to draw Bernabò to you. That you are not seeking a chance to kill him. That you wouldn't shit on his own doorstep.'

Blackstone remained silent.

'Damn you, Thomas. You risk too much. You know damned well he'll not be able to resist trying to kill you. Then the fault will lie at his door for breaking protocol with his brother and the Prince.'

'I can't answer for him. It's the gold we need.'

Killbere shook his head. It was obvious Blackstone wanted to draw the killer to him.

'It *is* more about the gold, Gilbert. For the war with France. What Bernabò decides to do is up to him but he cannot stop the Prince's dowry from being taken out of Milan. Besides, is it likely we're the only ones who know what the dowry is worth?'

'You think Verona is after the dowry?' Killbere gave it a moment's thought and answered his own question. 'These damned thieving noblemen. You're right. They'd slit their mother's throat and shove their fist down it if they thought she'd swallowed a silver penny. Aye, it's a prize worth having.'

Blackstone lowered his voice, pausing when Montferrat's men were in earshot. 'The Scaligeri aren't fools. It's a perfect time. Let the Pope's men raise the cross and scourge Visconti's forces while della Scala harasses and torments every Visconti village and town. Bernabò won't take to the field, not yet. His men will fight when they must, but he will stay behind Milan's walls. He daren't leave his brother when an English prince is due to be married in the city. It's the wedding that restrains him.'

'But for how long?' said Killbere.

Blackstone picked up the pace again. Even in the safety of Montferrat's castle there would be spies. To overhear the English King's Master of War might yield information of value that could be sold.

'The more of Visconti's men killed, the greater will be Bernabò's desire to take to the field. Taunt a mad dog long enough and it will break its restraining chain and attack. If he comes out, he'll be defeated, especially if Montferrat and Savoy reach agreement. It's up to us to keep him inside the walls by killing his enemies. That way, the Prince will be safe until after the wedding when we escort him and the gold home. After that I don't give a damn if the Pope's army and della Scala's men tear down Milan's gates and burn it to the ground.'

'Because by then, we and the gold will be long gone,' said Killbere. 'The Scaligeri will have taken a shit and sat on a thistle.' He snorted and spat. 'I like this idea more and more. Let's cause them grief. I'm all for killing any of these inbred, slithering rock lizards.' His grin was infectious.

Blackstone laughed. 'We leave at first light and seek them out.'

Killbere slapped him on the back. 'God, Thomas. I miss the old days. An army to fight. Men bellowing, lungs bursting. This will go some way to putting energy in my cock. There's nothing like fighting and killing to give a man an appetite for life.'

Blackstone brought his captains together and explained that they would be raiding and fighting, but he did not say against whom. Not yet. He would give his final orders about whom they would strike the next day, when they were clear of Montferrat's servants. Secrecy saved lives. The men rippled with eagerness, keen to put the night behind them and ride out. Each captain returned to their men and explained Blackstone's plan to strike where they must. No one had given Walter Mallin any tasks but he took it upon himself to check the men's horses.

John Terrel followed Mallin down the line of horses, carrying a bucket. Montferrat's stable hands had given every beast fresh straw and fed them, but Mallin wanted to ensure that no horse was lame or had suffered any unexpected injury. If Blackstone had decided not to stay in this place of food and shelter, then he would be riding man and horse hard.

Terrel's constant mutterings of complaint were largely ignored by the old horsemaster. His attention was focused on the animals now under his care.

'You would do well to learn what you can,' murmured the old man, a hand gliding across a horse's flanks.

'You treat me like a damned servant. One step removed from a slave. I'm a man-at-arms, not a damned stable hand.'

'You were a scum routier like the rest of us, Terrel. Were it not for Master Henry you would be cast out.'

'I joined him, did I not?'

'Aye, once you thought your skin would be safer by being with him rather than not.' He patted one horse. 'That cut has healed well. He'll be fine.'

'And my cut stings.'

'A sign of healing.'

One horse, belonging to the Gascon captain, Aicart, had shown some swelling on his rear leg days before and Mallin had made a poultice of witch hazel to reduce the inflammation. Aicart was a hard man who led his men from the front; he needed his horse to be fit and, with there having been no fighting, had asked Mallin to nurture the animal.

Mallin ran his hand over the horse's rump. He murmured soothing sounds to the horse whose ears pricked, head turning as much as the tethering rein allowed.

'Ease off that dressing,' Mallin told Terrel, who gave the horse's rear legs a wide berth in case it lashed out.

'I'm wounded,' Terrel complained.

'And I'm old. Get down there and peel it off slowly. You wanted a damned easy time of it – I'm giving it to you. Now do as I say,' he said, relieving Terrel of the bucket so that both his hands were free. 'Gentle, mind. He might still be tender.'

'Am I not tender, Mallin, you old goat? I suffer more than any beast and yet all I get is being stitched with a blunt needle by Will Longdon. Is my flesh not more tender than this horsehide?'

'You were rewarded because you killed them skinners. Do as I say or get yourself back in the ranks and leave an old man to do what he does best without listening to your whining.'

Terrel cursed and gingerly reached for the poultice. After the bandage was unwound, Mallin stooped and looked at the leg. 'Aye, he'll be fine, but we'll put on another for the night, just to be sure.' He passed the bucket to Terrel. 'Unwind the cloth, no need to squeeze the juice out. Wrap it so you could pass the thickness of a knife blade between leg and cloth.'

The horse's withers shuddered. It altered its weight from one leg to the other. Terrel held back.

'He's a dumb beast that needs care. He doesn't need another dumb beast pressing too hard on him. Do as I say.' Once again, he murmured a low comforting tone to the horse as Terrel did his bidding.

After ensuring that the poultice bandage had been bound properly, the old man patted the horse. 'Now then, let's get down the line and see the other mounts are ready for the morning.'

Terrel grimaced and stood up to rejoin the old man, who gave him a long hard stare.

'What?' Terrel complained.

'Bring the bucket.'

CHAPTER EIGHTEEN

The Marquis de Montferrat stood on the balcony of his sleeping quarters, gazing down into the courtyard sipping mulled wine brought by a servant. He pulled a blanket across his shoulders to keep the chill of the pre-dawn air and morning dew from settling onto his nightshirt. Blackstone had stayed behind after the previous night's meal while Killbere used the garderobe. Could Montferrat send a messenger? Of course. Once Blackstone explained what he needed, Montferrat said he would send three riders on different routes. Blackstone needed help. And Montferrat would do whatever was necessary to help the English.

In his bed that night he had lain awake listening to the scraping of metal on stone as Blackstone's men sharpened their weapons late into the night. Their low voices, little more than murmurs, hummed as they huddled in subdued candle- and lantern-light. Men preparing for conflict. Montferrat heard no sound of dissent or argument, as so often happened when fighting men were tightly confined, like Blackstone's men in the stables. He imagined the close-knit fighters discussing past successes and hopeful outcomes of the battles that lay ahead. He had eased into sleep accompanied by these sounds and then awoke as birds heralded first light. But it was not only the delicacy of birdsong that interrupted his slumber but the strike of iron hooves on stone from the courtyard below.

Montferrat watched Blackstone's men walking beside their mounts, leading them through the castle gates, their slow shuffling footfall accompanying the scrape of iron on stone. Horses snorted. Bridles jangled. No one spoke. Blackstone led his men on foot, his own horse towering over him, yet remarkably placid, defying its reputation. This was no grand exit. No fanfare. They slipped away without fuss into the approaching dawn, seeking out their enemy.

Montferrat shivered, but not from the chill air. He had fought enough against the Lords of Milan, Savoy and Verona, among others, to know how hard-won battles could be, but he had never faced men so determined to inflict ruthless and intense violence on an enemy like the English Master of War and his men.

He swallowed the remaining wine as the gates thudded closed on the last of the horses. He told himself he was fortunate he was a friend to Blackstone. He pitied those who were not.

Several hours later Blackstone and Killbere lay with John Jacob on high ground, peering over the hill's edge. Five hundred yards below, horsemen moved in a straggling fashion along the valley. They were spread out with no sense of order.

'How many do you see, John?' said Killbere.

'Thirty? Thirty-five? A patrol, do you think?' said John Jacob.

'Can't be anything else.'

'Whose men are they?' asked Killbere. 'Visconti's?'

The three of them had to shield their eyes against the sky's brightness despite the overlaying blanket of clouds.

'Can't be sure,' said John Jacob.

'Look at the man on the far side. He's carrying a pennon,' said Blackstone.

They fell silent again, each straining their eyes to make out whose blazon was being borne.

'Too far for me,' said Killbere.

'John?' said Blackstone.

'I'd say they were Visconti's men. Looks like their blazon. Can't be sure.'

Blackstone curved his hand around one eye, the tight circle focused on the pennon bearer. 'Visconti,' he confirmed after a moment of staring hard at the wavering banner. 'They're looking for signs of the Pope's men.'

'Or of della Scala's,' said Killbere.

Blackstone twisted and looked back at his men waiting in the belly of the ground below them. 'We'll shadow them as best we can,' he said. 'Renfred and his lads can skirt them when they return.'

'There might be no need for that,' said Killbere, drawing Blackstone's attention back to the Milanese horsemen. 'They're riding into a death trap.' He pointed.

'Damned if they're not half asleep,' said John Jacob. 'They've no advance scouts.' Out of sight of the horsemen, a thousand or more yards in the distance, around the contour of the opposite hills, a shimmer of movement disturbed the treeline of a forest. Dark shapes, barely distinguishable – men.

Blackstone studied the land. The opposite contours would draw the horsemen to follow its line around the forest edge. And that would give the ambushers the advantage of being on the higher ground. The hook-shaped forest would almost encircle Visconti's men. As he looked along the ridgeline where he lay, he saw the hills curved down onto narrower ground. Water glistened from a distant river, narrow enough to offer a crossing.

Killbere snorted snot and rolled onto his back. 'God's tears, Thomas, as keen as I am, is this worth our effort? Let the bastards kill each other.'

John Jacob looked at Blackstone. He nodded. Killbere was

right. 'We don't know how many are in those trees or whose men they are.'

'The more of Bernabò Visconti's men are slaughtered, the less he will restrain himself,' said Blackstone. 'Who knows how many he has already lost? There are few of his men down there, but if he sees this attack as a taunt too far, then the man's temper will drive him out of Milan with his troops. That creates fear. It might delay the marriage. More than that, it could make the Visconti hold back the gold.'

Killbere stared back down at the unsuspecting Milanese soldiers. 'They serve a monster, Thomas, and we are aiding and abetting him.' He picked dry snot from his nose, examined it for a moment, and then flicked it away. 'But...' He grinned. 'We cannot risk losing the gold.'

They slithered down from the hill's skyline and rejoined the men as Renfred and a half-dozen of his scouts returned. The German joined the other captains and they gathered around Blackstone, who drew a plan of attack on the ground. He explained what they'd seen from their vantage point. Visconti men were riding into an ambush. He laid stones to show the contours, broken twigs to show the extent of the forest and laid down an arrow of a few broken sticks to show their own route of attack. To the left of the hooked forest, a stretch of water meandered another half-mile in the opposite direction. Blackstone pointed to it.

'This is where we can kill most of whoever's in that forest once they attack the Visconti.'

'I'll wager they'll use crossbows first,' said Killbere.

'And then rush them on horseback,' said John Jacob.

Renfred pointed with a stick to the forest side of the water course. 'They've men there. No more than thirty, but it looks as though it's where they will stop any retreat. If Visconti's men turn away from that forest, they'll run straight into these horsemen.'

'And that will box them in,' said Killbere.

'And that's exactly what we would have done if it we planned such an ambush. That's where the circle is fully closed and Visconti's men overwhelmed,' said Blackstone, pointing a stick at the gap that led to the river.

Longdon pointed an arrow, indicating the snaking tear in the ground Blackstone had drawn as the river. 'How far from there to the forest?'

'A thousand yards,' said Blackstone.

'And cover for us?'

'None. We're in the open,' said Killbere.

'Then we need to fall back another two hundred yards from the crossing,' Longdon said, looking at Blackstone. 'You see why?'

The archer's eye had seen the benefit of drawing their enemy to the banks of the river. Men on horses would balk at a banked crossing, probably muddy, and be slowed by the obstacle, allowing the archers to kill them before they got across.

'If the Visconti men fight, and there's no reason to think they won't,' said Killbere, 'they'll break ranks when the men from the hook of that forest close in on them. Squeezing them. They only have one way to retreat and that's heading for the river.' His look at Blackstone was a silent question.

'We need to kill those horsemen before the Visconti's men get there,' said Blackstone, answering it.

'But how?' said Meulon. 'We have to get Will and his men behind them, and then have me and my lads take on those who break through chasing the Visconti.'

'Aye, we're too thin on the ground, Sir Thomas,' said Aicart.

The group fell silent. Their attack needed precision to assault their enemy, help the Visconti and break the ambush waiting by the river.

Blackstone pointed at Killbere. 'Gilbert, you take Renfred and his men. When Visconti's men are attacked in the valley, John and I will strike with ten men from their rear.'

'Those lazy bastards will lose a few before you get to them,' said Killbere.

'We're not here to wet-nurse them. Damned if I care that some of them will die. I just don't want a complete slaughter. Everything we're doing here is to stop Bernabò Visconti from turning his back on his brother and our Prince. We don't want him taking the field. As soon as the fight begins, then you kill the men at the river.' He gestured to Will Longdon. 'Will, you ride hard and fast and get to the place you need to be once Sir Gilbert starts his attack.' He nodded at Meulon. 'While he's doing that, dismount and take your position between Will's bowmen and the river. John and I will drive a wedge between the Visconti and whoever's lying in wait for them. Once we've done that, we'll pivot and ride for the river and they'll be in pursuit. Will, cut them down as soon as you can. Meulon, once we cross the river, we'll turn and stand with you.' He looked at his captains. 'Questions?'

There were none. Blackstone's captains dispersed back to their men.

Meulon nudged Will Longdon. His height and weight made little difference to the stocky archer's balance as he made a request. 'Listen, when you shoot over us, give my men a dozen yards before we reach the enemy, otherwise I'll have a shaft in the back of my neck. When we fought the Spanish, your arrows damned near creased my scalp.'

Longdon waved the arrow in front of Meulon's face. 'An arrowhead would bounce off your thick skull, Meulon. When a man bends his back into his bow, waiting for lumbering oxen to plough a field of battle, it's hard to see before he shoots.'

'Then open your damned eyes, Will. Slay the first rank of enemy but for pity's sake, don't drop onto my attacking line. It was too close in Spain. Too damned close.'

Longdon heard his friend's genuine concern. He nodded. They were bound to face brutal and rapid fighting. 'I'll have the lads put a twist on their feathers. That'll give the shafts more spin. It'll help with accuracy and distance,' he said, running forefinger and thumb along the arrow's fletching.

Meulon tapped Longdon's shoulder in thanks and turned to where his men waited.

Longdon called after him: 'We're always short of arrows. If one does strike your skull'—he smiled at the bear of a man—'bring it back so we can use it again.'

Blackstone and Killbere watched them go.

Killbere snorted and spat. 'Thomas, you give me the hind teat to suck on. The fight is with you. Damned if I should be the rearguard.'

Blackstone placed a hand on his friend's shoulder. 'Gilbert, did you not hear what Renfred said? You will be outnumbered. Is that not enough fight for you?'

Killbere shrugged. 'Ah, well, there is that, I suppose. Very well, Thomas, go and stir your hornets' nest. Remember, though'— he grinned—'I won't be there to save you if you fall off that bastard horse.'

CHAPTER NINETEEN

The Visconti captain, Mattia Marchesi, leaned forward in the saddle. He gazed down at the hoofmarks on the torn earth. No more than a dozen horses. More likely to be the enemy's scouting party. It might even be a small caravan of traders on their way east. He turned to look at his men following behind him. Cast out, given the dirty job of attacking small pockets of papal troops or Scaligeri camps. Enough to harass them. Barely enough to make any impression on their bigger force. Wherever they were. There had been no sign of them. But his master, Bernabò Visconti, had sent him and his men, and a dozen other small parties like theirs, to strike wherever they could, and send word back on enemy troop movements. The men behind him were watching for signs of the enemy, but they were tired. And resentful. If they were not held in check, it could be a deadly combination. He would not countenance discontent and they respected him enough to keep their complaints silent. As did he. He would not criticize Bernabò Visconti. Once they returned to barracks, a whisper of anything said against their Lord of Milan would end in a painful death. Visconti had kept the bulk of his men behind the city walls and Marchesi and the others knew that their comrades in Milan were going to benefit from the celebrations when the English Prince arrived. No lying out in the rain, soaked and eating salted meat for them. Going without fires for cooking. No, they would be dressed in their finery to show the English how a Visconti welcomes royalty. And when the gorging at the feasts was over, there would be enough food left to feed an army. And that wouldn't be him and the others. So much for comradeship. Bastards. Sons of whores. And they'd gloat when he and his men returned.

He drank from his wineskin. Snorted and spat. Even the wine in their rations was poor quality. Well, damn them, he'd have blood on his sword and that might earn him favour. Killing Scaligeri's men hadn't been a hardship. The Veronese were disorganized. In fact, he shouldn't complain. Their troops were poorly trained. They travelled in small groups, easy to follow, even easier to ambush and kill. Now Marchesi and his men had tracked these few horsemen who would camp by nightfall and then fall under their swords.

As he bent to loop the wineskin's cord back onto his saddle, a flutter of birds rose up from the forest three hundred yards to the right. No sooner had the flapping wings buffeted the air than lethal whispers hissed around him. His horse shied. A swarm of crossbow bolts. Some flying past. Others striking men and horses behind him. Three men fell, pierced by the missiles. Stunned into shock, the vital seconds gave his enemy the advantage. Horsemen surged from the treeline. Marchesi's hand was on his sword. How many? A hundred? More? Counting them wasn't necessary; there were enough to overpower him and his men.

'Ride!' he bellowed, spurring his horse forward towards the gap below the curve of forest that lay ahead, only to realize moments later that another twenty horsemen were attacking from there. He wheeled his mount. His men turned with him. In a desperate moment, he saw that the only escape route was to the river several hundred yards away to his left. Then riders appeared from a cleft in the land, sealing off that route too.

He spurred his horse at the second line of attackers, who had surged from the curved edge of the forest. They'd have to strike – hack their way clear and make for the gap beyond the trees, hoping their horses carried them through the enemy line and gave them a chance to escape. Shields raised, the men followed him.

He saw their attackers' blazon. Scaligeri!

Marchesi and his men did not lack courage. Or desperation. Fear gave men strength. They slashed left and right, but their enemy had closed ranks. Horses thudded against each other. If they couldn't break through, then the first line of horsemen that had attacked after the crossbows' bolts were unleashed would soon be upon them. They would be boxed in. Two more of his men fell wounded beneath the panicked horses. Reins hauled tight, spurs raking their beast's flanks, the Visconti men fought hard but they could hear the rumble and thud of attacking horsemen behind them. He dared a glance back and saw charging horsemen fast approaching. If they were more Scaligeri, then their lives were lost.

Blackstone came around the lee of the hill from where he had first observed the Visconti patrol and galloped towards the rear of the fight. The speed at which the Visconti men had been entrapped meant someone in the della Scala camp knew what they were doing. Like leaving a trail of breadcrumbs to entrap a bird, they had put a false trail down on the ground drawing the Milanese fighters into the ambush. And its execution had been swift. The Visconti were being smothered.

A yard behind Blackstone, John Jacob rode on one side and Aicart the Gascon captain on the other. Bezián, the 'priest killer' who had travelled with Henry Blackstone the year before, urged his horse to stay abreast of his captain. Blackstone had chosen well. The Gascons under Aicart's command were a force to be reckoned with, their ferocity unmatched despite their small numbers. Merciless in their killing of those who rode against them, they were as lethal as Will Longdon's bodkin points. They smashed into the Scaligeri ranks. Horses reared. Men fell, only to be trampled.

Marchesi gulped air. Sweat stung his eyes. He was no closer to escape than moments before, but whoever these men were, they were on his side. They looked like mercenaries. Had Bernabò Visconti sent them to bolster his patrol? There was no time for idle speculation. He rose in the stirrups and slashed down, cleaving an opponent's hand at the wrist. The man screamed. Marchesi barged him, slamming him with his shield, throwing him onto the ground. Defenceless, he would be dead in minutes.

Blackstone's impetus bludgeoned the huddled enemy. The bastard horse was a force of nature. Loosening the reins, he gripped with his knees and let it hammer blow the enemy horses with its misshapen head. Wild-eyed, the lesser beasts fought the bits between their teeth, veering away to expose their riders to a storm of hardened steel. The Scaligeri ranks broke free from the turmoil, attempted to regroup and turn back, but they placed themselves between Blackstone and the Visconti's second wave of fighters who attempted to pierce the massed horsemen. Chaos. Men screamed. Horses went down, flanks slaked with blood and sweat. Unsaddled men-at-arms tried to fight on their feet. And failed.

John Jacob roared to get Blackstone's attention. Hammer blows from a spiked mace were beating down on Blackstone's shield. Wedged between two of della Scala's men, he protected himself from the mace's fierce blows and slashed Wolf Sword across the second attacker who fell back, a foot caught in the stirrup, and was dragged by his panic-stricken mount further into the fray. Blackstone twisted in the saddle, rammed his shield beneath the mace wielder's chin and drove his blade into his exposed groin. The man screamed and fell.

John Jacob had fought closer to him. He mouthed something, but the bellowing of the fighting men drowned out his words.

A warning. He pointed his sword towards the far treeline. A hundred della Scala horsemen had burst from the forest, a final and desperate act to kill the Visconti and those who had dared to save them. Blackstone nodded, signalled his squire to follow him. He spurred the bastard horse towards the man he thought to be the Visconti leader. His back was to him. He slapped the flat of Wolf Sword's blade onto his helm.

The man turned, snarling, blade slashing, the strike anticipated by Blackstone and blocked.

'The river!' he said without thinking that the man probably didn't understand. '*Il fiume!*' he cried. Without waiting for an answer, he broke through what was left of the Scaligeri men. John Jacob and the others were already spurring away, following Blackstone's command.

As they turned their backs on the reinforcements approaching from the forest Blackstone saw a shadow, darker than the light that bathed the treeline. A lone horseman clothed in black. His surcoat bore a white cross. A man who inflicted God's fury on his enemies. Blackstone realized the man-at-arms had created the ambush and directed the fight and now gazed down without making any attempt to join the men he commanded.

What was it about this man?

Blackstone's memory taunted him.

He was sure he knew him.

CHAPTER TWENTY

Killbere and Renfred had manoeuvred their men into cover behind a cleft in the hill, observing the della Scala horsemen waiting to cut off any retreat from the fight. The veteran knight hunched low across his horse's withers like the men around him, their low profile concealing them from the enemy eighty yards away. They were downwind so, with luck, the ambushers' mounts would not detect their horses. The sudden attack several hundred yards away swept men's cries down to those in wait. The della Scala men broke cover, ready to cut off those under attack. Killbere waited until they had surged along the riverbank and taken position forty yards beyond the water. Now the overwhelmed Visconti men would see that any possibility of escape across the river and onto the open plain beyond was blocked.

The impact of Blackstone's attack from the rear of the fight reverberated down to Killbere's men. Killbere spurred his mount, the distant battle muffling the sound of his attacking horses. He saw out of the corner of his eye that as soon as he had surged forward, Blackstone and the Visconti had raced for the river. It was now essential that Killbere and Renfred's men inflict rapid violence on the enemy at the riverside, who were focused on the fighting in the distance. One of the della Scala men at the far end of the line saw Killbere leading the charge from their rear. He cried out a warning and yanked his horse's reins harshly, an act that made the horse next to him shy away, nearly unseating its rider. The momentary confusion gave Killbere an extra twenty yards. Despite being outnumbered two to one, the plan of attack had been straightforward. Half of Renfred's men would strike at the Scaligeri's backs to support Killbere, while Renfred would lead the others across their front. The della Scala men would be fighting in confusion, wheeling this way and that.

Killbere reached along the line of the men, slashing wildly at those unable to defend themselves, and as they recoiled from wounds and shock, Renfred's men boxed them in. Horses panicked, their riders barely able to keep control as they jostled each other, whinnying, heads plunging, snatching reins from their riders' grip. It made Killbere and Renfred's killing easier. When he reached the end of the enemy line, Killbere heeled his horse into the throng of horsemen who were now forced to fight both left and right as Renfred's men hacked at them mercilessly. Horses slipped and fell. Riders went down. Loose horses ran wild. Some splashed across the river through the ranks of Meulon's men waiting in position for the final assault expected from the far trees.

Killbere saw Blackstone break free from the fight and turn for the river.

'Back, lads!' he commanded.

Renfred's men cleared their fighting lines. Enemy bodies lay strewn. A severely injured horse lay dead, its rider trapped beneath its weight. Two of the ambushers escaped towards their comrades who they assumed were now chasing Visconti men towards the river.

Killbere saw one fall beneath Blackstone's sword; the other soon followed his fate, killed by one of the Gascons as his horse bolted into their ranks. Killbere's horse's hooves churned the bloodied ground as he spurred it into the water. The low incline that served as the riverbank soon bore the signs of their retreat to where Meulon and the others waited, shields at the ready. The German, Brun, held the line at the far end as Meulon waited in the centre.

Killbere's men slowed their mounts and guided them around those who waited on foot, their own mounts hobbled at the rear of Will Longdon's archers further back still. By the time Killbere and Renfred each took their place on either flank, the veteran knight saw that they had lost two men in the attack but the price had brought death and disarray to the Veronese and cleared the path for Blackstone and the others to hurtle into the river.

Blackstone's men slowed their mounts and eased them across the slippery bank and into the shallow water. That deliberate act gave their pursuers a chance to close the gap. It was down to thirty yards. As Blackstone and the surviving Visconti men stormed up the other bank, the ground shuddered from the wave of attackers. Yanking on their reins, they attempted to slow their galloping mounts. But a horse crazed with the scent of blood and being given its head only moments earlier took a great deal to slow. The first dozen trampled over the bodies of their dead comrades and plunged down the muddied bank. Some slipped, reared, threw their riders, leaving them helpless in the water as the horses bolted. Those unsaddled were left facing their following line of horseman, whose arrival on the mud-slicked bank created more turmoil as the riders cursed, brought their mounts under a semblance of control, leaned back in the saddle and eased their horses into the water.

Fifty slender shadows fell from the sky.

Bodkin-pointed shafts an inch thick, a yard long, tore into flesh. Horses and men screamed in pain. It was a slaughter. But it could not stop the weight of horsemen and their mounts from ploughing through water and up the other side through the swirling blood and arrow-riddled corpses.

Blackstone joined Killbere on the flank, ready to cut off any horsemen that might avoid Meulon who now strode forward ten paces, shortening the distance between his men and the attacking horses, ensuring that when the latter scaled the bank they had little opportunity to be spurred on to gather any speed. They would meet spear points and a shield wall.

The scrambling horses gained dry ground. Forty of Meulon's long stride lengths away. They came on. Twenty-five. Twenty. Now the riders could smell the stench of wet horse and men's vomit. But they had not yet spurred their mounts into a full-on charge.

Meulon knelt. Shields came together. Ten-foot-long spears were heeled into the ground: lethal spear points ready to pierce horse flesh. One man wounds or kills a horse; the second rises up and clubs its rider to death or drives hardened steel through the floundering body.

Meulon hunched. Will Longdon had left it late. He cursed him. And then, as he stared at the terrified horses fifteen yards away and braced himself for the onslaught that he knew would likely crush them, a shuddering wave of arrows fell onto the sweat-lathered beasts. His men leapt forward, stabbed and hacked, retreated, stood shoulder to shoulder again, and waited for the next wave. The maimed and dying beasts flailed and kicked, fighting for the last gasps of their lives, screaming pitifully. Unable to defend themselves, their riders lay dead. The next wave was caught in the obstacles made by the corpses. As Meulon strode forward, Blackstone and Killbere attacked the survivors from the flanks. Death encircled della Scala's men. They had no escape.

Marchesi held back his men. There was a lesson to be learnt here from a knight whose men were well practised in the art of killing. And yet he did not know who it was that had saved him.

Other than the sounds of pain from wounded man and horse, it fell silent. There was no celebration of victory. Blackstone's men went among the wounded and finished them off with sword or knife thrust.

Blackstone eased the bastard horse among the dead. His eye followed their attack line from where he was to the river, across the other side and all the way to where bodies littered the field close to the forest.

As his eye settled on the distant trees, the light began to play its tricks. The wind swayed the top branches; the shadows deepened. Not from lack of light, but from the black-clothed men that came out from the forest's depths. That same lone horseman who had remained in the trees when the Scaligeri had attacked now eased his mount forward. Behind him, a long line of men followed. And once they had emerged, another came and then another.

Blackstone's archer's eye swept across them. Close to five hundred men had seeped out of the forest. He looked behind him. His own men were stripping the dead of anything of value.

'Gilbert?'

'I see them. We won't live through the day, Thomas. And if there's one thing I want before I die, it's a shit.'

Blackstone's look showed sufficient surprise to make Killbere shrug. 'You have to be practical, Thomas. There's no time for other desires.'

John Jacob hadn't moved from their side. 'Sir Thomas?' he said, pointing his bloodied sword towards the line of men who had stopped their slow advance several hundred yards from the river where della Scala's men lay sprawled. The black-clothed men with their white crosses took on the appearance of a vast graveyard.

'Why've they stopped?' said John Jacob. 'They could overrun us easily enough.'

Blackstone shook his head. Again, there was that nagging doubt about the way the man who led them sat astride his horse. Almost casually, one shoulder slumped, as if leaning forward on his mount's withers. Something familiar.

They watched as the man's head half turned. He must have spoken to his men because they wheeled their horses. Those same disciplined columns which had emerged from the trees rode without haste towards the far end of the forest and the gap that had once been Marchesi's hoped-for escape route.

'That man is in command. He threw della Scala's men into the fray,' said Blackstone. 'He didn't want to lose any of his own. He hadn't counted on us being here to spoil his plans. They'll be hunting for Visconti men.'

'I don't give a damn who he hunts,' said Killbere. 'He's let us live today.' He turned his horse to go among the men and check for casualties as Blackstone stayed watching the dark columns snake across the open ground until finally the lone man who had remained eased his horse after them.

Blackstone glanced at John Jacob. 'Today wasn't the time or place, but I'll wager we'll come face to face again. And next time he won't be so generous to us.'

PART THREE

DEATH IN THE
MONASTERY

CHAPTER TWENTY-ONE

Henry Blackstone and Gifford had followed Prince Lionel and Count Amadeus of Savoy as they traversed the Mont Cenis Pass. An edge of uncertainty had caused Edward Despenser to send men ahead as a scouting party once they reached the charred remains of a goatherders' hamlet. Women were rebuilding the huts; one stood on a hillside tending a handful of goats. Amadeus hailed a man who approached him nervously.

Guichard, the goatherd, clasped his hands together as if in prayer, bowed his head and falteringly explained the events when Amadeus asked about the skeletons at the edge of the hamlet.

Henry was close enough to hear the conversation and the mention of his father's name. He glanced at Gifford. 'My father is clearing the way ahead,' he muttered.

'I doubt Despenser will be well pleased. Look at his face – he didn't know Sir Thomas was in the vanguard. He thought he was in command,' Gifford answered, his lips barely moving, wary of the horsemen around them hearing him.

One of the women turned her head from where she was laying woven grass onto a hut's roof. She appeared less cowed of the Prince and knights than the man who stood stooped in submission before them. 'There are more dead, my lord,' she cried, before continuing her work.

Her impertinence in not approaching the Prince before she spoke annoyed Despenser. He chastised her, but the Prince raised his hand to calm his deputy commander's ire. Despenser muttered something to the Prince, advising him to exercise caution as the peasants living so high in the mountains might be deranged.

'Woman,' said the Prince. 'Will you tell an English prince where the dead are and who they might be?'

She wiped a sleeve across her nose and clambered down the short ladder from her roof. Guichard the goatherd cringed as Melisende approached Amadeus and the Prince. 'This woman... she... she is my wife, lord,' he said.

She gazed up at the figure, whose height seemed even greater because his horse was so tall. There could be little doubt that the hundreds of men and horses that snaked behind him were following a man of great importance. She seemed overcome with sudden awe and bowed. The gesture appeared to please the man at his side, who had scolded her.

'You are the English Prince, lord?' she asked.

'I am. How would you know that?'

Guichard put a restraining hand out to stop his wife from saying anything more. 'Lord, we were told that... that you would travel this way.'

Melisende brushed his hand away. 'By the same man who did the killing and who saved our lives.'

'Woman, do you not obey your husband?' said Amadeus.

Melisende glanced at Guichard. She hesitated. And relented. 'Aye, my lord, I do. He is a good man. But sometimes his words falter.'

'Let him speak,' said the Prince. 'Today we are in no hurry.' He gestured for Guichard to continue.

Melisende nodded. 'Tell them, husband,' she said with a rare tenderness in her voice.

Guichard half turned, pointing in a vague direction beyond the hamlet. 'There are bodies lying at the bottom of the cliff and... and you will see a... a monastery, lord, and more dead. Killed by the English knight in the courtyard. They hang from the walls.'

'The monks did that?' said Amadeus.

'Sir Thomas gave them the instruction. As a warning to others.'

Amadeus turned to the Prince. 'Of course. It is Blackstone's way.'

'Barbaric, my lord,' said Despenser.

'But necessary, Edward.' He glanced at Amadeus. 'The pass is not patrolled.'

Amadeus had the courtesy to nod his acknowledgement at what was the gentlest of rebukes.

'Blackstone puts the fear of the devil in men's hearts,' said the Prince. He turned in the saddle and looked at Henry. 'Perhaps a few sous for these villeins?' he suggested.

Henry felt his neck colour. Did the Prince know he had been gambling and fighting in Chambéry? He could have instructed any of the other men who rode between him and the Prince.

'Highness,' said Henry, acknowledging the request. Less of a request, more of a command, he thought.

'Be generous,' said the Prince as Henry spilled out coins. He looked at the Prince, who held his gaze. It was a knowing look. Henry tossed the whole purse to Guichard, who caught it.

'Lord, bless you,' he said, bowing to the Prince, then handing the purse to Melisende without any sign of reluctance.

The Prince heeled his mount. 'Do not bless me, goatherd. Give your blessings to Sir Thomas Blackstone.'

When the Prince's cavalcade was within five hundred yards of the monastery, he drew up his horse. Torn flesh and eviscerated corpses were plain to see. Those hung low on the walls had

had their lower limbs chewed off by wolves. Eyes, scalp and faces had been pecked clean by ravens and crows. The Prince's eyes squinted against the light, trying to make out why some corpses were writhing.

'Do they still live?' he said, as if to himself.

'Scavengers feed on their bellies and chests, highness,' said Despenser. 'What you see are crows clinging on and eating. Making the corpses move.'

Prince Lionel winced. 'A clear message to anyone daring to strike at the monastery,' he said. 'Before we encamp, remove them. Find a ravine. Throw them in. Let the vultures and buzzards have their share of Blackstone's largesse.'

'Yes, highness,' said Despenser and called on a captain to detail his men to have what remained of the routiers cut down.

The men galloped towards the draped corpses to do the Prince's bidding.

'Master Henry,' the Prince called.

'Highness.'

'You and your man, here.'

Henry and Gifford eased their horses from the column and trotted forward to the Prince, who addressed Amadeus. 'You will have your pavilion pitched here. A prickly straw mattress does not become a Count of Savoy. It does not become a prince of the realm either, but it is fitting that he redeem himself in the eyes of the Lord for a life lived in comfort. We are only a few days from Milan. Best we prostrate ourselves in the privacy of a humble chapel.'

Amadeus smiled, understanding that the Prince had not imposed a monastic discomfort on him.

The Prince turned to Despenser. 'My Lord Edward, everyone else will camp here also. Including you.'

'Sire, I am responsible for—'

'We know, but our safety will be in God's hands tonight. And if we need further solace, Master Henry reading Petrarch's poetry will suffice. You may inspect the monastery and thus fulfil your duty to us.'

Satisfied that his authority was not being undermined, Despenser dipped his head in acknowledgement. His eyes, however, lingered on Henry. Whoever de Sainteny was he was certainly favoured.

The Prince addressed Henry. 'Announce us. Our compliments to the abbot. Tell him we will sleep there tonight and pray in his chapel. We will take mass and the sacrament with him. Arrange our quarters there, Master Henry: no finery. A cot and some food. And prayer.'

Henry and Gifford skirted the walls bearing the remains of the routiers killed by his father as Despenser's men set about cutting down the corpses. Henry tried to imagine the furious fight that would have taken place in the confines of the monastery's courtyard. Boxed in, no retreat, no quarter given. No respite from your effort, unlike the chance to regain breath and strength on the vastness of an open battlefield.

Gifford hammered on the gate, bringing Henry's thoughts back to the present.

Brother Jean, the abbot, was flustered. Over the years, the monks had offered hospitality to pilgrims and small groups of traders. In the past, Savoy's men had kept routiers away, but this recent episode of attack from brigands had brought home how precarious life really was. And as predicted by the scar-faced knight, an English prince had arrived at the gates. There had never been such turmoil in all the years he had been abbot at Mont Cenis.

In preparation, he had taken Blackstone's advice and brought his best wine from the barrel room. What remained of the slaughtered goats had been consumed by Blackstone's men and the women he had saved. All of this he related to Henry and Gifford as they followed him into a stone arched room. Low ceiling. A small window. A cot with a straw mattress and a bucket for a latrine. A bowl and cloth for washing. The only nod towards comfort was a brazier seated beneath the smoke hole in the roof. Other than that it was one step removed from a monk's cell.

The stone floor was cold underfoot, even through the soles of Henry's boots. He paced the room.

The abbot looked pained. He pointed to a dark corner. 'There is a door there. It leads to the small yard only a few paces from the chapel. It is more private than going through there,' he said, pointing to the door through which they had entered the cell.

Henry checked the two doors. 'There is no lock on either,' he said.

'For what purpose?' said the abbot. 'We are as one here.'

'Find a bench and a chair. Bring it here. The Prince can secure the doors from the inside.' Henry looked over the room again. Would a king's son be prepared to spend a night in such sparse conditions?

'It will do,' said Henry. Much to the abbot's relief. 'The Prince may intend to fast; if he doesn't, you must share what food you have, no matter how simple,' he instructed.

'Sir Thomas told me to offer our best wine. That I have done. The food is nourishing and we bake our own bread.'

'See to it that the Prince has privacy when he wishes to pray in your chapel.'

'My son, we follow the Rule of St Benedict and practise communal prayer.'

'Brother Abbot, that decision is for the Prince. When he arrives, ask about offering mass and the sacrament. He is a pious man. No ruffian like my—' Henry stopped himself in time. 'Like Sir Thomas Blackstone.'

The abbot pulled a face. 'My son, if I am faced again with such murderous creatures as came into this place, I would take the heathen Sir Thomas over a pious prince. He slew the devil's imps that day and saved many lives.'

Henry glanced at Gifford, who shrugged and smiled.

'Thank you, Brother Jean. My friend and I will sleep in the stable,' said Henry.

'Ah. Then you will have company. There is one other who has accepted our hospitality.'

CHAPTER TWENTY-TWO

The dimly lit stables revealed an elderly man hunched in the shadows, next to a donkey and a rouncey, both munching hay and tethered to wall rings. Spooning food from a pewter bowl, the old man sat against the wall with a saddle propped up next to him. He glanced up as a monk, sent by the abbot, escorted Henry and Gifford into the stables. Earlier, a novice monk had tethered their mounts further down the stables.

Next to the old man, whose cloak was of quality, as were his boots, were two chests and a yoke that fitted the donkey's back. He nodded a welcome.

'My friend, I am Henry de Sainteny and my companion is Hugh Gifford. We are to share these humble quarters with you tonight.'

The old man had sunken cheeks. His wrinkled skin was more like parchment and the veins in his hand pressed against bone. To Henry's mind, he looked to be in ill health. The fine clothing did not appear to match the ageing body. His cloak fell aside to reveal a bandaged leg.

The old man wiped away dribbles of gravy from his beard. 'You are a lord, Master de Sainteny? Must I raise myself and bow my head?'

The man's demeanour bordered on disrespect.

'Friend, there's no cause for rancour here. We are all common men. Are you any better?' said Gifford.

The monk, sensing aggravation, intervened. 'Messer Salvarini's kindness blesses us.'

'Why is that?' said Henry.

'Because I travel as an emissary of the Lord Jesus and all our saints,' said the old man, finishing his food. He extended his plate to the monk, who took it. 'I am a servant of God. I am a purveyor of sacred relics and artefacts. And I gave a valued gift to the abbot when I arrived.'

'And you are injured,' said Gifford, pointing at the bandage.

'Unhappily I fell from my horse yesterday. The infirmarian bound it so I shall be able to continue my journey in a day or so.'

Henry turned to the monk. 'Thank you, brother, we'll see to our bedrolls and share a plate of food when the Prince arrives.'

Henry noticed the trader's eyes flared for a moment.

'Oh,' said Henry, remembering. 'Tell the abbot that a knight who accompanies the Prince will inspect the monastery.'

'For what reason?' said the worried-looking monk.

'To ensure the building is safe. That you do not harbour anyone who shouldn't be here.'

'Only the three of you are here,' said the monk.

'Do as you're told,' said Gifford. 'It's for the abbot to question if it's to be questioned at all.'

Admonished, the monk left the stables.

'There is a prince travelling this route?' said the trader.

'A prince of England,' said Gifford.

'And why would he be crossing the mountains? The weather is still challenging. It's dangerous. Look at me. The damned donkey pulled on its rope and I fell on stony ground.'

'Our Prince is a master horseman and he doesn't pull a donkey along behind him,' said Henry, softening the jibe with a smile. 'And he travels to Milan to be married.'

'Then if he is to visit this humble monastery I hope he has a strong stomach. The food is passable at best,' said the trader. 'Why would royalty even bother coming here? I'd have thought he would be well served with servants and decent food.'

'He comes to pray. A night of contemplation.'

The old trader grunted. 'If I were a prince I'd stay in a warm bed and thank the good Lord for His blessing. That would be my idea of contemplation.'

Gifford shrugged. 'Who knows the thoughts of a prince? They are a law unto themselves.'

Henry pointed at the chests. 'May we know more about what you sell?' he asked.

'If you're interested in buying.'

'We travel with the Prince, but I gifted my purse to a goatherder who had lost everything.'

Salvarini coughed, lungs rattling with phlegm. He reached for a bottle of half-drunk wine, uncorked it and drank. Then he studied the two men who stood over him. 'I am a solitary man, unused to conversation. I intend no insult, but I must be cautious. What I carry holds great value to some men and is meaningless to others.' By way of apology, he reached next to him, picked up a full bottle of wine and handed it to Henry. 'Their wine is of a decent quality.'

Gifford turned over a bucket and sat on it as Henry squatted on his haunches next to Salvarini and glugged the wine. It spilled on his chin. He wiped his hand across his face and passed the bottle to Gifford.

'How often do you travel this way? Do you sell in France?' said Henry.

Salvarini eyed him. 'Are my travels of any significance to you?'

'No, but I have not come across a purveyor of relics before.'

'Young man, I have travelled to the Holy Land, the length and breadth of Italy and across the Holy Roman Empire. I visit monasteries and churches and show them fragments of the True

Cross, phials of holy blood, bones of the saints, relics that the divine have kissed. I am honoured and humbled to be able to do so.' He drank again.

Henry glanced at Gifford. Was this man genuine? He sounded as though he was at death's door when he coughed, as he did now after gulping wine.

'Can we see any of these things?' said Gifford.

'You doubt me?'

'I'm curious.'

Salvarini gave the request a moment's thought. His hands trembled as he opened one of the chests. With one hand holding the lid, he gestured with the other for Gifford and Henry to look inside.

Henry peered at the neatly laid out interior. Items were wrapped in dark red or purple velvet.

Gifford bent over. 'What is that?'

'A fragment of a saint's bone,' said Salvarini. He lifted two round-headed long nails, their uneven spikes pitted. 'Nails from the Cross.'

Henry hunched. The contents held his interest, as would a child's box of playthings to an infant. 'And this?' he said, pointing to a scrap of bloodstained linen.

'Torn from Christ's shroud.'

'And that lock of hair?' said Gifford.

'From St Catherine of Alexandria.'

Henry smiled and nodded. 'This is some treasure you carry, Messer Salvarini. I can understand why men of God and pious men alike would value these relics. But what of the poor commoners? What chance do they have of ever being able to enjoy the benefit of such revered items?'

'I have hand-crafted rosaries and manuscripts to aid them in their prayer.'

Henry caught his breath. 'Manuscripts? You travel to monasteries across Italy, you said.'

'Of course.'

'Then you must have heard of Don Silvestro dei Gherarducci?' he said, pulling free the manuscript page he stole from the bookshop in Paris.

'Gherarducci?' said Salvarini, nonplussed.

'Yes. He taught this illuminator,' he said, unfolding the page. 'Gherarducci: he's a Camaldolese monk and illuminator.'

'I don't know him. There are hundreds of monks in scriptoriums all over Italy. How would I know just one?' Salvarini began coughing. He pressed a linen cloth to his lips and wheezed into it.

Henry noticed the blood staining it. The old man was indeed ill, and it would kill him. He curtailed his excitement that he might find the young artist, respectful of what he now understood about Salvarini's health.

The old man realized Henry had seen the bloodied rag.

'It's hard travelling across the mountains,' said Henry.

Gifford had dipped a ladle into a water barrel and offered it to Salvarini. He took it, sipped the water, and then upended the bottle of wine. Once his breathing calmed, he nodded his thanks to Gifford.

'I travelled here because the high pass helps with my breathing,' he said, curling the rag back into a ball and replacing it inside his tunic. 'Why are you so interested in the monk who illuminated this page?'

'It's not a monk. It's a young woman. She... she has a gift given by God.'

Salvarini looked at the torn page. 'It is a work of splendour,' he said. 'Her name?'

'I don't know. But I must find her. Which is why I thought you might know where she is. It would be hard to disguise the presence of someone capable of doing this.'

The old trader nodded his understanding. 'Almost impossible, Master de Sainteny.' Salvarini gazed thoughtfully at the page and then at Henry. 'And what would you do if you found her?'

Henry shook his head. 'Declare my feelings.'

'But what if the Lord has taken back this gift? Denied her the blessing that allowed her to illuminate with such rare skill? God moves in strange ways that we cannot comprehend.'

'That doesn't matter. This work is... sacred. I am unlikely to even be considered by her. But I would try.'

'Do you believe she is beautiful?'

'She has to be.'

'What if she is not?'

'Expressing herself this way tells me her beauty would radiate from within her.'

Salvarini sighed and closed the chest's lid. 'She might be held in a castle or a monastery against her will. Such exceptional talent would not be allowed to be exploited beyond the walls.'

Henry folded the page and put it away. 'Then I would offer to release her and take her where she wanted to be.'

Salvarini's attitude had softened during their conversation. He placed a hand on Henry's arm. 'Young man, you are a dreamer.'

Henry smiled. 'Why should I not be?'

'Why not indeed? Without a desire for something beautiful, a man's life is mud-caked misery.'

The jangle of spurs and rustle of mail against fabric interrupted them as Edward Despenser stepped into the stables with two of his captains. Henry and Gifford got to their feet. Despenser shot them a look, then gestured for one man to search the stables to the right, and the other to the left, where Henry and Gifford's mounts were tethered.

'Who's he?' said Despenser.

'A trader of religious relics,' said Henry.

'Does he have no manners? Does he not stand when his betters enter?'

'He's old and sick, Lord Despenser. As you can see, his leg is bound from a fall.'

Despenser grunted. 'Open those,' he said, indicating the two chests.

'My lord,' said Salvarini, 'the contents are of great value to men of the cloth and those who cherish their belief in Christ.'

'I am a true believer, old man, but I need no fakery of yours to help me cherish my belief. Empty them.'

Salvarini made no complaint but painstakingly took each item from the two chests. Despenser's men returned and confirmed the absence of anyone else in the stables.

'The Prince will be here once we report back,' he told Henry. 'You're to take him to his chamber.' He moved next to Salvarini and examined the chests. 'You bear arms?'

'Only my knife,' said Salvarini, pulling aside his cloak to expose a sheathed dagger in his belt.

Despenser nodded and held out the palm of his hand. 'You'll have it back when we leave tomorrow.'

Once again, the old man didn't complain and handed the weapon to Despenser, who passed it to one of his captains.

'Very well,' Despenser said. 'Make no attempt to peddle these wares to my Prince. Understood?'

Salvarini bowed his head.

Despenser gave a final scornful look at the three men and left with his men.

The old trader began to repack the relics. Henry leaned across to help. Salvarini put an arm out. 'No, Master Henry. These are for my hands alone. Go and serve your Prince.'

Henry and Gifford left the old man to his work and stepped out into the evening light. Gifford sniffed the air. 'Storm's coming. Better we're sleeping in there rather than outside. For once we've drawn the long straw.' They walked across the courtyard; darkness was already closing in as black clouds smothered the distant sky. 'For a man who says he travels everywhere and makes a living out of what he does, you'd think he'd have known about the man you search for.'

'Not the man, his pupil,' said Henry.

'Still, someone that famous, and him being in the business, I'd have thought he'd have known.'

Henry nodded. He thought so as well.

CHAPTER TWENTY-THREE

The Prince rode into the courtyard followed by Edward Despenser, a groom and four personal valets on foot who bore a bedroll, blankets and other items of minimal comfort to dull the edge of his self-imposed hardship. The abbot, Brother Jean, stood with the monastery's prior and cellarer. Twenty of the thirty monks stood behind the abbot. Despite the humble nature of the monastery, the abbot had instructed the cellarer to ensure the best food and drink were made available for the Prince. Henry and Gifford stood a few yards behind the gathered monks.

Lionel needed no mounting box to alight from his horse. As a valet held the bridle, the Prince dismounted and faced the abbot's welcoming committee who, hands clasped, bowed their heads.

'I am Brother Jean. I welcome you to our humble home, highness.' He gestured to the monks beside him. 'Our prior, Brother Baptiste, and Brother Gabriel, who attends to our comfort, as frugal as it is.'

'We are not concerned with our comfort tonight but offer our thanks for your permission to spend a night in quiet contemplation,' said the Prince. He took in the gathered monks paying their respect. 'We hope we have not disrupted the monastery's routine. We know full well the discipline for those who follow the Rule of St Benedict.'

'You grace us with your presence,' said the abbot. 'I understand you wish to receive the Holy Eucharist?'

'That is so.'

The abbot paused. Questioning a prince had to be done delicately. 'We are simple monks, highness, who share our prayer as a community. Did you... have a thought when you would wish to receive the Blessed Sacrament?'

The Prince looked over his shoulder at the darkening sky. It would soon be sunset and vespers would be celebrated. He had no desire to be caught up in common prayer. He sighed. It promised to be a long night with little sleep.

'Brother Abbot, we have no desire to interrupt the Divine Office. Better we attend to this matter privately. Shall we say between daybreak and the first hour of daylight?'

The abbot considered his request. It suited him not to have the daily prayer cycle disturbed. He nodded his assent. 'Between lauds and prime, highness. I will await your presence.'

'Good!' said the Prince. 'Now, before this storm breaks, will you attend to us?'

'Yes, yes, of course. Young Master de Sainteny has chosen your quarters.'

The Prince smiled. 'Then we shall follow you and let your brothers return to their duties. We wish to detain them no longer.' He turned to Despenser. 'Return our horse tomorrow after lauds.'

Despenser nodded and instructed the groom to follow him and lead the Prince's horse back to their camp. The valets followed the Prince as the abbot led the way. The monks dispersed; Henry and Gifford bowed to the Prince and then fell in a pace behind him.

'We are supposing it will be the simplest of cells,' said the Prince.

'I fear it might be too simple, highness,' said Henry.

'Ah. As we feared. So be it. We did not expect finery. That is not the purpose of our vigil.' He glanced at Henry. 'You will stay close, Master Henry.'

Henry instructed Gifford to wait outside as the Prince stooped low below the door's threshold. When he stood upright, his head was barely a foot from the ceiling. Henry had arranged for the brazier to be lit to ease the dank smell of damp. For a moment Henry thought the Prince would berate him for choosing somewhere so austere, though what more could be expected eluded him.

'It will do, Henry. It's a step short of being a hermit's cave, but it's warm and will serve us well. It is important that we are ready to endure suffering in prayer. And to be seen doing so.'

Without waiting for any command from the Prince, the valets went about their work with the expertise of years of experience. Stripping the straw mattress from the cot, they unrolled the mattress they had carried from the Prince's pavilion. Covering it with a linen sheet and blankets, they then placed four pillows bearing the Prince's coat-of-arms at its head and unfolded an ermine-fur overthrow, more than twice the size of any blanket. Henry realized that he alone would be the one to suffer discomfort should the Prince demand his company long into the night.

The Prince dismissed them and settled on the stool, again organized by Henry, near the brazier. Henry hovered near the bench as the Prince took time to look around him.

'We have seen dungeons with more charm,' he said without accusation. 'But we will endure. Now. Wine? Did the abbot provide some succour for our vigil?'

Henry had put six bottles of monastic wine aside. He showed one to the Prince.

'Are we to drink like common hobelars from the neck of the bottle?'

'No, highness, the abbot provided two silver goblets.' He reached down and passed one to the Prince, who held it out for the wine to be poured. The muted sound of monks' chanting reached them, an eerie slither of sound as they attended to vespers. The Prince gestured for Henry to pour himself a drink. Once he had done so, he stood waiting for the command that he might sit. With a gesture, the Prince indicated to Henry that he should not keep asking permission before undertaking any action.

'Your Prince is weary, Henry. Already widowed and soon to be joined in marriage to one who is little more than a child.'

The Prince gazed into the brazier's glow. And in that moment Henry felt sorry for the man, not yet thirty years old, who had loved his wife, Elizabeth de Burgh. She had borne him a child, Philippa, and when his wife died five years ago, his child was only eight years old. Now he was to marry a girl a year older than his daughter.

And then the Prince stopped staring at the fire as if the memory had been put aside. He savoured the wine. 'What awaits us in Milan will be the most glorious celebration. It will seem endless. We can expect to be fêted with the richest of gifts. Far in excess of those bestowed on us in Paris. The Visconti do not hide their wealth; they flaunt it. If Violante could have travelled to England, we would have had a more dignified ceremony. But this is how we form alliances.' He drank. 'And our own coffers will be enriched. Your father awaits us after the ceremony as agreed?'

'As agreed, highness. He will take the dowry to your brother in Aquitaine.'

'Very well. Now, read. Share your love of Petrarch's poems. He too knew the loss of the one he loved. But let us not dwell in remorse. The third sonnet, perhaps, when he first fell in love with his beloved? Love is a binding force, is it not?'

Henry pulled the stitched pages of poetry from his tunic. 'I have only experienced such a feeling once, highness. I saw an illuminated page in a manuscript and knew there was a woman of beauty behind it.'

'A female illuminator? Does she still live?'

'I believe so. She is unknown to me, but she pulls me to wherever she is.'

'Then you will search for her?'

'When time permits. Yes.'

The Prince gave Henry an encouraging smile. 'So be it. If love eludes us, then the heart's journey in search for it is hastened.'

Henry turned the page and brought the lantern closer so he might read to the Prince.

'It was the day the sun's rays turned pale,
With grief for its maker when I was caught...'

Gifford waited outside the door, alert for anyone approaching the Prince's quarters. There was no need for concern about anyone in particular. Salvarini was injured and sleeping in the stables and it was unlikely any of the monks would show any interest: they were already at prayer. Perhaps a novice, not yet in the fold, might try to catch sight of a son of a king. A king was divine; the Almighty would also bless a son, and that might be enough of an attraction for someone to disturb the Prince. Gifford's eyes settled on the deep shadows, ears attuned to any sound beyond that of chanting prayers. There was no movement, no shuffling of sandalled feet through cloisters or along dark passages. Rolling thunder diminished the monks' chanting. He heard Henry's voice from behind the door. He was reciting something. Probably from that book he'd bought in Paris. Gifford pressed his ear to the door. What he heard made no sense to him. It was a foreign tongue.

The unyielding cold from the stone floor and walls seeped into his muscles. Gifford took a turn down the passage to keep himself moving. He walked ten paces back and forth from the door. It was going to be a long night.

CHAPTER TWENTY-FOUR

The brazier glowed, its heat stifling the air in the windowless cell. Hours passed until the prayers for compline ended and the monastery fell silent for the rest of the night. Since vespers the Prince and Henry had spent the time in conversation framed by the sonnets and their shared love of poetry. The Prince's tireless mind delved into the words and meanings with endless questions. Once the monks retired for the night, the only sound was the storm. Henry had fed the brazier as the Prince dozed and then, unwilling to risk waking him by returning to the stables, he huddled down, back against the door. The heady wine, the reading and the Prince's interrogation of each sonnet had tired him and he fell asleep. Soon after midnight, when the bell rang for matins, he stirred himself and fed the brazier again. The lantern spluttered, placing the cell into near darkness. Henry fumbled for a spare candle, lit it and checked on the Prince, who was snoring, tucked up under the warmth of the ermine bedcover.

The few hours' sleep had stiffened Henry's muscles, and he was tempted to retreat to the relative warmth of the stables. Knowing Gifford's sense of duty, he guessed that the man-at-arms was still outside the door. And if Henry was feeling the cold from the stone floor, then he would be colder still. There was nothing he could do other than to curl up again and hope that the next three or four hours until first light passed quickly.

When those first creases of light came, the bell for lauds woke Henry from his shallow sleep. Even more stiff from the snatched hours and night's chill, he cursed the brazier, whose heat had diminished to little more than a few glimmering embers. The Prince only stirred to raise his head from the pillow and, realizing that the monks still had an hour left for their morning prayers, turned over while muttering to Henry to wake him up before prime for mass with the abbot.

Henry's tongue was thick from the wine. His skin felt creased, his shoulders hunched. He yawned, shook himself and eased open the door, not caring any longer that it might disturb the Prince. There was only another hour to wait before he had to be roused from his cot. Gifford looked as miserable as Henry felt. He questioned what was needed with a tilt of his head towards the man he had sworn to protect.

'Hugh, you've been here all night?'

Henry closed the door behind him as Gifford readjusted his clothing from his crumpled night's half-sleep. One eye watching for shadows that shouldn't exist and an ear listening for a sound that didn't belong.

'Where else was I to go?' He rubbed a coarse hand over his face and shook his mind free of the night's cobwebs. 'Damned cold these monasteries. No wonder they spend most of the night praying. Probably the only way to keep warm. The Prince?'

'Still sleeping. Hugh, I need a piss.'

'I hope you're not asking me to hold it for you?'

Henry grinned. 'Hopefully, the Prince isn't expecting me to hold his.'

'Isn't there a bucket inside?' said Gifford.

'It's not for me to piss in a prince's pot. I need the latrine. Will you wait a while longer at his door?'

'Aye, though I'm not sure for what purpose. The only thing

I heard last night was the storm and rats scurrying. You'd best run for it. It's a damned cold rain out there whipped up by the mountain wind. The sooner we get to Milan, the happier I'll be.'

Henry tugged his tunic collar around his neck. 'Hugh, you have never been happy. Were it to happen the shock would kill you.'

'Then at least I'd have a taste of whatever's so joyous it'll slay me where I stand. Here, the grey misery of chanting monks and bitter wind freezing my arse kills any chance of it.'

Henry ran to the courtyard. There was a latrine near the stables that was little more than a cleft in the stone wall and a hole leading to a drain. Rain stung his bare head and dribbled down his neck. Sighing with relief, he glanced around the vast yard. The high walls' shadows swallowed any glimmer of first light. No one was about. The monks were locked in holy prayer again.

Adjusting his clothing, he felt the pangs of hunger. The Prince had deliberately fasted as a token of his vigil and that meant Henry had also gone without food the previous night. Even watery gruel and a chunk of bread would keep the hunger away. And no sooner had the thought crossed his mind than he corrected himself. He was certain the monks did not eat so frugally. The thought of food reminded him he had half a loaf of bread tucked into his saddlebags. He dashed along the wall to the stables. There was no lantern-light in the stables at this time of day when common men still slept. His eyes adjusted to the dim interior as he shook the rain from him. He could discern the shape of their horses and made his way to them, where his and Gifford's bedrolls and blankets had been laid out with the expectation of a warm night's sleep in the straw.

Salvarini's bedroll was empty; Henry assumed the old man had early business with the abbot, even though his chests were still there and unguarded. Before undoing the satchel and retrieving the bread, he plunged his hands into a bucket of water and sluiced his face, pulling his fingers through his hair.

He tugged free his spare shirt from the saddlebag and used it to wipe his face, then refolded it neatly and retrieved the bread. Dipped in wine, it would serve to stave off his and Gifford's hunger. As he turned, he saw Salvarini step into the stables and bend down to search for something in one of the chests.

'Signor Salvarini,' he called, 'did you get some sleep despite the storm?'

His greeting startled the old man, who jerked up from his task. Henry walked towards the stable opening. Salvarini's cloak was barely wet.

Salvarini, regaining his composure, said, 'You startled me.'

'I'm sorry: it was not my intention.'

'I didn't know you slept here last night,' said Salvarini.

'I didn't. I was with the Prince, but neither my friend nor I had any food.' He brandished the half-loaf. 'We need to quieten our grumbling stomachs.' He studied the old man for a moment. 'Your leg's strength has returned?'

'My leg?'

'You were striding briskly – I assume to avoid the rain.'

'Ah. No. I went to the chapel. I had hoped to join the monks at lauds. I was too late. I stayed along the side of the wall on the way back. That kept some rain off me. Now, I must wait until prayers begin at prime. Did your Prince not pray?'

Henry peered out at the swirling rain; gusts of wind whipped it this way and that. 'No, he will take the sacrament and mass privately with the abbot when lauds ends. Before prime, so I'd best be going to him, otherwise I'll be blamed for letting him sleep. We'll be leaving for our final days' journey to Milan afterwards.'

'And to search for the woman who has caught your heart?'

Henry's self-conscious smile prompted a look of sadness from the old man. He shook his head. 'Some things, Master de Sainteny, are not meant to be. An illusion, conjured by our own desires. Reality can be a harsh mistress.' He wheezed and caught his breath, then wiped his mouth with the back of his hand.

'I too had my heart snared, and I was asked how precious she was to me. And I answered the only way I could. That I would die for her.'

Salvarini started coughing, bent double, grasping the wall for support. Henry grabbed him before he fell to his knees. Salvarini's laboured breathing came in fits and starts. Henry eased him down and then reached for the water bucket and its ladle. Holding the old man's head, he tilted it and dripped water onto his lips.

Salvarini nodded his thanks as his breathing eased. He grasped Henry's wrist. 'Dying is a lonely business. And serves no purpose unless it is a good death in the service of others. Look at me. An old man peddling false relics to the gullible, desperate to be closer to the Almighty.'

He saw Henry's face at his admission.

He calmed himself. 'We all have to confess before we leave this world. And why cause distress to a good man like the abbot who believes in the bones of saints and the nails from the Cross? That is what comforts him.' He patted Henry's arm. 'Thank you. I must rest now. I hope you find what you seek and, if you do, that you protect her. With your life. That is love, young man. None truer. Now, go to your duty.'

Henry tucked a blanket around the old trader and left him lying with his back against the wall. He felt certain he would not be alive by the time he returned.

'What happened to the bread?' said Gifford.

'I dropped it. I was helping Salvarini. This cold and wet has affected him badly. I think he's going to die.'

'We're all going to die, Master Henry. Better if we have food in our stomach,' he said, picking off the pieces of dirt and straw, then tearing the half-loaf apart. He offered it to Henry, who shook his head.

'I'm not hungry any more. I don't want any,' he said.

'Why – did the horse piss on it as well?'

'It's the old man. He's close to death. I could feel it.'

Gifford shoved a piece of bread in his mouth, softening it with a swig of wine from the bottle Henry had retrieved from the Prince's cell when he returned from the stables. 'Good a place as any to die. Monks'll say a prayer for him and bury him. Better than the likes of me being left on a battlefield for the crows. He should think himself lucky.'

'I'd have stayed with him if I didn't have to be here for the Prince. No one should die alone, Hugh.'

'Aye, well, remember that when you next get me into trouble trying to protect you. I don't want you holding *my* hand. I don't want to die in the first place.'

The Prince's voice summoned Henry inside. It penetrated the wind that blew around pillars and beneath doors, its intermittent whistling reduced to moaning as it sought escape from the colonnade's roof timbers.

'Are you going with him?' said Gifford as Henry's hand rested on the door latch.

'To the chapel? He goes to pray and receive the sacrament. I don't think so.'

'Then he'll be going back to the others after that. I'm thinking he'll delay the column while he breaks his fast, but we'll be left with this stale bread.'

Henry saw a day of hunger approaching. 'Get to the kitchen, see what food we can buy.'

'Buy? With what? You gave your purse to a goatherd.'

The Prince called again.

'Hugh, tell them the Prince needs food for his journey.'

Gifford grinned. 'You'd lie in a place of God?'

'God will be busy looking down on a prince on his knees.' He pushed open the door. Gifford took a quick look around. He saw monks going back to their daily duties, heads down against the biting wind and rain, returning from their daybreak service. He headed for the kitchen.

CHAPTER TWENTY-FIVE

The Prince stood in linen shirt and hose, his cloak draped around his shoulders, the only item of clothing bearing any sign of his royalty. He had pulled a plain coif over his head, nothing more than a peasant would wear, and tucked his fair hair beneath it. His doublet and surcoat, resplendent with its intricately embroidered heraldic symbols and motifs, lay draped across the cot.

Henry gaped at the barely garbed Prince. 'Highness, the wind and rain. It's cold.'

'After we have received the sacrament, we will prostrate ourselves before the cross in an act of penance. You are to assist me. When we enter the chapel, you must take this cloak from us. You will stand back. Your presence is not to be felt. Understood?'

'Highness,' said Henry, realizing he was about to witness the most private of ceremonies.

'When we have made penance and stand to make the sign of the cross, you will drape the cloak around us and we will return here. Lord Despenser and the valets will return. You will not be required to attend our presence any longer. From now on we are a prince alone, chastised and blessed with no further need for poetry or private companionship. Our duty beckons us to Milan. Is that understood?'

Henry realized he and the Prince had slipped into an intimacy with the shared joy of poetry. It had been permitted by the Prince and had now been rescinded. Their roles would revert to royal prince and commoner. Henry bowed. 'I am here to serve, highness.'

Henry removed the sturdy chair that secured the door in the cell's corner, went through, checked that no monk lingered in the small courtyard and stepped aside for the Prince, who stooped low and strode towards the chapel, ignoring the wind and rain. To Henry's eye he appeared even taller than his actual great height. His back as straight as a lance, his head unyielding to the elements.

Henry strode ahead and opened the door into the chapel, closing it once he and the Prince were inside. The cut-stone floor was smooth from years of shuffling feet and knees that prostrated monks in front of the cross. Shadows flickered from the two candles on the altar either side of a polished brass crucifix. The holders for the tall candles were also of brass. There was no sign of silver or gold. The altar bore a pewter chalice for the wine, a plate for the Sacred Host and a missal. The abbot was already waiting by the side of the altar. Henry had seen mass celebrated in France and England when more adornment was usual. But here the abbot followed the Rule of St Benedict, which emphasized humility, simplicity and detachment from worldly possessions. Instead of ornate vestments, his garb was a plain linen ankle-length tunic with an unadorned stole across his shoulders, signifying his authority to celebrate the Eucharist. His chasuble, the outermost vestment, was of woven wool.

Henry held his breath. He and the abbot were to be sole witness to an English Prince's confession and act of penance. For a moment, he was transfixed. The Prince stood unmoving, hands clasped in front of him. The abbot made the sign of the cross, said something under his breath, a blessing of some sort, Henry thought, and then the abbot's eyes glanced his way. It was as if he had been struck. Caught in the moment, he had forgotten his instructions. Stepping behind the Prince, he reached up, eased the cloak from his shoulders and retreated to the back of the chapel, pressing himself into the shadows. He was too far back to hear any of the words muttered by the abbot, but the low hum of his voice was a soothing balm. Henry wondered if the arranged marriage would ever replace the affection the Prince had felt for his first wife. Perhaps it was this ceremony that the Prince needed to ease whatever grief he still bore for her. He knelt, the abbot at his side, a barely audible confession being made and absolution given so that the Prince would be in a state of grace before receiving the sacrament.

A sense of calm settled over Henry. His gaze shifted to the flowing shadows across the vaulted roof. He felt sleepy as the abbot's almost monotonous liturgy blessed the Sacred Host and wine and then offered the wafer to the Prince. Henry pressed his back against the wall. What was it that comforted him? The near silence? The chapel's spiritual atmosphere? It enveloped him, teasing from his mind the memory of his mother's death and that of his young sister, Agnes. He felt a lump in his chest. His heart contracted. Tears threatened. He fought an overwhelming urge to fall to his knees and pray for their souls. How often had he blocked that memory? To survive. How often had he seen his father fight back his tears when talking about them? Father and son sheltering behind a shield wall.

He wiped a hand across his eyes. It was time to concentrate on what he was required to do for the Prince. How long had his mind been wandering? The mass seemed to be over. The abbot made the sign of the cross and retreated behind the altar. The Prince took a few paces back, eased down onto his knees and then lowered himself face down on the stone floor, prostrating himself before the cross. The abbot retreated through a door behind the altar.

Silence. As heavy as snow. Broken only by the sound of a spluttering candle. Henry felt his breath trapped inside his chest. This was a moment of rare privilege not to be disturbed even by breathing. He sighed to ease the tension. Unsure what to do, he remained in the shadows. How long would the Prince lay prostrated?

A door creaked. A changing wind pressing against wood. The dull light shifted behind the altar as a cowled monk stepped into the chapel and around the altar to gaze down at the Prince. Henry felt a cold sensation ripple up his spine.

He stepped out from the shadows. The movement alerted the monk, who raised his head and pulled back the cowl. Henry stared at Salvarini. Knife in hand, he no longer looked like a dying man. Henry's rapid strides were borne of instinct. Yet no warning, no cry escaped his lips. The Prince's moment before God must not be disturbed.

Unaware of the intruder, the Prince had not moved. Salvarini faltered, as if not willing to lunge forward and kill the Prince. Henry's footfalls roused the Prince, who rolled clear as Henry got between him and the assassin, who sidestepped. There was no sign of an injured leg, yet his age meant he was still slow to react. He showed no sign of fear or hate or emotion.

Henry threw the cloak at him. Salvarini swiped it away with a sweep of his arm, the act exposing his body as Henry slammed into him, driving his knife deep into the old man's chest wall. Salvarini shuddered. Henry's weight bore down on him, driving the blade deeper as they fell to the floor. He pressed his arm across Salvarini's chest and arm to stop any attempt at striking back. The old man's frail body offered no resistance.

The door swung open. A gust of air swept in. Gifford, sword in hand, ran into the chapel. The Prince had not moved, the shock of the assault dulling his senses after his deep contemplation.

'Take the Prince!' Henry shouted.

Gifford placed his arm behind the Prince and hustled him away.

Salvarini convulsed, blood seeping from his mouth. His eyes fixed on Henry, who eased his weight from him and knelt next to the old man. The assassin's knife lay on the floor beyond his grasp. He made no attempt to reach for it. His breathing faltered. His gaze had not left Henry.

'You came here from Italy to kill the Prince. Who sent you?'

The dying man moved his head from side to side.

'Why then?' said Henry.

Salvarini's lips moved. Henry lowered his head to hear what he was saying.

'It... has to be... this... way.'

Henry cradled his head and wiped blood from his mouth. Salvarini nodded as if in thanks. His eyes closed and opened. His bloodstained teeth smiled. 'Find her, Master Henry.'

'What?'

'The girl...you seek... Find her... find... Elena.'

Henry didn't understand. 'Elena? That's the name of the woman? The woman I seek?'

Salvarini's shallow breathing diminished. He nodded his head. 'Help... her. I failed her... failed to protect her.'

'How could you know her name? How? Tell me. Where is she? How do I find her?' Desperation to find the answer before the old man died surged within him; he pulled Salvarini closer to him. 'Where-do-I-find-her?' Then his voice calmed, softening the urgency. 'Please...'

Salvarini nodded. 'Held... she... is held... by... he... who sent me... Guard her...'

Salvarini reached for Henry's face. His fingers brushed his cheek.

And then he was gone.

The shock of the failed assassination attempt in the sanctuary of the monastery's chapel rocked the abbot's composure. At the Prince's command Brother Jean sent a monk to fetch Edward

Despenser. Only he among the entourage was told: none other. Not even Amadeus would know of the attempt. Especially not the Count of Savoy whose men would usually protect the pass. His own marriage gave him ties to the French royal family. No one was trusted now. Despenser questioned Gifford, who explained he had left the kitchen and turned for the abbot's entrance to the chapel when he saw him slumped unconscious from a blow to the head. Alerted, he had tried to enter the chapel through the same door but it was locked from the inside. And that was why he had burst through the main door in time to remove the Prince from danger.

With due thanks he was dismissed.

Despenser blamed himself for not protecting the Prince, but Lionel dismissed any guilt. The knife used in the attack had been concealed in the false floor of one of the chests Salvarini carried. There was no evidence that the old trader had been sent by anyone. It might have been nothing more than coincidence that he had arrived the day before, suggested the Prince. An old man bearing an old grudge.

Henry, however, caused concern when he discounted that idea. He told the Prince and Despenser of Salvarini's final words, while remaining silent about the girl Elena. An unknown person had indeed commissioned the old man to kill the Prince, although Henry and Gifford questioned the choice of assassin. An ailing man, who had hesitated instead of completing the task. It was as if it had been destined to fail.

'It would appear,' said the Prince before departing for the camp, 'that Thomas Blackstone and his son make a welcome habit of saving our father's sons.' In gratitude for Henry's intervention, the Prince insisted that he and Gifford remain close to his person.

When the Prince and Despenser returned to the royal camp, Henry offered the relics in Salvarini's baggage to the abbot.

'They are cursed,' said the abbot, still visibly shaken that his monastery had experienced violence and attempted murder.

'They will be destroyed.' And he promised to say prayers of thanks for the Englishmen who had saved them from brigands and the attempt on the King's son's life.

Henry and Gifford rode out of the monastery's confines. The road ahead lay beneath an arched sky. Beyond it was a woman he sought. Henry felt certain everything that had gone before was now leading him to her. Fate had brought two men together and in delivering death to one had offered to the other a rare chance of fulfilling his heart's desire. It was a divine mystery that should not be questioned. For once Henry appreciated his Greek studies at university. The name Elena was derived from the Greek Helene, which meant shining light.

He spurred his horse, eager to close the distance between them, no matter how far that might be.

PART FOUR

A FEAST OF THE DEAD

CHAPTER TWENTY-SIX

Galeazzo Visconti's long silk tunic, rich with embroidered gold threads, rubbed against the sleeveless surcoat with a satisfying whisper of exquisite finery. The Visconti coat of arms stitched onto his surcoat creased as he moved, so that the image of a man looked as though it actually was being devoured by a viper. His soft calf-leather shoes were like a second skin, and despite his painful gout, their heels gave a soft *tap tap* as he approached his brother, who waited with his back to him, seated on a cushioned chair, drinking a goblet of wine.

Tall, burly, broad shoulders, trimmed beard, hair at his collar. A fighter. A diplomat. And a killer. Despite his vicious reputation, Bernabò was a contradictory character. He made treaties and broke them. He secured land and extended his domain through his wife's negotiation skills. Wealthy in his own right, he trusted only her, yet he was constantly unfaithful. Of his thirty-six children, sixteen were illegitimate. Fourteen of the bastards survived since the scar-faced Englishman had taken revenge on two of his illegitimate sons. Bernabò bred like a bull. He fought like one. And the frustration of not leading his army in the field was an itch he couldn't scratch. The Pope had excommunicated him for seizing the Church's territories and declared a crusade against him. Were it not for the wedding and the need to keep the bulk of his men in Milan as a show of force to impress a young English Prince, he would ride out and face his enemy.

The servant who escorted Galeazzo onto his brother's balcony overlooking the city bowed and returned to his station with as much haste as was dignified in the presence of the Lord of Milan. His master's molten-lava temper could erupt uncontrollably if he were challenged, and the servant knew that Galeazzo Visconti's presence meant just that. A challenge. A servant was a convenient whipping post. Or worse.

'My brother's footsteps tell me he is in haste to deliver a lecture or a complaint,' said Bernabò without turning around.

Galeazzo stood to one side of his brother. Bernabò did not wear such elaborate and richly adorned clothing. His leather tunic was smeared with blood, flecks of which had splattered onto his neck and beard, staining the collar of the linen shirt he preferred to wear when hunting rather than silk. His black hair was matted with sweat and his grubby hands, dirt-caked, were tainted with dried bloodstains.

Men or animal's blood? Galeazzo wondered.

'I had a wonderful boar hunt. Thank you for asking,' Bernabò said before Galeazzo had a chance to speak. 'Where else am I to draw blood while the bastard Pope harasses my men? I am caged, brother, by you and the promise I made to stay for the wedding. I'm at war, dammit. I should be hunting Scaligeri and the Pope's brigands.'

Galeazzo refrained from making any comment. He was three years older than his brother and, being the elder, held a slightly more senior position in their joint rule. His natural disposition was to embrace art and culture. He didn't share Bernabò's bloodlust but that did not stop the forty-eight-year-old Galeazzo from being as ruthless as Bernabò when it was demanded. The two of them had had their older brother Matteo assassinated thirteen years before when they wrestled control of the city from him. And what a city it was.

Milan had dominated northern Italy for a thousand years. It outshone Paris, which, despite its claims to being the city of education, philosophy and intellectual exchange, had fewer paved streets or fountains than Milan. The city, spilling far beyond the ancient Roman walls, gave shelter to a hundred thousand citizens who drank clean water and were served by hundreds of public ovens that daily fed every district with fresh bread milled from wheat grown around the city. The Milanese had access to hospitals and churches. How many cities in the world housed thousands of monks from all denominations or settled legal disputes with a similar number of lawyers?

Galeazzo was the embodiment of Milan. He embraced a wealth unlikely to be matched across Europe. The twenty thousand silver pennies minted every year fed an economy of artisans whose reputations for quality stretched far and wide. Men of war and imperial palaces throughout Italy, Provence, Germany and beyond coveted its renowned armour, swords, helmets and mail. Milan had unbelievable wealth and increasing power.

And it also had Bernabò Visconti.

This crude, violent man held the city in his grip. His laws were strict and kept the peace, allowing citizens to walk the streets without fear of robbers. But fear there was: of Bernabò's reputation for lethal anger and instant punishment of anyone deemed to have transgressed any laws, whether being drunk in public at night or stepping in the path of his pack of hunting dogs. The penalty varied: being flayed, blinded or buried alive – or worse. Whatever desire for excessive punishment that occurred to Bernabò was gratified. He once roasted alive an insolent priest in a cage above a fire pit. The stench of burnt human flesh hung over the streets for days.

And now Galeazzo's nose twitched at his brother's stench. None of the rooms opening onto the balcony offered any waft of perfume, or the cloying smell of sex from one of his notorious orgies; this was the stink of death and stale sweat.

'It is your war, brother. Not mine. I work to forge alliances and you take a blade to them.' He suppressed his frustration. This was not the time to challenge Bernabò. 'There are two thousand guests arriving. They'll be coming through Porta Snesa. Does that mean anything to you, brother?'

Bernabò shrugged. 'You're here to complain about the bodies, aren't you?'

'Ah. You've guessed. Seven men hanged from balconies. A hundred paces apart. Their flesh ripped by whips. A welcoming sight for Amadeus who leads Lionel, the English King's treasured son, and his entourage to be wed. Here. At the cathedral. And they will arrive in three or four days. If, that is, they do not turn back in disgust when word reaches them of your barbaric display! Get them down, Bernabò. I will not tolerate you sabotaging this wedding.'

Bernabò pushed back the chair and faced his brother, anger spilling like the wine as he pointed the hand holding the goblet. 'Oh fuck off. I'm not trying to stop your cursed wedding. Those men lost eight of my hounds when a pack of boars turned on them. They were stupid and careless and an example had to be made of them. I'll take them down tomorrow. The crows need to eat.'

Colour flushed Galeazzo's face. His temper was barely contained. 'Bernabò, listen to me carefully. When my son's bride Isabella was brought here, those years ago, one of your bastard sons tried to have her poisoned and—'

'I knew nothing about that!'

'So you say. And he paid the price. I put our family at the heart of French royalty and now I will do the same for my daughter with the English Crown. Do not try to undermine this marriage. Do not. I warn you.'

'You're feathering your own nest, Galeazzo. Not my family's.'

'I bring respect and—'

'And I enforce it with blade and whip. My city obeys my laws.'

'Calm yourself,' Galeazzo said gently. Bernabò's tipping point was a constant unknown. Only Bernabò's wife, Beatrice Regina, could approach him when he lost control. But she was not here, and he was close to the edge. 'I ask for harmony at a time when we must both show the Prince and dignitaries that we are as one. You are essential, Bernabò, to the success of these next days. Let them see us stand together. Our families joined by dignity. Our troops resplendent.' He smiled, his voice liquid gold as he purred. 'And our wealth on show.'

He let the image of the wedding's grandeur seep into his brother's thoughts. 'Think on why we are graced by the English King offering his son.'

'The money. Two hundred thousand is a goodly sum.'

'Beyond that, Bernabò. See how this union helps not only my family but yours.'

Bernabò scowled. As far as he was concerned his brother's influence in the English court would outstrip anything that might be of benefit to him. 'My family does not marry into the English or French courts. No, I do not see the benefit.'

Galeazzo prompted him gently. 'The English King seeks alliances. He wanted his son Edmund to marry into Flanders. The Pope stopped that. So the English lost a vital alliance against the French. Now, he sends another son to us here.'

Bernabò snapped impatiently. 'Do not treat me like a dullard. I know all of this.'

'But not only for the money, Bernabò; there is more that benefits him. Think about the rancour the English King feels towards the Pope. When Lionel marries Violante what do you think our fine young Lionel has been ordered to do?'

Galeazzo waited like a teacher drawing out an answer from a pupil.

Bernabò smiled. 'Ah, I see. He will turn his displeasure towards the Pope by siding with us here.'

Galeazzo concealed his sigh of relief that his brother had finally seized the truth. 'Yes, dear brother. Lionel will commit the several hundred men that ride with him and pay for any of the free companies of mercenaries who roam through our domain.' He paused. 'You see now why we must stand in harmony and exploit everything we can from this marriage. For both our sakes.'

Bernabò calmed. He grunted. Slurped what was left of his wine. Thought about it. He shrugged and nodded. 'We will. They may be royalty, but they are paupers at our door.'

'Exactly, my brother.'

Bernabò considered the immediate future, which was as far ahead as interested him. 'A celebration the likes of which not one of them will have ever witnessed, never mind experienced. A Visconti wedding and celebration.'

'Yes,' said Galeazzo, relieved. His argument and his brother's consumption of wine had won Bernabò over. He placed a hand on Bernabò's shoulder by way of farewell and strode to the door. He turned. A bite to his demand. 'Take the bodies down, Bernabò. Tonight.'

The flung goblet followed a curse and struck the hastily closed door.

CHAPTER TWENTY-SEVEN

Blackstone and his men picked their way back through rolling countryside, careful not to run into the overwhelming force led by the black-robed knight. The fight against della Scala's men had made an ally of the Visconti captain, Marchesi. They escorted him and his few remaining Visconti men-at-arms towards Milan now that they were too few to engage their enemy. Will Longdon applied what care he could to Marchesi's wounded men on Blackstone's orders.

'Thomas, I am unclear why we're heading for Milan instead of rooting out the Scaligeri,' said Killbere. 'I am not fussy who I kill. If they are declared an enemy, I'll send them to the devil. You said we would not offer ourselves to those murdering Visconti bastards. Saving a handful of Marchesi's men is but a sideshow if we are to root out della Scala's men.'

'Gilbert, I'm supposed to be inside the walls when the Prince and Henry arrive.'

'You planned this?'

Blackstone shrugged. 'No. It was all uncertain. But if I could find a way in then I can find out how the gold is to be delivered and where. It might only be after the wedding. I had considered it before we left the monastery, but there was no safe way I could pass through the city gates without the risk of being exposed. And then I'd be killed. Now I have a way in.'

'With him?' said Killbere, cocking his head at no one in particular among the riders behind them.

'Yes.'

'Ah, then that is why we have not declared who we are. To him, we are English and Welsh skinners being paid by someone, whoever that might be, to help Visconti keep della Scala's men from raiding.'

'Yes.'

'Now that's a wonderful plan, Thomas,' said Killbere, unable to keep the sarcasm from his voice. 'Except he'll be able to describe our blazon no matter how muddied, and as soon as he does that—'

'It will be too late. I'll be inside the walls.'

'It will be too late because they will squeeze the walls of that city like a wine press squeezes grapes in order to catch you.'

'By now, the Prince will be at Turin, perhaps beyond. He's less than eighty miles from Milan. In two or three days he'll be entering the city. The Visconti will not be looking for me. They will be preparing to welcome the Prince. And even if Marchesi describes my blazon, there is no evidence it's me. I could be any man who once served under the Blackstone banner and then sold my sword.'

'Thomas, I used to think you a clear-thinking man. Now I see you have received too many blows to your head. You are who you are. They will look for you.'

'By then I will be with Henry and the Prince and they won't dare risk taking me.'

'I'll come with you.'

'No, Gilbert, you must command the men. I'll send word. I'll take one of the new men with me in case the Visconti eyes are sharper than I hope they are and remember any of us from when we last caused them harm.'

Killbere shrugged. 'Who? There's not much choice. Brun is as big as Meulon. Terrel is wounded.'

'Aye, then I'll take him. He'll help me with my plan.'

'Terrel? He's a damned liar who's always looking for the easy way out,' said Killbere.

'He'll do.'

'Who else? Mallin, he's too old... but he could be useful. No one gives a second glance to an old routier who could pass for a beggar at any time of the day.'

'No, he has to look after my horse. I daren't risk taking it inside the walls. We've spare horses from della Scala's dead. We'll use theirs and I'll take the Gascon.'

'Bezián? The priest killer? We still don't know how steadfast are the men Henry brought to us.'

'I like him. You said he fought well against della Scala's men.'

'Aye, but if he comes across a wayward priest molesting woman or child in the celebrations, he'll gut them.'

Blackstone smiled. 'I like a man with a sense of purpose.'

Killbere sent John Jacob to get Terrel.

'Me? I'm wounded,' he whimpered. 'I'm not fit to ride any distance, Master Jacob.'

'Sir Thomas wants you. He has his reasons.'

'Aye, but I'll be no good to him in a fight. My wound still weeps.'

John Jacob reached under Terrel's tunic and tugged it up. 'The bandage looks clean enough. It's a minor wound.'

'Minor? It gripes like a thousand scorpion stings.'

John Jacob looked concerned. 'So many?'

'Aye. I get no sleep with it. You can ask Mallin; he'll tell you.'

John Jacob's solemn expression offered sympathy. 'You know what that means, don't you? When a wound bites like that?'

Terrel shook his head.

'It means it's well on the way to healing. Get a damned horse saddled and ride to where Sir Thomas is waiting.'

Blackstone had left his men under Killbere's command encamped within an hour's ride of the city gates, taking advantage of an enclave of wooded hills. The hills provided both a good defensive position from their height and a means of rapid escape in case of a forceful attack.

'He should have taken me with him,' said John Jacob as he and Killbere watched the distant figures of Blackstone riding with the Milanese captain and his wounded men. 'Terrel, of all people. I swear the man's a charlatan.'

'Perhaps that's what Thomas needs for his purpose.'

'Still, Sir Gilbert, it would be best if I was at Sir Thomas's side.'

'You know how he is, John. We'll never change him. Damned if I didn't give up twenty-odd years ago when we landed in France. Stubborn as a damned mule and a skull twice as thick.' Killbere lost sight of the riders. 'Let's hope the Visconti don't find him. Likely as not he'll kill them and then the entire plan and the marriage collapses.'

Blackstone had told Bezián and Terrel about his plan to enter Milan. The Gascon showed no sign of concern, but Terrel tried once more to be excused from the venture. He was ignored.

'You will groan as we ride,' said Blackstone. 'Not too much. I don't want Marchesi thinking I have mewling infants fighting for me. I will use you to get to the hospital. So, remember, when I suggest we strike out for the hospital, you can show your pain. Not too much. Enough to be convincing.'

'It will require no acting skills, Sir Thomas. I am in sufficient pain to be of use to you.'

'Good,' said Blackstone. He looked at Bezián. 'Questions?'

Bezián shrugged. Being chosen by the King's Master of War was privilege enough and needed no questions to be asked. Except one.

'Do we kill those who try to stop us? Anyone of rank? No matter who?'

'If we have the choice of running, we will. If not, yes. We don't wish to draw attention to ourselves. The Visconti aren't stupid. Once Marchesi reports to Bernabò he'll be looking for me. If I cannot reach my son or the Prince, then I'll use one of you to carry a message to them.' He studied the Gascon's calm demeanour. A man unconcerned that he might be riding into a death trap. 'Any more questions?'

'No, Sir Thomas. I just wanted to check who I could kill.'

Terrel shook his head. There was no escape from what was obviously an act of madness.

They made their way to Marchesi and his depleted group and the wounded men.

'If I am to take you to Lord Bernabò, I still have no name with which to present you to him. If you are men of a free company, you serve someone,' said Marchesi.

Blackstone reassured the Milanese captain. 'He knows me. We have met before. I was sent to protect his patrols like yours. That way, he keeps most of his men inside the city walls. He needs them here for the wedding. Now, let us ride. Your men need help. You decide how we enter the city. We follow your command.'

For years, Marchesi had been leading men, but the man who had rescued him now appeared to be the one giving the orders.

They rode at a steady pace towards the city that dominated the countryside. The imposing city walls showed square, no-nonsense merlons. There were no swallow-tailed crenellations here like the battlements in Florence or Verona. Blackstone remembered how formidable the city was from the last time he had barely escaped with his life. A city as unyielding as the man who ruled it.

'Some gates are closed because of the wedding,' Marchesi said. 'We go through Porta Renza. It will put us in the eastern side of the city, so will take us longer to reach Lord Bernabò's *castello*.'

Blackstone nodded. The *castello* was in the city's north-west. Ahead of them was a stone bridge over a moat that was a tributary of the Seveso and beyond the bridge stood the fortified gates. Traders and peasants thronged the approach but cleared when Marchesi shouted for them to stand aside. The Porta Renza's guard commander ordered the gates opened when he recognized who led the men.

The gate commander looked at Marchesi's travelling companions. 'No weapons on the streets, Marchesi. Not with these crowds. Our guards and the likes of you is all right. Them, I don't know.'

'They saved our lives, Salvatore. They ride with me to Lord Bernabò.'

'All right. Your responsibility.' He waved through the riders and as Marchesi's horse moved forward the guard commander tapped the horse's withers. 'Good to see you back safely, old friend.'

Bezián cast a glance at Blackstone when a main thoroughfare was revealed, crowded with Milanese and visitors, jostling each other as they walked. Vendors, their stalls and carts laden with fresh food or bread, cried out, offering their wares. Merchants dressed in silk and less privileged citizens in rough wool rubbed shoulders as they clogged the street beneath tall stone buildings, wooden balconies strung with drying clothes. Colourful cloth awnings, rolled ready to be unfurled for shade when the sun blessed the city, hung beneath the balconies. The hum of voices muted the sound of a flute player. Bernabò's guards manned the entrances to some of the side streets, controlling where the crowds could move. An old woman carrying a basket of vegetables and bread chastised a soldier for blocking her way to her house. He relented and let her pass. Marchesi forced his horse through the crowds, calling them to stand aside. Guards raised a hand in greeting, then answered when he asked which streets he could use to avoid the crowds.

'It's a hell hole to escape from should we have to,' said Bezián.

'It serves us well enough. The wedding has drawn in more outsiders. These crowds are better than a shield wall for us.'

They followed Marchesi for another two hundred yards before he turned down a guarded street, the soldiers standing aside for him. Here, there were no throngs of people, only tradesmen carrying out their work on various buildings.

'Do you know where we are?' said Bezián. 'It's a warren. Worse than Lyons or the back streets of Paris.'

'And both would give half their treasury to have what this city offers. I know we've turned north-west. Bernabò's castle is at Porta Giovia. Remember whatever you can. These streets have landmarks. We'll need them if we run into trouble.' Blackstone pointed. 'What's the name of that church?' he asked Marchesi.

The captain half turned in the saddle. 'The San Lorenzo Basilica.'

After a minute riding on, Blackstone lowered his voice and told Bezián and Terrel, 'That's one place we'll use if we must.'

Bernabò's *castello* loomed in the distance. Streets ran left and right across the gates. 'We don't want to be taken inside there,' said Blackstone. 'We'd never get out alive.' He looked around, making certain his nod to Terrel went unnoticed by the others.

Terrel slumped across the horse's withers. His prayer to the Virgin Mary whispered through gritted teeth.

It was almost an act too far. Bezián saw Blackstone's alarm. The Gascon backwalked his horse a yard, reached out and as if in a comradely gesture, gripped Terrel's shoulder. Genuine pain made Terrel grimace. Bezián lowered his head next to his ear. 'Not too much, you damned fool. They might insist on taking us inside the castle and treat you there.'

'Marchesi,' Blackstone said. 'Is Lord Bernabò expecting you to report directly to him?'

The horses came to a halt. 'I have to speak to my superiors and then he will summon me,' Marchesi said.

'Then let me take the wounded on to the hospital. My man needs attention. I don't want him dying on me.'

Marchesi looked back at his own men, bloodied and weak from the fight. He checked the hunched Terrel. 'It will take some hours before I am seen,' he said, weighing up his options.

'Then I suggest I take them and return to be at your lord's command.'

'Very well. You know the way?'

'I'm sure I do.' Blackstone's mind sought the answer he needed. It had been years since he had been in Milan. The more familiar and confident he sounded, the better. But not too confident. 'I can't remember which one is the closest to here.' He dragged names from his memory. 'The Ospedale del Brolo or San Simpliciano?'

Marchesi had enough on his mind reporting back to Bernabò about recent events without questioning the offer made by the man he thought to be a mercenary. He pointed away from the castle. 'Del Brolo. They'll see to everyone. When you return, tell the guards I am expecting you.'

The able-bodied men followed their captain towards the gates as Blackstone heeled his horse to face another street. The seven men who followed muttered among themselves, obviously pleased not to face the Lord of Milan's wrath at their failure to die in battle protecting his domain. The streets fanned out before them. Blackstone felt uncertainty nudge him. He had no idea where he was. Bezián glanced his way. Blackstone shrugged. 'The further away from the *castello*, the better.' He turned to one man who was nursing what was left of his arm. 'You know the way?'

The man nodded.

'Then lead on. We'll follow.'

The injured hobelar nudged his horse past Blackstone. The wounded followed. Blackstone and Bezián, with a worried Terrel, brought up the rear. After turning down one avenue and then another, Blackstone carried on in another direction, letting Marchesi's men go their own way.

'What now?' said Bezián.

'A back-street stable, an inn, and a place to sleep. We await the Prince's arrival.'

For the first time since setting out on this dangerous journey, Terrel smiled.

CHAPTER TWENTY-EIGHT

Bernabò Visconti turned away from his favourite view of his city. His balcony ran the length of his upper quarters and from there he could see beyond the *castello*'s walls across the city's rooftops. The bee-like hum of voices from those in the streets below swelled and faded and music echoed from one of the many courtyards as musicians rehearsed for the wedding. Bernabò had handed over arrangements for the forthcoming ceremony to his brother, whose chamberlains, advisers and various other household officials were experienced in arranging sumptuous feasts and celebrations. Massed drums and trumpets quickened the pulse as their staccato beats and fanfares soared high above the walls, disturbing flocks of pigeons from the multitude of roofs. The birds rose, swirled, held together and resettled onto one of the castle's ninety-foot towers. The pigeons of Milan had been at home in the city since Celtic tribes had quarried and laid the first stones a thousand years before.

'My lord?' said a servant.

Bernabò turned. Marchesi was escorted onto the balcony.

Bernabò dismissed the servant and took stock of his patrol company's captain. 'I'm told you fought off della Scala's attack,' he said, pouring wine into a goblet.

Marchesi was unsurprised that the news had already reached
Bernabò. His superiors would have relayed their information
after questioning him.

Bernabò's unflinching stare held his captain rigid. Despite his
wounds and weariness, there would be no respite until the full
facts were delivered to Lord Bernabò and then his fate would be
decided. Failure could be easily punished. Marchesi had served
Milan and his lord for twenty years; he was liked and trusted by
his men; he had earned the right to command a long time ago.
Even so, despite old victories, a new defeat could bring harsh
punishment.

'My lord, we fought hard against an overwhelming enemy.
The Scaligeri had greater forces behind them. The Pope's men.'

'Uh-huh,' said Bernabò, seemingly disinterested as he
sipped his wine and stared down sixty feet to the main
courtyard where household officials were harrying servants
loading carts carrying the hundreds of benches and gilded
chairs through to the city centre and the Palazzo dei Visconti,
where the great feast would take place after the ceremony.
Bernabò's wife and family resided there, and it was where
he attended to administrative and legal business and spent
time with his wife, Beatrice. Family and his own privacy were
keenly separated. It was here in the fortified *castello* at Porta
Giovia that he felt at home. His soldiers were billeted here;
the steam from his horses stabled below, rising on a winter's
morning, was as fragrant to his senses as any woman's
perfume. His six thousand hounds were kennelled throughout
the city, citizens of Milan compelled to care for them. His
favoured 150 hounds were kept at the *castello*, pampered by
diligent huntmasters and servants who, like those in the city,
knew violent death awaited them should any dog suffer injury
or lack of care. The stronghold was where his orgies went
undisturbed and the screams from the torture chambers in the
castle's depths were for his delight alone. The stronghold was
his. It was where he belonged.

'Come here,' he said, without turning to address the captain directly.

Marchesi's hesitation was slight enough not to be noticed. His lord and master was peering down into the courtyard and it would take little effort for Bernabò to throw him over the edge. Swift punishment for a perceived failure on the battlefield. Marchesi kept a yard between him and the Visconti lord.

'What do you see?' said Bernabò.

A quick nervous glance showed Marchesi the hive of activity. 'Faithful officials attending to your bidding, lord.'

'I trust my officials, Marchesi. They work with their best endeavour to please me and abide by the strict standards I set. A good man attending to his duties is well rewarded. Those who cannot meet my standards are reduced in rank, dismissed, or face a lingering punishment.'

Marchesi's throat was dry but he involuntarily swallowed hard. Bernabò faced him. 'What happened, Marchesi? How is it you and a handful of your men survived? You killed della Scala's men and yet an overwhelming force of papal cavalry did not strike you down.'

'I cannot say, lord. The company of men who joined us in the battle fought with a fierceness that the Pope's men perhaps did not care to face.'

'I'm told they entered the city with you.'

'Only their captain and two of his men. One is injured, and I sent them with my wounded to del Brolo. Their captain wishes to present himself to you. I do not know who pays for him and his men.'

'Who else would support us?'

Marchesi was at a loss. 'Montferrat is against us, so too the Lords of Ferrara and Rimini.' He shook his head. Respected and feared in equal measure, Bernabò Visconti always took the field with his men, unlike his brother. It was a mystery what strangers would put themselves in danger on behalf of the Lord of Milan.

'Perhaps they are *condottieri* who wish to impress you and seek your favour. But he's a *condottiere* known to you. That is what he tells me.'

'I pay no *condottieri* in this war.'

'He's an Englishman.'

'Giovanni Acuto? I am still negotiating with him.'

Acuto was the Englishman John Hawkwood, but he fought for Pisa and no firm arrangement had yet been made to have him switch sides.

'You are certain he is English? Not one of the German *condottieri*?'

'No, the Germans ride mostly with the Pope. Lord, I am at a loss. This man speaks our language, and he knows your city.'

A wild thought pierced Bernabò's mind. 'Describe him,' he said, a part of him sensing the answer before it was given.

'Tall as you, my lord, and as broad. He is fast with his blade and—'

'A scar. Here. Down his cheek.'

Marchesi stumbled in uncertainty. 'Yes, my lord. His blazon is a gauntlet grasping a sword.'

'Below its crossguard,' said Bernabò with muted certainty. And then, to be certain, 'You saw his shield?'

'Battle-scarred. Whatever was written was unclear,' said Marchesi, now wary he was stepping into dangerous territory.

'*Défiant à la Mort*,' said Bernabò without a glimmer of surprise in his voice, his thoughts reeling back to when he had Blackstone under his knife, only for him to escape. The goblet fell from his fingers. It clattered into the courtyard below. He ignored it. His gaze settled on the rooftops. Somewhere in this sprawling spider's web was his enemy. Had he used the defence of Visconti troops purely to sneak inside these walls? If so, why?

Bernabò stood erect and looked down at his captain. 'He won't come here, Marchesi. He will seek sanctuary with the Prince and then he cannot be touched. Find him. The Prince arrives late tomorrow. The man who saved your life is the English King's Master of War, Sir Thomas Blackstone, and he is in my city.'

CHAPTER TWENTY-NINE

Terrel was not smiling for long. By the fifth attempt at finding stabling and a bed, it was clear that Milan's swelling population had secured what accommodation was available. He knew better than to complain aloud. Blackstone and the Gascon, Bezián, trudged on foot, leading their mounts through the twisting streets. Blackstone was gaining information every step along the way. Roads and passages remained blocked by Visconti's guards. Blackstone mapped his journey so far in his mind, like a track through a maze that meandered here and there. He would use these side streets as a way through the city's web. Wherever possible Blackstone kept their distance from Visconti's men guarding the roads and passageways, which was one reason he was guiding their mounts on foot, their swords wrapped in their bedrolls and obscured on the side away from a guard's prying eyes.

'We've gone a long way across the city, Sir Thomas,' said Bezián. 'We're south-west from where we left Marchesi. Are we not to contact the Prince and Master Henry?'

'We are, if we can get close enough when they arrive. Every hostelry along the route we've travelled is taken. So that confirms what the innkeepers have told me. The Prince will be greeted down here at the Porta Ticinese. See how the road is wider here? And more soldiers.' He nudged his horse into the shade of a building, ignoring the curses of those he pushed aside. No ordinary citizen argued with a man-at-arms. He took a drink from his wineskin and passed it to Bezián and Terrel. 'The crowds have to be accommodated on the principal streets, and from what I can tell, most of them will line the route, but the largest crowds will be at the various piazzas. That suggests that the Prince will ride from the gates in the south-west through the city and into the Visconti palace. He won't be quartered in the *castello*. That's Bernabò's private domain.' He took back the wineskin from Terrel. It was lighter. Blackstone made no comment, but Terrel's guilty look told him the man-at-arms knew he had been greedy.

'Then we should try to get as close as possible to the palace,' said Bezián.

'That's my plan – if we can find someone to take us in. It won't be long before Bernabò knows I'm here, and I've no desire to end up in his dungeons again.'

Blackstone called out to a street trader nestled further along the cool passage. Neither Bezián nor Terrel knew what was being asked. Blackstone checked something the trader said, and bought a small basket of wild strawberries from his cart by way of thanks. Blackstone shared them with his companions. As they each slurped the sweet flesh, Blackstone gestured down the main street.

'Traders are being pushed off the main route. This is where the Visconti will ride down with the Prince. The fruit-seller says it's a mile and a half from the gates to the palace, so somewhere'— he sucked the flesh from the last strawberry—'along this route we have to make sure Henry sees one of us.'

'Not the Prince?' said Terrel, wiping his hands across his gambeson. He frowned. 'Master Henry?'

'Terrel, think about it,' said Bezián. 'When was the last time you met the Prince?'

'Don't be stupid – never.'

'And when did you last see Master Henry?' Bezián patiently asked.

'When he left for Bologna.'

'So Master Henry would recognize you?'

'Of course! I served him as did you and the others.'

'But if Sir Thomas has just told you we must catch his eye, what does that tell you?'

Terrel had to reflect a moment before answering. 'That he never left for Bologna.' A candle flame flickered in his mind. 'So, Master Henry went with the Prince.'

Bezián flicked the strawberry's stem and leaf away with the shake of his head.

Terrel defended his slow take-up of the facts. 'I was not to know that Master Henry rode with the Prince.'

'No, Terrel, you weren't, but you understand we must now decide how best to attract my son's attention.'

'Aye, Sir Thomas. I understand.'

'Good. Then let us continue on our way,' said Blackstone, ignoring Bezián's glance of disbelief in their companion's slow-witted ways. 'We are all tired and hungry,' he said with consideration for Terrel. 'And once rested and fed, our thoughts will be as sharp as our blades.'

As Blackstone led the way again, he heard Bezián mutter behind him. 'Providing the blade has not rusted beyond repair.'

The owner of the Locanda del Falco Nero was as shrewd a businessman as Blackstone was a leader of men. Yes, his inn had room for their horses and the riders could sleep in the one remaining stall, but he was holding out for another day until those desperate enough would pay far more than his usual charge for livery, bed and food.

'How much?' said Blackstone, hiding his shock at the prices once he was told how much the owner wanted.

'Ten *soldi* for a mug of wine, another twenty for a bowl of soup and bread,' said the smug innkeeper. As he continued to rattle off his prices Blackstone realized they were at least five times the going rate.

'And look how close you are to the Palazzo Visconti,' said the owner.

Blackstone nodded as if in agreement. 'And that is why Amadeus, the Count of Savoy, sent me here to check that this area is safe.'

The innkeeper raised his eyebrows.

Blackstone brushed the dirt from the blazon stitched on his tunic. 'You see this? Do you know what this is?'

'I do not.'

'Have you ever seen such a blazon before?'

'In truth I have not.'

'I am the Count's scout. How else would I have been allowed into the city bearing arms if I was not?'

'My Lord Amadeus?' said the innkeeper, impressed. 'The one who brings the English Prince to our Lord Galeazzo?'

'Yes. But lower your voice. I am not supposed to take anyone into my confidence about this matter'—he paused—'of life and death.' Another pause to let the man swallow hard. Was this a threat? 'Because only the most trusted can be told of our mission here,' said Blackstone, nodding towards his two ruffian-like companions.

The hesitant innkeeper looked from one to the other. He was not yet convinced. 'I am no fool: do not take me for one. If you are Amadeus's men, you would be billeted in the *castello* with Lord Bernabò's soldiers.'

Blackstone laid a conspiratorial hand on the man's shoulder. His voice lowered. 'There are a hundred of us scattered throughout the city. We are billeted in inns everywhere. Two or three men at a time. It is our job to stay in the background and to observe who helps and who... hinders us. There are those on the streets who will make their dislike of the English known.'

'No! Lord Bernabò would have them skinned alive.'

'If they can be caught,' said Blackstone. 'His men guard the route; it is Amadeus's men brought into the city this morning who will patrol the back streets watching for these malcontents. There'll be some who will make a great profit from the honour being bestowed on the Visconti family.'

'A fair price given the importance of the day,' the innkeeper protested.

'I agree,' Blackstone assured him. 'I would not see a hard-working man lose the chance to make a profit. I have a gold florin to pay for our lodging and care. One florin now and one more when we leave.'

The innkeeper's mind raced, instinctively assessing profit and loss. The florin was a rare coin, seldom seen in day-to-day bargaining for food and lodging. Three men would eat and drink a great deal, but he'd water down the soup and the wine. He'd make a profit. And having the gold florin would enhance his reputation. In that moment a few local *soldi* seemed paltry by comparison.

He resisted the urge to snap the coin from Blackstone's hand. He laid open his palm.

Blackstone placed it and watched the greedy man's fingers curl over it.

'For another I'll kick out travellers taking up three beds.'

'We'll sleep with the horses,' said Blackstone. 'Remember our being here must not be mentioned.'

The innkeeper's head bobbed. 'You will honour me by telling Lord Amadeus that I served you well.'

'He'll be told,' Blackstone assured him.

'I will have my servants look after your horses.' He scurried away.

'Innkeeper,' Blackstone called, making him turn and face him. 'Do not water down the wine or the soup. And bring us fresh bread and meat. See to it now.'

The innkeeper hunched. It was likely he'd make less profit than he had thought.

Blackstone let the stable hands lead their horses into the yard and thence to where other mounts were tethered. Unlike the monastery, these stables had separate stalls, and once the horses had been tethered and unsaddled the three men stripped their swords from their bedrolls. Blackstone searched the low roof timbers for a place to conceal them.

'Bezián, cup your hands.'

The Gascon pushed his back against the stall wall and did as Blackstone asked, taking Blackstone's foot into the stirrup he'd made. Blackstone slid his sword behind a broad chestnut beam. 'Terrel, hand me Bezián's sword, then your own.'

Once the swords were concealed, Blackstone huddled in the only empty stall, which was to be their sleeping quarters. 'We'll eat and then go back on the streets.' Sweeping aside straw and dirt he scratched a line in the dirt with his knife. 'The Prince comes in here at the Porta Ticinese. The locals call it Porta Snesa.' He drew a route down to where he placed a stone. 'This is the palace, and here'—he scratched a mark in the dirt a short distance away—'is where we are. Three hundred yards as an arrow flies.'

Bezián put two stones along the marked route. 'Sir Thomas, you told us to watch for places where we could attract Master Henry's attention. I think it will be difficult with the crowds who will line the street but what about in the piazza at this church?'

'That's the Basilica di Sant'Eustorgio. I noticed it too – a good choice.'

'Especially if whoever's there can stand here at the far corner to attract Master Henry's attention,' said Bezián, marking the dirt where the scratched line turned a corner.

Blackstone nodded. 'All right. I saw a side street next to it as well. We could double around the back streets if we needed to.'

Bezián pointed at the second stone. 'This is another place I think one of us might have a chance to attract attention. The San Lorenzo church is closer to the main route and might not have as many people standing between its steps and the road.'

Blackstone knew Bezián had studied the route as carefully as he had done. It was a good start. He looked at Terrel. 'Did you see any better place for us?'

Terrel made a show of concentrating at the scratched dirt. He shook his head. 'I did not,' he said. 'I agree with Bezián. These are the best places.' He kept his eyes down studiously, hoping he wasn't going to be questioned further. The route to the stables had baffled him. Milan teemed with people, soldiers and a hundred streets that spun out from every corner. It was better not to lie and offer any other suggestion because he had none.

By the time darkness had fallen, each man had a clear idea of where they would stand and how then to slip away through the back streets where they hoped Marchesi's search had not yet reached. It was a certainty, Blackstone had told them, that the Visconti captain would be hunting for them.

Terrel was anxious about being captured if Marchesi's men found him, but he still settled to sleep that night, his thirst for money overcoming his fear of being caught. Having witnessed the throngs already gathering in the streets, he knew there was a way to make easy gains. His knife was honed and his greed as sharp.

CHAPTER THIRTY

The next morning Blackstone guided Terrel and Bezián on foot back to where the vantage points offered them their best chance of catching Henry's attention. Blackstone needed Henry to ask the Prince to send for him so that he could get into the Palazzo Visconti. The gold was due to be delivered after the ceremony. How, by whom and where? was what Blackstone needed to know.

Bezián decided to take the Basilica di San Lorenzo Maggiore, which was near the Ticinese Gate. This would be the first opportunity for Henry to see any of them. It was also where soldiers were already billeted in strength. Groups of twenty at a time clustered along the main thoroughfare, ready to stand along the entire length of the route. Bezián was careful to keep a dozen paces behind them and mingle with the Milanese and incomers as he spied out how to reach the basilica later that day without causing friction among those who would already be in place. With his back against a corner of the church, he let his gaze wander up and down. He needed luck to be on his side. He waited. And watched. It was going to be difficult.

Blackstone stayed for an hour with Terrel at the Basilica di Sant'Eustorgio, which was half a mile from where Bezián would be and the closest vantage point to where they were staying, a few hundred yards from the palazzo. Flocks of pigeons swooped from its domed roof, as nervous and excited as the onlookers, who knew they were about to witness history taking place in their city. Blackstone and Terrel stood half hidden by the portico's columns, behind the gathering soldiers readying to line the route. Here, the crowds would gather more densely than anywhere else along the route. It was open spaces such as this one at Sant'Eustorgio, and also at San Lorenzo, where any surge from the crowd would push onlookers into the procession and so it was here where there would be more soldiers.

'Terrel, you'll stand back well away from those soldiers. When the procession turns that corner...' He pointed along the length of the road where, four hundred yards away, there was a curve that would bring the procession into view. 'When they turn that corner, everyone here will be looking that way. You move down the side of the piazza. That will place you as close as possible to the riders.'

Terrel nodded. But he wasn't happy. It was risky. He would be breathing down the necks of the soldiers guarding the procession's route.

'The side street here will be closed off,' said Blackstone. 'The crowds will be cheering. That's when you make yourself known to my son. Do you remember what was agreed? What to call out to him?'

'I cry out de Sainteny and Locanda del Falco Nero.'

'That's all. Nothing more. It will be meaningless to anyone else. But it will tell him where to find us.'

'We don't know what side of the column Master Henry will be riding,' said Terrel. 'I won't be able to hail him if he is not on this side.'

'Which is why we chose these two basilicas. One over on that side of the street, this one here. Either you or Bezián will have the best chance. I might choose the wrong side as I move behind the crowds. I'll be looking for a break and a chance to draw his attention, but if I fail, then I can do nothing more than wait for you back at the stables. One of us should be able to catch his eye. Whatever happens, as soon as he rides past, get back to the inn.'

Terrel nodded his understanding and watched Blackstone move in the direction of the city gates and Bezián. And do what for the rest of the day? he asked himself. He shrugged. Do what you want. There are wine-sellers and food stalls in that packed side street. Enjoy yourself, said the answering voice in his head. He peered around the increasing crowds. Better to make sure he had a way out if things went wrong. He sidled alongside the church where people were already packing the narrow street, jostling forward and carrying food and drink. If he had to run for any reason, that street would be a barrier. Terrel's sense of survival turned him back to the church where a steady stream of people were coming and going.

He stepped into the vast, cool nave. Those who had entered ahead of him were kneeling on the stone floor. Light from the doors was swallowed by the huddled people and the several side chapels that also had their share of worshippers. The pillars running along each side cast even deeper shadows than the gloom of the nave. Faded frescos loomed on the side walls. Terrel edged his way towards the altar. He had robbed a church once and knew there would be a sacristy somewhere in the back, as well as a rear side door to the outside. Satisfied that he now had an escape route should anything go wrong, he edged his way back to the heat of the day. It was time to watch if Milanese thieves were as adept as those in any English city.

As time passed and the sun moved, Terrel inched his way around the columns, shielding himself from the direct sunlight. Looking down the street, he could see the crowds now pressing behind the soldiers guarding the route. He had spotted three thieves at work. A skilled family, by the look of it. The youngest, a child six or eight years old, wormed his way through the crowd, causing the intended victim to berate him while a girl, a few years older, deftly cut the purse from his belt. With well-practised sleight of hand, she passed it to an older boy. He, in turn, edged away towards the side street, passed it to an older man, perhaps their father, Terrel thought. Then he slipped into the church. Terrel followed. In one of the side chapels a burly man, someone who looked as though he didn't belong to the family of thieves – if they were a family – stood at the back wall, took the purse and slipped it into a satchel. Then the father figure slipped back out into the crowd.

Terrel believed they were targeting only this section of the crowd and would leave before the thefts were noticed. And if thieves had their chosen spots, then all along the route there would be other gangs at work. He heard the distant sound of trumpets and then the rapid beats of drums. A hum of anticipation rose from the crowd. How long would the thieves dare to work this piazza? If he was doing the purse cutting, he'd have taken his time and waited until the procession got closer. Then everyone's attention would be on the approaching cavalcade.

He left the church before the 'father', as he called him, turned with the crowd once they had heard the welcoming fanfare for the Prince, as yet still out of sight a mile and a half away at the Ticinese Gate. Terrel held back, using a pillar as if it were a boulder in a stream, forcing those leaving the basilica to swirl around him. The burly man was still in the church.

Terrel waited, eyes flitting around the people in front of him, looking for the thieves at work. There were too many people. And then he saw the child worming his way into the crowd. His eyes followed him, as a predator stalks its prey. The thieves would work quickly, taking as many purses as they could as the people craned their necks to catch sight of the procession, jammed against each other, unaware of a tug or a push against them. Terrel reassured himself his knife was still in his belt. Dare he wait until Henry Blackstone rode past with Prince Lionel before he killed and seized the money?

CHAPTER THIRTY-ONE

The spectacle of Galeazzo Visconti's welcome for the English Prince awed the crowd who gathered along the route from Porta Ticinese. Galeazzo and his wife Bianca with their son Gian and his wife Isabella sat astride immaculately groomed horses resplendent in caparisons woven with gold and silver thread and the Viper of Milan blazon. As splendid as the spectacle was, Galeazzo's efforts to impress Prince Lionel were also a crass display of wealth. Horses, women and shining armour were all adorned with jewels. Eighty young women attended the Visconti household, all dressed alike in bodices of scarlet with white cloth sleeves embroidered in colourful swirls and sashes of interwoven gold and silver threads stitched with semi-precious stones which had each cost a hundred florins.

By contrast, the Prince was dressed soberly. His silk surcoat was emblazoned with his crest and a fine thread of green that rose from its hem to spread across his shoulders. It was as if a mighty oak, tall and strong, presented itself to the Milanese. His train of several hundred snaked behind him, far beyond the gates. Only the Prince rode forward at the walk to meet Galeazzo. Despenser and the other accompanying knights held back, riding slowly to close the gap so that when the formality of being greeted was over, they would be in attendance again.

Blackstone was on the same side of the route as Terrel and he couldn't see Bezián across the street now that the spectacle had begun. Galeazzo's son had a retinue of thirty knights with him and blocked his view. As Blackstone shifted position to get a better vantage point, he looked at Isabelle, the thirteen-year-old child – as she was then – he had brought to Milan eight years before to marry into the Visconti family. He remembered the brave girl who had endured so much on the journey, now a young woman who had already lost a child in its infancy two years after arriving in the city. Perhaps her life of comfort might offer some succour for that grief.

Blackstone's weight and height parted the stubborn crowd. No one raised any objection once they took the measure of him. The horses blocking his view were nudged aside by their riders as Galeazzo and the Prince prepared to take the lead in the long procession. He saw Bezián raise his arm further back in the crowd. Blackstone signalled him so that they could identify each other. Bezián's hand turned, gesturing in a circular motion. Blackstone looked behind him. Soldiers were filtering through the crowd nearest the gate and would reach him soon. More of Visconti's men were moving across the gaps in the street behind the church. He looked back to Bezián, who indicated he was heading back in the direction of the stables, for he too had soldiers moving through the crowds around him. Church bells pealed across the city. Blackstone gazed down at the procession, which was now on the move. Trumpeters had turned, their long instruments adorned with the Visconti tasselled blazon, to walk as an escort between onlookers and the cavalcade. Drummers led the procession, striking a solid single beat. He craned his neck to see where Henry might be. Beyond the Prince and Galeazzo, the Visconti entourage followed and then came Despenser. Blackstone kept a watchful eye on the soldiers moving through the crowds and those in the street. One figure was directing the soldiers. Marchesi. They were searching for him. Once again, he dared to stay where he was and lean out to see if there was any sign of his son. His gaze settled above the heads of the escorting trumpeters, searching out riders who followed. At first he didn't recognize him. Henry now wore a surcoat bearing Prince Lionel's royal blazon. So too the man who rode beside him, Gifford. Blackstone realized that somewhere along the journey the Prince had rewarded Henry and brought him even closer into his circle.

Soldiers were closing in, checking men in the crowd. If he stayed any longer, they would find him. The best hope to reach Henry lay with Terrel. If Blackstone could get to where Terrel stood in the piazza before the soldiers' search reached them, he or Terrel would have a last chance to attract Henry's attention. Blackstone hunched to lessen his height and nudged his way through the crowd towards the street behind the church. There were still plenty of people milling in the back streets to help obscure him from Marchesi's men. He gauged the distance to the corner. Half a mile. Several minutes before the procession hove into Terrel's view. And then another half-mile before they reached his position. Blackstone shouldered his way towards the street. He had fifteen minutes at best to reach Terrel's location and be there when the procession reached him. He cursed under his breath. There wasn't enough time.

Terrel had no intention of losing the prize in the thief's sack. He had stayed under the portico watching the efficient gang at work. Every time a purse was cut, it was passed on to the man in the church. How long would it be before they moved on further down the procession route to steal from those crowds? The best chance he had to take the sack of money was in the gloom of that ill-lit church. He looked down the street. The rhythmic *thump-thump-thump* of the drummers beckoned the eager crowd to lean forward, their voices babbling with excitement as the first horses turned the corner.

He was on edge. If he was going to kill the thief with the sack, it needed to be done as the procession drew level. The crowd would all be looking at the spectacle and the church would be empty. He would kill and run. He already knew where the side door was at the back of the church and then he'd work his way back to the stables before Blackstone or Bezián returned and secure the stolen coins in his saddlebags.

The child was still weaving among the onlookers. The girl cut the purses. The older man took them into the church. He was only ten feet from where Terrel stood by the side of the pillar. He looked down the road. The front riders were closer. His attention had been on the thieves. Now he saw trumpeters dressed in Visconti livery walking along the flanks as drummers beat out their single incessant beat. The first horses bore the Prince and next to him was the man he determined to be Visconti. Despite being distracted by the gang and losing a few minutes, Terrel's attention was snared by his shock at the spectacle and the unbelievable wealth it projected. He had never seen anything like it. Was everyone in Milan rich? All those cut purses. Did they contain silver deniers or gold florins? Panic seized him. He couldn't see the small boy or the girl. Had the cheering crowd swallowed them? Stepping beyond the pillar, he looked both ways. There was no sign of them. Other figures were moving two hundred yards on the opposite side. Soldiers disrupting the crowd. He looked along the route on his side of the road. Past the piazza where he stood, men were forcefully pushing through the crowds, causing the same disruptive ripple. Soldiers were working their way in his direction.

Riders passed by. Men and women dressed in finery. Prancing horses. And then he saw Gifford and Henry Blackstone, who rode on the side nearest to Terrel. Fifty yards. Where were the thieves? Thirty yards. His eyes scanned the crowd. Twenty yards. There! The older man had cut through the crowd and got behind him as he slipped into the church. Henry Blackstone was level with him. Terrel cupped his hands around his mouth and bellowed over the noise of the crowd.

'De Sainteny!'

Henry Blackstone's head snapped towards him.

'Locanda del Falco Nero!'

As Henry scoured the crowd, Terrel plunged into the cool darkness of the church, knife in hand.

CHAPTER THIRTY-TWO

Blackstone ran through the back streets, weaving his way towards Terrel and the church piazza. The tide of people shuffling in the confines of the narrow streets forced him to seek a riskier route. He turned back to a broader passage, where Marchesi's soldiers were in force as they, too, followed the procession's progress. Marchesi's men in the crowds were moving slower than those in the street where Blackstone was now. These soldiers were forging a path through the slow-moving tide of Milanese. At every alley leading down to the procession's route, Blackstone saw it getting ahead of him. The basilica loomed above the rooftops. A burly character pushing his way through the crowded street turned into Blackstone's path, causing them to collide. The slow-moving crowd, the heat of the day and the frustration of trying to make progress in a packed city tipped the man's temper. He cursed Blackstone. Grabbed a handful of his gambeson and drew back his fist.

The man's strength and heavy build were no match for Blackstone's speed. He let the man pull him forward and headbutted him. His knees sagged. Blackstone punched him once and he fell. Voices were raised. A woman screamed. The crowd scattered.

The cry came from behind him. 'Blackstone!' He turned. Marchesi, now visible in the churning crowd. Blackstone stepped over the fallen man and ran hard for the basilica's side door on the far side of the church.

Terrel blinked in the gloom as he stepped into the church from the bright sunshine. He couldn't see the thieves, but as his eyes adjusted, he saw they were making their way down the nave towards the rear door. He ran after them, not realizing bystanders near the doors had seen him. The resounding cacophony of the bells stopped the thieves from hearing his approach. The decoy child was being tugged along by the cut-purse girl. The older boy was at their side while the father figure strode alongside the gang's satchel-carrying leader. The father turned to urge the girl to keep up and saw the looming figure of Terrel with a knife twenty feet away. His jaw dropped as he snatched at the man next to him. By the time he turned, it was too late. Terrel pushed the girl and young boy aside. As they fell, the older boy struck at Terrel but a hard and fast punch to his face floored him. The father backed off, scared of the sudden violence. He was not a fighter but the man with the satchel was. He swung its weight in an attempt to stop Terrel. It caught the side of his head despite Terrel's arm deflecting it and the forceful strike knocked him off balance. His momentum carried him into the gang leader, knocking him to the ground. Terrel's wound from his fight on the mountain pinched as both of them scrambled for the bag. Terrel lay half across the burly man, trying to bring his knife hand around to plunge it into the squirming man's neck. The snarling satchel man rolled and threw a lucky punch, knocking Terrel off him. Undeterred, Terrel twisted away and was about to lunge as the man turned, reaching for the bag. Shadows and a surge of footfalls crossed the light slithering across the stone floor. Somewhere beyond Terrel a door slammed. Men shouted. Before Terrel could strike, a dozen men forced themselves past him and grabbed the burly man, kicking and punching as he curled and tried to escape the vicious blows. Two men seized Terrel and lifted him to his feet. The sudden mayhem confused him. What was certain was that he had lost the satchel.

These men jabbered and threw gestures as rapidly as the punches. They smiled at him, slapping his back. Terrel realized they thought he had tried to stop the thieves from escaping. They hauled the burly man to his feet. Others had grabbed the rest of the gang. No sooner had they been apprehended than soldiers stormed into the church from the rear. The vigilante crowd holding the gang greeted them with a dozen voices, all proclaiming that the gang had stolen purses, proved by the bag being held high. Terrel didn't understand a word but gestures made towards him needed no interpretation. The gaggle of men stood between Terrel and the soldiers. And then he saw Marchesi pushing his way through his men. Terrel ducked and turned away, hoping not to be recognized.

An iron grip clutched his shoulder. He winced and looked up at Blackstone's face.

'They're saying you stopped a thief,' Blackstone hissed. Then he smiled. 'And that's saved us both.' Blackstone hauled him away from the baying crowd and Marchesi and his men.

Terrel cursed his bad luck. A bag of coins had been denied him. Worse still, Blackstone now thought he had committed a good deed. Through no fault of his own his reputation was getting the better of him.

CHAPTER THIRTY-THREE

Henry Blackstone and Gifford waited until darkness before leaving Prince Lionel's entourage. They made their way the short distance to the inn, where they hoped whoever had called his name was a friend. Henry had not seen who it was that cried out when he rode past the Basilica di Sant'Eustorgio, but the message was clearly aimed at him.

'We could be walking into a trap,' said Gifford. 'For all you know, there's someone holding a grudge from the last time you were here. They called you by name. Who would do that?'

'We'll soon find out, Hugh. There's the inn.' They pressed themselves against the corner of a building. 'And the rooms are lit. So, are we to meet someone staying there?' He studied the building, as yet undecided how to approach. A night watch passed close to the inn, their lamplight showing the stable doors ajar. 'Or there?'

Gifford nodded. 'First place to look. Remember, we only have our knives. Let's not get into a brawl. There'll be plenty of drunks in every tavern and inn while these celebrations are on.'

'Not here. Lord Bernabò tolerates no man on the streets feeble with drink after dark.'

Gifford glanced around the shadowy streets. 'Then that's a

worry, Master Henry. If the night watch questions us, who's saying they won't want to try and please him? They run us in and we won't see the light of day again.'

'Oh, you'll see daylight, Hugh, but you'll lose a hand or foot at his pleasure.' He sensed Gifford's unease, his eyes scanning the passageways that led in and out of the street. 'All right,' he said quietly. 'Let's find out who knows me and wanted me to come to this place.'

They crossed the street and waited outside the stable doors. A groom came out, carrying a bucket of horse manure. Gifford stopped him. 'Who's in there?'

The boy didn't understand.

'You forget where we are, Hugh,' said Henry, and asked the same question in Italian. The lad answered. Henry let him pass.

'Three men,' said Henry.

Gifford eased his knife free. 'Then let's see if they're friendly. Step through and I'll cover your back. I'll pull closed the door behind us.'

'No, leave the door. It would warn whoever's in there.'

'Master Henry, we'll be exposed at our backs.'

'We tread carefully and move through shoulder to shoulder. That way, we will have a better chance of defending ourselves should this be a trap.'

Gifford was unhappy, but nodded his assent.

Easing into the stables, they looked down the row of horses, the sheen of their coats caught by lamplight at each end. There was no sign of anyone. Henry and Gifford edged forward. They were barely ten paces inside the stable when the door slammed closed behind them. They swirled around, but all they saw was a shadow ducking away. They turned back to face Blackstone and Bezián, brandishing their swords at their chests.

Gifford cursed. Henry's sudden look of regret for not listening to his guardian man-at-arms was plain.

'You are easy to kill, Henry,' said Blackstone.

He and Bezián lowered their swords. Blackstone resisted the urge to embrace his son, having taught him a harsh lesson. 'Master Gifford, you turned your back on an open door.'

'That was my fault,' said Henry. 'Hugh advised a different approach. I insisted we move through the stables together.'

'Then you would be responsible for his death as well. You must learn, boy. Fighting men have an instinct that shouldn't be ignored.'

Henry bowed his head. Blackstone softened. 'All right, Henry. It's good to see you.' He embraced him. Gifford and Bezián acknowledged each other.

'You too, my lord.' Henry beamed. 'Bezián. Was it you who called out to me?'

'It was me, Master Henry,' said Terrel as he joined them.

Henry concealed his surprise that the man he considered the weakest and least reliable of the men who had joined him in France was there at the heart of his father's enemy.

'And he killed two skinners on the pass,' said Blackstone.

Gifford caught Bezián's glance. Clearly, there was some doubt about that.

'We saw two men hoisted on the roadside when we came across,' said Henry.

'And I took a wound for my trouble,' said Terrel.

'Then you've served well,' said Henry.

'The Prince?' said Blackstone, leading them to the stall.

'Eager to be married tomorrow. The wedding gifts are said to be of great value,' said Henry. He caught his father's enquiring glance. 'There's been no mention of the gold dowry.'

'Sir Thomas, there was an attempt on the Prince's life at the monastery,' Gifford said. 'Master Henry saved his life. The Prince is in his debt.'

Blackstone looked at his son. 'Then before I make myself known to the Prince, it's time I heard everything that happened on your journey from Paris and who might have sent the assassin.'

★

Once they had listened to Henry and Gifford's retelling of events at the monastery, the men considered what had happened. Bezián was the first to offer an opinion.

'The attempt was ill-planned,' said Bezián. 'As if it were destined to fail.'

'When he lay dying, he wouldn't tell me who had sent him. But he said something strange, that it – I mean his death – had to be the way it was. Bezián's right. I think the old man sacrificed himself.'

'If so, then he was trying to save someone,' said Blackstone. 'Someone held by the man who sent him to kill the Prince.'

'Makes no sense,' said Gifford. 'Master Henry and I have thought about little else on the ride from the monastery to here. An assassination has to succeed if you're trying to save someone.'

Henry remained silent. He had still not shared with anyone the old man's final words asking him to save a woman called Elena. The pull of the illuminator's whereabouts still gripped him, but it was his mystery to unravel.

Blackstone reached for his mount's rein and tethered it to the stall. It was already saddled and Wolf Sword's scabbard concealed once again in the bedroll. He slid the blade out of sight. 'Lead us to the palace now, Henry. Are we able to get past the Visconti guards?'

'Lord Despenser has his own men at the south gate.'

'I'll wager the Prince made that demand, did he not?' said Blackstone.

Henry faltered. Of course. The Prince knew his father would need to join him in Milan.

'He did,' admitted Henry.

'Then lead us to him.'

CHAPTER THIRTY-FOUR

Once Henry took Blackstone and the others past Despenser's sentries at the palazzo's gate, Bezián and Terrel led the horses to the palace stables. The Palazzo dei Visconti was a warren but Henry knew the way to the Prince's quarters through the dimly lit corridors.

'Lord Despenser guards the Prince since the attack in the monastery. But he cannot stop me from seeing the Prince. His highness has ordered that Hugh and I remain close to him. Despenser's men will be at the foot of the stairs in the next hallway.'

'And you think they will block you from seeing the Prince?'

'Despenser hovers like a bird of prey. He won't be pleased to see you. He's already aggrieved I have gained favour in the eyes of the Prince.'

'Well, he is a renowned Knight of the Garter: that's a significant honour. Our King has great affection for him. He's due our respect. But you saving the Prince has wounded his pride. If he cannot get past that, then he is a lesser man.'

Henry nodded and led the way along the passage to where shadows flickered from oil lamps on the walls. Edward Despenser stood at the bottom of the stairs with four of his men.

He stared hard at the dishevelled Master of War, resplendent as he was in his own surcoat and blazon. His bejewelled sword belt reflected the oil lamps' glow. He looked what he was, a knight of great standing, used to being in the company of royalty. He was thirty-two years old, six years younger than Blackstone. Stocky, he reached Blackstone's shoulder, but it was obvious he was a fighting man by the way he carried himself. He raised a hand to stop them. Henry, Blackstone and Gifford halted ten feet away.

'I have not been informed of your presence in the city,' said Despenser. 'Nor have I been commanded to allow you to attend the Prince.'

Blackstone stepped forward, closing the gap between them. Despenser was no common man-at-arms to be commanded to step aside. His courage on the battlefield and loyalty to the King and his sons were beyond question. He, in turn, had the highest respect for the King's Master of War. Two men of renown facing each other. Yet courtesy would go only so far if Despenser refused Blackstone access to the Prince or challenged his authority to commandeer the gold dowry.

'And yet the Prince ordered that your men stand at the south gate. What other reason for that could there be if not to bring me here into the palace and prevent a confrontation with Visconti's men?'

'The gate is one matter, the Prince's quarters are another.'

'Lord Despenser, your journey here with several hundred men under your command has served our Prince well. It was my duty to ensure the route was clear. No one knew how many routiers might have been crossing into Italy. My few men were able to move quickly and sweep up any challenges along the way. That the King tasked me without your knowledge reflects no disrespect for your command.'

Despenser grimaced. 'We saw the result of you clearing the route. A savaged routier ripped apart by wolves; men's bodies hanging from a monastery wall, torn to the bone. It was a sight not welcomed by the Prince. Or me.'

'With respect, I did not intend to please you or the Prince. We meant it as a message to those who sought to pillage and rape.' He paused, letting his gaze settle on Despenser, who still appeared to be hesitating in allowing him to go past his men. Blackstone lowered his voice so that the humiliation he was about to deliver was heard only by Despenser. 'My lord, you are not privy to the King's command or my arrangement with the Prince. Do your duty and step aside so that I might do mine.'

Despite the dim light and shadows across Despenser's features, Blackstone saw the insult strike home. There was little more than a twitch of muscle in Despenser's shoulder as he restrained his instinct to reach for his sword. He blinked twice and then turned on his heel for the stairs and the Prince's quarters. Blackstone, Henry and Gifford followed. As they passed the stony-faced men-at-arms guarding the stairs, Gifford smiled and winked at them. If a French army couldn't stop the King's Master of War, a renowned knight of the realm had little chance of success.

Prince Lionel dismissed his personal servants when Edward Despenser announced Blackstone, who strode into the Prince's quarters with Henry a step behind. Both bowed before the Prince, who smiled at finally meeting his father's Master of War. He nodded to Despenser to leave the room, who then joined Gifford waiting outside.

'Highness, I see you are well.'

'Thanks to your son, Sir Thomas.'

'Good fortune favoured him, highness.'

'Our good fortune was having him close to us. Beyond that, he has been a pleasant companion with his love of poetry.'

'A gift I don't share,' said Blackstone. 'That was bequeathed by his French mother.'

'And now, Sir Thomas, we are close to our marriage and you have crept into the city and our company. We won't ask how that was achieved. Master Henry's accounts of your fortitude and enterprise serve as sufficient testimony.'

'I hope he has not exaggerated.'

'Quite the opposite. He related your exploits with due modesty.'

'Highness, my presence here has put you in a difficult situation. Bernabò Visconti searches for me. We are old enemies.'

'And we are to marry his niece. There will be no conflict, Sir Thomas. Lord Galeazzo would tolerate no interference. We must discuss more important matters, and if you have to leave the city to undertake our father's instructions, we will arrange safe passage.'

'Then you know where the gold is and how it will be delivered.'

The Prince settled himself in a fur-draped chair. The marble side table supported a glass decanter of wine, and a half-filled glass. Blackstone knew that the Prince's chamberlain had ensured the Prince's food and drink had been tasted. What no one had bargained for was a physical attack like that made in the Mont Cenis Pass monastery.

The Prince sipped the wine. 'As part of our dowry, we receive certain towns and domains here in the north. Once we are married and the celebrations end, we will travel to one of these towns, Alba, which is, I'm told, south of here. The wedding gifts and the gold florins will be escorted there by Visconti's men.'

Blackstone pictured the countryside in his mind's eye. An enemy could easily arrange an attack if they wished to stop the dowry from reaching the Prince and then England. If the Prince was not with the escort – if he was already in Alba – that would make it seem as nothing more than an attack by brigands.

'Highness, what is important is that we must ensure everything along the way is as it should be. We should bring Lord Despenser into the King's plan. If I'm to get the gold back to your brother in Bordeaux, I might need to call upon his help. If you remain in Alba, then I can use him.'

The Prince took little time to consider Blackstone's proposal. 'Master Henry, summon Lord Despenser.'

Henry turned for the door. Outside, Gifford waited, as did Despenser. 'My lord, our Prince summons you.' Henry stepped back as Despenser strode into the room. Despenser cast a glance at Blackstone, then bowed his head to the Prince as Henry closed the door on Gifford, whose raised eyebrows questioned him. Henry's only response was a smile.

'Lord Edward,' said the Prince, 'Sir Thomas suggests you are told why his presence here in Milan is of importance. We agree.' He tipped his head in Blackstone's direction for him to explain.

'My Lord Edward, have you had sight of the two hundred thousand gold florins promised as part of our Prince's dowry?'

'I have not. They plan to deliver it to Alba when his highness leaves after the celebrations.'

'Do we know how it is stored?'

'In a vault here in the palace.'

'But how many chests? How heavy? How will they transport it?'

'I don't know.'

'Do your men guard it?'

'The Visconti men guard it.'

Blackstone thought for a moment, deciding how much Despenser should be told. He decided to lay a false trail so that his own long-term plans could be put in place. 'I have to get that gold across the Alps and back to Prince Edward in Bordeaux. The French are already preparing for war.'

Despenser looked uncertainly at Blackstone and then the Prince. 'Highness, I am to accompany you from Alba back to England. Your territories here will be under English control, but the dowry is to return to the King's treasury. That is what the King commanded me.'

'And that was what the King wanted you to know. Now we believe you must be told the truth of Sir Thomas's mission. At the first opportunity, he will take the gold back to Aquitaine.

You will stay with us in Alba for as long as the King demands it. And that way, people will believe that our dowry remains in our possession.'

Despenser was quick off the mark. 'Sir Thomas is renowned for riding with only a hundred men. Half of which are archers. That leaves few fighting men-at-arms. If the Pope's forces find out that he is carrying the gold, they could overwhelm him. These forces might be antagonistic towards the King. Or if the Visconti know he is leaving the country, then they too could strike against him and claim that brigands were to blame for the attack. It is a risk too great to take.'

The Prince looked at Blackstone to answer Despenser's concerns.

'Let me worry about how my men fight should it come to it, my lord. I need to know what will be required when I take the two hundred thousand gold florins. They'll be heavy. Now, can you take me to the gold? So that we can assess it?'

Despenser winced. 'Would that not show a lack of trust in the Visconti?'

'I suspect Bernabò Visconti knows where I am. Were it not for the Prince's protection he would have me dead by now. I have no respect or trust for the Visconti. Either one of them. They are the Vipers of Milan and Prince Lionel does them great favour by marrying Galeazzo's daughter. War with France is coming. We need the gold.'

Despenser had no argument left. He nodded. 'I'll take you to it.'

CHAPTER THIRTY-FIVE

Blackstone sent Gifford to fetch Bezián and Terrel from the stables so that they could join the party visiting the vault. Lord Edward Despenser led them through the lower floors of the palace, twisting this way and that, their journey illuminated by wall sconces burning oil. They descended a staircase that spiralled deep below the Visconti palazzo, the humidity increasing the deeper they went underground. It brought them into a broad space, cobbled underfoot, and large enough to accommodate half a dozen guards who, until they heard the descending footsteps, had squatted on benches and stools in the dismal, airless room. They stood, waiting to see who it was that approached.

As Despenser spoke to the senior man commanding the guard detail, Blackstone studied the iron grate; locked and bolted, it spread across the entire length of one wall. The gold was held in little more than a prison cell. The near darkness behind the bars showed a sturdy, heavily timbered table with four iron chests lurking in the gloom. The flames from the room's torches barely reflected the curved steel bands that straddled the boxes.

The guard commander made no protest at Despenser's request. He unlocked the gate, swung it open and stood aside, instructing two of his men to go into the cell-like vault and put a torch on each wall bracket. The wax-soaked jute heads flared and spat, light from their flames arching across the ceiling. The guards then pulled back to stand by the far wall as the English Lord Despenser led the others into the room. Each chest was twenty inches long, twelve high and wide. They had a handle at each end, two iron rings on either side. The chests had a flat box lock that secured their lids.

Despenser unwrapped four keys from a velvet wallet, each as long as the breadth of a man's hand. The small disc at the top of the barrel bore the Visconti crest. Further down the barrel were three staggered bars, or teeth, on either side.

'Each chest has its own key,' said Despenser. 'And it must be placed correctly into the lock so that the wards align and turn cleanly.'

He showed each key to Blackstone. At the top of each key was a number stamped into the metal no bigger than a smith's mark. Blackstone looked closely at the Roman numerals, I, II, III, IV. Milanese blacksmiths were renowned for making intricate locks for the nobility.

'I see no marking on the chests to use the correct key,' said Blackstone.

'Lay the palm of your hand on the curved steel band and you will feel a punch mark.'

Blackstone did as Despenser suggested and then held out his hand for the keys. He slotted the appropriate key in each lock. Blackstone lifted the lid on the first chest. It was full to the brim with florins. Every coin gold, renowned for its purity and consistency. Blackstone picked up one of the inch-wide coins. Like all the others, it bore the image of St John the Baptist holding a sceptre and a scroll, and on the other side, the Florentine symbol of a lily. It made him think of Father Torellini, the priest who represented the Bardi family, Florentine bankers who backed the English King in his wars against France. He dropped the coin back onto the pile.

'Henry, Gifford, open them. Bezián, you and Terrel as well. A chest between you.'

The men-at-arms lifted lids, exposing the same amount of gold. The coins choking the chests glittered blood red in the torchlight. The men gazed down at the unimaginable wealth that lay before them. Terrel laid his palm across the top of the coins, a small act of reverence. He caught Bezián's stare of disapproval. Should anyone other than Blackstone touch the gold Lord Despenser would regard them as thieves. Terrel ignored Bezián's accusatory stare, the gold's wealth seeping its warmth into him.

Blackstone stared at the problem that lay before him. It was an easy calculation to make. Two hundred thousand split between four chests. Each chest containing fifty thousand and likely to be too heavy for any man to lift alone. Even two men would struggle. Blackstone closed the lid on his chest and gripped the handle with both hands. Despite his strength, the chest was a dead weight. Perhaps, he thought, someone like Meulon and he might be able to lift it, but they would not be able to carry it far. Each chest would weigh at least the same as a hogshead of wine, and that was three hundredweight, and that was a hundredweight more than Meulon or him. That's why there were rings on either side so that a metal shaft could be passed through and four men could take the strain. To return this gold to Bordeaux would be a slow and laborious journey. And he had already decided some time ago that getting across the Alps was too risky. What was certain was that, no matter what route Blackstone chose, once word got out about the wealth being carried, it would attract men of violence from far and wide.

'Sir Thomas?' Despenser broke into his thoughts. 'Have you seen enough?'

Blackstone nodded. 'Close the chests,' he told the others.

As Bezián slammed down his chest lid, Terrel winced, snatching away his hand just in time, the rim of the lid striking his hand.

'Move your arse, Terrel,' said Bezián.

Terrel nursed his fist, letting the belligerent Gascon shove past him to join the others shuffling out of the vault. None of them saw him slip the snatched coin into his tunic. At the first opportunity he would use it to buy his way out of Blackstone's service. The Master of War had too many enemies. It was only a matter of time before he and his men would face overwhelming odds and die where they stood. Honour and glory were as far removed from what Terrel desired as were the stars in the sky. Gold bought freedom. And he would seize it.

Blackstone accompanied Despenser to the Prince's apartments. The tall man now looked frail in Blackstone's eyes. His narrow face seemed hollowed by fatigue – or was it a sense of grief? he wondered. His hair had been recently brushed, resting on his shoulders. His neatly combed beard flowed down from his chin, a cascade of fine hair that looked as if it belonged more to an older man than a youthful twenty-nine-year-old prince of the realm. What was the sadness that haunted his eyes? Widowed with a thirteen-year-old daughter, he was marrying a child only a year older than her. There was no doubt in Blackstone's mind the man's sensitivity was being tested. He was dressed in an ermine-fringed night robe, ready for bed and a night's fitful sleep before the grand ceremony the next morning. The hours of darkness would soon disappear and reveal the glaring light of day and the focus of thousands of people to fall on him.

'Highness, my apologies for disturbing you again,' said Blackstone.

'You and Lord Despenser have assessed the gold?' Prince Lionel asked him.

'We have,' said Despenser. 'Sir Thomas and his men examined each chest.' He cast a disparaging glance at Blackstone. 'And he now holds the keys. Highness, it will be a challenge to move such weight over a great distance. Your journey home will take far longer than we anticipated.'

Blackstone remained silent. Better to let the Prince's second in command have his say. His status had already been dented by Blackstone's presence in Milan.

'We leave for Alba after the ceremony and feast,' said the Prince. 'We will make ourselves known to the citizens of the city we are gifted as part of our dowry. Then we will begin the journey home after a few weeks so that our bride might be presented to our father and his court. The first part of the journey will pose little difficulty. A hundred miles to Alba? Less? Three days' journey? Were the gold not so important to our brother's efforts in France, it could remain with us and be guaranteed safety on the way back by you and the hundreds who accompany us.'

The Prince turned his attention to Blackstone. A note of weariness entered his voice. 'We sacrifice our dowry for the good of our beloved brother and his fight against the French. Sir Thomas knows full well that it cannot wait until we return. There is an urgency – not so, Sir Thomas?'

'It's why the King sent me to your side, highness. I must find a way to get the gold into Prince Edward's hands. But Lord Despenser's men and mine will escort the gold from here to Alba. That takes it out of the hands of Visconti and any risk that they could arrange an attack by brigands and seize it back. They would not risk attacking it with you and your bride on your way to Alba.'

Despenser restrained his irritation at being usurped by Blackstone. 'Highness, the King's Master of War is always willing to take risks, but if he and he alone is to take the gold back to France once we reach Alba then, as I have said, it risks the gold being seized by enemy forces. Cannot an arrangement be made with your brother for us and the gold to return together? Better we protect it. It will be impossible for Sir Thomas and his few men to get it back to Bordeaux in good time. He knows it can't be done.' With that he turned his attention to Blackstone, challenging him to give the Prince an answer.

'Well, Sir Thomas? Can you give our brother what he needs for his war chest? Is there a way?'

'Yes, highness.'

'Then share it,' said Despenser.

'No, my lord, it's better only I know how we are to give Prince Edward the means to fight on.'

'You dare suggest I would betray such information?'

'No, only that you would challenge my decision, and I am not here to be challenged. I am here on the King's orders. How I get the money he needs to fight the war is my responsibility and mine alone.'

Blackstone's answer bordered on insult, and it stunned the Knight of the Garter into silence. Despenser's ill temper threatened to boil over. The Prince's gentle tones and forgiving smile calmed his second in command.

'Dear friend, our father and our brother have stood where you stand now. Why do you think the King honoured Sir Thomas with his heraldic blazon *Défiant à la Mort*? He is a man who defies those who do not see the way ahead as he does. It is best to allow him to go his own way.'

The Prince turned his attention to Blackstone.

'Sir Thomas, your manner might be tempered when addressing a knight of Lord Despenser's standing and reputation.'

Blackstone dipped his head, acknowledging the gentle rebuke. 'Highness. I know reputations are hard won.' His flattery stroked Despenser's pride – but only for a moment. 'But reputations alone do not win battles, give the King what he wants... or save a prince's life.'

The jibe was as sharp as his archer's knife. And it found Despenser's heart.

Without a moment's hesitation, the Prince raised his hand to stop the insults from gaining momentum.

'Good night, Sir Thomas.'

Despenser gritted his teeth.

'Goodnight, highness,' said Blackstone. He turned and locked eyes with Despenser. 'And to you, my lord.'

The weight of the door closing behind Blackstone was as sullen and final as a coffin lid slamming into place.

CHAPTER THIRTY-SIX

Darkness surrendered to glow-worm light in the narrow slits of stair windows. The apartments and greater salons were effused with warm reflections on their windows. For those who kept windows open for the night air, the flickering candles and oil lamps threw shadows across walls and ceilings. Murmurs quietened as lords and their guests went to bed later than usual, the excitement and anticipation keeping them up past their usual time to retire.

Below the encircling walls, the vast courtyard bustled with silent intensity. Here, servants were preparing for the feast that would follow the marriage ceremony. Tables had been joined into long seating arrangements. The high table where the Prince and his bride would be seated accompanied by the Visconti and special guests like the venerated poet Petrarch stretched across the breadth of the yard. From where they sat, they would look at two long rows of tables, left and right of them down the courtyard. Trolleys were laden with embroidered tablecloths: vast swathes of fine linen; gold and silver platters; goblets; eating knives; bowls for hand washing. As soon as first light crept across the sky the tables would be wiped dry from the morning dew by the palazzo's servants and then laid under the keen eye of the household officers. The *camerlengo* was responsible for all the servants in the palace and it was his responsibility to ensure the celebratory feast was everything his master Galeazzo Visconti demanded. The palazzo hierarchy dictated every household officer's authority and responsibility. The *camerlengo* would oversee the fine detail of the seating and the tableware. The menu and wines would be the responsibility of the *maggiordomo*. Servants would be flogged if his exacting demands were not met. It was a seamless operation executed by an army of servants with their chain of command from the *maestro di casa* to the *scalco*, who controlled the kitchen staff, to ensure the event reflected the power and wealth of the Visconti. A feast that would showcase the Visconti status.

Nothing more than ghostly whispers from the fevered preparations in the courtyard reached up to where Henry Blackstone stood leaning over a balcony that ran the length of the third floor. He watched in silent admiration as a thousand candles faltered like fireflies in the breeze and then recovered their strength as men and their shadows moved efficiently about their task. Henry had slipped out of the modest quarters given to him and his father. Gifford was quartered with Bezián and Terrel in the stables. Henry relished the moment as he reflected on his journey since absconding from Oxford University the year before, the men who rode and fought with him, the reconciliation with his father... and now, to be in Milan at such a historic occasion: it put flesh on the bones of his young life's journey.

'*Mon petit chevalier.*' A voice behind him.

Henry swirled around. A woman stood half in shadow. Elegant, refined, she did not move, letting the half-light capture her mystery. Henry's heart pounded. He knew exactly who it was. Eight years before, he and his father had escorted the young French Princess Isabelle, no more than a child, to be married here. And his companionship had pleased her, and earned him the term of affection *mon petit chevalier*.

'My Lady Isabelle,' said Henry, bowing.

She stepped into the glow of the wall lantern. Her long flowing silk gown, its rich blue colour swallowing the light, was square cut above her breasts; the wide sleeves flared from the elbow. He saw God's miracle in the girl changing into such a beautiful young woman. She wore a delicate gold necklace; pearls interwoven in her braided hair; a brooch, sapphires and rubies; rings that flared with the light. He gazed at her delicate features. He remembered her eyes. And her gentle voice. He couldn't help but smile, a grin that felt like the village idiot who'd been given meat instead of pottage for his supper. She reached out her hand. He took it as tenderly as if he was holding a wounded songbird. He stared at this young woman he hadn't seen in all the years that had passed. He too was no longer the twelve-year-old son of the English Master of War who had taken the arduous journey with her.

She smiled. 'My heart is still French, Master Henry, but here I am known as Isabella.'

'How did you know I was in Milan?' he asked. There had been no contact with the Visconti.

'The procession,' she said, standing with him at the parapet and casting a glance down the preparations; then she turned to face him. He towered over her; she reached up and plucked a strand of hair from his shoulder. 'I heard your name called. I sought you out. How could I not after the journey we endured together?' She blew the hair away into the night. 'You took a blow to your head in a skirmish outside of Chambéry. Do you remember?'

'Of course. The scar remains.'

'And you were so brave about it,' she said, reaching up, easing his head down so she could run her fingers into his hair and feel the scar. Satisfied, she withdrew her hand. 'And it has not made you dim-witted?' An enquiring look that teased.

'There are those who claim it has.'

'Oh, they're jealous.'

'There's not much to be jealous of.'

She shrugged, as uninhibited as a sister might be, not a high-ranking noblewoman. For a moment Henry thought of the sister he had lost.

'When my brother Charles brought you into the room in Paris and I saw you for the first time I thought you might have been nothing more than the son of an Englishman who was our enemy. But my brother said you read books and that cheered me.'

'He was generous. He gave me a book on chivalry.'

'You still have it?'

'I do.'

'And since my brother became King of France you will once again wage war against him.'

'We waged war against him and your father long before that. We will always fight France for our King. I doubt the war will ever end. We're at peace now but your brother looks for it to continue.'

'And does such animosity come between us?'

'It could never do that.' The conversation had taken a direction he had not anticipated. Doubt caused him to hesitate.

'I'm pleased, Master Henry. We shared too much for it to do so. But your father is here.'

He felt she was probing for information. He remained silent.

'Of course he is,' she said, answering her own question. 'We all know. Bernabò Visconti had men searching for him, but his brother has reined in his desire to capture your father. This wedding is too important to disrupt with violence. And besides, it would be a terrible diplomatic incident if Bernabò did anything foolish.'

'My lady, is this a warning?'

'No. It is letting you know that my husband's family are two sides of the same coin, but one is more aware and considerate of the situation than the other.' She sighed. 'You will always be the companion and trusted friend from our time together.

I am pleased I heard your name called. I remember it being your mother's name. You travelled with the Prince from Paris, which means you did not wish your father's name to be associated with you.'

'My lady, you're asking why I'm here. I'm with the Prince.'

'I'm pleased you're here, but it made me wonder why you did not use your father's name.'

'Because I did not wish those who travelled with the Prince to know my true identity until it was the right time. I was there to be close to the Prince.' He was about to reveal the attack on the Prince's life but thought better of it. 'As I was to you when we travelled, I am a companion to the Prince. We share a love of poetry. Of Petrarch.'

'Ah, and he will be at the high table tomorrow,' she said. She leaned over the parapet and pointed. 'There.'

Henry felt as though a small hurdle of uncertainty between them had been overcome. His suspicious mind had urged caution with Galeazzo's daughter-in-law, but it was quickly supplanted with a new hope. 'Can I meet him, do you think?'

She looked surprised. 'Petrarch? No, don't be silly, Henry. He is an honoured guest.' She saw his disappointment. 'I am sorry.'

'May I not aspire to meet the great and the good?'

'You can have the aspiration, but the reality is a different matter.'

'I met your brother, the King.'

Her voice had that same teasing lilt. 'But it was he who summoned you. You do not ask to see a king or this country's greatest poet. These men are above us all.'

'I shared quarters with an English prince.'

'Henry, my affection for you was born many years ago but even I cannot get you close to the high table. And I will wager even your Prince would not. I can do many things since I married into the Visconti but that's not one of them.'

It was his turn to shrug nonchalantly. 'It was worth a try.'

'Of course. You know it is unlikely we will be able to see

each other again before the Prince leaves Milan with his bride. My husband and his family would disapprove if they learnt I had even approached you. Or that Sir Thomas Blackstone's son was also in Milan under a different name. They would think the worst. That there is a plot of some kind.'

'I'm sorry my presence may cause you problems.'

She touched his arm. 'You forget, it was I who sought you out.' She turned to leave and go back into the shadows. 'If there is anything in my power that I can do to return what you and your father did for me, you only have to ask.'

Henry's smile of regret said enough. He shook his head. 'I am content to know you are happy.'

She studied him a moment longer. 'Very well then.' She extended her hand.

He bent and kissed it. He held on to her slender fingers a moment longer than he intended. He cursed his slow-witted mind. He straightened. 'There *is* something you can do for me.'

Again, she looked surprised. Again, the enticing smile. 'Now I am intrigued.'

Henry unbuttoned the top of his gambeson and fumbled inside. He tugged out the picture he had torn from the illuminated manuscript in the Paris bookshop. He unfolded it and showed it to her, making sure the light caught the exquisite work.

'Her name is Elena. She is an illuminatrix. I don't know where she is. I thought perhaps a monastery. She was taught by Don Silvestro dei Gherarducci.'

Isabella studied the page, tilting it so the light could create its own magic. 'I have heard the name Gherarducci.'

'You have? I believe the woman might be in a Camaldolese monastery.'

Isabella folded the page and handed it back.

'A woman's hand did this? You're certain?'

'So I'm told, yes.'

Isabella shook her head. 'The Camaldolese follow the Rule of St Benedict. Perhaps she is in such a monastery near here.

I will try and find out what I can.' She noticed Henry's concerned expression. 'What is it beyond the beauty of this work that calls you to her?'

Once again, he was reluctant to tell her of the assassination attempt on Prince Lionel. But Salvarini's final words to him still infused him with a quiet desperation. 'I believe she is in danger, and I was asked by another to guard her.'

Isabella touched his face. 'Once again you are *mon petit chevalier*,' she whispered. 'I will search her out for you.'

And then, as silently as she had arrived, the shadows took her.

When Henry returned to the room he shared with his father, Blackstone's bedroll was empty. The common latrine down the corridor was unoccupied, so wherever Blackstone was, he was not close to their sleeping quarters. Henry resisted the urge to go out into the night to find him, convincing himself that if his father had wanted his company, he would have invited him. Besides, his thoughts had been snared by the hope that Isabella might find information on the illuminatrix Elena. The young woman whose deft hand created such beauty might be closer than he thought. If anyone had the means to seek her out, it could well be the child he had accompanied to Milan and was now a woman of importance. He curled into his blanket and, with an imaginary image in his mind's eye of the beautiful girl he would find, fell into an untroubled sleep.

CHAPTER THIRTY-SEVEN

Earlier in the night, a common servant had bumped into Blackstone in a narrow, poorly lit corridor. The woman grovelled, bent double, fearful of being punished for her clumsiness, her hands grasping Blackstone's in supplication as she begged forgiveness. Clear thinking told him Bernabò would not make any attempt on his life while he was under Prince Lionel's protection, but instinct overrode logic when it came to survival. An unexpected thrust from a concealed knife by one of Bernabò's killers could end his life and the political upset in the aftermath of his death would be for others to unravel. He had blocked the woman's hands as she grasped at him. The slip of paper fell from her fingers. She raised her head, stared at him wide-eyed. He released her, and she scuttled away. He unfurled the folded note. Holding it close to the wall lantern, he read its summons.

Blackstone edged his way through the palazzo's labyrinthine corridors. Disembodied voices carried along cross passages as the palazzo's servants went about their duties. The smoke from burning torches and oil lamps snaked along hallways and into the dark recesses where Blackstone moved just as silently. The citadel had doorways into outer yards that gave him access to the gates that led into the city. It was easy enough to time the route of the palazzo's guards and slip out through a postern gate without being challenged. The well-lit, quiet thoroughfares would guide him north-west to Porta Giovia and Bernabò Visconti's castello.

Somewhere in the cloistered city, he heard the distant chant of monks, their solemn rhythmic voices enticing lost souls. He kept close to the walls of the buildings. Dogs barked. Once, a voice cried out, enquiring who was there. Blackstone was long past the house by the time the dog stopped barking. Streetlamps lit every road in Milan. The only darkness lay between buildings. When night watchmen's shadows loomed from another street, he pressed back into darkness and then continued on to the meeting place designated by the unknown author of the note. The soaring city walls blocked out the sky, denoting the strength and authority of the Visconti family, a visible symbol of Bernabò Visconti's controlling power. Blackstone increased his stride. It would take thirty minutes to reach the meeting place. Monastic bells near and far denoted the night's hour. For all he knew, it was a trap. A ploy to draw him out. The bait was simple. Your men are in danger. And where to meet. The writing was clean and strong. A man's hand. Unsigned. Anonymous for safety.

He reached the corner and stopped to check his sense of direction. He needed to go west, away from Bernabò's citadel. The meeting place was ten minutes further on at the Porta Vercellina. Blackstone turned into another street. A sudden screech as two alley cats fought. No different, he thought, than him and Bernabò Visconti.

Monks' chanting grew closer, their voices rising somewhere ahead, thin as reeds in the wind now as they finished their hour of worship in their chapel. He turned a corner. A monastery's walls rose before him, their forbidding shadows adding to the mystery of what was to some a place of fear and confinement. Blackstone stepped into the darkness and waited. Rather than confront whoever had summoned him to meet on the far corner of the monastery, he held back, letting the clouded night sky cast its own black mantilla on the street. Nothing moved. His eyes sought the pillars that could conceal a man. The shadows did not move. A stray cat, tail upright, a battle flag of confidence, strutted out of the monastery's iron gates behind which lay the gardens, no doubt a favoured hunting ground. The cat faltered. Then stopped. Were its senses warning it of danger? Blackstone watched the cat. Its back arched and it crabbed sideways. Away from the building on the opposite side of the street. And the shadow that moved in a doorway.

Blackstone used the buildings as cover. Knife in hand, he pressed into a narrow passage. Ten yards further on, he saw that whoever was waiting had not moved again. If he continued, his approach, no matter how rapid, would alert those who waited and give them the advantage. There was a simpler way to flush out whoever was concealing themselves.

'Here,' he said quietly.

He heard the intake of breath. Blackstone took two rapid strides into the next doorway a moment before the man ventured a step away from his concealment. Shadow hid his features but he was ready to fight. Knife held low. He crouched as he walked, step by slow step towards where he thought Blackstone's voice had been.

'Come out,' the man said. 'Show yourself.'

Blackstone watched from the darkness. The man drew level and was then past him. Blackstone took only a couple of silent paces, grabbed the man's collar and kicked his legs from beneath him, forcing him to his knees and his knife an inch from the man's face.

Without hesitation, the man dropped his knife, raised his hands and whispered. 'Sir Thomas. It's Marchesi.'

Blackstone pushed him forward so that he stumbled onto hands and knees, and moved away so the Italian couldn't roll and attempt an attack, watching as he did so for anyone else who might be part of an ambush.

'I'm alone,' Marchesi hissed, loud enough for only Blackstone to hear. He recovered his knife, sheathed it and, without wasting a moment longer, hid in the darkness. The only dull light reflecting on their faces came from the main street lantern.

'Am I to believe you have information about my men's safety? A Visconti captain betraying his own lord and master?' said Blackstone, so close he could smell the wine on Marchesi's sour breath.

'I would not tell you anything that would cause harm to my people. You saved my life. I am honour bound to repay you. Lord Bernabò knows you are in the city.'

'I saw you searching for me.'

'I did my duty, but I did it slowly. I saw you in the crowd.'

'Then you have already repaid the debt.'

'Sir Thomas, I did not know who you were when we rode into the city and that you were my lord's sworn enemy.'

'A vendetta exists between us.'

'I know nothing of it.'

'Is he threatening my son and the men with me in the city? Is he laying a trap for us at the wedding ceremony?'

'Not here, Sir Thomas. Beyond the walls. Your men who rode to our rescue. They are to be ambushed and slain.'

Blackstone's mind calculated the odds of such an ambush taking place. Killbere would have chosen defensive ground and close to the city for when he and the Prince went south to Alba. They would be waiting.

'Then you have information that comes directly from Lord Bernabò,' he said.

Marchesi's fear was obvious. Furtive looks up and down the street. 'If I am seen, I'll be questioned. And that would lead to my death. I heard everything from when he spoke to one of his commanders. He knows your men have set up camp less than an hour south-west of the city walls.'

'And you told him,' said Blackstone.

Marchesi shook his head. 'I had no cause. They are no threat to any of our men.'

'Then who?'

'A farmer saw and betrayed them.'

It was always a risk to be in enemy territory, Blackstone knew that. It would not be the first time locals had betrayed fighting men. 'Then you stand a traitor to Bernabò. Visconti men will die because of what you have told me.'

Marchesi shook his head. 'No. Lord Bernabò would not risk using Visconti men. Not now, not with his brother's alliance with the English King. Later, perhaps, yes, he will search for you and wage war against you. He wants you dead, but that day will have to wait. He's using condottieri. Three hundred of them, well paid, who will strike by the time the ceremony takes place.'

The information placed Blackstone in an impossible dilemma. His first duty was to secure the gold, accompany it to Alba with the Prince and Despenser's men as escort. But he should be with Killbere and his men, who would remain ignorant of the planned attack against them. Even though they had chosen their ground well, the odds were three to one; many of them would be killed or maimed. And the greater risk was that survivors would be brought inside the city to be tortured and executed. Once the Prince left the city, Blackstone knew Galeazzo would not be able to rein in his brother. The moment the viper Bernabò's grip embraced any of Blackstone's men, he would expect Blackstone would once again return to the city to save them.

'You'll go to them?' said Marchesi. 'Slip away tonight. Warn them.'

Blackstone fell silent. He shook his head. 'I cannot. My duty is with the Prince and to serve the King.'

'Sir Thomas, three hundred against so few...' He let the sentence die on his lips.

'They've fought such odds before,' said Blackstone, resigned to his men's fate.

Marchesi could do no more. 'I have done what I could, Sir Thomas. I must get back.'

'Marchesi, you have repaid your debt with honour.'

He saw the dark shape of the man's head nod, and then Bernabò's captain slipped away.

The next day Blackstone looked on as Prince Lionel of Antwerp, Duke of Clarence, was married to Violante Visconti on the porch of the church of Santa Maria Maggiore in the presence of nobles and others of great importance. The Prince towered over the diminutive Violante and to Blackstone's eyes, who stood far behind the heaving crowds, it looked as though a giant had brought a child to a celebration. Which, in truth, was the reality.

Bernabò and his wife followed his brother's entourage who turned their horses for Galeazzo's palace and the feast that awaited them. Their horses' bridles and saddles were decorated with jewellery as were the rich silk garments worn by the Visconti and their extended family. Blackstone watched the man he wished to kill more than any other. He saw no sign of anyone who might be one of Bernabò's thirty-six children or of the dozen and more surviving illegitimate children. Blood vengeance still ran through Blackstone's veins. He had slaughtered two of those illegitimate sons, who had been responsible for his wife and daughter's death. The vendetta would never die until either Bernabò or Blackstone lay dead in a pool of their own blood. Vendettas could take a lifetime. Blackstone was not impatient. For now his duties lay elsewhere.

The procession moved towards the palazzo's courtyard and the prepared feast, an extravagance that would go on late into the night. It suited Blackstone. Henry would keep watch on Bernabò's movements while he, Gifford and Terrel lightened the Visconti's burden of gold and took it under their own protection. He would not wait for the Visconti troops to arrive the next morning to escort it to Alba. He would be one step ahead.

Blackstone turned for the vault and the gold. Church bells pealed in celebration, a death knell for those who would be slaughtered beyond the walls.

CHAPTER THIRTY-EIGHT

To any observer, Killbere's camp looked settled. Those watching saw smudge fires and men moving among the trees. The *condottieri* had been well paid by the Lord of Milan. Their orders were to kill Blackstone's men, strip them of whatever wealth they carried as booty for their efforts but to keep a handful of them as prisoners and deliver them into the city. The mercenary raiders were a mixed group of Germans, Hungarians and Englishmen. Disaffected men free from the restraints of fighting for the Holy Roman Emperor or a distant English King. They numbered 312 hard-riding hobelars who sold their swords to the highest bidder. They had served the Veronese lord, Cansignorio della Scala, against the Visconti; now they sided with his enemy and fought for Bernabò. They waited as their scouts reported back. Everything they'd observed told them Blackstone's men camping in the trees were bored, and had set few pickets. What horses could be seen were tethered to one side in the forest. The rising ground was the only consideration: a long incline from the flat ground up to the trees. They would launch the attack straight across the open plain for five hundred yards from their concealed position on the reverse side of a hill. It would no doubt rouse the men in the trees but they would have little time to defend themselves once the charging horses crested the incline and tore through them. They had received a warning about the presence of archers, but they disregarded them as a threat due to the trees hindering their movement.

The vicious ruffian who led these men was a rogue Englishman who had fought in Italy for several years. A common thief and murderer, he had proved himself an efficient, callous killer. His blackened broken teeth hid behind a matted beard. Squat-built, muscled in chest and arms, with bulbous nose and patchy bald head, he was one of the Almighty's ugliest creatures sent to roam the earth. Such features added to his reputation. His real name was Richard Bell but in order to increase his status he had taken the name *Il flagello del Diavolo*. That grandiose title, 'The scourge of the Devil', proved an attraction to those who paid good money for the most dangerous of men to undertake their bidding.

He looked along the line of horsemen. Bernabò Visconti was a man to please. This attack would bring more glory and wealth. And Thomas Blackstone was not with his men. That fact alone gave Richard Bell more than enough confidence. He relished the thought of taking a handful of Blackstone's men to the Visconti. His status would grow even more.

The self-proclaimed Devil's Scourge snarled a command at his men. The extended line of horsemen, swords drawn, shields on their arm, spurred their horses to the gallop.

Meulon walked among the men. He had sent Brun to the far end of the camp, as Killbere had instructed him. The line of men who lay flat ready to rise up would be the first line of defence. Shields, spears and halberds. Behind him Killbere, William Ashford and John Jacob stood ready in the trees. Walter Mallin had kept half a dozen horses hobbled and tethered in plain sight. The rest of the horses were far back on the fringe of the rear treeline.

Will Longdon and Jack Halfpenny's archers were close by, ready with arrows nocked, their line extended. When Killbere gave the command, they would shoot in a high arching curve over the trees for their arrows to fall 250 yards away, right on the edge of the incline. Once again, a whisker away from Meulon's shield wall.

'And here they come,' said Killbere to Bezián, who stood ready at his side.

Getting into Milan on the eve of the royal wedding would have been difficult, but not to leave. Blackstone had sent Bezián out when it was still dark to warn Killbere. By first light, the veteran knight had prepared Blackstone's men to lure in the mercenaries. Their slow demeanour, the campfire's smoke creeping into the trees' canopy, indicated men showing little interest in their own defence. Lazy men who thought themselves safe hiding in the trees.

The shuddering tremor of over three hundred galloping horses tightened men's grip on sword and mace. The *condottieri*'s over-confidence had blinded them to the shape of the incline. That was the very reason Killbere had chosen it as a defensive position. At either end of the rising ground, the curved hill forced any en masse approach into a funnel. Horsemen would lose their extended line of attack and instead bunch up, sixty or seventy riders at a time, as they forced their mounts into the space.

It was the perfect killing ground.

'Wait!' Killbere called out to Longdon and Halfpenny, who were blind to the attack and depended on the veteran knight's judgement when to shoot. 'Wait!' he called again.

The horsemen's extended line changed shape. The riders saw their mounts would falter on either flank of the incline. They had no choice but to check their horses' speed as the leading edge of the attack reached the base of the incline. Horses barged each other as they jostled for position. They went from galloping to cantering and eventually had to trot. Those at the back cursed and fought the reins, eager to push through and reach the men they came to kill. Every second lost in the charge gave Blackstone's men a chance to ready themselves. Unbeknownst to the mercenary force, Blackstone's men were already well prepared.

Lathered in sweat, the first eighty horses crested the rise. As the horses scuffled for their footing Meulon's men ran the twenty paces forward and thrust their spears into the animals' chests. Some screaming beasts surged forward, driven mad with pain; others fell back into the crush behind them.

'Now!' Killbere bellowed.

The sudden rush of wind above their heads became a sinister whisper of fluttering yard-long arrow shafts that fell where planned: behind the first row of horses. The arrows found flesh and bone, striking the riders and their mounts with bone-crushing velocity. As those horses floundered it stopped the frontal attack's momentum. Hooves thrashed; mounts fell and rolled, crushing men. Those at the rear tried to force their way through the bloodletting. Agonized shrieks mingled with the whinnying of horses and unwounded men bellowing to keep the attack going.

Enough of the horsemen broke through.

Meulon retreated to join Killbere's men, who raised their shields. Their line of defence stretched as far as their numbers allowed through the trees. Every trunk and sapling between them was as good as adding another man to their ranks.

Bezián took two strides forward as a wounded horse faltered, its rider struggling to keep his seat. He hacked at the horse's throat, whipped away the blood-soaked sword and caught the falling rider with a downward blow that half severed his head from his neck. Bezián sidestepped, rammed his sword point into the muscled thigh of another rider, twisted the blade, felt it strike bone, withdrew the hardened steel and rammed it again into the screaming man's groin.

Killbere and John Jacob worked as a deadly partnership. Jacob forcing his shield high, a horseman striking down with little effect as Killbere thrust his sword point into the man's armpit. Blood slathered men and horse. Rivulets of blood sluiced John Jacob's shield. As riders fell, men either side of Killbere rushed in to kill.

Meulon gathered his men, Brun on his left flank down the line, he on the right. Big men forcing the attackers apart. Spear and sword jabbing and cutting. Shields high, step forward; shields lowered, thrust and kill.

Time and again, the whisper of goose-fletched arrows passed overhead and fell into those slithering on the incline. The attack was already faltering. Horsemen had careered through Killbere's ranks on pain-maddened mounts only to be met with Killbere's rearguard: William Ashford and Aicart with Renfred and his men; only twenty men holding the cut-off point for horsemen who might be fortunate enough to fight their way through. Longdon and Halfpenny's archers were further back still.

Killbere bellowed to regroup. There could be no gaps in the line of defence. They had stopped the first wave of attack. The blood-soaked ground between where they stood and where determined mercenaries still urged their horses forward was littered with dead and writhing horses and mutilated men. Half a dozen of Blackstone's men lay dead, crushed under hooves or bludgeoned and hacked by sturdy men who used their horse's strength to turn this way and that, catching footsoldiers off balance and scything them down with sword and axe.

Killbere raised his sword. The captains saw the signal.

A howl of defiance swept through the trees.

Killbere and the men stepped forward a yard at a time, killing everything in their path. They dispatched the wounded. Stepping around the carnage, they reached the crest of the incline. Below them at least a hundred lay dead. In the distance, eighty and more riders were galloping away. Along with the bodies in the trees Killbere and the men had killed close to half of the mercenary force sent against them.

The Devil's Scourge had joined his namesake. Eyes staring skyward.

Raptors gathered.

Scavengers landed.

A feast of the dead.

PART FIVE

ILLUMINATRIX

CHAPTER THIRTY-NINE

The smell of burning flesh wafted across the vast courtyard. Fat dripped and sizzled into the hot coals. Boar, calf, suckling pigs, goat, fowl – all were roasted on a spit for the celebratory feast. The air was infused with fragrances to disperse the odour.

At the high table, the Prince and the slender figure of his child bride were flanked by her father Galeazzo and his wife Bianca of Savoy on one side and her uncle Bernabò and his wife Beatrice Regina della Scala on the other. Petrarch, the renowned poet and scholar, sat further along next to Amadeus, Count of Savoy. Several Italian noblemen, landowners aligned with the Visconti, were also seated with them.

Henry had watched the tables below being prepared the previous night and they now had honoured guests sitting on long benches. The guests' clothing of fine silks and brocade fluffed and rustled like the peacocks they were. Men were seated at one table, women at the other. Gold and silver cutlery adorned the tables; a hundred servants were in attendance as others ferried food from the spit and the kitchens.

The constant stream of food being brought to the table demanded stamina of the diners. During the feast, eighteen courses were presented, sixteen of those meat and fish, then cheese and fruit. Each course had fifty dishes, half of meat, half of fish. The feast began with suckling pigs, flames coming from their jaws, before the gorging continued with roasted calf, quail, partridge, duck, herons, beef, plump capons, roast kid, salted ox tongue, eel and lampreys. Paste made of powdered egg yolk, saffron and flour with real gold leaf gilded the meat accompanied by rich sauces.

The food flowed constantly from the kitchens and as each course was presented, gifts were brought before the Prince at the high table. Two greyhounds, with collars of velvet and silken leads, one each for the bride and groom. Twelve bloodhounds with gilded chains. Goshawks and sparrowhawks, their bells of silver-gilt and enamelled buttons on their covering bearing the Visconti blazon.

The night wore on. The food unending. It was an orgy of greed. More gifts came, of specially made suits of armour for the Prince and twelve great rolls of gold brocade, twelve of silk from the looms of Milan. By the tenth course Galeazzo had presented the Prince with a variety of horses, led into the courtyard a dozen at a time. Saddles of gilded leather, with lances and shields and six steel helmets, two of silver-gilt, one of pure gold. Six destriers, great war horses embellished with gilt bridles, velvet reins, silk tassels followed.

By the time the cheese and fruit were brought the Prince had received an ermine-lined coat covered with pearls, with a ruby brooch with diamonds. As the feast finally slowed, Galeazzo Visconti's head groom brought forward two magnificent breeding horses. One was called 'Lion', the other 'Abbot'. And the Visconti did not forget the noblemen who accompanied the Prince. Crested helmets of silver-gilt and another seventy-six horses were presented to them. It was a night that scribes of the day recorded for history.

What was not recorded was the attempted killing of Thomas Blackstone.

*

'There's enough food left over to feed an army,' said Terrel as he made his way to the vault with Gifford. 'I stood there watching like Sir Thomas said for me to do. I can tell you my stomach growled so damned loud I was worried they would hear me down in the courtyard. It was torture is what it was.'

They made a turn down the narrow staircase towards the lower depths and the vault. It was barely wide enough for a broad-shouldered man to descend without having to twist his body to accommodate the twisting stone walls.

Gifford followed Terrel down the spiral staircase. 'But you did as Sir Thomas asked?' he said.

'Who are you to question me, Gifford? Go about your business coddling young Master Henry or find him a bloody wet nurse so he can suckle on the tit.'

Gifford grabbed Terrel's collar. The gravedigger turned thief turned routier twisted violently. The narrowness of the stairs restricted his movement. Gifford held him fast against the curved wall. Terrel's feet scrambled for purchase on the narrow steps.

'Listen to me, sewer rat. No one coddles Master Henry. If you didn't watch Bernabò Visconti as Sir Thomas asked, then we are blind as to what he might do. Did you watch him or were you standing on that balcony scratching your balls and thinking of your stomach?'

Terrel twisted himself free, stumbled down two steps, steadied himself and faced the stocky man-at-arms. His knife pointed at Gifford's stomach. 'Touch me again and I'll gut you like the damned fish served at the feast.'

Gifford backhanded him. 'You talk too much.'

He fell back, arms outstretched for purchase on the smooth stone wall, the knife clattering away. Dazed, he spat blood.

'You want to kill a man, Terrel, you save the words until after the deed is done.'

Terrel raised a hand in an act of submission. 'All right, all right, you bastard. Yes, I watched him.'

Gifford nudged him forward. 'Then get down to the vault and tell Sir Thomas what you saw.'

They spiralled downwards to where the Visconti guards stood away from the iron gates, which were now open. Blackstone and Henry were checking the caskets of gold florins when Terrel and Gifford emerged into the room.

'They look happy, Sir Thomas,' said Gifford, meaning the sullen-looking guards.

Blackstone raised his head from the third chest of coins, slammed closed the lid and instructed Henry to lock the chests. He stepped out of the caged vault to where Terrel and Gifford waited.

'They challenged us taking the gold, but I have a document with the Prince's seal releasing it to me,' said Blackstone.

'And I'll wager Lord Bernabò will not be well pleased when he hears of it,' said Gifford. 'You did as I asked?' said Blackstone.

'Aye, Sir Thomas. I bought two strong mules to haul the gold. Got them in the stables.'

'Terrel? You watched Lord Visconti?' said Blackstone.

'I did. He ate like he was starving. His appetite would kill a lesser man. He's built like a bull and he—'

Gifford interrupted him. 'Sir Thomas doesn't care how much food he ate. Make your report.'

Terrel suppressed his sullen anger. 'Near the end when the Prince was given two more horses, the man we rode with, March... Marcha...'

'Marchesi,' Blackstone said.

'Aye, him. He came to the table and said something to Lord Bernabò. It was not good news. Lord Bernabò looked as though he had pissed his hose.'

'Did he leave the feast?' said Henry.

'No, Master Henry, but he had both his arms on the table and his fists kept clenching as though he was strangling someone.'

'Then I'll wager he had word that Sir Gilbert and the men have killed the skinners he sent against us. He'll not contain his fury. Right, let's get to it before the night ends.'

'We're to move those chests of gold, Sir Thomas?' Terrel asked.

'No, they are,' said Blackstone. 'Henry, tell them what's needed.'

Henry approached the uncomfortable-looking guards. There were eight of them and they were clearly caught between the instruction of the English Prince who now rightfully owned the gold and Bernabò Visconti who, despite his brother's cautionary advice not to interfere in the matter of the dowry, commanded these men.

Terrel smirked. 'Their balls will be squeezed now.'

'And you'll lose yours if you don't get back up to the room above. There's a trapdoor. Go and open it,' said Blackstone.

Terrel's uncertain look was matched by that of Henry and Gifford.

Blackstone pointed past the Visconti guards into the depth of shadows of the extended room. 'You think they carried that weight down those steps?'

Terrel and the others stared into the gloom. It was obvious that only Blackstone had noticed the chain pulley further back, and that meant there was a trapdoor above.

Terrel grinned. 'Aye, Sir Thomas, I'll have it open,' he said, turning for the steps.

With the appearance of whipped men, the guards obeyed Henry's instructions. From an alcove in the wall, they took down iron rods and slipped them into the rings on either side of the chests. With a man on each corner, four men lifted their cargo to the pulley. By the time the second chest had been moved, the wooden trapdoor above had been hauled open by Terrel.

'Gifford, go to Terrel. Watch for any of Bernabò's men approaching. Henry, take four of these men and have them ready to move the chests. I'll bring the others when the vault is cleared.'

Henry and Gifford left Blackstone alone as the guards manhandled the final chests and hoisted them up. Blackstone gestured for the men to join the others in the hall above. When they reached the chests, Gifford closed the trapdoor.

'All right, Henry and Gifford will go with the first trip to the stables…' Blackstone fell silent. The hall where they stood extended into the darkness. Somewhere in the blackness echoed the sound of two hefty doors being opened. Approaching footfalls gathered pace. Several men strode towards them, looming out of the darkness bearing oil-soaked flaming torches. Shadows danced. They came closer. The man who led them was Bernabò Visconti. Sword in hand.

CHAPTER FORTY

Bernabò Visconti halted twenty feet in front of Blackstone. The guards who had hoisted the gold stepped to one side, drawing their swords. Henry, Gifford and Terrel armed themselves and half turned, protecting each other's backs.

Blackstone did not draw Wolf Sword.

'It must end,' said Visconti. 'This blood feud between us. It must be settled.'

'Does your brother know of your intentions?' said Blackstone casually. 'Do you have his permission to attack us?'

Blackstone locked eyes with him. Bernabò faltered at his calm defiance. Spittle formed at the corner of his mouth. He was fuming, barely able to contain his temper. It was exactly what Blackstone wanted. Bernabò strode forward, closing the gap between them. And still Blackstone did not draw his sword. For a moment, it looked as though Bernabò might raise his arm to strike.

'It ends tonight. Here!' Bernabò spat.

Blackstone knew Bernabò must have been told his attempt to destroy Killbere and the men had failed. A final twist of the knife into the tyrant. Blackstone was as calm as Bernabò was enraged. It taunted him even more. It would be only moments before the rage broke through whatever slender barrier held it back.

'Dismiss your men,' said Blackstone. 'Let this be between us. Have them light the hall behind you. I need space to kill you.'

Bernabò's huge shoulders trembled. Eyes bulging and teeth bared, he nearly choked on his own spittle. Without turning, he commanded the men with him: 'Light the lamps!'

There was a moment of uncertainty that forced Bernabò to half turn. His snarl was enough to spur the men to obey. While he stared at Blackstone, the men went back into the darkness and touched their flames to wall sconces swollen with oil. As the lamps flickered into life, the cavernous underground passage was bathed in half-light that reached for the ceiling, leaving a dull glow below their illumination.

Bernabò moved slowly backwards, keeping his eyes on Blackstone, who had not moved and had still not yet drawn his sword. The Visconti lord was now far enough away to be standing in what was to be the arena where the two bitter enemies would fight. The light settling across him was a hood obscuring his face, but the flames in the wall sconces caught his eyes.

He was forty yards away when his voice boomed and echoed, dismissing his men.

The chest bearers edged around Henry and Gifford and strode back to where Bernabò waited. They joined the men who had accompanied the Lord of Milan and slunk away further down the passage until the unseen doors were heard being closed again.

'Go,' said Blackstone without turning his head.

'Leave you here? Alone?' said Henry. 'We cannot trust them.'

Blackstone's voice remained calm. 'Go now, close the doors behind you. We'll attend to the gold after I have killed him.'

Henry's voice rose in frustration. 'I won't leave you! Don't you see this is a trap? He's wearing mail.'

'I said leave me, Henry. Do as I say. Take the others and go.'

Still Henry protested. 'And if his men return? You'll be killed. I won't leave you!'

Blackstone pivoted and slapped him. 'Obey me, boy!'

Henry fell from the blow. His lip split. His look of disbelief turned to anger.

'Get him out of here, Gifford.'

The man-at-arms grabbed Henry's arm to help him up, but he pulled it away petulantly. Henry strode away with Gifford at his heels and also Terrel, who was trying to hide his desire to escape the killing room as quickly as he could.

The door slammed closed.

'So that is your son. He should have stayed; then I could have finished with the Blackstone family.'

Blackstone drew Wolf Sword and his archer's knife and unbuckled his scabbard belt. Bernabò unencumbered himself from his own scabbard, his dagger, long, narrow, sharply honed and pointed, held low in one hand. Blackstone strode forward without hesitation. Bernabò stood rigid. An immovable rock waiting for Blackstone's attack. Within sword's length, Blackstone feinted, pivoted on his heel and lunged with his knife. It caught the top of Bernabò's hand, bare below the long mail sleeves. The wound was superficial but served the immediate purpose of forcing Bernabò to drop his dagger.

The feint exposed Blackstone to Bernabò's rapid reaction. They were too close for a sword to be used. Bernabò's fist holding his sword's handle punched Blackstone, who turned in time for the blow to miss his jaw and smash into his left shoulder. Bernabò's bull strength was enough to numb Blackstone's arm. His knife fell from unfeeling fingers. The pivoting momentum carried him into Bernabò and, despite the pain streaking down his left arm, he barged the solid man back onto his heels. As he staggered, Blackstone swung Wolf Sword in a fast arc, meaning to cut Bernabò's leg from under him. Such a blow would have downed him and a death blow would have followed a breath later.

Bernabò dropped his shoulder, pushed his blade down and Wolf Sword struck honed Milanese steel instead of flesh. The two men stepped back from each other, swords raised in the high guard. Blackstone strode forward, slashed down, turned his shoulder the moment Bernabò parried and, with a swift sidestep, struck fast. The sword's point caught Bernabò's arm, high near the elbow. Fast and powerful enough for the blade to penetrate his mail. It was another superficial wound, but one that would bleed. Blackstone's agility gave him an advantage over Bernabò, whose mail-clad bulk made him slower. A flurry of blows forced Bernabò to back-step, trying to keep his balance, block every strike and find an advantage. It came a moment later. The damp walls had dripped moisture onto the stone floor and, when the old injury to his leg gave way, Blackstone slipped on the wet stone. He fell sideways onto his left arm. Had it been his sword arm, the strike that followed would have cleaved him from shoulder to chest. Bernabò grunted with effort, bent almost double as he struck down. Where Blackstone had been a second before, there was now only the edge of his blade. Bernabò's sword slid along its length, hitting the stone floor. It sparked and clanged as Blackstone rolled clear. Bernabò shifted his weight and struck repeatedly; Blackstone had to block and absorb the power of the blows without being able to parry. If he was to counterattack he'd have to give Bernabò the chance to get past his guard, but in doing so ran the risk of falling under his blade. It was a chance he had to take.

Blackstone stepped back and to the side. A deliberately slow move that opened his body to a straight lunge. Bernabò didn't hesitate. Blackstone's sword was to one side. Bernabò sprang forward, the effort making his weight fall on the front of his foot. The point of his blade caught Blackstone's gambeson. Blackstone felt the scorpion sting as it pierced his side. A flesh wound. A sacrifice. Bernabò would close in now. His balance was already on the front foot. It carried him forward. Blackstone's knife had been lost at the start of the contest, but his bunched fist struck Bernabò so hard between the eyes it shattered his nose.

Bernabò gasped. Staggered back. Blood ran into his beard and mouth. His eyes flared. He spat blood. Rage took him. He was losing control. Blackstone returned to the high guard. Sweeping the blade towards Bernabò's head, he knew the experienced fighter would duck. It was exactly what Blackstone wanted. As Bernabò hunched, his sword arm dropped and Blackstone struck his target cleanly. The clay lamp shattered, spilling oil onto Bernabò's head and face. It was a distraction he could not have anticipated. His natural reaction made him half turn, his free hand wiping the oil from his face and eyes. Blackstone jabbed at his thigh. Enough to pierce muscle. The leg folded. As Bernabò dropped, he had the presence of mind to raise his sword to stop the killing blow he knew would come.

It never did.

Blackstone's fist gripping his hilt twisted, driving its pommel into the side of Bernabò's head. A fleeting sense of sweet justice for the wife and child he had lost because of Bernabò's scheming those years before added strength to his blow. Wolf Sword's pommel was embossed with two halves of a penny. One his wife had carried, the other Blackstone. When she was murdered, he had melded the two into the sword's round pommel.

Bernabò fell back. The sound of his body hitting the stone floor echoed with a dull, resounding thud. His sword flew from his grip. His feet squirmed in the spilled oil. His arms flailed. Dazed, he tried to lift his head. Wolf Sword hovered over his chest. Bernabò was helpless as he blinked in the dim light at the towering shadow that stood over him.

'Your vile corruption will rot below with the worms.'

Bernabò showed no fear. His hand raised. 'I yield.'

'I don't care,' said Blackstone, tightening his grip, ready to plunge it into the man's barrel chest.

The crash of doors opening behind him saved Bernabò's life.

Lord Edward Despenser's voice boomed down the long passage. 'Do not kill him, Blackstone! The Prince commands it!'

Blackstone didn't move. Did not lift the sword point off Bernabò's chest. Made no sign of turning away. Did not look at those who approached behind him: a dozen and more by the sound of their footfall. The light changed. Flaming torches held by these men cast a fiery glow across the body lying at his feet. He sensed Despenser close to him. There, not half a stride behind him. And yet he had not tried to reach out and restrain Blackstone's sword arm.

'Thomas,' said Despenser in a conciliatory tone, any antagonism between the two men abandoned. 'He must live. You have bested him. Let that humiliation be his punishment.'

Still Blackstone did not move. He stared down at the man waiting to die; his voice was calm. 'And he will never forget it. He will always seek revenge. Our vendetta is not ended.'

For a heart-stopping moment it looked as though Blackstone would ignore the Prince's command. He pressed the blade with the barest of effort into Bernabò's mail above his heart. The point separated the links.

'If your heart beat any harder it would reach out to the tip of my blade and I would remain innocent of killing you.'

And then he stepped back, withdrawing Wolf Sword.

Bernabò didn't panic. Easing himself away, he got to his feet and retrieved his sword. Blackstone waited. Would this be a counter-attack? Despenser stepped forward and levelled an arm between the two men.

'This night is done, Lord Bernabò. What remains between you will be settled another time.'

The battered and bloody Visconti gave a final killer's glance at Blackstone, then turned on his heel, limping back the way he came.

Blackstone looked at the men who had arrived in time to save Bernabò's life. Despenser, a dozen of his men, Henry, Gifford and Terrel. The blood on Henry's face from his father's earlier blow dried now. Blackstone showed no sign of welcome to any of them. He glared at his son. It was likely he had run to Despenser.

'Have your men lift the gold and secure it,' he said.

The men stepped aside as he cleaved his way through them.

CHAPTER FORTY-ONE

Voices echoed through the corridors of Galeazzo Visconti's palazzo. Angry voices, muted by thick walls, rising in threats, punctuated by slamming doors. Hurried footsteps along stone floors. Beyond the palazzo, as first light edged into Milan's streets, hooves clattered as hundreds of horsemen left the city. For a brief time, the city fell silent. Citizens who had heard the exodus delayed leaving their homes until satisfied the sounds did not foretell of violence on the streets.

The Prince's physician treated Blackstone's wound, objecting when he insisted on the wound being cleaned and packed with herbs. The bleeding was staunched while a frantic search was undertaken for an apothecary who might have yarrow or plantain. Finally the physician's servants brought what Blackstone had demanded and the wound was bound. Blackstone insisted the bandage be tight so that there was no weakness when he stood and stretched. One contest had been fought; others would follow.

And then the Prince summoned him to his quarters. The long night's gluttony and few hours' sleep before being awakened by news of the attack on Blackstone had etched haggard lines into his face. He hadn't yet had his hair attended to by his valet and his loose robe exposed a long silk chemise. His night attire suggested that whatever had gone on in the privacy of his quarters had taken the Prince from his bed. There were no servants in the room. Despenser stood by the door. Blackstone faced the Prince, who sat on a cushioned chair sipping wine. He grimaced and belched.

'The food was rich. It takes time for it to settle.' He drank more wine. 'Sir Thomas, your wound is bearable? It has been attended to?'

'It's a minor wound, highness, and attended to with great care. My thanks for sending your physician.'

The Prince nodded. 'We learnt of the assault against you and summoned Lord Galeazzo to explain. In order to maintain harmony and mutual respect between our two noble houses, we expressed grave concern about Bernabò's egregious behaviour and asked Lord Galeazzo to demonstrate his loyalty and commitment to our relationship by addressing this issue with the utmost urgency. It was not only a personal affront but a stain upon the honour and hospitality of his great house.'

The Prince's gaze settled on his father's Master of War.

'I should have killed him,' said Blackstone.

The Prince's calm broke. 'No, you should not!'

'Highness, he came intending to kill me.'

'Your vendetta is known to us. That is a personal matter. This assault was a greater issue, an insult to us and our father.'

'It was more than our personal hatred, my lord. I believe he had learnt that the *condottieri* he had commissioned to attack Sir Gilbert Killbere and my men who are camped beyond the city walls had failed. That enraged him.'

The Prince looked to where Despenser stood. 'My Lord Edward? Did you know of this?'

'I did not, highness.'

'And how did you learn of it, Sir Thomas?'

'Someone close to Lord Bernabò warned me. I sent one of my men to alert Sir Gilbert.'

'The act of sending them against your men was an act of violence against England. You should have come to us with this information.'

'Highness, you had more important matters to attend to. Your marriage is of great value to the Crown. And Bernabò would have denied any involvement, which is why he used skinners. I thought it best to attend to the matter in my own way.'

'A way that teeters like a man on a high ledge, Sir Thomas. One wrong move and disaster can strike.'

'Highness, there are men who need to be killed so that others might pass by safely.'

'Like those on the pass, Sir Thomas, so that we might pass safely?'

Blackstone remained silent.

The Prince sighed. 'Well, Lord Bernabò has left the city. He's gone to fight against Cansignorio della Scala and the Pope's allies. It is not an argument involving his brother Galeazzo. We will not be caught in the middle of a war that is not of our father's making.'

'Highness?' said Despenser.

The Prince beckoned him to speak.

'What now? How are we to proceed? We leave for Alba. If Sir Thomas is to protect the gold, I think we should know how that is to be achieved.'

'Yes,' said the Prince. 'It's time we know of your plans to get the gold back to our brother in France.'

'My men will join us once we leave Milan. Once we are at Alba, I'll make a final decision about how to get the gold past our enemies. Della Scala or Bernabò Visconti. Both are a danger, but neither will attack until I leave Alba. Your presence assures us of that.'

'That's still not an answer,' said Despenser. 'You strike out with our Prince's dowry but you deny him an explanation.'

'Because I do not yet know how to achieve it,' said Blackstone, the lie easily told. 'Word will have already spread about our route and what we carry. Until I know for certain how I can safeguard it, what I do must be done in secret.'

'No, Sir Thomas, that time has now passed,' said the Prince. 'We trust you, but Lord Despenser is correct. It is our dowry and we must be confident that it will be safe. How will you get it to France? Back across the high pass? That way is probably the most dangerous of all. What of a ship from Genoa? We can bring influence to bear if it's a ship you need.'

'And risk a storm? Or the unreliable word of a ship's master? Milan is aligned with Genoa,' Blackstone said.

'They would not dare seize a ship we commissioned,' said the Prince.

'Highness, Milan supports Genoa, and Genoa is allied with France and Aragon. How easy would it be for Bernabò to make an arrangement with Spain? His hands would be clean just as he hoped they would be after his skinners had slaughtered my men. An Aragonese ship meets that from Genoa. The gold is exchanged. A lie is told such as pirates raided and stole the cargo. And we lose everything and the damned French have us by the throat. No, sire, I beg you leave this to me. I will get the gold where it needs to be.'

The Prince's irritation was obvious. 'You try us. We are tired and we have already drawn us back from that ledge I spoke of. You must inform us of how you will safeguard the gold.'

Blackstone let the Prince's irritation settle into a disgruntled scowl.

'By putting my life and those of my men between the gold and those who would seize it.'

It was obvious that Blackstone was not going to tell the Prince or Despenser what his plans were.

The Prince squirmed, suppressed another nauseous belch and with a flick of his wrist dismissed Blackstone.

'You would try the patience of the Almighty and tempt the devil himself,' said Despenser through gritted teeth.

Blackstone lifted Arianrhod the Silver Wheel Goddess from beneath his collar. 'That's why the Almighty gave me her for protection.'

Stepping past Despenser he closed the door behind him.

CHAPTER FORTY-TWO

Henry Blackstone had run to Lord Despenser and warned him of the impending fight between his father and Bernabò Visconti. He knew it would cause further displeasure from his father. Once Despenser's guards had secured and protected the gold, as his father had commanded, Henry instructed Gifford with a curt reprimand not to seek him out. He wanted to spend the night alone. Seeking comfort in a bottle of wine, he returned to the balcony whence he could see the remains of the great feast being cleared away. His swollen lip stung as he drank, as sharp as the humiliation he had once again suffered at the hands of his father. His desire to stand and fight once again rebuffed. Once again shown to be a disobedient son in front of fighting men when all he wanted to do was stand at his father's side. His love pushed aside because of his father's hatred for the man who had hidden in the shadows when his mother and sister were murdered. Why did his father not accept that, like him, Henry wanted Bernabò Visconti dead for what he'd done? Denied the chance for vengeance, he had been reduced to the status of a child again. Did his father not realize how much he still blamed himself for not being able to save them those years ago? He had only been a boy, but the terror had stayed with him. The desperate plight of his young sister clinging to him as the Jacquerie stormed the manor house. The slaughter that went on around them. And then his father and the men rescuing them, only to have a Visconti assassin squirm his way into their lives and kill his mother and sister. Did his father not understand the burden he had carried these past years? It never left him.

He drained the wine and threw the bottle against the wall.

He gripped the balcony wall, knuckles white with despair, tears stinging his eyes. Cursing silently for all the years he had tried so hard to live up to his father's expectation of him. Whatever that was.

'Master Henry?' said a voice tenderly.

He turned as Isabella stepped onto the balcony. He dragged a hand across his eyes, embarrassed to be caught in his self-pity.

She stepped closer to the wall and looked down. 'I too find the smoke from the incense and the candles sting my eyes. It was very difficult trying to eat.' She disarmed him with a smile. 'My husband and his family take great pleasure in entertaining their special guests. Your Prince has been honoured more than any other.'

'It's been a long night for everyone,' Henry said.

She nodded, staying where she was, gazing down at the scurrying servants. She glanced at him. 'It can also cause tension. Everyone wishes that the Prince is embraced in goodwill and that nothing overshadows that. My husband's father had a furious row with Lord Bernabò. There was a great deal of anger between them.'

He decided not to admit being in the vault when Bernabò Visconti had stormed in. 'Was there trouble?'

She glanced at his cut lip. But said nothing. 'Lord Bernabò left the city with his men and the Prince summoned Lord Galeazzo.' She shrugged. 'Yes, there was trouble.' Now she studied him more carefully. Was her brave young chevalier involved? 'Do you know what happened? No one will tell me.'

He faltered for a moment. She was part of the Visconti

family now. Was there anything he could tell her she wouldn't find out eventually? Would it make any difference? If the Prince had summoned Galeazzo, then the assault would soon be known.

'Lord Bernabò tried to kill my father.'

The news didn't appear to have any effect on her. Always the calm one, he thought. A true princess trained from childhood to never reveal her innermost doubts or feelings.

'He is a violent man. Your father was injured?'

'Wounded, but nothing serious. Lord Bernabò was also hurt. My father was close to killing him but I had fetched Lord Despenser, who stopped it on the Prince's orders.'

Her lips parted so slightly, he barely heard the gentle sigh of understanding that escaped past her lips. 'Ah, I see.' Her forefinger hovered close to his lip. 'And were you fighting?'

'I was not.' He lowered his eyes. 'My father struck me for disobeying him.'

'Obedience is a hard taskmaster. I too felt its sting when I was young.' She stepped away from him, looking over her shoulder. Concern wrinkled her brow.

A young servant appeared half in the shadows. A handsome boy with auburn hair and a face as pretty as any young girl's. 'My lady,' he said, his voice a whisper.

Isabella nodded and made a small gesture of assurance. 'I cannot stay long,' she told Henry. 'My ladies-in-waiting are watching the stairs for me. My husband sleeps, but I should not be away from his side.' She waved the young man away, shooing him into the shadows. 'Stefano is my most trusted servant.' She smiled. 'He worries that I might anger my husband.'

Henry felt the lump in his throat tighten. Danger was everywhere and, it seemed, embraced everyone. 'I'm sorry that I have placed you in this situation.'

'I am here because I said I would help you. It's difficult to approach you openly. You understand?'

'Of course.' His heart picked up a pace because if she was

here, then she had news of the woman he sought. Good news or not?

'There is no Camaldolese monastery anywhere near here. But there is a rumour that a woman had skills in demand by the monks at the Abbey of Santa Maria di Rivalta Scrivia. It could be a rumour only, I do not know. Women sew, make clothes and embroider. It might be nothing to do with your illuminatrix. And di Rivalta Scrivia, being a Cistercian monastery, does not allow women inside the walls. It is very strict.'

This news was the closest Henry had ever been to finding the woman whose artistic skill had enraptured him. He dared to hope.

'Such a woman could not create her masterpieces from a house, or a room in a castello. She would need paint and brushes, and someone to grind the minerals into the colours she would use. It is not something a person would undertake alone. She would need help from apprentices or assistants. Where would they have found such a woman?'

'I don't know, Master Henry, but there is the Abbazia di San Marziano, which is a few miles away from the Abbey of Santa Maria and they have their own scriptorium. Would this lady you seek not be there? Perhaps that is where the monks sent their manuscripts. I think so. Yes?'

'My lady, I don't know where these places are.'

'They are on one of the routes to Alba where your Prince must go.' She smiled. 'A prince needs rest. The Abbey of Santa Maria di Rivalta Scrivia is known for its hospitality to travellers.'

She extended her hand. He pressed his injured lips to it, ignoring the sting.

'I am in your debt, my honoured lady.'

'No, mon petit chevalier, I am forever in yours.'

And Isabella Visconti, the French Princess, slipped away into the darkness and out of his life once again.

CHAPTER FORTY-THREE

The Prince's cavalcade extended the length of the main street. He would leave the city the way he had entered. Lord Galeazzo waited patiently at the Porta Ticinese with his wife, Bianca. This would be the last time they would see their daughter until Prince Lionel invited them to his palazzo in Alba. The marriage would not be consummated for at least two years when Violante would be best suited to be with child. The Visconti expected to be invited before the Prince returned to England to present her to the English King. That was providing the previous night's disturbance had not soured their relationship. Bianca had chastised her husband when she learnt of Bernabò's attack. His behaviour had risked everything that she and Galeazzo had carefully planned. Chastised or not, Galeazzo would take only so much criticism before banning her and her ladies-in-waiting to their chambers. The earlier argument with Bernabò had drained him. And this morning his gout had flared, more painfully than before the extravagant feast.

Behind him, horse bridles jangled as the noblemen's mounts shook the flies from their eyes. Their riders muttered soft curses to keep them steady. They shared Galeazzo's impatience at being kept waiting but dared not express their thoughts. They too were suffering from over-indulgence at the feast and the humid air added to their discomfort. It was already after terce and the delay was an obvious gesture of the Prince's displeasure.

Blackstone had overseen the loading of the gold onto the sturdy mules. He made sure it was seen by the Visconti servants. The Prince's wagon remained loaded with his pavilion and other comforts. The numerous gifts would be sent on to Alba when the Prince was in residence. Blackstone shifted his weight in the saddle. His wound was an irritation to be ignored. Terrel was stationed behind Blackstone to escort the paired mules while Gifford and Henry were to be on the other side. But only Gifford was there.

'Where is he, Gifford?' said Blackstone.

'I don't know, Sir Thomas. Lord Despenser summoned him to the Prince. I was told to take my place here.'

Blackstone had decided to have the gold a dozen horses back from the front where the Prince and Despenser would lead the column. Like the unfortunate Visconti family, he too had given cause to offend the Prince, and now the Prince had summoned his son. There was nothing to be done but to wait.

Edward Despenser ushered Henry into the Prince's quarters. Henry bowed. A valet was fussing over the Prince, attaching the gold chain around his chest that held his riding cloak across his shoulders, and ensuring it was draped correctly over his embroidered silk doublet. As he did this another valet eased riding gloves onto the Prince's outstretched hands.

'Enough,' said the Prince. The servants moved away. 'Master Henry, we have summoned you to make a suggestion which we hope might please you.'

'Sire,' said Henry, dipping his chin respectfully.

'We recognize your clear thinking when you summoned Lord Despenser. Your action averted a situation that would have caused diplomatic harm to our presence here.'

The Prince waited for a response from Henry. He gave none.

'Very well. We travel to Alba where we will stay for... however long we decide. That is yet to be determined. Our young bride will have her own quarters as is proper and right, and she will have her servants in attendance day and night. We will, of course, wish to share our love of poetry with her.' The Prince made a final adjustment to his cloak. 'But she speaks no English, her French is passable, and so we will share what we love in the poet's language. We desire your company, Master Henry. Your education at Oxford speaks well of your character, and will be helpful in furthering her knowledge of scholarly matters. A temporary tutor is what is required. You will become part of our household for a period of time. We will, together, educate young Violante in the ways of beauty from the written word.' The Prince glanced up at Henry. 'You will ride behind me and Lord Despenser.'

'Yes, highness,' said Henry.

The Prince gave a nod of dismissal. Henry hesitated. The Prince caught the brief uncertainty. 'Yes?'

'Sire, may I speak freely?'

'Our suggestion does not sit well with you?'

'It's a great honour, sire. I hoped that I might be given some... some leeway to be absent for a day or two on the journey.'

'Absent? From us?'

Henry brazened it out. 'May I approach, highness? There's something I would like to show you.'

The request caused a look of surprise from the Prince. Despenser's protective instincts made him step towards Henry. The Prince looked at Despenser and shook his head. He beckoned Henry to him. Henry took out the folded illuminated page and showed it to the Prince. He saw the Prince's surprise.

'A young woman's hand did this, highness. She was a student of Don Silvestro dei Gherarducci. I am searching for her. I have her name and I have found an abbey where I think she might be.'

The Prince fingered the illuminated artwork. 'And where is that?'

'Highness, on our way to Alba. There is a route that would take you past a monastery called the Abbey of Santa Maria di Rivalta Scrivia.'

Despenser interrupted, 'Highness, I have already planned our route.'

Henry quickly jumped in to strengthen his appeal. 'The abbey is well known for its hospitality to travellers.'

The Prince raised his eyes to acknowledge Despenser's concern. Looking back to Henry, he said, 'And you believe a monastery would allow a woman – even one who clearly has the love of the divine in her heart – to practise her art in such a place? The shining light of our good Lord does not alter the fact that she is a woman.' He folded the page and handed it back. 'Such things are not possible, Master Henry.'

Henry did not take the folded page. His hand hovered, forcing the Prince to hold it a moment longer. 'Highness, a few miles from di Rivalta Scrivia is a smaller abbey, the Abbazia di San Marziano. They have a scriptorium. That abbey is for women. I believe the monks commission work from the scriptorium there. I believe that is where I will find her.'

The Prince considered Henry's enthusiasm, clearly held on a tight rein, but earnest in its honesty.

'And what would you do if you found her?'

Henry had no wish to tell the Prince everything. To explain what the would-be assassin had told him, that the girl needed guarding, would tip the Prince towards Despenser, who would not wish to risk the possibility of any dangerous situation.

'I don't know, highness.'

The Prince still held the folded page. He reopened it, stared at the illumination. He looked at Despenser. 'You will change our route, Lord Edward. We wish to avail ourselves of the hospitality of the monks at di Rivalta Scrivia abbey.' He folded the page and handed it to Henry. 'There are times, Master Henry, when pursuing beauty is reason enough.'

CHAPTER FORTY-FOUR

Two hours after Prince Lionel led his cavalcade out of the gates of Milan, Lord Edward Despenser called out a warning as horsemen appeared in the distance. Despenser was alert to a surprise attack especially as the route had been altered and they were carrying two hundred thousand gold florins.

Blackstone spurred his horse forward; sidling alongside his son for a moment, he looked at him. Henry stared back but then turned away. Blackstone ignored him and drew up next to Despenser.

'They're mine,' he said. 'It's Killbere and the men. They've been close by since we went into Milan.'

'Then they'll join the column?' said Despenser.

'No, my lord, I'll take my two men and join them. We'll act as outriders. Put your men in my place to flank the gold. My scouts will ride ahead and make sure the way is clear.'

'Then you know the route, Sir Thomas?'

'Aye, my lord.' He chopped the air with the flat of his hand. 'Straight ahead to Alba and the Prince's new possession.'

Despenser took pleasure in contradicting him. 'No, Sir Thomas, we ride for an abbey near the town of Tortona. Your son has persuaded the Prince to alter our route.'

Blackstone felt the jibe and glanced back at Henry, who ignored his father's scowl. 'How is it my son has any influence on a prince of the realm?'

'They share a love of poetry.'

Blackstone knew Despenser was drawing out the pleasure of pitting father against son.

'So my son's silver tongue drips sweet words to enchant the Prince? Is that it? He has an education, my lord, but I don't think he has the wit to divert a prince from his destination.'

Despenser smiled. 'How little you know your son, Sir Thomas. He pursues a woman. Did you not know that?'

Blackstone had no answer and Despenser knew it.

'He found an illustrated page. By a girl's hand. Someone he claims was mentored by a master artist. There's an abbey near to where we travel. He showed the Prince and his highness was touched by the beauty of the work. Beauty and poetry, Sir Thomas, they can lead men... and boys astray.'

'I can see you are not so easily persuaded, my lord.'

'Indeed I am not.'

'I'm pleased to see you know your duty. A tender heart that appreciates such a gift is beyond common men such as you and me.'

Blackstone had reduced Despenser's status. An insult that could not be easily challenged without him appearing to be precious about his social rank. Blackstone suppressed the anger he felt at Henry disrupting the journey. His own duty was to deliver the gold. His son's whim – a pursuit that was little more than a fawn chasing morning mist that disappeared as soon as the sun warmed the land – had put another day on the journey to Alba. Blackstone smiled. He was not prepared to show disloyalty to his son. 'My son is blessed with a heart as gentle as the Prince's.' He gathered his reins. 'I'll ask him to teach you a better understanding of the poetry he shares with the Prince. Be patient with him. It takes time to teach those with little comprehension.'

With another insult delivered he spurred his horse the mile beyond the column to meet Killbere and his men.

He would deal with Henry later.

Killbere snorted as Blackstone questioned Gifford.

'You knew about this woman?'

'I did, Sir Thomas.'

'For how long?'

'Since Paris.'

'And you thought I should not know of it?'

'I thought it unlikely Master Henry would be serious enough to pursue it.'

Blackstone studied him for a moment. 'You don't believe that, Gifford. You have been at his side since he was at Oxford. You know damned well the lad has wayward tendencies.' He paused. Gifford had not lowered his eyes as he was being questioned. 'No, you knew he would pursue it but you remained loyal to your charge. Very well, that's as it should be. But in future remember why we are here. All right, he needs you, Gifford.'

'Lord Despenser has kept me from him now that he rides close to the Prince.'

Blackstone sighed. 'All right, Gifford, I'll make certain you rejoin him. I need you to use your judgement and steer him clear of behaving like a damned fool.'

'Sir Thomas, he's a headstrong young man.'

'And you have more sense in one curled fist than he has in his brain. I'll make no complaint if he ever comes before me with a few lumps.'

'Thank you, Sir Thomas, but I would not wish him to think I was the one who told you about the woman.'

'He won't. Lord Despenser took that pleasure.'

Gifford dipped his head and returned to the men.

Blackstone glanced at Killbere, who smiled. 'He likes women. We've all pursued them.'

'Dammit, Gilbert, don't encourage him.'

Killbere pointed to where Mallin was taking his time bringing Blackstone's horse on a long rein to where they waited. The Prince's column moved slowly past half a mile away.

'It was a good fight, Thomas. A pity you could not have been with us.'

'I couldn't risk alerting anyone. Bezián served the purpose in warning you.'

Killbere looked over to where the Gascon waited with the others. 'Aye, he's proved his weight in some of that gold you're carrying. Fought hard and fought well. I count ourselves lucky he was at our side. And you?'

'Arguing with Despenser. He's rigid in his thinking.'

Killbere tugged free a heavy purse and tossed it to Blackstone. He waited as Blackstone pulled open the ties and spilled a few coins into the palm of his hand. For a moment he didn't understand why Killbere had given him the purse. He studied one of the coins more closely. And then a few others.

'That's right. They're minted in Verona. When the lads stripped the skinners every purse had Veronese coin in it. So, were they Visconti men or not? And if they weren't then how did your man inside Milan know about them?'

'I don't think he did. All he knew was that Bernabò was using skinners.'

'And if those men we killed were in della Scala's pay?'

'Then there's an arrangement of some kind between Bernabò and della Scala.' Blackstone handed back the purse. 'In this part of the world we have no allies. If we are fortunate, Alba will give the Prince the safety he needs with his new bride and we can be on our way.'

'Before we abandon the Prince you must let us explore if there's a decent brothel in the town.'

'First we have to ride to an abbey. A place called Tortona. Do you know it?'

'Tortona? Didn't we pass along that route those years past when we left Florence to go back to France?'

'I don't recall.'

'Ah, well, if it's the place I'm thinking of... Tortona... there was an abbess. A fiery woman with the face of a pinched arse. Aye. I tried to seduce one of her novices. If that's the place I'm thinking of.'

'We'll know soon enough.'

Mallin reached them. 'Sir Thomas. He'll be glad to see you. He can have someone else to bite and kick.'

The bastard horse lowered its ugly head and swung it hard as if he'd understood Mallin. And that was why Mallin had brought the unpredictable beast forward on a long rein. Blackstone approached it cautiously, hand extended for it to catch his scent.

'He hurt you?'

'No, I watched his habits. He caught one of Will Longdon's young archers with a blow of its head. The lad was on his way to the latrine and the beast knocked him so hard he damned near ended up in the shit pit.'

Blackstone and his horse stood their ground facing each other. 'Very well.' He passed over the reins of the horse he'd been riding. 'Take the horses we used in Milan to Lord Despenser's men. We need our own mounts.'

Mallin nodded his understanding and went along the line of men where the horses were tethered.

John Jacob joined Blackstone and Killbere. 'And young Henry?' he said.

'With the Prince,' said Blackstone.

'With the Prince,' Killbere repeated. A statement that begged to be a question. 'Of course he's with the Prince, John. Where else would he be?' And gave Blackstone a querulous look. Blackstone shook his head.

'God's tears, Thomas, you've had a falling-out.'

'I struck him. He's not spoken to me since.'

'With good reason? I mean you striking him.'

Blackstone sighed and took a handful of reins, pulling tight so he could mount without the bastard horse's yellow teeth biting him. 'There's much to tell, and I'll explain as we ride. Right now we must find the route we need and send Renfred and his men out to scout ahead.'

Killbere and John Jacob looked at each other. The gold's journey had begun and Blackstone and the men were its keepers. A storm was brewing not only between father and son but with Despenser, and now there was an uncertain route. There would be more trouble ahead. Of that both men were certain.

CHAPTER FORTY-FIVE

Henry Blackstone was in the Prince's pavilion on the first night of the journey towards Alba. After two hours of meandering exploration of French and Italian poetry, the Prince retired, excusing Henry from his companionship.

Making his way through Despenser's tents, he headed for where his father's men camped. Firelight sprinkled the dark fields and he saw the warm glow of flames light up Meulon and Will Longdon as they fussed and bantered over a blackened iron pot of food on the flames. Neither man happy with the other's efforts. They watched him approach, Meulon's grin widening behind his thick beard.

'Look what the night creatures spat out,' said Longdon as Meulon gave Henry a suffocating hug.

'Will, Meulon, how are you? Good to see you.'

'It looks as though you travel with princes these days. How are we common folk meant to behave in such company?' said Meulon. Both men bowed at the waist.

Henry clasped Longdon's extended arm and pulled the muscled archer into an embrace. 'I keep a prince company at his request because I am familiar with the books my mother gave me and an education granted by the King. Who am I to deny a prince? I see you still argue like an innkeeper and his wife.'

'My cooking needs no interference and this damned oaf keeps feeding the fire when what I need is slow-burning embers,' said Longdon.

'And all I want is food that is cooked through,' Meulon answered. 'So, Henry, it's been a long journey since we last saw you.'

'Placed by my father to listen for discontent in the Prince's camp in case there were people who opposed the marriage.'

'And we hear there was trouble,' said Longdon.

'Some. In the monastery at the pass. We saw your efforts at clearing the way for the Prince.'

'Scum that needed to be taught a lesson. We're good teachers.' Longdon grinned. 'Seems you did better than us and saved the Prince, though. Good work, lad.'

'It's good to have you back with us, Henry, even if we know you sleep on a feather mattress at the feet of the Prince should he need a night poem to help him sleep,' said Meulon.

Henry looked up at the bear of a man. 'One day I'll wrestle you down, you know that.'

'I look forward to the contest,' said Meulon.

'Aye, but he'll be an old man wrapped in blankets on his deathbed when that happens,' said Longdon.

'True enough,' said Henry. 'Now, I must find John Jacob and Sir Gilbert.'

The two men's expressions became more sober. 'Unless the world has changed these past twenty-odd years, I wager you'll find them with your father,' said Longdon.

'You poke me with a bodkin point, Will.'

'Aye, and there are times men need it to face Thomas Blackstone's displeasure.'

'He knows?'

They nodded. 'Chasing beautiful women is no crime, lad, but

when it distracts him from his duty, he was never going to be pleased.'

'Gifford?'

Meulon dipped the ladle into the pot and blew on it. 'Despenser. He's the one who told him.'

'I fear I need your shield wall, Meulon.'

Meulon slurped, fanning the hot food. 'Much good that would do you.'

Longdon and Meulon watched sympathetically as Henry took a breath and nodded at the inevitable confrontation that awaited.

As he passed through the knotted groups of his father's men at their fires, some eating while others readied bedrolls, they hailed and welcomed him. The warmth he felt being back with them had nothing to do with the night air or heat from the flames. Then the shadows thinned as, in the near distance, he saw the familiar bulk of his father. Blackstone stood like an obelisk facing him, as if he had been aware of his son's approach from the time Henry had left the Prince's tent. Waiting, staring in his direction, flanked by John Jacob, who knelt at the fire, and Killbere, who was eating from a pewter plate.

'My lord,' said Henry, remembering to address his father correctly in front of others.

Blackstone ignored him, except for an unsmiling nod of his head. Killbere ran a tongue over his teeth, picked out a piece of gristle and tossed it into the fire. 'Ah, our Prince's companion returns.' He put down his plate and stood to embrace him. John Jacob placed a firm hand on Henry's shoulder.

'Master Henry, one day I won't recognize you. You grow taller and broader.'

'It's only been a few months, John.'

'Feels longer,' said the man who had chaperoned Henry as a boy.

Killbere belched and pulled up his belt. 'Henry, I have business to attend to at the latrine pit. I'll bid you goodnight. We'll catch up with all our stories when nature's demands cease troubling my bowels.'

John Jacob had his back to Blackstone as he looked at Henry. 'And I need to check the picket lines.' He gave a slight grimace. Father and son needed time together. With a final squeeze on Henry's arm, he and Killbere walked off into the night.

Henry waited until they were out of earshot. 'Father. I cause distress to those we both love dearly.'

'They know when to stay silent and let men get on with their business. Something you need to learn. Sir Gilbert thinks I was wrong to strike you.'

'So do I. A son wanting to stand with his father when facing danger should not be punished.'

Blackstone did not invite Henry to sit or to share the food simmering in the pot. His hands rested on Wolf Sword's pommel, his gaze unyielding. 'I don't doubt your intentions, what I will not tolerate is disobedience when a fight is about to start. You disobeyed me three times. I don't want anyone at my side in a fight who cannot obey a command and who refuses in front of other men. Gifford and Terrel would have obeyed immediately had they been in your place. Those are the men I want with me in a fight.'

'They are not your son, my lord.'

'Oh, now I am your lord. Our intimacy alters with your petulance.'

'I am trying to honour you with every breath. And every breath leaves me choking with failure.'

'Because you don't listen. Because you fail to understand what needs to be done when the time for it to be done arrives. You ran from that vault and warned the Prince and Despenser of the fight between me and Bernabò. I would have killed the man who, years ago, had one of his bastard sons plot the murder of your mother and sister and the death of the Princess Isabelle. He deserves to die. And you stopped me.'

'Perhaps you could not see the consequences of killing him.'

'I did not care about what happened when he was dead. Whatever trouble came my way, I would have dealt with. It was not your decision to make.'

They fell silent. The wood crackled in the fire. Henry longed to return to the Prince's cosseted world of the royal pavilion. But he had not yet been dismissed and knew he had to endure more of his father's displeasure. As if grasping a sword's honed blade, he took a deep breath and seized the moment.

'About the woman I seek.'

He got no further. Blackstone levelled an accusatory finger at his son. 'You damned fool. You disgraced me in front of an honoured lord, a Knight of the Garter, who now sees the King's Master of War as a hapless idiot who cannot control a wayward son. A son whose smooth tongue and whimsical infatuation with a non-existent spectre steers a column of men and the vital gold they carry off route. You appealed to the soft heart of a good man when you should have used your brain and thought of what was important. A safe passage on a planned route, not deviating into unknown territory to suit your selfish desires. You put Lord Despenser at a disadvantage and served me ill.'

Henry swallowed hard. There was to be no respite.

Blackstone had not finished. 'You caused Despenser to dismiss Gifford. Your man. Who serves to protect you.'

'I need no protection. I can look after myself.'

'You need protection *from* yourself! And now I will address that matter.' Blackstone's voice, muffled in frustration and anger, offered no opportunity for a reply. 'You will have Gifford at your side, Henry. I swear I will not have you running like a damned lone wolf, causing mayhem when there are matters of importance to attend to. Come with me.'

He stalked away from the fire. Henry picked up his pace in order to follow. It took no time at all to reach Lord Edward

Despenser's pavilion. Despenser was sitting on a stool. Stripped of his jupon, boots and sword belt, he wore a surcoat bearing his coat of arms. He stood as Blackstone reached him.

'My Lord Despenser. My son has the Prince's ear. Neither of us can change that. But I want his man Gifford to return to his duty.'

'I saw no need to have him waiting around like a stray dog,' said Despenser.

'You would defy the King?'

Despenser looked uncertain. Blackstone pressed on.

'The King ordered my son's protection. Gifford is Warwick's man and has served him and the Crown loyally. If you wish to have a scribe write to the King, telling him why you have dismissed Gifford from his duties, then I shall withhold my request.'

Despenser knew he had no choice in the matter. He looked past Blackstone's shoulder to where Henry stood obediently. 'Then I shall return him to his duties,' he said.

Blackstone nodded, turned away and gave Henry a withering look. 'Do your duty. Stay with the Prince until you are dismissed.' His voice lowered to a whisper. 'And then abandon this nonsense. You are a scholar. Behave like one. You are trained to think. And try to remember you are my son.'

Henry stood, feeling even more humiliated. He had no objection to Gifford returning to be his shadow. In fact, he was pleased to have the uncomplicated man's company. All his focus now lay in finding Elena, the elusive woman who he was sure would infuse his life with her beauty.

That thought was enough for him to put everything else aside.

CHAPTER FORTY-SIX

The Prince rested as he had promised at the Abbey of Santa Maria di Rivalta Scrivia; Henry rode on the extra miles to the Abbazia di San Marziano. Gifford rode with him.

'My father spoke to you?'

'He did,' said Gifford.

'He is not well pleased.'

'He is not.'

Henry smiled. 'Cheer up, Hugh. Our quest is almost done.'

'It's not my quest. You're the one running after a woman who might not even exist.'

'Ah, you should see the sunrise instead of the sunset in your thoughts.'

'I would be glad to keep the daylight for as long as I can. That way I can see where I'm going and not be running into the night like a blind man on a narrow path.'

'You'll see. She will be everything that leaps from that page.'

'And what happens then? Your father escorts the gold while you're trying to seduce a girl touched by the divine into your bed?'

Henry shook his head. 'I would do no such thing. A creature of such beauty needs my protection.'

Gifford frowned. 'Protection? From bathing in the divine light? Who is it that would harm her? The devil's imps wouldn't go near such a place. They have business elsewhere.'

'Before Salvarini died, he asked me to find her and to guard her. That she was being held by those who sent him to kill the Prince.'

The information felled Gifford into silence. Henry Blackstone was on more than a quest to find a beautiful girl; he was riding into trouble. 'Can't you see this for what it is? A dying assassin encourages you to find the girl you are looking for. He's sending you into a trap. And me with you. Are you thinking clearly? How would he know she was in an abbey? How can you know it might be the one we approach? There are convents and abbeys in Italy thicker than fleas in an inn's bed. This becomes more tangled the more you tell me.'

'You sound like my father, Hugh.'

'Then use your head.'

'Listen to me. Salvarini urged me to save her. To guard her. She is being held against her will, on that I'll wager.'

'And you think an abbess has her locked up? That an abbess sent him to kill the Prince? Master Henry, are you losing your mind? The man was a charlatan.'

Henry slowed his horse. 'Don't lecture me, Hugh. I don't know who's holding her or why. But the same people sent Salvarini to do the killing. The abbey might be controlled by a lord of a domain.' He became exasperated at Gifford's lack of understanding. 'I'll find out when I locate her.'

He spurred his horse.

'You think to find the man behind the killing? Why didn't you tell Sir Thomas? Or Despenser? Or the bloody Prince instead of spouting poetry through the night!' Gifford shouted after him.

Henry turned in the saddle. 'You don't have to ride with me. Go back!'

Gifford dug his heels into the horse's flanks. 'Merciful Christ, I must be paying off my sins,' he muttered to himself.

*

It was still light when they reached the abbey. The clear sky silhouetted the looming walls.

'We should ride around the walls,' said Gifford. 'We need to see if there have been horsemen travelling here. If you think there's an enemy within this place, then we must prepare ourselves.'

Henry was quiet. The end of his quest might lie beyond the abbey's gates. Who else? Urging his horse into a walking pace, he skirted the walls, eyes down, searching for signs. Gifford followed. By the time they had ridden around the abbey, the light was fading. There had been no sign of horsemen's tracks.

'Now it's time,' said Henry. 'You wait outside with the horses.'

Gifford dismounted. 'And let you walk into a trap?' He handed his reins to Henry. 'Tie them to that tree. I'll knock.'

Henry had no choice but to obey. As he tied off the horses, Gifford's fist thumped the postern gate next to the abbey's main door. He waited.

'You think they're at prayer or sleeping already?' he said.

'Either,' Henry answered. The towering walls held them in twilight shadow.

Gifford kicked the door with the toe of his boot. 'Come on, come on...'

Moments later, they heard women's voices. Two of them. One fearful, the other calming. A peephole latch slid open. A woman's face. Pock-marked, eyes screwed up at the sight of Gifford. Her head covered in a wimple. A voice behind her, asking who was at the gate. The senior woman turned away and quietened whoever was behind her, telling her to return to her duties. And the older woman's eyes scrutinized Gifford again.

She spoke hurriedly. Irritation in her voice. Questioning.

Gifford sighed. 'Damned woman is chattering too fast. I can't follow. You do it.' He stepped aside, allowing Henry to take his place. Gifford listened as Henry's gentle voice charmed the woman. There appeared to be some agreement between them. The woman nodded and closed the latch.

'What now? They won't let us in?' said Gifford.

'She's gone to fetch the abbess. If we're permitted entry, we must leave our weapons here.'

'Out here? Any damned vagabond could thieve them. As well as the horses. I say we take horse and weapons inside. Leave them in the yard. That way, they stay safe and we're not unarmed like two damned pilgrims looking for refuge. We don't know what awaits us in there.'

'I'll try.'

'Good. Tell her you're with an English prince. Or that you are friends with one of the Visconti's wives. Better still, tell her you're Henry Blackstone. Your father fought for Florence. He'll have passed somewhere along the way. That should be a sharp reminder – sharp as an assassin's dagger.'

'Hugh, these nuns live in isolation. They'll know nothing about that. If we're lucky, the only contact they'll have will be with the monks at Santa Maria di Rivalta Scrivia.'

'And if she's not here?'

'I don't know.'

'Then I suggest you abandon the idea and return to your father and ride with him.'

'And if I find her here and she needs protection?'

Gifford gave him the same unequivocal reply. 'Return to your father and ride with him.' Henry was about to argue, but once again they heard women's voices approaching. The latch slid aside. A woman, younger by ten years than the previous inquisitor, who had looked to have lived sixty years or more, pressed her face to the gap. She had rosy cheeks. Her face scrubbed. She looked well fed. 'I am Abbess Lucia and I am told you are enquiring about one of our illuminatrices.'

'I do, Mother Abbess.'

'This house is known for its scriptorium. We have many fine illuminatrices here.' She studied the young man closely.

Henry pulled out the torn page and held it in front of the open latch. The poor light didn't disguise the quality of the illumination. He saw the abbess react. His heartbeat quickened. This was the place. He knew it.

'What interest do you have?'

'A prince of England has expressed interest in the skill and beauty of this work,' Henry said, smothering his own desire with a lie.

The abbess scrutinized him a moment longer. 'Very well,' she said, confirming his belief that the woman he sought was inside. 'We do not allow men to be alone here. You will be chaperoned.'

'We understand.'

Hearing that there was more than the one man making the enquiry, she pressed her face further into the gap and peered to see Gifford.

'No weapons are permitted.'

'We ride with the English Prince who is now married to a Visconti. We must protect our horses and weapons. I would ask that you allow us to leave them in the yard.'

Her eyes had flared when Henry slipped into the conversation his association with the Visconti. Perhaps these nuns were not so isolated after all.

'We are a poor house. We work to feed and clothe ourselves.'

It was a blatant request for money. Henry caught on.

'I was hoping to make a payment for disturbing you this late in the day. I know it is almost time for vespers.'

She smiled. This man at her gate was sharp-witted. She nodded. The latch closed. A bolt was thrown. The main gate opened.

'Hugh, bring the horses,' said Henry as he stepped into the abbey's yard while unbuckling his sword belt.

The abbess was short and plump. The younger woman who hovered in the background was plain-looking. Her features, visible beneath the wimple, were creased from working in the sun. Her hands rough and calloused. The abbess looked as though she did no manual labour.

Gifford secured the horses and weapons and stood respectfully a few paces behind Henry, who fumbled for his purse, spilled coins into his hand and passed them to the abbess, who appeared to be more than satisfied by his generosity.

The abbess had turned into an atrium flanked by arched cloisters on either side. He could make out carved images of animals on the columns' capitals. Ahead of them, the façade of the basilica, the main building, seemed to be where the abbess was taking him. Henry hovered at her side. Gifford and the younger nun followed.

'Is Sister Elena in the scriptorium? Will I see her before vespers?'

'Elena? There is no Elena here.'

Henry's throat tightened. 'This is her work, isn't it?' he said, holding the torn page in front of him.

'It is. You mean Sister Magdalena. She is renowned. It is widely believed that the Almighty blessed her.'

'Magdalena? Yes, yes, that's her. Elena. I misunderstood her name.'

They walked into the arched basilica. It was nearly dark. The church lacked windows, except for ones positioned at the east and west. For a moment, the sound of shuffling nuns entering from the far side of the church's side doors distracted Henry. Vespers would soon begin. The abbess veered away, pushed open a door that led into a plain cut-stone corridor, more humble than the vaulted church. Darker still, lit by small wall sconces.

'Was she not influenced by Don Silvestro dei Gherarducci? That is what I was told.'

Abbess Lucia ignored his question. 'Why are you so interested in Sister Magdalena?'

He hesitated. How could he explain that the woman he sought needed his help?

'I am an admirer of beauty.'

'A nun does not show herself to the world. She is married

to Christ. Why do you think she wears a wimple? You come here with lust in your heart?' She stopped. There was a door ahead. Her demeanour had changed. Henry had said the wrong thing.

His thoughts raced, trying to save the moment. 'I admire the beauty of the good Lord that shines from within the artist. That is what I meant to say.'

The shadows deepened. Her round face took on the look of a malevolent cherub as she stared up at him. She nodded. 'Very well.' She pushed open the door, which led into another corridor. All that could be seen were two empty cells, possibly used for novices, and a door at the far end with a small hatch. The abbess stepped aside. 'She is in there.'

Henry hesitated. He had expected the woman he sought to be in the scriptorium. The way ahead felt forbidding. Gifford pushed past them.

'Let me look at this place,' he said. He stepped into the narrow passage. He stopped at each darkened cell. Inside each was a palliasse. Nothing more. Abandoned. Satisfied, he beckoned Henry to join him.

'Nothing to worry about.' He nodded towards the door and its hatch at the end of the corridor. 'Go ahead. I'll stay at the door with the abbess just in case she's on the side of the devil and locks us in here.' He grinned. 'We would disappear without a trace.'

Henry pressed a hand on Gifford's arm. 'Thanks, Hugh.'

As his guardian returned to stay at the only way in or out, Henry ventured towards the hatch. Why was Elena, or rather Magdalena, down here? A heavy wooden bar bolted and barred the old iron door. Was she a prisoner? Is this what Salvarini meant when he said he should guard her? This place already constrained her. He had to know what was going on and why he had been sent here. And why such a skilled illuminatrix was kept from the other nuns. He reached for the hatch. His hand hesitated. He called her name. 'Sister Magdalena. May I speak to you?'

He heard a shuffle inside.

A muted voice agreed to his request.

He edged open the hatch. His mouth dry. His expectations pounding in his chest. A glimmer of light appeared. And then became brighter as the glow from a candle inside exposed the inside as a bare cell. A straw mattress on a plain frame. A small stand where a bible was open. He could see no sign of paint or brushes or pens. A foul scent lingered. Stale like any underground cell but fetid. The stench of a human trapped alone in a small space.

His throat dried. 'Sister Magdalena?' he whispered.

A shadow came between the door and the candlelight. A hunched old woman, her wimple dirty, the scapular draped across her front stained with food. She raised a twisted hand to shield her eyes, trying to see who beckoned her. Disease distorted her face. Leprosy.

Henry gasped, trying to match the sight with the image of the young beauty he had carried with him. His attempt to speak failed him. He fumbled for the torn page. Suddenly the abbess was at his side. Startled, he stepped away from the door.

The abbess smiled with a kindness kept for those who came face to face with a world they could not comprehend. 'She is an anchoress, young master. She will die in there, devoting her final years to our Lord and his teachings.' She eased closed the hatch. 'We did not abandon her when she caught the *morbus sacer*.'

Henry tried to settle his thoughts. The term meant 'sacred disease'. A punishment from God for sins committed.

'Blessed and then condemned? What sins could she have committed here?' he whispered, unable to grasp the loss of his ideal.

The abbess shrugged. 'She was a beautiful young woman. Her work cherished and desired by church and layman alike. Noblemen paid great sums of money to possess her illuminations.'

Henry gripped the torn page that had brought him so far, only for him to be met with a loss that bordered on grief.

The abbess nodded. 'Completed twenty years ago.' With a slow movement, she slid the hatch closed. 'That person no longer lives.'

PART SIX

ASSASSINATION

CHAPTER FORTY-SEVEN

Blackstone's men were encamped outside Alba's walls, which encompassed soaring towers spearing to the heavens throughout the city. The bulk of Despenser's men were beyond them, spread further across the open meadows, there being so many travelling in the Prince's cavalcade. Blackstone's captains were inside the city walls with him. The gold was secured in the Duomo di San Lorenzo's crypt. The ancient cathedral was as impregnable as the Visconti vault in Milan. On the edge of a piazza, in a grain store, Blackstone was examining the cart that had been laden with some of the Prince's travelling comforts. Now it was empty and exactly what Blackstone needed.

Killbere swept his gaze across the piazza and the city's walls. He leaned on the wagon's side, working a twig around his gums, clearing any pieces of rogue food from their recent meal. He spat some flecks away. 'Since we've been here, I feel less safe than if I were in Milan. The Prince might have been gifted it, but it's still a Visconti city. The people here are loyal to them. The servants in the citadel are Visconti's, the blacksmiths, the monks, all of them. If they ever decided they didn't want to be ruled by an English prince, they could rise up and slaughter the few men we have here. Our blood would be running in the gutter before the men outside could breach the walls.'

Blackstone studied him for a moment. 'It's a city that was ruled by Galeazzo. Not his brother. Have you seen anyone show disrespect? Or raise their voices other than when we rode through the city gates with the Prince, and they were lifted in welcome?'

'I have not.'

'Have any of the women turned their face from you?'

'They have not.'

'Or urchins cast a rotten piece of fruit?'

'Very well, Thomas. I understand. But when I'm caged like this and the Visconti stench is trapped within the walls like an open shit pit, then I'm on my guard.'

'Then rest assured, old friend, we'll soon have the wind in our faces and leave the stench behind.'

'Not before time. We have spent too many days worrying about our young English Prince and his gold. Let's travel back and ready ourselves for war.'

The sound of iron-shod horses clattered across the piazza. Henry and Gifford rode into the square; their horse's slow pace seemed to reflect Henry's mood.

'He doesn't look happy,' said Killbere. 'He's been gone two days.'

'Then I'll wager that means his quest for the girl was nothing more than a night phantom in his befuddled brain.' Blackstone sighed. 'He inherited too much romance from his mother. She filled his head with poetry. I swear it does no good in a world where a man must have his wits about him.'

'He's drawn to protecting the weak and those in need of help. That's what he believes. You cannot blame him for that, Thomas. You know where that comes from. He was only a boy when he tried to save Christiana and Agnes. When a boy loses his mother and sister the desire to help others stays as deep in his chest as would one of Will's bodkin points. And you cannot blame only his mother. He has your stubborn determination to go his own way.'

Blackstone pulled aside a plank in the wagon's floor. 'My path is clear. I see the way ahead. He takes so many wrong turns he lays a false trail for himself.'

'Then it's time you shared with me and the lads what we're going to do with the gold.'

Blackstone looked around the square. The towers were already casting long shadows. He had remained silent about his plans because he wanted to consider all the risks involved. 'Yes, it's time.' He looked to where Henry and Gifford had dismounted near the Prince's quarters in the town's citadel, inherited, like the town, as part of his dowry. 'Now that I know he's back and I don't have to go chasing after him.'

Killbere hawked and spat. 'There speaks a man who condemns his son at every turn.'

Blackstone clapped him on the shoulder. 'A man who vowed to the woman he loved he would keep his son from danger. Fetch our captains. It's time to go through my plan.'

Henry and Gifford plodded up the steep staircase leading to the Prince's quarters. Despenser's guards ushered them on to the fourth floor where they were told to wait by one of the captains. The Prince was being advised of how much territory he had been gifted. Most of it consisted of fertile land with ancient vineyards and crop fields. Trading in wine and grain would further increase his coffers.

After an hour of waiting Despenser came to the door, saw Henry and ushered him inside. He left the Prince and his poet-loving companion alone.

'Highness,' said Henry, bowing to the Prince, who stood at a table covered in unfurled maps with a heavy silver goblet holding each end in place.

'Master Henry!' He waved an arm, beckoning Henry to move

closer. 'You find us settled in our new home for a while. We are told Alba has one hundred towers. A surfeit of generosity from our gracious hosts.'

Henry's forced smile did not go unnoticed.

'You did not return to the abbey, so we thought you'd found the young woman and you had lingered,' said the Prince.

'It was not as I had imagined, highness.'

'Had you gone to the wrong abbey?'

'No, the woman who illuminated that manuscript was there. Everything I had been told about her was correct. A master had tutored her and her work is renowned.' He winced.

The Prince watched the younger man's discomfort. He remained silent for a moment longer, then said kindly, 'It was not to be then?'

Henry shook his head. 'She is now an old leper, and anchoress, kept in near darkness with barely enough candlelight to read holy scripture.' He paused. The image was etched on his memory. 'So bent and crippled. So lost to the world. Her beauty and her skill, both gone. I don't think she will live for much longer. Highness, I beg your forgiveness for asking you to divert from your route in order for me to seek her out.'

'You sought beauty. As do we, Master Henry. It was the correct decision. And you experienced her divine-given skill through that page of manuscript. That alone proves your quest was not in vain.'

Henry felt a surge of warmth towards the Prince, who had had his own share of despair in his young life and who was generous enough to include Henry in his passion for poetry.

The Prince's voice lifted. 'Let us discuss more of Petrarch. Come to us after compline. Our thoughts will be settled from prayers. The town asleep, the citadel free of scurrying servants. We take a light meal before retiring, and spend an hour or more finding solace and understanding in the great man's words.'

There was a timid knock on a small door behind the Prince. The Prince hesitated, raised a hand to stop Henry leaving. 'The servants. They use these stairs.'

'Highness, does Lord Despenser know about this?'

'Come!' said the Prince, beckoning whoever was on the other side of the door. 'He has a man downstairs.'

A servant entered carrying a silver tray bearing a carafe of wine and a goblet.

'Sire,' Henry said, watching the man place the tray on the side table, deferentially keeping his eyes lowered. 'Has this wine been tasted?'

The servant bowed and left the room.

'Your concern is touching. To ease your apprehension, the answer is yes. The stairs run directly from the kitchens to our quarters. There are no other rooms leading off these stairs. Our cupbearer and chamberlain taste my food and drink in the kitchen. Despenser's man guards the bottom door and he lets the servants through.' He smiled. 'We are as cautious as is possible. Life is not without risk, Master Henry.' Again the pause that expressed the Prince's compassion. 'As you well know. Now. After compline, you will share some time with us and we can also discuss how you are to act as tutor for our Lady Violante.'

Henry bowed his head. The Prince's generosity and compassion had eased the mixed emotions of humiliation and bitter loss. 'I look forward to it, highness. Thank you for your kindness.'

Blackstone's captains sat hunched in a semi-circle, facing him, their backs against the duomo's crypt walls. The darkness was lit by lanterns. The caskets of gold sat like an altar between Blackstone and the men: Killbere, William Ashford, Meulon, Will Longdon, the Gascon Aicart, John Jacob and Renfred. They had completed the tasks Blackstone had set them when they first arrived in the city.

'John, you have the chain?'

The sturdy man nodded. 'Yes, Sir Thomas. A blacksmith cut it into manageable lengths as you asked.'

'William?'

'I have the clothes you wanted. Poor quality, but they will fit. A washerwoman rid them of lice. She pounded so hard for the single denier I gave her – had I given her more the cloth would have been in shreds. You asked me to choose one of my men to take with me, wherever that is to be. I'll take Bullard. He's strong, dependable and doesn't talk a lot.'

'Renfred? You found a sturdy beast to haul the cart?' said Blackstone.

'There's a slaughterhouse at the far end of the city. Easy to find when the wind blows. I bought an ox. Saved it from the knife. It'll be grateful enough to haul anything you want day and night.' He grinned. 'It's in a stable in the next piazza. I've paid a stable lad to watch it.'

Blackstone looked at Meulon, who nodded.

'We found a carpenter. It was difficult to convince him. But he was happy to be paid. We had no idea what size to ask for.'

'I said we should have paid for a bigger size,' said Longdon. 'If we could have put Meulon inside, then anyone could have fitted, but this oaf was too superstitious.'

'It's bad luck to measure a man for a coffin before he needs it,' said Meulon.

'But we could have kept it for when you did,' Longdon insisted.

'Did you get one?' said Blackstone patiently, looking at the two men, so opposite in stature.

'We did,' said Longdon. 'We thought that the length should be determined by picking out a man on the street and the width that of a man who enjoyed meat and wine in excess. A short broad coffin.'

'Then we have almost everything we need,' said Blackstone. 'The chain goes into the boxes that hold the gold. The gold goes in the wagon's false floor. The Prince's personal effects were there during the journey. It's padded and lined in leather. We pack it with straw, then nail down the planks. We use one chest with enough gold coin covering the chain to fool any inspection. There have been enough prying eyes since Milan to know that I escort the gold in the chests on the mules. If there's to be any attack, it will come to me.'

Ashford looked at Blackstone. 'Then me and Bullard are to be dressed as villeins. What do I tell Bullard?'

'I'll have a document written in Latin. It will be meaningless. Information that I believe the conflict in Italy will worsen and that we should keep an eye on the French gathering their forces while I am here. My son will write it. It is something that, should the worst happen, can be surrendered. We'll conceal it beneath the coffin.'

'So, I'm to carry a dead man in the back of the wagon?'

'A body we have yet to find,' said Renfred.

Blackstone looked at the Gascon, Aicart. 'I gave you the task. Discretion was needed. Do we have a body?'

'It was not easy, Sir Thomas. People cling to their dead as surely as if they were alive. I was fearful that I would not find one but then I came across a small church where some villeins had gathered there to hear prayers being said by the priest over a labourer who had fallen while repairing a roof. He had no family. I paid the priest. We packed him in salt and bound him in cloth. If we take the wagon to the back of the church we can put him in the coffin.'

'Then we're ready,' said Blackstone. He addressed Ashford. 'William, you and Bullard are returning pilgrims and pilgrims are afforded safe passage by Knights of the Tau from Lucca. You'll travel on the Via Francigena. You go south for the coast route. Then on to Lucca. The Knights of Tau will be on the road. They align themselves with Florence. And Florence is where you'll take the gold. Twelve or fourteen days and it will be safe. Once you have delivered the gold you'll be given good horses. Make your way to Bologna. It's held by the papal forces. We'll meet there and then return to France where we are needed.'

The men's surprise was obvious.

Killbere spoke for them all. 'Thomas, this is gold for the fight in France. We're tasked with getting it back across the Alps and into the Treasury. You send it, unescorted, to Florence?'

'I decided we cannot risk the journey home. We are too few. The road too dangerous. I was uncertain how to get the gold back safely. The journey to Florence is a hundred and fifty miles closer than going back to Bordeaux. When we were with Montferrat, I sent a messenger to Father Torellini and the Bardi Bank in Florence. They support the King's wars and when they have the gold, they will issue letters of credit. The King and Prince Edward will have the money they need for the conflict that's coming. As William and Bullard play their part, we will travel this side of the mountains. It's open ground. If there's to be a fight, that's where it will happen. There is to be no word of this to the men. As far as anyone is concerned we carry the gold on the mules. Start loading it into saddlebags and transfer it to the wagon.'

The men were silent as they stood. He looked at each in turn. 'We place ourselves between the Prince's gold and anyone who desires to take it.'

'Then yet again we are to be the bait,' said Longdon with his broken-tooth grin.

'Would we have it any other way?' said Killbere.

The men stood and filed out to finish what had to be done. Killbere held back. His sombre mood was for his friend.

'Thomas, you are risking everything.'

'I know, Gilbert. But everyone knows I accompany the gold. That's what they believe. Don't you think word has already flown from Milan? And from here? Bernabò is out there waiting.'

'And he'll want the Visconti gold back,' said Killbere.

'We head north towards Verona.'

'We'll draw della Scala to us.'

'And see if the Pope's ally plays a treacherous game.' Blackstone grasped his friend's shoulder. 'And if he seeks overall power here. He will be more dangerous than Bernabò.

CHAPTER FORTY-EIGHT

Henry and Gifford saw no sign of Blackstone and the captains as they made their way to the stables.

'I'll get us food from the kitchens,' said Gifford.

Henry strode across the piazza. The light was fading. The lanterns glowing from the stables offered a welcome sanctuary from the turmoil of the past few days. At least, he thought, he was still in favour with the Prince. That would take his thoughts away from the disappointment and his sense of failure.

Both horses had been unsaddled, and each given a feed bag by stable hands. Henry laid out his own and Gifford's bedroll and blanket across a bed of dry hay. As he crouched to fuss over the bedding, he saw a figure approaching half in shadow further down the stalls. Henry's sword belt lay next to his blanket. He reached for his knife. If the figure who was coming his way was an enemy, the knife would prevail better than a sword in the narrow confines of the stable. He stood, using Gifford's horse next to his to block him from being seen. He peered across the horse's withers. The figure stooped, as if looking for someone. Every few strides, he would bend and peer between the horses. He was no stable hand. Young. An easy gait. Not as tall as

Henry, who ducked and crawled back under his own mount so that the first bedroll the stranger saw would be Gifford's.

Henry edged closer, a hand soothing his horse's rear leg, steadying any nervousness. The figure reached Gifford's mount, saw the bedroll, and stooped low. Henry stepped out, grabbed the man's shoulder and had his knife point at his throat.

He gasped. 'Stefano!'

The terrified youth stumbled back the moment Henry released him. Henry raised a palm to reassure him. He had last seen Isabella's trusted servant back in Milan, and now he was here. Henry's surprise caught him off guard. 'The Lady Isabella is here in Alba?'

The trembling youth clasped his hands across his midriff. He bowed, raised his head, shook it and, swallowing hard, gasped that she was not. Henry took him by the arm, guiding him to sit on an upturned rundlet. He reached for his wineskin and offered it to him. Stefano took a mouthful, swallowed and wiped his mouth with the back of his hand. Now he was calmer, he peered up at Henry, who loomed over him. Henry pulled up another rundlet rather than intimidate him.

'How long have you been here?' he asked.

'I came yesterday.' Stefano looked over his shoulder, still nervous. 'I beg your forgiveness, Master Henry. I did not wish to alarm you.'

Henry smiled. Stefano had been the one who had been alarmed. 'I am cautious, Stefano. I can't be too careful when I am in a city once ruled by the Visconti. Why are you here?'

'I serve my Lady Isabella.'

'Yes, I know that,' said Henry, forcing patience into his voice. 'But why are you here?'

'She sent me to you.'

Henry waited. Perhaps the lad would only respond to one question at a time. Would it help to prompt him further? 'Then why did she send you? To give me a message?'

'Yes. Exactly, Master Henry.'

Henry waited. There was nothing more forthcoming. 'Now is a good time to tell me.'

Stefano swallowed, eyes fixed on Henry's face, focusing to aid his memory of the message he had to remember. 'My Lady Isabella remembered you asking about the illuminatrix. She has thought more about it. It was the name Elena that you gave her. My lady thinks you didn't hear correctly when you were told to guard her.'

'I don't understand,' said Henry. His chest was tight again, just as it had been when he searched out the monastery. 'There was a woman. Her name I thought to be Elena. Events proved otherwise. What is it I have not understood?'

'My lady says you speak our language with great skill, but she asks if it is possible that you did not hear the request as the man who gave it intended.'

Henry thought of the dying assassin who'd lain in his arms. His rasping breath, those last words. 'What does your mistress think I did not understand?'

'The message you were given. Did the man say "*guardala*", that you should protect this woman, Elena, or is it possible that you heard the word "*garda*"?'

In his mind's eye, Henry saw and heard Salvarini give the warning. To go to where the woman he was seeking was being held by those who had sent him, the assassin, to kill the Prince. Salvarini had used his desperate search for the illuminatrix to send him to find a different woman. The old man had used his dying breath to save someone else. A woman called Elena.

'It's possible I did not hear him say "*guardala*",' Henry admitted, realizing that he had been fooled – blinded by his own desire at the time.

Stefano nodded. 'Then, Master Henry, would he be telling you to go to Garda? The lake? Could that be it?'

'Yes.'

'Then my mistress remembered a lady by the name Elena, not

yet betrothed, held against her will in the great *castello* at the lake. Her family have been stripped of their title and lands with barely a servant remaining, forced into impoverishment by the Lord of Verona.'

Henry's throat dried. 'Cansignorio della Scala.'

Salvarini. Who was he? A remaining loyal servant obeying a tyrant in an attempt to save a helpless young woman? Sent by that tyrant to assassinate the Prince?

Stefano watched Henry.

'Have I done as my lady asked?'

Henry nodded. 'No one could have done it better. Return tomorrow and give my thanks to your lady. You have served her better than any other.'

Stefano's face beamed at the compliment. 'I am instructed not to return to her if you don't know the route.'

'Then you know the way?'

Stefano nodded.

Henry pulled the boy's hand towards him and pressed his purse into it. Then he closed the servant's fingers over the offering. 'This is my reward. You have also done me a great service. Now, find a tavern and eat and drink, and tomorrow meet me here. Understand?'

Stefano nodded obediently. He stood and bowed and went into the piazza, turned a corner and was gone from Henry's sight. Henry considered what course of action to take. To ride off at first light for where the Scaligeri castles braced both shores of Lake Garda would further inflame his father's anger. To go to him and explain the mistake about what he thought he had heard made him look more foolish than the quest he had undertaken. But not to tell his father about the della Scala plot? That might invite disaster. He thought of the Prince. Despenser needed to be told. If Henry's suspicions were correct, the Lord of Verona had sent Salvarini to assassinate the Prince in the monastery.

Gifford arrived with bread and meat. Henry's look of concern was plain to see. 'What?'

'Leave the food, Hugh. Find my father.'

Gifford put down the food on the rundlet. 'What's wrong?'

'I have important information. I must find Lord Despenser.'
He strode out into the piazza.

'Is there nothing more I can tell him?' he called.

Henry turned. 'Find him!'

And then he ran.

CHAPTER FORTY-NINE

As Henry turned the corner to the Prince's lodgings, he heard the dull thump of a door banging in the night breeze. It was the citadel's kitchen door, which opened onto a side street. Instinct made him turn for it. The narrow passage was empty. Whatever activity remained in the city was confined to the piazzas and they were mostly empty as the citizens returned to their homes and prepared to attend to their prayers.

Henry ventured into the kitchen's entrance. There was supposed to be a guard at this door and another at the base of the rear stairs. The dull light inside the kitchen flickered with shadows from a cooking fire. Fat dripped hissing into the fire from the spit. Pots bubbled. Steam rose. Evening prayer would have reduced the number of servants but it should not be this empty. Knife in hand, he ventured further. The darkness deepened. He strained his eyes. His foot caught on a body on the floor and he lurched back. Two men. One of them Despenser's, the other a servant, his grease-smeared leather apron telling Henry he worked in the kitchen. Ignoring the failing light, he strode ahead to where the stairs would be. A dogleg turn, the steep narrow steps illuminated by wall sconces. More than enough light to see the sprawled body of the second of Despenser's men. Henry scrambled over him and pounded up the twisting stairs, shoulder banging on the stone wall at every turn. A coiled, fear-gripped choking ascent, lungs heaving.

The Prince's rear door was open. Desperate to ensure the Prince's safety, he went straight into the room. Warm pockets of candlelight spread their glow into the corners of the room. The Prince lay on his bed, convulsing. Mouth wide, struggling for breath, eyes staring in horror. Specks of foam spurting from his mouth. Henry strode across the room to him. A shadow came from one side and struck him hard. The blow glanced off his shoulder. The pain spurred him to raise an arm, pivot and strike out blindly. His arm was knocked away by his assailant. A masked figure, fast on his feet. Henry blocked the attack, an attempt to grip his throat. Henry grasped the arm with one hand as he tried to plunge his knife into his attacker. The man's weight shifted, allowing his arm to tighten around Henry's neck. The stench of the man's stale sweat filled his nostrils. Henry twisted free, his knife arcing towards the assailant. A leather-clad cosh swung again. Henry hadn't moved quickly enough. The left-handed blow caught him by surprise and hit the side of his head. Henry staggered. The assassin ran. The entire attack had taken place in silence.

He lunged for the Prince, throwing his weight across his body, trying to stop his body from arching. His foot caught a small table. It fell over, tumbling a silver platter of food and a goblet of wine onto the floor. Moments after, guards hammered at the Prince's door, demanding if all was well.

'Here!' Henry called. His voice hoarse, groggy from the blow.

The locked door gave way under a guard's shoulder. They stormed into the room. One of them punched Henry on the nape of his neck, two more dragged him to the floor. More guards were pounding up the main staircase.

Henry heard muted shouts as he slipped towards

unconsciousness, a part of him instinctively curling to protect himself from the flurry of blows and kicks.

And then he fell into the silent void.

A cool, wet cloth dabbed his face. He hurt. His ribs felt bruised. It was painful to breathe. He coughed, his hand finding that of the person bathing his face. His gambeson had been removed, his shirt had been opened, as if someone had examined his injuries. He saw Gifford's face staring down at him. His guardian dabbed more dried blood from Henry's scalp.

Henry focused. Where was he? It felt like a monk's cell. Bare walls. A candle on a small wooden table. He tried to remember what had happened.

'Where am I?' he said, his throat dry.

'Drink,' said Gifford, easing Henry's shoulders from the cot he lay on. He trickled wine from a clay flask between his lips.

Henry raised a hand. It was enough. Gifford laid him back down. 'They think you poisoned the Prince. Despenser had you thrown into this cell. Sir Thomas is with him now. And if Despenser does not see reason, then I fear your father will attack him. Him, a knight of the realm. That's why he sent me to you. I'm here to cover your arse again, Master Henry, in case we all end up at the end of a rope.'

Henry's eyes cleared. He focused on the door. The grated iron cage showed him two of Despenser's men sitting on stools beneath wall sconces. One guard tore apart a piece of bread from a loaf and dipped it into his clay beaker. Both of the men were watching Gifford's ministrations.

Blackstone and Killbere faced Despenser in the Prince's quarters. His body had been removed by the monks from the Duomo di San Lorenzo. Lines were etched on the knight's grim countenance. The Prince had died while under his care.

'You know damned well my son caused no harm to the Prince.'

'And yet he was found trying to smother the Prince! It was only the servants who knew of that staircase and yet your son used it to reach the Prince. Why wouldn't he have used that door?' Despenser insisted, pointing to where the guards had broken into the room. 'Since we left Paris, your son has been continually in the Prince's presence.'

'He saved his life on Mont Cenis!'

'Or so he claims! What if the old man stopped *him* from attacking the Prince?'

Blackstone took a threatening step towards Despenser, but Killbere blocked him.

'My Lord Despenser, you accuse the son of the King's Master of War,' said Killbere. 'You have no evidence. Even a blind man can see he came across the assassin and tried to stop him.'

'Did he? I am not convinced,' said Despenser. Tempers were running high, constrained for the time being, but it would take only a spark of ill-chosen words to ignite violence.

'What reason would my son have to kill the Prince? He was devoted to him. They shared their love of poetry. The Prince gave him leave to look for a woman he sought. He even had you change the route to this place.'

'And does that not show your son's cunning? To insinuate himself with the Prince? To gain his trust? There was no woman! It was a feint. A way to contact an accomplice who helped poison the Prince. Him and the Visconti!'

Spittle flecked from Despenser's anger.

'Merciful Christ,' said Blackstone. 'Have you lost your mind? The Visconti needed this marriage. They wanted an alliance with Edward! Why would they kill him? For what purpose?'

'To stop the alliance. To seize back the gold. It is not Galeazzo I have in mind, but his brother. You remember that, don't you, Blackstone? Can you forget Bernabò's hatred for you, your family and the English? He's done it before. The French Princess? We know he had a servant try to poison her.'

'And I stopped it.'

'And a wolf never changes. Now he plunges the knife of discontent into his brother's back. He seizes the day.'

Blackstone's voice became calm, reasoned – full of menace. 'You harm my son, Lord Despenser, and you will know why our King chose me as his Master of War.'

Killbere's gnarled fist gripped Blackstone's arm. He saw the cold fury. He whispered, 'Thomas. He has no proof. He cannot harm Henry. Step back from this.'

Blackstone gave him an accusing look, as if Killbere had betrayed him.

Killbere smiled. 'Because if he did, he would feel my blade through his throat.' And with that, he turned his glare on the esteemed knight, Edward Despenser.

Despenser was no coward. He saw the moment needed to be won without bloodshed.

'Your son conspired with a Visconti spy. He rode into the city yesterday. He waited and spoke to your son in the stables. Stable hands witnessed this. We believe your son took from him the poison sent by Bernabò Visconti. This spy then went to a tavern using money given to him by your son. Money, we suspect, paid for delivering the poison. The evidence mounts against him, Blackstone. Justice must be done.'

'Where is this spy?'

'Captured, tortured and confessed.'

'I'll speak to him,' said Blackstone.

'He succumbed to the pain.'

'So there is no evidence.'

Despenser remained silent.

'Then my son's life is in your hands and you will have to explain to the King how his son came to murdered. An explanation good enough to satisfy him why you could not protect him.'

Despenser was no fool. He saw the predicament that the Prince's death placed him in. If, however, Blackstone's son *was* innocent, and had tried to save the Prince, then Despenser could suggest that he had allowed Henry Blackstone to stay close to the Prince as an added precaution. A decision that could have saved the Prince's life.

'And once you decide, what will you do next?' said Blackstone.

'We must accord a prince of the realm the highest dignity in death. Pavia is close. He will be taken there. It is Galeazzo's city. Until we can arrange his body to be returned to England, he will be buried in the Chiesa di San Pietro in Ciel d'Oro. It is a renowned place of worship.

'And Bernabò?'

'I take the field and join forces with the Pope's men against him.'

'Then I must do what I came here to do and escort the gold,' said Blackstone.

'A long and dangerous journey back to England.'

Blackstone didn't contradict him. 'And I will need every man. Including my son.'

Despenser walked the knife edge of decision. Blackstone was an adversary he would prefer not to have. And even though most of Blackstone's men were outside the walls, they would fall on his own men, commoner and nobleman alike, if they were given the order.

'Then let us speak to him and hear his version of events.'

Henry Blackstone was on his feet in the cell as he faced Despenser. Blackstone and Killbere stood behind Despenser. Gifford waited outside the cell, holding Henry's gambeson. It was obvious Henry had taken a beating. He explained everything that had happened from when he left the Prince, and of the invitation to return. He explained Stefano's role. That his mistress Isabella had sent news of where the real woman he sought was being held.

'You say he confessed?' said Henry.

'He did. That you conspired together to kill the Prince. That he brought you poison. That he would help you eliminate the guards.'

'It saddens me he suffered such great pain,' said Henry. 'What man wouldn't confess to stop the agony? He was nothing more than a simple boy. Lady Isabella trusted him completely. She sent him to guide me to where the woman I'm still looking for is held. That is all. You have caused the death of an innocent. I was coming to warn you before I saw the guard was not at his post at the kitchen door. I believe Cansignorio della Scala planned and executed the assassination. That is the link between what happened here and at Mont Cenis.'

'The Lord of Verona? Another illusion,' said Despenser.

'There was a message intercepted by Montferrat on our way to Milan. Sent by the French,' said Blackstone. 'We believed that the message was intended for the Scaligeri. Perhaps, Lord Despenser, you should heed the information. The evidence is mounting against della Scala.'

'He is an ally,' said Despenser. 'He fights Bernabò.'

'We think he is bought and paid for by the French,' said Killbere. 'The skinners who attacked us at Milan were paid with Veronese coin.'

'It serves della Scala to have you believe it was Bernabò Visconti,' said Blackstone. 'The numbers against Bernabò increase with your men. The division splits Galeazzo from his brother. The Visconti are weakened. They start to lose territory. Domains that della Scala wants.'

Despenser fell silent in thought. He raised his eyes to Henry Blackstone.

'I did not kill the Prince, my Lord Despenser. I tried to save him. Stefano was innocent. The assassin is already long gone. And I question why the assassin spared my life. I would have killed him had I the chance. He was strong and quick on his feet. I was not fast enough. Why did he only strike me down? The only purpose that serves is for it to be thought that I was responsible for the Prince's death.'

Despenser's eyes betrayed his conflicted thoughts.

'Why leave me alive otherwise?' said Henry.

Blackstone stepped forward so that he could face Despenser. 'Think back. The French send a letter warning that I am in Italy. The root of this evil lies with them. If della Scala has created division on the orders of the French, then whoever conspired to kill the Prince wanted to weaken our King. Weaken a warrior king with grief, have the gold seized, and then go to war. See this for what it is.'

Despenser still seemed uncertain. But then he surrendered. He nodded his head and turned on his heel.

'I have matters to attend to. Do your duty, Sir Thomas. Safeguard the gold. I release your son to your care.'

The guards followed Despenser, scuffing up the stone staircase.

Blackstone looked his son up and down. 'Well, you did your best to save him.'

Henry's smile said differently. His best was not good enough. As usual, his thoughts added.

Blackstone sighed. 'So, there's a woman involved after all. And you believe she needs rescuing.' He glanced at Killbere.

'Not for the first time, Thomas,' said Killbere, with a knowing smile.

Blackstone remembered when he was a sixteen-year-old archer who rescued the young girl, Christiana, from a castle in another place, in another time.

Blackstone lifted aside Henry's open shirt. 'Your ribs are bruised. Nothing more. Can you ride?'

'I can.'

'Then you expect me to give you permission to seek out this woman you believe is being held against her will?'

'A man's dying words. A man who sacrificed himself. Yes. I understand now what he was asking of me, but Lord Despenser killed my guide. I don't know the way.'

'I do,' said Blackstone. He placed a hand on his son's shoulder. 'You offered your life for the Prince. No man can ask anything more of another. Sleep now, and rest. Rise at first light. I have a letter I need writing. We leave together at sunrise.' He turned away and then thought better of it. Turning back to face his son, he said, 'I'm proud of you.'

Henry watched as his father left the cell. Killbere lingered a moment longer. His smile and the nod of his head meant more than any words.

Gifford waited at the cell door as Killbere went past him.

'Get him some food. Make him rest,' said Killbere. 'This is one night he won't be chasing tavern whores. Given young Henry's taste for trouble, a brawl over a whore would not please Sir Thomas.'

Killbere made for the stairs.

Gifford looked at Henry.

'I hope he's right,' said Gifford, throwing Henry's gambeson to him. 'Horseshit draws flies as surely as you attract danger.'

'It's not over yet, Hugh.'

Gifford sighed. 'I know.'

CHAPTER FIFTY

They left at dawn. As they crossed the bridge Blackstone tossed three of the chest keys into the river. The fourth was tied with cord beneath his shirt. The creaking ox-drawn wagon went ahead of the men. William Ashford and Bullard would share the walking duties alongside the beast yoked to the wagon. Four miles beyond Alba, Ashford guided the wagon bearing the vital gold hidden beneath the corpse's coffin onto a southern route, heading for the coast.

Blackstone and the men rode on. He watched the wagon turn.

'We should have had a priest say a prayer for its safe delivery,' said Killbere. 'My bowels quiver at the thought of that gold leaving our care.'

'William served the King before me. He knows the risk. He can deal with any challenge. There are places they can stop along the way and enough pilgrims on the route going in both directions.'

'Another mystery I have yet to understand. Why take a damned long trek across mountains, facing all that nature can throw at you, to try and find salvation? I'll bend the knee to be shriven, but then I'll find salvation with an accommodating nun. That's the best kind of religion for a man.'

'I was thinking of asking you to accompany the gold.'

Killbere's shock and disgust silenced him. He gagged as he tried to find a response.

Blackstone continued. 'You would enjoy a quiet journey along with all the other pilgrims seeking redemption for their souls. No fighting along the way. Father Torellini's men waiting to escort you into the city. A city renowned for beautiful women.'

Killbere raised a hand to stop the provocation. 'God's tears, Thomas. You insult me. Flay me alive rather. That I should dress as a common peasant, stripped of your blazon, defenceless. You would heap such shame upon me?'

The wagon disappeared from view. Blackstone turned in the saddle. The men behind him had also kept their gaze on Ashford and Bullard's departure.

'Don't worry, Gilbert. If anything happens to that gold, I'll be the one wearing a common man's garb. I'll be the one stripped of my privileges given by the King and Prince Edward. You're right. I'm taking a dangerous risk.'

Killbere let the creak of saddles and jostling bridles comfort his thoughts. 'Thomas, we are few and we're setting ourselves on the road to draw out an enemy, whether it be the Visconti or della Scala. We can be sure of one thing. They will be in far greater numbers than we few have ever faced. The further we go carrying those chests, the more chance William has of reaching Torellini. Your decision was correct. And if they strip you of honours and privileges, well, then I... I will be with you.'

'And wear common garb?' said Blackstone.

'No, Thomas, I will visit you in prison.' He guffawed so that the bastard horse swung its head and tried to bite his mount. He shook his head and blew snot from each nostril. 'What chance do you think we have? We'll likely be dead long before the gold gets to Florence. And if it doesn't? It will be no concern of ours.'

'You're a comfort, Gilbert.'

'I am known for it.'

Blackstone spurred his horse. 'Then let's close the distance between here and whoever's waiting to seize our precious cargo.'

The first two days revealed no threat. Renfred and his scouts rode in long looping searches ahead of Blackstone's men. By the third day, they had reached Piacenza. Blackstone instructed the men to encamp outside the city walls while he approached the guards at the city's main gate.

The guard commander stepped towards him, arm raised, but retreated as the bastard horse lunged its head towards his outstretched hand.

Blackstone tightened the rein. 'Send word to your *podestà* that Sir Thomas Blackstone wishes to enter the city for the night.'

'You have business here, Sir Thomas?'

'None that concerns you. I am passing through. I'll bring in several men with me. I'll need stabling and lodgings. See to it.'

He turned the bastard horse back to where the men hobbled their horses and prepared for the night ahead.

'I'll wager the authorities know damned well why we're on the road,' said Killbere.

'And once they see those mules, they'll know for sure,' said John Jacob.

'That serves our purpose,' said Blackstone. 'You and John with me inside the walls. We take Henry and Gifford with us. Mallin and Terrel to tend the horses. Who else?'

'Meulon and Bezián, in case there's any trouble,' said Killbere.

'That'll do,' said Blackstone. 'We flood the streets with any more armed men and they'll have extra guards watching us. See to it, John. And we double the pickets from now on when we camp.'

John Jacob wheeled his horse.

Blackstone and Killbere dismounted and walked their horses further from the men.

'You're worried,' said Killbere. 'It won't help.'

'The first three days on the route south to the coast are the most difficult for William and Bullard. Once they get to the sea, the road is easier. Ten more days and they'll be under escort at Lucca.'

Blackstone looked beyond Piacenza's walls.

'And what of our way ahead?' said Killbere. 'That's where we must put our thoughts. Renfred hasn't returned.'

Blackstone nodded. 'He'll scout as far as he can. There are two armies out there, and we have to make sure we meet the right one. Bernabò's or della Scala's. We turn north tomorrow towards Verona. We have the mountains at our back. It's the open ground that poses the greater risk.'

Blackstone knew that ahead of them Bernabò Visconti's army would be striking key places held by the papal forces. Roving bands of Cansignorio della Scala's troops would be skirmishing, laying ambushes and trying to draw Visconti into a place where he might be overwhelmed. Two dangerous men vying for control over swathes of territory. Each as vicious as the other. Both having murdered their own blood to secure their authority.

'I know you, Thomas. You gave in too quickly to Henry in agreeing to go after this woman.'

'You think he knows why?'

'Sometimes men who have great learning, an education from the finest universities, are as dense as cow shit.'

Blackstone smiled. 'My son is stupid?'

'No, his desire to help those in need blinds him. Especially if it's a woman. That is where his thoughts lie. He's not looking beyond that. We head towards the Scaligeri bastards rather than the Visconti bastards because we believe Cansignorio della Scala sent an assassin to kill the Prince. And if he's supposed to be an ally of the Pope and against the Visconti, then he will believe we go to him for protection. For the gold. And if my thinking continues along this twisting route, then we will get close to the girl and perhaps, God willing, kill the bastard.'

Blackstone smiled. 'And we need no education to kill those who cause us harm.'

CHAPTER FIFTY-ONE

Blackstone followed the city guards into the piazza, where the *podestà* waited with several other officials flanked by guards. The welcoming committee was to show his status and had little to do with honouring Blackstone. Like every other city, such officials were often outsiders, men voted for by the city's council to bring impartiality to the governing of the city.

A page stepped forward, bowed and addressed Blackstone. 'My lord, Signor Corrado, the *podestà* of Piacenza at the service of the Commune.'

The senior figure, dressed in flowing robes of blue and red embroidered with silk, bowed as Blackstone brought his horse to a halt. He looked down at the flock of peacock-dressed officials. The *podestà*'s gold medallion of office swung free; he grabbed it with his free hand, the other held a staff of office.

'Sir Thomas Blackstone, we are humbled by your visit to our city. We are here to accommodate your needs. How may we be of service?'

Blackstone eyed the city councillors. He wondered where the *podestà*'s home province might have been. Piacenza was neutral in the Visconti conflict. For as long as it suited them, that is. Blackstone suspected that the man governing the city was likely to have once been the Visconti's choice to govern here. That fact posed no threat. If it was true, it added to Blackstone's hope that news of his journey bearing the gold was already being spread far and wide.

'I need secure stabling for our horses and a cargo we're carrying,' said Blackstone, feeding the lie about the gold.

'It has already been arranged,' said the *podestà*. 'Accommodation is provided for you and your...' He glanced nervously at the unsmiling men who stared down at him.

'My men stay with their horses. We pay for food and drink. A bed and a meal for me and Sir Gilbert Killbere, who rides at my side.'

The *podestà* bowed again. One councillor took the hint from his brief glance and ordered two of the guards to lead the way to the stables.

'We appreciate your generosity, Signor Corrado,' said Blackstone, and followed the guards. They were led across two different piazzas towards a smaller *campo* where stable hands and a farrier lived in houses alongside the yard.

'You could almost see the spittle running into his beard,' said Killbere. 'He was salivating, wanting to know what our cargo is.'

'Good. Let them suspect what we carry. We'll see what approaches are made once we are settled at the inn.'

Mallin glanced uncertainly at Terrel as the two men brought up the rear. Terrel was checking the houses and side streets. Piacenza might be the one place he could put his escape into action. The River Po lay to the north. How far was that from where they had entered the city? The river carried barges and boats. Trade went up- and downstream, and Piacenza was on the main trading route. Instead of trying to slip away from Blackstone and the men on a horse, a boat would carry him further afield in better time.

'Do you have lice in your braies? What are you looking for? You think we're going to be ambushed here? Would Sir Thomas bring us into such a place if it wasn't safe?'

Terrel's lie slipped easily from his lips. 'I'm looking to see if anyone is watching us. What people see, they can sell to those who might be interested.'

'For pity's sake, Terrel, there are none here with the wit to suspect what we carry. They might like to know, given they are poor wretches trapped in their lives in this *campo*. Little more than villeins.'

The wood and stone stable had a gap wide enough to accommodate double doors had there been any. Its open-fronted entrance led into a space that could take in twenty horses, with tie rings in the wall on both left and right: one of many modestly sized stables scattered around the city. The stable hands ran out to take care of the horses. Blackstone issued a warning about his horse, telling them it must be kept separate from the others. He steered it into the stables, dismounted and followed a small boy to where his horse would be kept. Blackstone secured a rope halter over its misshapen head and ran its length through the wall's tie ring. For once, the belligerent beast made no objection and allowed him to remove the bridle and bit. Blackstone remained wary. It would not be the first time the horse conceived in hell had lured him into a false sense of security. He unsaddled the beast and edged around the back of the horse. As far as it could, it swung its head to watch him. It waited until he was almost clear and then lashed out with its hind leg.

Blackstone was quick enough to sidestep, cursing the wilful animal.

'One day that beast will kill you,' said Killbere, walking to where Blackstone backed away.

'Given the choice he'd prefer to bite and kick our enemies, Gilbert. If we're in a fight, I'll take him over any other war horse. The men are settled?'

'Aye, just waiting your orders.'

Blackstone went to where the men had arranged their mounts, boxing in the mules bearing the chests.

'Do we leave the mules loaded, Sir Thomas?'

'There are enough of us here to ease their burden, John. They need food and drink like the rest of us. Make sure there are always two men watching through the night. Henry, you and Gifford take your watch around the streets here. Not far, just enough to see if anyone is gathering who might have violence on their mind.'

Henry nodded. 'There'll be a night watch.'

'Even so. Best we keep our own eyes open. John, you and the others stay here. Sir Gilbert and I are at the inn. There'll be people interested in what we carry. Keep anyone asking at bay. We'll see who shares our lodgings. If I'm right, then word has already flown from Milan. Those who are interested will want to make sure. We'll keep them guessing. I'll have food sent here for you all.'

'We need to replenish all the men's wineskins,' said John Jacob.

'Very well.' He looked to where Mallin and Terrel were carefully lying out their saddles into the straw, a ready pillow for the night ahead.

'Walter, you'll check the mules. We don't want any of them going lame or getting sores from the weight of the chests. Terrel, once Mallin has done that you go with him and buy three firkins of wine. John will give you money. The stables will have a handcart.'

'Aye, Sir Thomas,' said Mallin.

'You can manage to haul a cart?' said Blackstone, wondering for a moment if he was asking too much of the older man.

'No need for insult, Sir Thomas. I'm not a one-armed man with a broken leg needing a crutch.'

Blackstone apologized and made an excuse to ease the insult. 'I meant no such thing, Walter. I was thinking it might prove awkward to manage the three, even with two men pushing. They'll be heavy.'

'That is why I have Terrel with me. He's stronger than he looks.'

Terrel looked put upon but had to smile like the others. 'Where would Walter be without me at his side?' he said.

'A happier place,' said Bezián, causing a ripple of laughter among the men.

Mallin stepped closer. 'You jest at his expense, Arnald, but he helps do what must be done to care for Sir Thomas's horses. And your horse. He might lift and carry for me but if you wish to take his place, then I'll see how long you last without complaint, squatting in horse shit and scraping it from their hooves. A horse goes lame, you walk. Remember that.'

Bezián was suitably admonished. He raised a hand in surrender.

'Then once you're ready, Walter, you and Terrel go and buy the wine,' said Blackstone. He and Killbere walked into the square. At a respectful distance, two of the guards remained waiting to escort them to the inn.

'Old Walter might not have many teeth, Thomas, but he can give a nasty suck when it's needed.'

Once Mallin was satisfied the mules showed no sign of injury or weakness, he and Terrel ventured into the city. Terrel dragged the small two-wheel handcart. Cluttered houses, as in all walled cities, pressed close together, throwing shadows into narrow streets and passageways.

'You should not let the men speak to you with disrespect,' he said to Terrel as they left the *campo* and took a passage leading to a piazza.

'They have always thought ill of me. Especially Bezián.'

'Ignore him. All of them. Stand and face them. You've proved yourself on this journey. There are dead men lying on a mountain pass, food for crows, because you killed them. Drunk or not, those bastards could have got the better of you.'

Terrel strode north. Had anyone suspected how he had stumbled on those men and how they had been killed? Skinners so drunk they were barely able to stand. He knew Killbere doubted what had happened.

'There are times I don't want to argue,' he said. 'It doesn't take much for men's tempers to rise. Then a knife in hand kills one man or the other. I just want an easier life with less bad blood.'

Mallin was keeping pace as best he could, one hand on the cart's side. 'What's the hurry?'

Terrel wanted to reach the river before dark. Securing passage on a barge either up- or downstream depended on there being daylight before bargemen pulled their boats ashore for the night. There was still enough daylight left for him to get hours away from Piacenza and Blackstone's desire to entice men to come for the gold they carried.

'We must find wine-sellers before it's dark. Better we stay in the open piazzas, and it's safer,' said Terrel. He could taste the freedom that lay at the edge of the city. The gold florin he had tucked away would buy more than escape. Whatever destination beckoned once he'd reached the river, the gold would buy him lodgings and a woman to care for him. By the time he'd spent it all, he would be wearing finer clothes and have secured employment that did not demand riding with battle-hungry men.

'There'll be no tavern willing to sell us wine there,' Mallin complained. 'What are you thinking? We should look in some of those side streets before curfew is called. That's where we'll find the wine for the best price.'

Terrel, unwilling to show his true intention, agreed. 'Then let's go as far as we can, staying in the open, and work our way back. I'd feel safer doing that, wouldn't you?'

Mallin begrudgingly agreed, but there was something about Terrel's haste that caused him to suspect he was being led in a direction that suited Terrel. And as they concentrated on finding their way through unfamiliar streets both failed to see the two rough-looking men following them.

⋆

Killbere sniffed the cooked pork on his eating knife. 'It smells better dead than alive, Thomas. They cook food differently here. This is good.' He shoved a large piece into his mouth, chewing happily.

Blackstone bent to his own food. Their table at the inn was well placed to view the rest of the room. Smoke clung to the ceiling from the tallow candles. Men ate and drank. All of them looked to be passing through the city. There were those who were obviously traders, and others who could be men willing to hire themselves to provide protection for those traders. There were minor officials who shared a common table. Clerks and scribes. No drayman or farrier would be eating in this inn. The food was good but beyond the purse of local workers.

'The fowl is good. It's duck. Cooked with wine and spices. And the bread is fresh,' said Blackstone. 'Cities like this are prosperous. They attract travellers on the main routes and those who bring in goods from the river.'

'Aye, no wonder so much is fought over in these parts,' said Killbere, dipping torn bread into gravy.

'Yet no one has asked us anything. A greeting usually comes with a question about where we have travelled from or are going to.'

Killbere looked around the room. No one glanced their way. 'Innkeepers depend on goodwill as well as good food. Perhaps there are too many strangers here for them to care.'

'Or because they already know who we are,' said Blackstone. 'In the corner. One man is facing us, another has his back to us. The former is eating like a famished dog. As if time is not on his side.'

'Is he looking at us?' said Killbere.

'He has one eye. A scar over the other. An old wound. An eye lost in battle or in a tavern brawl. Short, squat. He's trouble. The innkeeper has spent a lot of time at his table. When we leave glance his way. Don't make anything of it.'

Killbere pushed away his empty plate. He picked his teeth and belched. 'Then we should reconsider where we sleep tonight.'

Blackstone downed the last of his wine. 'Did you think I would take a bed when we are supposed to be carrying that much gold? That was for the benefit of those who arranged these lodgings.'

Killbere wiped his knife clean. 'Ah. Then my thoughts of a soft bed and perhaps the company of a whore are not to be.'

Blackstone spilled coins onto the table. 'Not tonight, Gilbert. Now that they have seen us here they will think we are ready to take to our beds. Find the back door. Tonight we must be awake and alert.'

'The river?' said Mallin.

'Of course, that's where the cheapest wine is going to be. That's where they trade. There'll be warehouses. They bring wine for everywhere.'

'We have enough *soldi* and *denari*,' said Mallin. 'We should find a merchant at the market; there's no need to drag ourselves to the far end of the city. We'd be away from the stables for too long. Piacenza has its own wine. No, no. Look. There are market stalls over there. They're closing for the day. We go straight there and buy what we need.'

Terrel hesitated. To disagree was likely to expose his true intentions. Reluctantly, he nodded.

He held back as Mallin bought the wine. The old man didn't haggle too long. The three firkins were heavy, but small enough to lift easily into the cart. Mallin and Terrel took a handle each and began to pull the cart. Terrel's escape now lay far behind him. Every step took him away from his plan. When would the opportunity present itself again? After ten minutes of silence as they pulled into a quiet, narrow street, Terrel stopped.

'I can't go back, Walter. I cannot.' He let go of his grip on the handle and stepped forward of the cart. The sudden weight forced Mallin to ease his handle down.

'What is this? Can't go back? What does that mean?'

'I don't fit in with these men.'

'You rode with skinners in France before Master Henry led us. You've fought hard and well since. Sir Thomas would not have taken any of us had he not considered who we are. No man has strength only. We all have weaknesses.'

'Can you pull the cart?'

'What?'

'Are you strong enough?'

Mallin looked uncertain. The conversation was taking an unexpected turn. He bent, picked up both handles, and took a few steps forward. It was slow and he felt the weight. 'Of course,' he said. 'But you will come back with me.'

Terrel shook his head. 'I'm sorry, Walter. I must get to the river.'

'And do what? Beg for help? You're no beggar, but you don't have enough money to pay for a passage.'

'I'll manage,' he said, not willing to expose himself for the thief he was.

Mallin grabbed his arm. His grip was strong enough to pull Terrel forward on his toes, bringing Terrel's face close to his own. 'Listen to me!' he hissed. 'Together, we are strong. Blackstone's captains are fair-minded men. Those who serve are loyal. Loyalty, John,' he said, using Terrel's first name to try to bring him into the fold of the close-knit fighting men. 'You belong with the men who embraced you. Master Henry, his father. You even saved Killbere's life in France. See things for what they are.'

Terrel pulled Mallin's hand away. 'Why do you think I run? Because I know how things are. Walter, I thank you. But I must go.'

He ran down the street, turned a corner and was out of sight.

Mallin stood in disbelief for a moment. Then he picked up the cart handles and heaved his way forward.

Terrel slowed to a walk. A man running aroused suspicion. Then he stopped. He was disoriented. The narrow alleyways and passages with their overbearing buildings obscured the way to the piazza, where he could get his bearings for the river. He walked twenty yards forward but saw only an ever-darkening passageway. Turning back, he found himself at the junction of the street where he had left Mallin. There was no sign of him. He stepped into the street and looked towards where Mallin would have gone. In the distance, barely visible in the fading light at the far end of the street, he saw the cart rocked forward and two men assaulting Mallin. The old man was trying to defend himself.

Terrel ran towards them. They were using clubs on Mallin, shouting questions he couldn't understand. He saw Mallin go down under the blows. He bellowed a warning. 'Hey! Bastards! Stop that!' He tried to remember some of the Italian he had heard. '*Fermati! Fermati!*'

The men stopped beating Mallin and turned to face him. Terrel looked for an escape route. The men got closer. Terrel's mouth dried. They were scrawny men. Not men-at-arms – common thieves. Crouched like alley rats as they scuttled towards him. Mean. They bore no weapons except their clubs and knives in their belts. He pulled his knife free, but they kept coming. One of them grinned. They were going to beat him to death. He knew he would not be able to fight off the two of them. Fear for his own survival loomed. Terrel pulled free the gold coin. He held it high. 'Gold!' he shouted. '*Oro!*' They stopped. Terrel backed himself against the wall and hurled the coin as far as he could away from him. It clattered and rolled somewhere in the distance.

The men chased after it.

Terrel ran for Mallin and hauled him to his feet. 'I'm all right, all right,' Mallin muttered, taking his hand from a bloodied scalp wound. He looked dazed and stared at Terrel. 'You came back.'

In that moment, Terrel knew his dream of escape had gone. He cursed himself. He had bought his life and Mallin's at the cost of his freedom. He got between the cart's handles and hauled it upright.

'I'll take the cart. We must get back,' was all he said.

The two assailants returned to the men-at-arms who had commissioned them. They made no mention of the gold coin. Instead, they said the man they questioned admitted what the Englishman was carrying.

John Terrel's actions had once again saved a life. And without knowing it he had served Blackstone's purpose by drawing out his enemy: sacrificing the stolen florin made it easy for the assailants to believe that Blackstone was transporting gold.

CHAPTER FIFTY-TWO

Terrel got Mallin back to the stables as a lamplighter put a flame to the single lantern at the entrance to the *campo*. John Jacob helped the unsteady Mallin from the handcart. The wound on his scalp needed attention, but the bruises to his face and arms from where he had tried to defend himself would heal in their own time. He didn't want any fuss made, but agreed to having his wound cleaned.

John Jacob settled him on a stool. 'Gifford, get some water and find a cloth,' he said.

Henry squatted next to him. 'Who did this?'

Terrel, fearing that his absence in the attack might be exposed, said, 'Two men. Purse-cutters. They weren't men-at-arms.' His eyes settled anxiously on Mallin, who didn't meet his gaze. Would he tell them what happened?

'Aye, two of them,' said Mallin.

Gifford put a pail of water down, squeezed out a cloth and handed it to Henry, who attended to Mallin's wound.

Meulon turned to Terrel. 'You fought them off? You weren't injured?' The gathered men looked from Terrel to Mallin. Anyone involved in a fight would bear some evidence of it.

'He was taking a piss in a doorway,' said Mallin. 'When they saw him coming, they ran.' He coughed in pain. 'Must have seen his dick in his hand.'

The men laughed. The uncertainty broken. Terrel smiled.

'They came hard and fast,' said Mallin, 'but they weren't trying to kill me. Sounded to me like they were asking me something. Stupid bastards must have known I don't speak their tongue.'

'What do you remember? Any words they used?' said Henry.

'They were insistent, right enough,' said Mallin, giving the assault some thought for a moment. 'I remember "*roba*" and... er... "*cose porti*". Aye, them words they used more than once.'

Henry stood up. 'I think they were asking what cargo was being carried on the mules.'

'Then they still don't know,' said Bezián. 'If Mallin couldn't understand them then they got no answer.'

Terrel remained silent. His actions had given the attackers the information they needed.

'Even so,' said John Jacob, 'if there're people desperate to know, then we must be ready. Meulon, you and Bezián guard the stable's far door. It's dark enough down there to stay out of sight. Henry, you and Gifford use this handcart and block the entrance. Ten feet away from this opening. Put the firkins either side. Find rakes and pitchforks. Lay them across them either side. Whatever you find will do – create an obstacle for anyone attempting to reach the mules.'

'And my father? Shouldn't we send word?' said Henry.

'And lose time trying to find him at night? No. Sir Thomas is where he is.'

Henry didn't argue. None of them knew if an attack was imminent.

'And me and Terrel?' said Mallin.

'Are you steady enough on your feet?'

'Aye, I've got paste in my saddlebags to treat the horses. I'll pack some of it on the wound. That'll do for now. What else hurts won't get between me and any thieving bastards coming through that gap.'

'Then you and Terrel hide the chests under straw and stay with the mules. If whoever's coming arrives in numbers and gets past us, then let them take the chests.'

'Let them take the gold?' said Mallin.

'Yes,' said John Jacob. Only Blackstone and the captains knew what was in those caskets. Chests of cut chain and a covering of coins in one chest was not worth two men ignorant of the contents losing their lives.

Mallin nodded. Terrel followed him to where the mules were tethered. As they got out of earshot, Mallin grabbed Terrel's arm. 'I heard what you called out to them bastards. They wouldn't run for a denier or a handful of *soldi*. But they would run for a gold florin. Was that it? Was that what was going to take you away?'

Terrel nodded.

Mallin loosened his grip. 'The next time you thieve gold, take enough to save yourself as well.'

'I tried.'

Mallin chuckled and tapped his shoulder. 'You didn't try hard enough, lad,' he said.

The *campo* was silent. Those who lived in the houses had their shutters closed. The couple of stable lads slept in the hayloft, thankful the men below had not brought them into whatever trouble was coming their way. A stray cat strolled fearlessly from the side passage across the small square towards the narrowest of alleys. Its nightly routine uninterrupted. Its territory already fought for and won.

The stables were in darkness. John Jacob and the others were out of sight. Sword in hand, their shields already taken from their saddle bindings and resting next to them. The handcart was where John Jacob had instructed it to be. The firkins, two on one side, the third on the other, sat a few feet away from it, rakes, tines upwards, and pitchforks' hafts laid across. A simple obstruction to make attackers lift their feet and slow their advance on the stable entrance.

The scrape of boots on stone heralded the killers' approach. A flaming torch held at their rear cast long shadows ahead of the huddled men. There were twenty hard-looking ruffians. They bore no blazon. Their swords were already drawn as they eased into the small square. Whispered uncertainty made them slow, edging forward towards the opening. Halfway across the *campo* they faltered. They brought their torchlight forward. That was when they saw the cart and the obstructions, telling them they were expected. Stepping around the cart allowed only one or two men at a time, but it also exposed them to the threat of a surprise attack from inside the stables.

There was more whispered uncertainty. They had not expected the men inside the stable to be alerted. They made a decision. Two men darted forward to haul the handcart away, two more bent to throw aside the rakes and pitchforks as their companions gathered at their backs to storm the opening.

Men at the rear cried out in pain. The others spun around. Four of the men writhed in death throes. The torchbearer faltered; shadows merged into a mêlée of confusion.

Blackstone and Killbere were silent killers. Striking without mercy, they felled the men whose backs were to them and then cut into those who swirled to face the unexpected attackers. The torch was dropped, leaving a dull glow from the *campo*'s lantern which was barely enough to distinguish men's faces. Sparks tumbled across the ground as men kicked and trod on the burning torch.

No sooner had they turned to face the gruesome efficiency of the attackers behind them than bellowing men surged from the stables. At the far end in the darkness, a door burst open and two more men emerged. The attackers' plan for a surprise assault had become a terrifying ambush.

Men tried to flee, turning this way and that in their panic. Henry and Gifford cut down two of them. Three more men ran for the narrow passage, but Meulon met them with deadly skill using a pitchfork as a spear, while Bezián unleashed rapid sword strokes that were too fast to even be seen in the dull light.

By the time the abandoned torch had been extinguished so too were twenty men. What remained of the burning embers spluttered and died beneath their spilled blood.

Blackstone and Killbere had arrived at the square and seen the handcart set in front of the opening. Realizing the men inside expected an attack, they waited in a darkened doorway at the far side of the square and let the killers walk into the trap.

'Sir Thomas,' said John Jacob with a broad grin as he stepped over a body. 'Why am I not surprised to see you?'

Blackstone wiped Wolf Sword's blade free of blood. 'John, we thought this place was too good to be true. Only one access, away from the main piazza. An open front and a place at the inn far enough away to separate us.'

'You had warning?' said Killbere, toeing one of the dead men.

'Aye, Sir Gilbert. Terrel and Mallin were attacked. We learnt enough to arm ourselves and be ready.'

'Then Piacenza is not so neutral after all,' said Henry.

'Would the *podestà* risk doing this? I think not. Word had already reached here of when we left Milan and it would have been one of the officials who arranged our accommodation. Corruption worms its way everywhere.'

'This one still lives,' said Bezián as he bent over one of Meulon's victims.

'Bring him into the light.'

Meulon bent and hauled the man beneath the *campo*'s wall lantern. Meulon's pitchfork had pierced his lungs; he was close to death, eyes staring wide at the men who peered down at him. He looked no different from the other men.

'Skinners,' said Killbere.

'Aye, but who sent them?' said Blackstone, stooping to search the man's face. Blood spurted from the corner of his mouth. Blackstone wiped it away. 'Who sent you here?'

The man's eyes stared in disbelief at his own impending death. His lips moved. Bubbling froth.

'He's drowning in his own blood, Thomas,' said Killbere, bending over. He jabbed a finger in the man's chest. 'Meet the devil or the archangel. Speak the truth and your soul goes to the light.'

'Was it Lord Bernabò?' said Blackstone.

The man's dying gaze turned to Blackstone.

'Cansignorio della Scala?' Killbere asked.

The man tried to speak. His eyes blinked closed and open. There was no sense to be made from the gurgling sound. He convulsed.

'Gone to the devil,' said Killbere.

Blackstone stood. 'For all we know, they're skinners working for themselves.' He looked at the jumbled bodies lying in the square. 'Drag them in line. We'll lay them out and challenge the *podestà* in the morning.'

'And until then?' said Henry.

'Get some sleep,' said Blackstone.

CHAPTER FIFTY-THREE

When the morning ushered in the first creeping rays of sunlight trying to find a way through the buildings, Blackstone's men went among the dead. They stripped anything of value, although there was little of it. They emptied every purse. Terrel kept his panic under control as he searched for the two men who had attacked Mallin. If they were among the dead, then one of them would still have his gold coin and if any of Blackstone's men found it, then it would not take long for Blackstone to work out how a dead skinner had a gold florin on his person. As he checked the last of the men relief overcame panic. The two assailants were not among the dead. They must have been paid by these killers to get the information they needed, he reasoned. Better that than risk being seen themselves by the night-watch officers, a chance encounter that would have instigated violence against Piacenza itself.

The *podestà* trembled as he stood looking at the dead men laid out in the *campo*. Locals leaned from their windows or skulked in doorways as the city officials tried to avoid stepping in the blood that mired the dirt. Blackstone and Killbere faced them.

'These men came in the night to kill us. They were in your

city, Signor Corrado. Piacenza is neutral. Am I to believe you had no part in this?'

'You must believe that!' said the *podestà*. 'I have never seen or heard of these men before. No large group of men such as these came through our gates. They must have come in twos and threes over days.'

'*Condottieri*,' said Blackstone. 'Paid by someone to lie in wait for us here. If I am to believe you know nothing about these men, can you tell me who might?'

The savagery of the wounds displayed on the corpses made one of his officials turn and vomit. The *podestà* covered his nose with a lace-trimmed, scented cloth. The stench of the dead seeped into the confined square and the cloying smell of the vomit added to the unpleasantness. He shook his head. 'I cannot help you, Sir Thomas. I offer my heartfelt apology. Piacenza is unused to violence such as this.' He cleared the phlegm from his throat and spat to one side. A gesture common to a latrine cleaner, not a dignified senior official.

'You will bury them at the city's expense,' said Blackstone.

Signor Corrado was about to suggest that the dead would have had money on them but changed his mind when he saw Blackstone's expression. The array of grim-faced men behind Blackstone bolstered the *podestà*'s view that to argue might unleash more violence on the city. He nodded.

'You can sell the dead men's horses to defray your costs.'

Corrado dipped his head. 'I am grateful, Sir Thomas. I will have the bodies removed.'

'And do it quickly. I leave for Verona in the hour.'

There was nothing more to be said. Blackstone waited. The *podestà* looked uncertain. He bobbed again and turned away with his officials.

'Well, if any of these wretches are playing both sides then telling them where we're going should flush out those who want the gold and us dead.'

'We must plant information that draws attention to us,' said Blackstone. 'These cities have more whispers flying over their walls than bats in a bell tower. There's no reason anyone would even know about Ashford and Bullard's journey.'

John Jacob hovered, waiting for Blackstone's instructions. 'We ride today, Sir Thomas?'

'Have the horses saddled and we'll get the chests back on the mules.' He placed a hand on Killbere's shoulder. 'Then you and I go back to the inn.' He toed a dead man's head to one side. 'Recognize him?'

'Our one-eyed fellow diner,' Killbere said. 'Then perhaps he was staying there as we were supposed to.'

The inn was quieter than the previous night. The innkeeper was burly enough to deal with troublesome guests, but the two men who faced him across the counter were not to be trifled with. Especially not the one who towered over him. He looked particularly mean. And he had asked if the innkeeper remembered him. How could he not?

'I remember you eating here. Your room went unused. If you're here to complain about me putting someone else in there, I can't afford to have a room empty.'

'The city paid for that room. You were not out of pocket.'

The innkeeper shrugged. 'So what? There was money to be made.'

'I don't care about the money. I want to know who the one-eyed man was at that corner table.'

The innkeeper kept his eyes down, his hand sweeping a cloth across the wooden counter. 'I don't have time to take notice of who's here or there.'

'But you remembered us,' said Killbere.

Another shrug. A casual toss of the cloth into a bucket. 'I don't remember him.'

'He's dead. Him and nineteen others,' said Blackstone. 'The city is digging a mass grave as we speak. They would have room for one more. Did he stay here?'

The innkeeper was cautious. 'He paid for a room, yes.'

'Did you let others use it when he didn't return last night?'

'No. He paid double the rate.'

'Show us,' said Killbere.

The reluctant innkeeper could only nod and lead the way. As they reached the base of the stairs, he slapped an urchin across the back of the head who was sweeping the floor. 'Out of the way!'

The child moved, eyes down, hands clasping the straw broom's haft.

At the top of the stairs, the innkeeper turned down a narrow passage. He opened a door and stepped aside.

'This is his room?' said Blackstone.

The innkeeper nodded.

'What have you taken?' said Killbere.

'Nothing. I expected him to return.'

Blackstone went inside the room. Killbere dismissed the innkeeper. Once inside, they closed the door. A wooden-framed bed held a straw mattress. A folded blanket, unused. A stool. A candle. The smell of stale woodsmoke permeated the small window in its badly fitted frame. Street sounds reached inside the small room. A hook on the back of the door held a cloak.

Blackstone took it down while Killbere pulled back the mattress to check if anything was concealed.

'He's paid extra for a piss pot,' said Killbere. 'He must have been thinking he'd have a bladder full of wine after killing us.'

Blackstone felt the hem of the cloak. Something rustled under his fingers. A poorly stitched seam, already fraying, let his fingers tear it apart. He pulled out a grubby folded parchment, the wax seal broken. He unfolded it. There was a neat script on it, in Latin.

Blackstone offered it to Killbere. 'It means something official,' said Killbere, taking it from Blackstone. 'This is good parchment, but I can't make out the seal.'

'Me neither. We'll get Henry to look at what's written,' said Blackstone.

Killbere handed it back. 'There's nothing here. Where are his saddlebags? We need to find his horse.'

Downstairs, they saw the innkeeper outside rolling rundlets of wine down the ramp into his cellar. Blackstone called the urchin to him.

'Where does the innkeeper stable the horses for the men who stay here?'

The nervous child glanced towards the innkeeper. Killbere offered him a small coin. The child snatched it and pointed down the side street, alongside the inn.

There were twelve rooms at the inn but only stabling for four horses. The horses tethered there had their saddles and saddlebags lodged on frames at the end of each stall. Except one.

A stableman entered with a handful of bound hay. He dropped it when he saw the two armed men. Killbere raised a hand to calm the man's worried expression.

'We mean no harm. Are you the *stalliere*?'

He nodded.

'Signor Corrado is helping us find a one-eyed man who stabled his horse,' Killbere lied. 'Is it this one?' he asked, patting the horse's rump.

'It is, lord,' said the stableman.

'Then where are his saddlebags?'

'He took them with him to the inn.'

Killbere looked at Blackstone. 'Your turn, Thomas.'

Blackstone frowned.

'Pay him something. A couple of *soldi*. I paid the urchin.'

'You gave him a *quattrino*. Barely enough to buy a piece of fruit.'

'It was better than nothing. He gave us information worth a menial coin. This man has confirmed the saddlebags should have been in the skinner's room. Open your heart and your purse, for pity's sake.'

Blackstone handed over two *soldi*. The stableman's gratitude was obvious – now he would be able to buy extra loaves of bread.

'There,' said Killbere as they stepped back into the street. 'Don't you feel a warm glow in your vitals at being generous to a poor bastard who shovels horseshit all day?'

The innkeeper didn't see Blackstone and Killbere arrive back at the inn. As he bent over a rundlet, he felt a sharp kick on his backside that sent him sprawling over the small barrel and down the ramp into his cellar. When he came to, he stared up at Blackstone and Killbere. The shorter of the two men was sitting on a firkin, drinking from a jug of wine.

Blackstone put his boot on the innkeeper's throat. 'The man's saddlebags. You took them from his room.'

The sprawled man, arms splayed wide, croaked a reply. 'He asked me to look after them.'

Blackstone applied more pressure.

'All right, all right. Yes. I took them early this morning when he hadn't returned.' He pointed behind his head.

Killbere stepped around him. He couldn't see any stored saddlebags.

'Where?'

'In the barrel,' the innkeeper said.

Killbere saw the most obvious barrel in the cellar. It was surrounded by firkins and rundlets. He lifted off the lid. It was empty of wine and big enough to hide the saddlebags and a few other stolen items as well. He hauled out the leather bags. 'There's a cache of stolen items in here,' he said.

Blackstone drew his archer's knife. 'Any of those belong to the one-eyed man?'

A fervent shaking of the head was convincing enough.

'Have you taken anything out of those bags?'

'I swear I have not. There was no time.'

Blackstone looked at Killbere, who opened the saddlebags. 'If he had taken anything he wouldn't have left what's here.' Killbere slung them over his shoulder.

'Stay where you are until we're gone,' said Blackstone, and followed Killbere up the ladder to the street. They tipped over two rundlets and pushed them down the ramp in rapid succession.

The man's cry told them one of the rundlets had found its mark.

The bodies in the *campo* were dragged onto carts; blood smears scored the dirt. Henry looked at the Latin inscription on the document Blackstone had taken from the dead man's cloak.

'It's a safe-conduct pass for whoever carried it.'

'He doesn't need it any more,' said Killbere.

'And the seal? I examined it again. It looks like it comes from Verona to me. That broken ladder there where the seal was cracked open? I think that's part of the della Scala blazon,' Blackstone suggested.

'Yes, perhaps,' said Henry. 'You see this ink? It's gone brown. I've seen documents like this when I was at Oxford. Originally, it's dark blue or black and it fades. This type of ink is common here. The della Scala's chancellery might use it. They would issue the pass.'

Blackstone pulled out a small box about the size of a man's palm from the dead mercenary's saddlebags. When he unwrapped the silk, Henry saw it was a reliquary of gilded silver adorned with semi-precious stones. Blackstone handed it to him.

'There are marks on the bottom.'

Henry turned it and scrutinized the mark on its base. It was an impression about the size of a thumbnail. 'I'm not sure, but I think this came from a church in Verona. It appears to be the Basilica of San Zeno. See here?' He turned it so Blackstone and Killbere could see the etched image of a figure holding a fishing rod. 'That's the church's symbol of peace. St Zeno is Verona's patron saint.'

Killbere's face crumpled. 'How is it you know this?'

Henry smiled. 'I went to university.'

'Well, don't sound so damned clever about it.'

Blackstone took the reliquary back. 'Thank you, Henry. Go and tell John to ready the men.'

Henry left to do Blackstone's bidding as the veteran Killbere, whose comment was nothing more than a gentle jibe, gave him a pat on his shoulder.

'Well,' said Blackstone. 'The bastard had a safe conduct and a gift from della Scala.'

'A gift? He thieved it more like.'

Blackstone turned back the corner of the fine silk. The Scaligeri family device of a ladder against a crimson background pointing to an eagle was imprinted on its corner.

'Perhaps,' said Killbere. 'Easy enough to steal a piece of silk when taking the box.'

'What if this is a reward from della Scala and he and Bernabò are using the same skinners?' Blackstone said. 'Della Scala was recruiting. Visconti sent them against you when I was inside Milan's walls.'

'Skinners can play both sides right enough.'

'So can Italian tyrants.'

They fell silent as the men led out their horses, ready to leave Piacenza.

Blackstone tossed the dead man's saddlebags aside. He beckoned John Jacob and handed him the reliquary. 'Put this in my saddlebag, John.'

His squire took the carefully wrapped box from him. 'We're ready to leave, Sir Thomas.'

Blackstone nodded. John Jacob returned to the men.

The thump of another dead body being thrown onto the cart drew Blackstone's attention.

'Enemies working together for a common cause. Why not? Montferrat thought the message from France was heading for Verona.'

'But why, Thomas?'

'Bernabò would not dare have the Prince killed, but if the French convinced della Scala that the marriage to Lionel gave our King more influence here, then it might be in his best interests to arrange the killing.'

'That would also suit Bernabò by stopping his brother from marrying into our royalty, but the finger is going to point at him,' said Killbere.

'That too works in della Scala's favour,' Blackstone said. 'Edward Despenser has already committed his men to fight against Bernabò.'

'Then it all points to Cansignorio della Scala.'

'And the skinners? Are they playing both sides or is there any chance Milan and Verona have agreed an unholy treaty?'

They fell silent for a moment. Mallin brought Blackstone's horse out on a long rein keeping it clear of the other mounts.

'If I was playing dice with the devil, I'd say both stand to benefit,' said Killbere. 'One takes the gold they think we're carrying, the other takes you as the prize. Della Scala gets the gold. Bernabò gets you.'

Blackstone tugged the reins tightly so he could mount without being bitten. 'Then we'll only know when we bait the bastards.'

PART SEVEN

THE TRIAL, THE DUEL & FIRST BLOOD

CHAPTER FIFTY-FOUR

William Ashford had served the King years before joining Thomas Blackstone at the King's request. The responsibility placed on him by Blackstone sharpened his determination to serve both the Master of War and the King himself as the ox-cart creaked along the well-worn path towards Florence. Ashford took it upon himself to explain to Bullard why they had been given their mission. The wagon concealed secret documents that had to reach the King's supporters in Florence. These documents were vital for their King because war would soon break out in France again and those in Florence needed the information in those documents. It was a lie, of course, but there was no need to burden a simple man-at-arms with the truth. If anything went wrong and torture followed, then the only thing that would be lost were the documents Blackstone had concealed beneath the body in the coffin. Bullard was a sworn man to Blackstone and the responsibility of being chosen to accompany such documents added to his pride.

They had reached Sestri Levante and turned from the coast road up into the mountains. Another four or five days and they would reach Florence. So far, there had been no trouble. The pilgrims travelling the same route back to Rome where their pilgrimage had started were few, and those they encountered were moving slowly after their arduous round-trip journey. How many of those who started that journey had survived was anyone's guess. Bad weather, injury and illness would have taken its toll. But spiritual redemption and penance might have unburdened those who made the pilgrimage, so at least, Ashford believed, their souls were prepared for God when they succumbed along the way.

The pilgrims travelling towards the Alps for their crossing into France strode with a determined pace. There were few of them. Ashford and Bullard counted no more than twenty a day, often men walking with a companion, sometimes lone pilgrims unwilling to even raise their eyes from the road at their feet. Only once did someone block their way ahead. The empty road showed no other travellers except for three down-at-heel men who looked in need of food and whose horses were of poor quality. Ashford thought them to be skinners who had abandoned whatever business they had been engaged in and were seeking a way back to France. They didn't seem to offer much of a threat – in fact he thought they were begging. And he and Bullard both carried a knife at their belts beneath their cloaks in case they had to urgently defend themselves and their cargo – their weapons were concealed beneath the wagon seat in a hidden compartment.

Bullard played his part as he stood at the ox's side: an illiterate pilgrim returning from France, carrying home for burial the body of a dead fellow seeker of redemption. He did not try to obstruct the two men who dismounted and approached the wagon.

At first Ashford was reasonable with them. 'We have some food we can share with you,' he said. 'There'll be a monastery ahead who will replenish what we have.'

'What else do you have, pilgrim?' one said as he clambered onto the back of the wagon. Ashford cast a quick warning glance at Bullard, who would have to deal with the third man, who remained mounted. It was now evident that these were robbers who had eluded the Knights of the Tau, responsible for guarding the Via Francigena and ensuring the safety of pilgrims.

'We have nothing but the clothes on our back and a few extra in our packs,' said Ashford, watching them. The first man had spilled out the packs while the other reached into the open coffin and the rope-bound corpse wrapped in cloth. 'And poor brother Timothy, our dead companion whose leprosy finally claimed him.'

The thief snatched back his hand. And then he thought about it. He turned to his companion. 'Help me haul this coffin off. Pilgrims are devious bastards.'

Ashford realized he dare not risk the compartment being found. These men looked as though they would strip every plank from the wagon.

'Let me help you, brother,' said Ashford, climbing back to the first man. As the thief looked up, puzzled, about to demand Ashford stay where he was, Ashford plunged his knife into the man's throat. The thief on the ground stared up, one hand on the coffin, the other going for his sword. Ashford kicked him hard. He sprawled back. As Ashford jumped down, Bullard snatched the mounted man's reins, yanked them hard, pulling the horse's head down and throwing its rider off balance. He reached up, grabbed the man's cloak and, as he hauled him down, thrust his knife into the rider's chest. Jumping free from the tumbling body, he rammed the knife home again as it hit the ground.

Ashford and Bullard's victims lay dead where they fell.

Ashford checked the road. There was still no sign of anyone.

'Take anything they have of value. Cut their purses and check their saddlebags.'

There was little to be had from the dead men. What coins they had, Ashford and Bullard pooled into one purse. The saddlebags yielded tired clothing and stale food and some trinkets and religious artefacts that had obviously been stolen from other pilgrims. They would keep a few of them. They would be helpful to convince others, should they be asked, that the two men on the ox-cart had visited religious sites along the way.

Ashford and Bullard worked with lean efficiency. They threw the men's bodies into gulleys, obscured from sight by brush and bracken. Their saddles followed. Then they turned loose the three horses.

Ashford and Bullard resumed their journey.

The only sign remaining of the brigands was their blood seeping into the dirt.

They pressed on, fearful that other adversaries might be on the road ahead but in greater numbers. Skinners or Visconti men ranging far and wide: it made no difference. Any more than a handful of belligerent men and they would be hard-pressed to defend themselves. They had covered a great distance. By starting before dawn and travelling until the moonlight was obscured by clouds, they were getting close to Lucca. At night each man would take it in turns to keep watch, and then sleep, lying beneath the wagon that kept the dew from them. Ashford would stare at the hefty planks above his head and imagine the multitude of gold coins that lay hidden there. Above the fortune of concealed gold, a dead man thwarted anyone's attempt to search the wagon.

Over the days, he and Bullard had gathered returning pilgrims who accompanied them on their way. Ten men, sometimes more, other days less, road-worn but with the fire of redemption in their eyes, strode alongside the trundling wagon. A hand on the sturdy wood to aid their pace. The heavy wheels creaking over every yard, a welcome reminder they were getting closer to home.

As night fell, they would tighten their grip on the side of the wagon to help them from tripping on the stony road. They were determined to keep up with the two men, who had explained their urgency to keep going as long as the day and moonlight permitted: they had a friend to bury. But when Ashford halted for the night, freeing the willing beast from its yoke so that it could rest and graze, their fellow travellers slept far enough away from the dead man so that his spirit might not rise in the night and haunt them. Such superstition was welcomed by the dead man's guardians.

The threat came one morning when Ashford had readied the wagon and set off earlier than usual, leaving the other pilgrims still wrapped in their blankets further back along the road. He had sensed they were getting close to Lucca as the road had turned inland through wooded hills. In the distance, olive plantations and vines clung to the rolling hills. That meant the city could be reached by nightfall. They were so close and yet Ashford could not shake off the fear of robbery that was a constant companion. It was heightened that morning when he saw several armed men on a track higher up, riding in single file along what was little more than a scar on the hillside. They were shadowing his route, and then they disappeared from view as the track descended through a wooded glade.

He called to Bullard, whose turn it was to walk alongside the lumbering ox. 'Armed men somewhere ahead.'

Ashford eased open the loose board beneath him that concealed their weapons. He laid Bullard's sword and knife on the side of the wagon and covered them with sacking. Bullard nodded that he saw what Ashford had done. Another mile went by and as they turned a corner, they found those same riders blocking the road. Bullard slowed the ox. Ashford climbed down, hand resting where his sword lay concealed. Bullard eased back to the opposite side. One of the horsemen came forward.

'Pilgrim, it looks as though you need an escort to where you're going.'

'We're slow, but we are content with that,' Ashford answered. 'We have the good Lord to watch over our journey.'

The rider's companions came closer. Their dark woollen

cloaks concealed their weapons and made the men look ominous. Ashford's hand reached under the sacks to feel the grip of his sword.

'I know what you carry,' said the rider, 'and we will ride with you.'

'I carry a dead friend who needs Christian burial,' said Ashford.

'Who died of the pestilence,' added Bullard.

The man who addressed them smiled. 'You play your role well, but that's a lie, and pilgrims should not tell untruths.'

Ashford and Bullard fell silent. The moment to fight was near.

The man swept his cloak aside, exposing a surcoat bearing a red axe on a white field.

Ashford and Bullard's hands went for their blades.

CHAPTER FIFTY-FIVE

Blackstone's men rode at a steady pace until dusk. They camped and started again at first light the next morning. They were a day away from Verona. As the sun rose on that final day, it exposed the low hills and a castle three miles away. Despite its small size, the swallow-tail castellated tower indicated that it belonged to della Scala. Probably no more than an outpost watchtower. Blackstone's instinct had made him call a halt. Except for the screech of a high circling buzzard pestered by crows and the jangle of horses' bridles waiting patiently as their riders scanned the horizon, it was silent. The air was already heavy with expected heat.

Renfred and his scouts rode back towards the column of men. They were breathless from their fast ride.

'We skirted beyond the hills. There's a large force approaching from the east beyond that watchtower, too far to count. If we continue in this direction, Sir Thomas, then we ride into others who lie in wait hidden from the road. It's an ambush. An army of... I don't know, three hundred men maybe.' He turned in the saddle and pointed at the rolling landscape. 'Most are out of sight behind the hills.'

Blackstone stared into the distance. Rows of vines on one

side of a far hill caught the morning light, but on the opposite hillside, across the valley, olive groves clung to the shadows of sackcloth grey beneath their branches.

'They have crossbowmen in those olive groves,' Renfred said.

'Good place for them, Thomas,' said Killbere.

'Were you seen?' Blackstone asked his scout.

'No.'

'And can they see us from there?'

'No. There are no more than fifty or sixty of them but they have pavisiers. So when the bowmen have shot and are readying again, the men shield them. Pavisiers will protect the bowmen but it also means that if you attack you have both to fight. You have to ride along the road between those hills and then any lookout they have would see you.'

'Even if we get close enough for Will's archers, if their bowmen stay underneath the olive trees, it affords them some protection,' said Killbere. 'And we'd be exposed on three flanks. Front and both sides.'

'And we can't charge past those olive groves without exposing ourselves to the men behind the hill,' said John Jacob.

Killbere leaned on his pommel. 'Can't make a run for it and can't go around them.'

Blackstone looked around him. There was a small forest of mixed beech and oak trees half a mile behind them. 'All right, we get the horses back in those trees and stand our ground. If they want to risk bringing their bowmen forward, then our archers will deal with them. The forest covers our rear.'

'Thomas, we could be sitting on our arses longer than it takes for a whore to decide to become a nun.'

'Or the other way around,' said Will Longdon, who had sidled his horse forward.

'We don't know who the riders from the east are,' said John Jacob, 'or how long it will take for them to reach us. With luck, it could be della Scala. We're closer to Verona than we are Milan.'

'There's nowhere to run either way,' said Killbere. 'We don't know who's out there.'

'Then we should provoke those who are waiting for us to ride into their trap,' said Blackstone. 'And kill as many as we can.'

Killbere grinned. 'Bring the bastards to us.'

'Yes. All right: Gilbert, form up the men in front of the trees. Will and Jack's archers on the flanks. Renfred, your men ride with me. You take us around their rear and make sure we have a fast ride back here. John, pick another ten men. We'll sting their arse and force them to give chase.'

Henry had heard the conversation. 'May I ride with you?'

Blackstone looked at his son. 'You hold the centre with Sir Gilbert.'

Killbere grinned. 'Can't have you falling off your horse when they give chase, Henry. You've a maiden to rescue.'

The men laughed at Henry's discomfort.

'You'll soon forget the woman when these bastards give chase,' said Killbere. 'You and Gifford stand with me.' Killbere heeled his horse. 'Ride hard and fast, Thomas – who knows how many will come at us this day? We'll need the devil at our back and angels on our shoulder.'

Henry cantered after Killbere, with Gifford at his side. 'We're thirty miles from the lake near Verona. A fast ride and I could be there by nightfall.'

'Tame your desire, Master Henry,' Gifford said. 'Before we think on that, we need to survive this day. Do as Sir Gilbert said. Put the girl out of your mind.' He looked at Henry, who had not answered. 'You understand? You wanted to stand with your father: well, that time has come.'

Henry nodded. They rode on to take up their positions.

Will Longdon went to his archers. John Jacob wheeled his horse to pick his men.

Renfred pointed out the way he thought best to slip behind the waiting enemy. 'Look to your left, Sir Thomas. That hill will give us cover until we sweep wide behind them. They're looking to where they expect us to be.' He pointed towards the olive groves that gave way to the road ahead. 'Their bowmen won't move from their cover. It'll be the mounted men who'll give chase.'

'Then stay close to me and John. We need you to take us in and bring us out.'

'Aye, Sir Thomas, I shall do that.'

Blackstone saw Longdon and John Jacob gathering their men. They soon joined him.

'We ride behind whoever's out there and bring down as many as we can. Once we've cut into them we turn back for here.'

He waited for questions. There were none. He spurred the bastard horse to take the fight to his enemy.

Killbere rode into the trees, dismounted and tethered his mount. 'Mallin! Terrel! Double-tether and hobble those mules. Cover their eyes. We don't want them running scared.' The ground was soft underfoot and gave way under his weight. His foot caught layers of dry leaves and broken twigs. Years' worth fallen from the trees.

'Captains! To me!'

Henry ran with the captains to Killbere, who stood looking along the treeline. He checked the canopy.

'The breeze is at our backs. Have the lads build fires a hundred yards ahead of our lines. Plenty of dry leaf and branches. Be ready to smother them with greenery. When these bastards attack, they'll ride into our smoke. Light them on my command.'

They turned back, calling for their men. Henry strode across to Gifford.

Killbere snorted and spat and wiped a sleeve across his beard. His eyes scanned the open ground in front of where they were to make their stand. It would be a thin line of defence. There weren't enough of them. If they were as outnumbered as

Renfred had reported then they would be overrun. He looked further into the woodland. If they had to fall back, that's where they would make their stand. They'd lose use of their archers, who would have to fight hand to hand, but the trees and undergrowth would hamper those attacking.

Killbere gathered an armful of dead wood and dragged it forward to where the men were preparing their meagre defence. One thing was certain in his mind. If the other force Renfred had seen riding from the east were unfriendly, then no matter how many fires they lit, or arrows they shot, they would be overwhelmed.

He turned to Henry to see a strained look of uncertainty on the younger man's face. 'Are you fearful?'

Henry swallowed hard. He shook his head. 'I'm not.'

'Then you're a damned fool. My arse pinches and my balls squeeze tight every time. It's fear that keep you alive.' He grunted. 'God's tears, lad, face death and spit in his face. Fear only leaves you when the killing starts.'

Renfred and his men led the way around the low hills that shielded them from the enemy waiting in ambush. They drew up when they saw the horsemen gathered on the reverse side of the hill. Had Blackstone continued on the route to Verona as planned they would have been waiting until Blackstone's column had got into crossbow range from the olive grove and then crested the hill and swooped down.

'How many do you think?' said Blackstone.

John Jacob studied the huddled mass of horses and riders. 'Hard to say from here. They're bunched up. Those men there look to be their rear ranks.'

'Sir Thomas, from the tracks we saw, there have to be three hundred, perhaps more. I think we're looking at about a hundred of them – perhaps a few more,' said Renfred.

'I think you're right,' said Blackstone. 'Then the others must be beyond them and out of sight.' He grinned. 'These hundred will serve our purpose. Once we draw them under Will's arrows, that'll thin them down.'

John Jacob gestured towards the unsuspecting men. 'A lot of them are not yet mounted. That means they didn't see our approach on the road like Renfred said.'

'It also means they knew the route we were taking to Verona,' said his German captain.

'This is a well-travelled road. Not difficult to play the odds that we would be on it. And paid informers in places like Piacenza earn their keep betraying travellers,' John Jacob said.

'Especially if they think they're carrying a king's ransom in gold,' said Blackstone. 'Do you see a blazon or a banner?'

'Nothing yet. Perhaps they're skinners,' said Renfred.

'There'll be enough routiers among them, following a leader, but crossbowmen don't get paid by skinners, they serve powerful men,' said Blackstone. 'If it's the Visconti they'll raise their banner so we'll know who's killing us.'

'They won't be expecting anyone coming from their rear. They're interested in the road over the hill,' John Jacob said.

'Then we ride in slowly. As if we're going to join them,' said Blackstone.

The men nodded their understanding.

Blackstone took an extra turn of the reins and heeled the bastard horse into the open.

CHAPTER FIFTY-SIX

The men who waited in ambush were unprepared. They sat in small groups, each man holding the reins of his horse. Others walked through the gathered men, trailing their mounts. The huddled mass was waiting for their lookouts to warn them of Blackstone's advance along the road from Piacenza. No banners were visible as Blackstone approached, riding calmly two hundred yards behind their rear ranks.

A few of the ambushers stood and looked. They returned Blackstone's greeting of a raised arm showing he was there to join them. That he was no threat.

Not for another hundred yards.

And then he spurred the bastard war horse, drew Wolf Sword, and lifted his shield.

Bernabò Visconti and his captain, Marchesi, were out of sight as they waited beyond that first group of men that Blackstone saw. Bernabò had only joined his captain once word had reached him of Blackstone's fight in Piacenza and then him leaving for Verona. The 250 men that he brought to join Marchesi's fifty had been gathered with haste. Marchesi was a dependable captain whose own men were loyal and continued to patrol and harass bands of the papal forces or Cansignorio della Scala's men. In contrast, other than the contracted Genoese bowmen, the mercenaries Bernabò had pulled out of his army fifty miles to the west and brought here were the scum of the earth, but they served his purpose. He knew Blackstone's strength, and even though outnumbered, there was no doubt Blackstone would put up a fight. Bernabò would throw in these *condottieri* first.

Bernabò and Marchesi had remained saddled, as had Marchesi's men. The *condottieri* in the rear ranks lacked the same discipline. Had Bernabò or Marchesi been closer to them instead of around the next curve of the hill waiting to pounce, they would have felt his wrath and the tip of his steel-tipped lash.

The ripple of violence swept towards him and Marchesi in a wave of screams and cries of alarm. Horses whinnied and mounts jostled.

'We're being attacked, Marchesi!' said Bernabò.

'Della Scala's men?' said Marchesi as he gained control of his horse, panicked by the other mounts' fear.

'Them or Blackstone!' Bernabò spurred his horse hard, the rowels drawing blood. The beast's head reared, its eyes widened as its reins were yanked hard and turned towards the screams.

Blackstone cut a swathe into the hapless mercenaries. A dozen fell from Wolf Sword and the crushing force of his horse. As he tore into them, John Jacob and Renfred's men followed him into the fray. It was a slaughter. The men on the ground had no chance against the violence unleashed on them. John Jacob stayed close to Blackstone's shoulder. Renfred wheeled his men, flanking Blackstone, cutting off any attempt to attack his blind side. The sheer weight of horseflesh pounding into the terrified men created mayhem. The mercenaries ran for their lives, abandoning their mounts. Few escaped the strike of iron-shod hooves and honed blades sweeping down on them. The loose horses reared in panic and added to the turmoil. By the time men had clambered into their saddles and armed themselves, Blackstone's men had wheeled their mounts, leaving pain and terror behind them.

Bernabò and Marchesi and their men cantered into view around the blind side of the hill. Marchesi bellowed commands for the *condottieri* to mount. Fearful that Bernabò would inflict his own punishment on them and bellowing curses, they climbed onto their panic-stricken mounts. Like a pack of squabbling wolves, Marchesi herded them as Bernabò yelled out his commands. The paid killers struck out after Blackstone, already long gone and out of sight.

Bernabò and his own troops, with Marchesi at his side, followed the mercenaries. 'If those bastards falter, cut them down,' he commanded and, heeling his mount, joined the stampede to wherever Blackstone and his men had run to. It took little time to see what awaited them. Galloping around the edge of the hills and into the open ground, first the smell of smoke reached them and then the sight of drifting, curling fumes from a dozen fires spread a hundred yards ahead of the ranks of men waiting for them. They saw the last of Blackstone's attacking force disappear through the smoke and into the forest beyond.

The *condottieri* faltered. Some riders hauled their horses away. But Bernabò's men were ruthless. Those that tried to evade the attack died in their saddle. The others learnt the lesson after four of the mercenaries lay hacked and slumped across their horse's withers.

Bernabò slowed his mount. 'Hold back, Marchesi. Let them take the brunt of it. The English will have their archers waiting.'

The Visconti riders slowed their horses, watching as the men ahead rode, yelling to bolster their courage. Spitting out their fear and hatred for those waiting to kill them.

Death came quickly enough.

A withering, unseen fluttering in the sky plummeted through the veil of smoke.

Bernabò wheeled his horse. He and his men were out of the longbow archers' range.

'On! Ride on!' he demanded of those who survived the first onslaught.

Better to face the half-screened enemy than turn back and face certain death at the hands of Bernabò's troops.

'Wait,' he demanded of Marchesi and his own men. 'The archers will loose again, and then we ride hard at them.'

He brought up his shield, drew his sword, and looked over each shoulder as his men formed up behind him.

More men in the haze ahead went down as the next cloud of yard-long arrows fell into them. There was no choice for the survivors. Ride on hard and fast. Bernabò Visconti was on their heels.

Blackstone, John Jacob and Renfred, with their men unscathed from their attack, quickly hobbled their horses and ran for the men standing in a staggered line. Killbere stood with Henry and Gifford at his side. The veteran knight appeared unperturbed.

'Your sword is blooded, Thomas. You caught them unawares then?'

'Aye, the bastards were sipping wine before they choked on their blood.'

They kept their eyes on the shifting smoke. It was clearing. Now they could see the killing field beyond the smoke. Two waves of horsemen.

'Skinners first and then the biggest bastard of them all,' said Blackstone.

Killbere laughed. 'Merciful Christ, Thomas, they are nothing but a ragged-arse scavenging bunch of thieves and vagabonds. Let's go to them and bring them down.'

He hefted his shield, ready to stride forward. A distant cry, a command from Will Longdon on one flank, echoed by Jack Halfpenny on the other, for the archers to shoot broadhead shafts into the flailing beasts. A painful wounding and death for the brave horses that would throw their riders.

Blackstone looked at Henry, who fixed his gaze on the carnage now less than two hundred yards ahead. No words were necessary. When the young Blackstone had fought his first terrifying encounter at Crécy, a boy of the same age, sixteen-year-old Edward of Woodstock, Prince of Wales, stood in the battle's vanguard. His father, the King of England, had looked on and refused to remove him to safety. Blackstone knew that decision took courage.

Now he had to drink from that same fountainhead.

'Forward!' he shouted.

As one man, they all stepped five yards ahead of the archers to take the brunt of the attack.

Horses fell screaming in pain. Their riders kicked free from the stirrups. They were disadvantaged, but that did not lessen their will to live and the only way to do that was to kill the men who lunged towards them.

Blackstone, Killbere and John Jacob were as formidable as a broadhead arrow point. Blackstone used his strength to hack his way forward, his shield slamming faltering men aside onto Killbere and John Jacob's blades as they stood two paces behind him. The killing was methodical. A steady, stride by stride, merciless ritual of death. Blackstone had no time to look for Henry and Gifford. Out of the corner of his eye, he saw Meulon thirty yards away slamming his shield against attackers as Brun then rammed down a blade into them. Bezián was further forward than most. He attacked flailing horses, ramming his sword into their chest or blinding them, and as riders tried to dismount he scythed his blade across arms and exposed throats. His shield long since abandoned, he danced this way and that, avoiding the dying horses' death throes and their iron-shod hooves that cracked the bones of helpless fallen riders as they tried to raise themselves from the ground before being slain by the Gascon.

Henry had not advanced as far as Blackstone or Killbere. Taking blows on his shield, he was warding off an attacker. Gifford had sidestepped a mercenary, struck him with his shield and when the man fell kicked his head with such force that the man's neck breaking was as stark as the sound of dry twigs snapping underfoot. Then Gifford hamstrung Henry's opponent. Henry hesitated, sucking in air, sweat stinging his eyes.

To hesitate was to die.

'Kill him!' Gifford yelled, moving forward to block another attacker.

The downed man's eyes widened. Teeth bared. Severed hamstrings sending flames of pain through him. Henry rammed his sword point into the man's open mouth.

Above the cacophony of rising screams of pain, he heard Blackstone shout a command.

'Shield wall! Shield wall!'

Bezián half turned, saw Blackstone, Killbere and John Jacob make a stand, shields raised. He looked across the dead and dying. More horsemen. They were struggling to breach the carcasses of the dead and the disarray of the wounded horses. Some beasts stood shivering, unmoving, slaked in their riders' blood. Shocked into immobility.

Bezián jumped over the dead to retrieve his shield and then joined the others. Will Longdon's archers were running from the exposed flanks to take up position at the rear of the captains and their men. The horsemen leading the new assault were 150 yards away.

Blackstone wiped an arm across his sweat- and bloodstained face. 'That's Visconti,' he said.

'And enough men to finish us,' said Killbere.

Blackstone turned, eyes searching out Longdon. A flight of lethal shafts might stop them being overrun. 'Will! Hurry, man!'

He caught sight of a blood-splattered Henry. He was bent

over, vomiting. All of them had done the same at some time in their lives. No sooner had he turned back to face Bernabò's armour-clad frame forcing his way towards him than distant blaring trumpets rolled across the open ground. Its effect was immediate. Bernabò reined in his horse. He shouted a command. The attack faltered. Wheeling his mount, he turned away, followed by his men.

Blackstone stared hard across the sun-streaked fields. Bernabò Visconti had drawn up his men and now faced the extended line of horsemen that had appeared.

'That's della Scala's banner,' said John Jacob.

'Then why in the name of the Almighty doesn't he swoop down and finish the job? Thomas, for pity's sake, he's sitting on the ridge.' Killbere stepped forward, dropped his shield, and let his sword dangle from its blood knot. He cupped both hands and bellowed. 'Kill them, you stupid bastard!'

The tableau beyond them did not change. Bernabò Visconti and his men didn't move. Neither did della Scala on the hilltop. And then, without haste, Bernabò cantered his men away from the battlefield, returning to the hills that would shield him and his men from sight and from where he could retreat.

'God's tears!' Killbere hissed. 'There goes the chance to kill the evil bastard and leave him for the crows.'

Blackstone snorted and spat. 'Perhaps that's not what della Scala wants. Remember what we said, Gilbert? Bitter enemies with a common cause?'

Killbere looked from Blackstone to the forest, where they had secured the mules. 'Aye. Then now we must see how true it is.'

A phalanx of men trotted down from the ridge towards them. They did not draw their swords. Their banner fluttered.

'I think we'll soon find out. That's Cansignorio della Scala himself,' said Blackstone.

CHAPTER FIFTY-SEVEN

The Lord of Verona drew up his horse beyond the dead and dying. The group of men with him held back ten paces. His banner remained unfurled, the weight of its blood-red material barely able to flap in the breeze. He was twenty-eight years old. His upper body, barrel-chested, bulged with muscle. The band of muscle across his back and shoulders made him look squatter than he was as he sat on his war horse. He wore an open-face bascinet, edged with gold and silver and sporting red and white ostrich feathers on its crown. The silver bridle and inlaid reins, and the intricately decorated saddle, made him – in Blackstone's eyes – another peacock flaunting his wealth and authority.

Blackstone waited. Wounded horses spasmed in their death throes. Dying men groaned pitifully, soon to be despatched with a knife thrust.

Della Scala's thick, dark beard, trimmed close to his jaw, parted as he smiled.

Killbere lowered his voice. 'Let's not forget that he murdered his brother barely ten years past to control Verona, Thomas. And if he did that as an eighteen-year-old, then see that smile as being of a wolf about to pounce.'

Blackstone loosened Wolf Sword's blood knot and slid its

blade into his scabbard. 'If we are to judge what men do when they are young, Gilbert, we all have sins to atone. You forget, our King seized power when he was younger still.'

'Aye, but he didn't slit his brother's throat to do it.'

Blackstone picked his way towards della Scala.

'Mind how you go, Thomas. It's not only men's guts on the ground that might cause a fall. The words you choose can tumble you into a bear pit.'

Blackstone caught Meulon's eye and made a slight gesture, enough for the throat-cutter to know he was to go among the wounded enemy and kill them. The big man pointed to six others to accompany him.

Cansignorio della Scala watched as Meulon began his work. 'You should let them suffer more, Sir Thomas. They're only paid men. They have no loyalty.'

Blackstone stood a few paces away and peered up at the man whose eyes stayed on the killing. 'We are all paid men one way or the other, lord. And who's to say our loyalty is any more noble than one man fighting alongside another?'

'Your loyalty is undiminished,' said della Scala, returning his gaze to Blackstone. 'But lessons should be taught. And the word of it always finds a way to reach beyond the killing field.'

'As word of my journey reached you? Or is your arrival a fortunate coincidence?'

Cansignorio della Scala sighed. 'News of the death of an English prince is fleet of foot. And then to hear that the King's Master of War rides north creates a curiosity. Is it not fortunate that I arrived when I did?'

'Look about you. Fortune already favoured me today,' Blackstone said.

Della Scala nudged his horse. 'I offer you and your men sanctuary so they may rest and treat the wounded. And safe passage for the cargo you carry, of course. Better it be kept without the threat of being seized.'

'And are you not seizing it, my lord?'

The wolf grin creased della Scala's face again. 'Only until we are sure it can be delivered safely to the... er... proper authorities.' He teased his reins, turning the horse. 'When you're ready, Sir Thomas.' With a final glance at the men being mercifully killed. 'You should have let them suffer,' he said, his voice tinged with regret.

Blackstone had lost five men in the fight. Two were from Meulon's command, three others those who fought in line with John Jacob and Killbere. Before leaving the field Blackstone had his men buried, their shallow graves covered with stones. Crows were already pecking the enemy dead.

Della Scala's men formed a column on either side of Blackstone's with della Scala leading the way with his banner and captains.

'We have his men either side, Thomas,' said Killbere, 'which tells me he has no intention of allowing us free passage. The bastard threatens us.'

'And heavily outnumbers us,' said Blackstone. 'To fight him would show our hand. It was our intention to deliver what he thinks to be the gold directly to his door.'

'Aye, but now the murderous whoreson treats us with disrespect.'

'My friend, we must endure some insult if we are to achieve our aim and discover who sent an assassin to kill our Prince.'

Killbere grunted. 'Him or Visconti, it makes no difference. Despenser is ready to join the Pope's forces. We should invade the damned place and be done with both of them.'

'Then, before you start a war between the English and della Scala, let us keep our wits about us and see what happens when we reach Verona.'

Killbere placed a finger on each nostril and blew free the snot. 'And Henry? How far do we go to find the ghost of a woman he's determined to seek out?'

'If the woman exists, and she's held by della Scala, then the assassin at the monastery who gave Henry the message points the finger at della Scala being the man who sent him.'

'And then?'

'We draw him out of his castle and kill him on the field of battle.'

Killbere grunted with satisfaction. 'Then I am a happy man. And it will be you who starts the war.'

CHAPTER FIFTY-EIGHT

Della Scala led the way, until late that day they saw the shimmering light of the vast lake in the distance.

Henry turned to Gifford, his voice constrained to barely a whisper as the goal he sought appeared. 'Hugh. Feast your eyes. That must be Lake Garda.'

Gifford looked to where the plain appeared to merge into the water. Either side of the lake, hills rose steeply, and in the distance those hills became high-peaked mountains. 'It's a natural fortress. Wherever she's held, there's no saying how you would reach her. She might be in a damned shepherd's hut up in those peaks.'

'No, della Scala has her. Scaligeri has four castles around the lake. She's in one of them.'

Gifford sighed. 'Aye, but which one? And by the look of our direction of travel, we're not going to any of them.'

Della Scala had turned east on a well-travelled road, leaving the lake behind them.

They spurred their horses into a canter, forcing peasants and the loads they carried to step aside. Henry risked questioning Blackstone. 'Lord, do we know where we're going?'

Blackstone looked back at his son. 'There seems little doubt we're riding for Verona.'

Henry felt despair grip him. So close and soon to be too far from the lake and for him to find Elena.

'It might be for the best,' said Gifford.

'Or not,' Henry answered. 'If the girl is in danger.'

'I fear Sir Thomas has more pressing matters on his mind,' said Gifford. 'The gold travels with us and we are being taken into a city. Easy enough to contain the men. He won't want that.'

As the day's light softened, Blackstone saw the distinctive swallow-tailed crenellations topping a castle's walls. Below those walls a broad river moved lazily, its surface tinged by a setting crimson sun. The river curved down to where the men waited, and then beyond, making a long, slow loop. They were at the bottom curve of the river, which meant they had the castle to their front, the river to their left and right. Their only way to retreat should they have to would be to travel back directly behind the way they had come. It took no experienced general to know that the two arms of the river stopped any retreat on either flank and that an overwhelming force could block their route out.

On this side of the river, meadows bled into forests and a stone beach reached into the water. A three-arched bridge constructed of brick with the same crenellations on its walls spanned the river and led into the castle. Della Scala had slowed the pace. The day's heat made every man sweat and the cool air from the flowing river refreshed tired riders. It had been a long day. A battle had been fought and Blackstone's men needed food and rest and to have their wounds attended to.

'Castello degli Scaligeri. This is where the Lord of Verona lays his head,' said Killbere.

'Damned if the place doesn't look impressive,' said John Jacob.

Blackstone turned to Will Longdon. 'Will? To my eye, it's a hundred and forty yards from this side of the river to the other.'

'Aye, near enough. Another twenty paces to that gate in the wall.' Longdon grinned. 'If I keep my bowmen this side of the river I could cover you if there was a need.'

'Thomas, we'd be hard-pressed to fight our way out from inside should we have to,' Killbere said. 'Even with the help of Will's lads.'

Blackstone was looking to the side of the river from where they approached the bridge. 'We must make our own decisions, Gilbert. The river protects the northern approach to the castle and if della Scala ever needed a quick escape, then he would use this bridge. He has other castles to run to. And if that was ever his plan, then we can also use it to escape if we must. We retreat through that gate if we have to and Will slows anyone giving chase. It might not come to that. Let's hear what della Scala proposes. If he invites the men inside, then they're vulnerable to crossbowmen on the walls. If he suggests leaving them outside, then there's only a handful of us for him to hold in the castle. If that's his plan. Gilbert?'

'Aye, right enough. If I were him, I'd have us and the captains taken inside. That would tell me he felt confident about overwhelming the men left without those who command them.'

Della Scala drew to a halt and conversed with his immediate staff. Horses swished their tails against the heat and flies. White streaks of sweat smeared their flanks and they champed the bit, eager to be allowed down to the river to drink.

Henry turned to Gifford, his voice tense with excitement, hushed so that no one else other than his companion could hear. 'Hugh! She's here! I know it!'

Gifford looked puzzled. 'So now you're a soothsayer? You see what normal men cannot?'

'I think she was held in one of the castles at the lake but

now there's official business being conducted here. Important business. And if it has something to do with her then she would have been brought here.'

'You're guessing all of this? I doubt the woman even exists. You must keep your boots on the ground and your head out of the clouds, Master Henry.'

Henry smiled. His mood lifted. 'You'll see.' He nudged his horse forward. 'My lord,' he said, addressing Blackstone. 'You see that banner?'

Blackstone had paid little attention to the flags lofted high above the swallow-tail walls. The breeze along the river unfurled them. Alongside the familiar red and white banner bearing the Scaligeri's blazon of a ladder, a second flag fluttered in the breeze. Its deep purple field was adorned with a golden cross and keys.

'That's a papal legate's banner,' said Henry. 'If there's a delegation inside then that means an ecclesiastical judgement is imminent. There is no other reason for them to proclaim their presence.'

Blackstone regarded his son. 'And I'll wager you think it has something to do with the woman.'

Henry nodded. 'An ecclesiastical court has to be convened to pronounce on the legitimacy of taking over domains held by another. It fits with everything I was told in Milan.'

'Damned lawyers,' spat Killbere. 'Priests and lawyers. Mother of Christ, a plague on them both.' He glanced at Henry. 'And you were set to become one.'

'A lawyer has his uses, Sir Gilbert.'

'A kick up the arse has its uses.'

'Whatever's going on it will be conducted in Latin,' Henry said.

A shared look of dismay passed between Blackstone, Killbere and John Jacob.

'And you are the only one among us who can speak Latin,' John Jacob said.

'Why else did I study so hard at Oxford?' Henry had the grace to smile.

'You were whoring in Oxford,' said Killbere. 'And I doubt you were sweet-talking whores in Latin.' He shook his head and then nudged his horse closer to Blackstone, his back to Henry. He lowered his voice to barely a whisper so that only Blackstone could hear. 'Thomas, if they discover that we delivered chests of scrap metal, we might require your over-educated son to argue our case to the damned priests.'

Blackstone glanced past his friend, checking to see that Henry hadn't heard. 'It won't come to that, Gilbert. We'd be dead before he uttered a word intelligible to our ears.' He sighed and raised his voice. 'All right, Henry. You will accompany me.' He drew breath. 'And don't look so damned pleased with yourself.'

One of della Scala's captains rode down the column to Blackstone. He spoke rapidly.

'I think he said that you, me and John are invited to join the Lord of Verona inside the *castello* along with my captains,' said Blackstone, glancing at his son for confirmation.

'And that he would provide a surgeon to treat the men's wounds,' Henry added.

The captain remained aloof, waiting for a reply. He then pointed to the mules and once again spoke rapidly.

'And the gold is to come with us,' said Blackstone.

Blackstone answered the messenger, picking his way through the Italian. 'Greet your Lord della Scala and offer my thanks. Tell him a few others will accompany me, as will our cargo, but that my captains stay with my men on this side of the river.'

'There you have it,' said Killbere. 'The bastard wanted to strip our men of their captains. He's up to no good.'

The messenger looked at Killbere, not understanding what was being said.

Killbere smiled at him, dipped his head and made a small gesture of respect. 'Your Lord of Verona is a treacherous whoreson, and given the chance, I would happily castrate him myself.' Another smile and a nod of the head.

As the insult was delivered, the men kept a straight face. Blackstone signalled for the messenger to leave.

'John, bring the captains forward. They need their orders. We take Mallin and Terrel inside with us to tend our horses. I don't want this belligerent beast kicking one of della Scala's grooms to death. Henry, you and Gifford as well. Keep your ears open, Henry. We might learn something we're not supposed to know.'

Henry watched his father's orders being carried out. The despair he had felt at the lake had gone; now his stomach squirmed with hope that he might be closer to what he sought. What had begun as a quest to find a woman who created beauty on a manuscript's page – a quest that had turned to ash on his tongue – had turned into a journey to solve the mystery of a dying man's words. Words which might soon prove to be true.

The light was fading. Burning torches and braziers were lit on the high walls. Illumination flared in the tower at each end of the wall facing Blackstone. Shadows moved along the parapet's walkway bristling with men.

'Gilbert, once we are inside, you and the others get up on those walls. We need to know what lies beyond them.'

The bastard horse's hooves clattered across the bridge. Blackstone would soon find out if the risk he had taken would expose the Lord of Verona's involvement in the Prince's assassination. But if it did, how would he kill Cansignorio della Scala and escape?

CHAPTER FIFTY-NINE

Blackstone followed the Lord of Verona into the Corte d'Armi; the vast courtyard of packed earth underfoot had cobbled and paved walkways around the four sides of the *castello*. The high crenellated walls loomed against the darkening sky. Light flickered from windows on the one side of the castle. This would be the residential part of the fortress. The windows with their pointed tops and columns and small balconies showed della Scala to be a man who mixed the strength of cut stone with an eye for beauty. Blackstone appreciated the skill required to create the decorative surrounds cut by master stonemasons and carvers. The Italian lord was renowned for making Verona one of the most beautiful cities in northern Italy, spurred on perhaps, Blackstone thought, as a rival to Milan.

It was obvious to Blackstone that the place was formidable enough to defend itself and sustain life for those inside its walls. Towers, six storeys tall with windows and arrow slits, buttressed the corner walls. Food smells from kitchens across the courtyard mingled with the acrid smoke from a forge. Garrison troops manned the walls and gates. Burning torches and lanterns were being lit around the yard. Liveried servants ran forward to secure della Scala's horse as his captains rode on across the far side of the yard to the stables. One servant tried to reach for Blackstone's bridle but the bastard horse swung its great head and knocked the man off balance.

'My horsemaster will take care of it,' Blackstone told him as della Scala cast a disapproving look at the assault made on one of his servants, an assault that added, in his mind, to the belligerent reputation of its rider.

'Blackstone, with me!'

The command had the bite of noble authority. Now secure in his castle, the Lord of Verona did not need to offer polite conversation.

Blackstone turned to the others. 'Gilbert, make sure the men stay close to the gold. Walter, take my horse.'

He dismounted and handed the reins to Mallin, who had jumped down to ease the bastard horse away from the other mounts. With a final nod to Killbere, Blackstone followed Cansignorio della Scala through an arched entrance and double heavy doors into the great hall.

Blackstone took in the expansive room. A fire blazed despite the night's warmth, the room's stone walls casting their own chill. Long cut logs were stacked beside the fireplace, in which stood an iron brazier grate the length of a man. Massive chestnut beams across the ceiling straddled the width of the hall. Tapestries hung on every wall, colourful and richly woven; the della Scala coat of arms in carved stone loomed over the fireplace. A smooth lime-plastered wall bore a religious fresco. A statue of the Madonna and Child stood in a corner beneath a window, the Virgin's mantle washed in a blue pigment. A large brass cross embedded with precious stones was displayed on a wooden cabinet. It was a room expressing the Lord of Milan's devotion.

Blackstone was twenty paces behind Cansignorio and stopped as della Scala pulled free his helmet and tossed it onto the heavy wooden table, avoiding a carafe of wine and ornate glass goblets. He watched as della Scala bent over, allowing the valets to pull free his mail. They scurried away as the broad-shouldered man tugged and loosened his sweat-soaked linen shirt from his chest. Blackstone studied him. The slab of muscle across his back complemented his deep chest and muscled arms. Della Scala waved away a willing servant waiting to pour and tipped the wine into the goblet himself, ignoring the spill settling on the tabletop. He quaffed a mouthful, stared at Blackstone and snarled.

'You attacked my men on your way to Milan. You think I don't know that?'

'They were *condottieri*. Paid men. You brought in savage killers from France. I saw some results of what they did on my way here. I didn't kill any of your men.'

Della Scala stared at Blackstone. He spat a grain of pressed grape and refilled his glass. Then he poured another and offered it to Blackstone.

'What game were you playing?'

Blackstone drank before answering. 'I needed to stop Bernabò from escalating the fight against you. The more of his men you killed, the more likely he would abandon Milan and that might have risked the Prince's wedding from going ahead. Killing a few of your mercenaries was a small price to pay to ensure nothing stopped the wedding.'

Della Scala looked away.

There stands a guilty man, thought Blackstone.

Della Scala sprawled into a half-backed chair draped in fur. 'I can afford to lose men like that. They were of poor quality. They had a simple job to do, and that was to harass Bernabò Visconti's men. I side with the Pope's forces. You should remember that, Blackstone.' He turned to look at the blazing log-fire.

Blackstone watched him. He appeared confident that no evidence pointed at his involvement in the Prince's death, yet an innocent man would have surely passed comment. Blackstone decided now was not the time to accuse him. Despite the absence of solid proof against him, Blackstone would find the right time to issue the challenge. Not now, though.

'Is that why there's a papal legate here?'

Della Scala turned his attention away from the flames. 'You saw the flag.'

'If you fight for the Pope, then perhaps you seek better recompense for your efforts,' Blackstone suggested, hoping to draw out the reason for the Church to be involved.

Della Scala ran his fingers through his matted hair, swirled the residue of wine from his glass and tossed it into the fire. The flames spat. He refilled the glass. Blackstone had only drunk half of what he had.

Della Scala shrugged. 'No, that is another matter. There's a court hearing. A land matter. I need to secure another domain. It's complicated.'

Blackstone watched as he sipped his wine. Complicated because of what Henry had found out? A failed assassination in a mountain monastery. An ageing assassin. A guardian trying to protect the welfare of a vulnerable woman? Who was the old man and who was the woman? What relationship did they have? A man, by all accounts, who willingly sacrificed his life rather than kill a prince of the realm. Henry's search and Blackstone's suspicion that Cansignorio della Scala was responsible for or at the very least involved in the assassination had caused father and son's worlds to collide here in the Castello degli Scaligeri in Verona.

An idea formed in Blackstone's mind how he could bring the accusation into the open.

Della Scala put the empty glass down on the table and stood. 'Tomorrow I would like to see the gold you carry.' He wiped a sleeve across his moist beard. 'Such a treasure needs to be kept safe. As I said, we must make sure it reaches the proper authorities.' This time there was no smile creasing his face. He turned his back and strode for a door in the far corner. 'Your men will be fed and given a place to sleep. I have already sent my physician across the river to treat your men's wounds.'

And no doubt have him report back on how my captains have prepared a defensive position, thought Blackstone.

He drained the glass. His stomach growled. He needed food.

CHAPTER SIXTY

Killbere and John Jacob had followed Mallin, leading Blackstone's horse into the stables. Grooms waited but steered clear of the bastard horse. Was it their sixth sense or had news of the beast's temperament already reached them? They guided the other mounts into individual stalls, bedded in deep hay with netted feed bags already in place hanging from the wall.

Terrel led the two mules into their own stall. The sturdy animals showed no sign of discomfort or fatigue and immediately began to chew hay from the feed bags. The grooms secured the other mounts, dragging the saddles onto wooden stands and then rubbing down the horses.

Killbere gestured to the encircling walls. 'Before we do anything else we get up onto the walkways and see what lies beyond.'

Henry and Gifford went together. They climbed the angled stairs to the walkways beneath the swallow-tail parapet. 'Keep your eyes sharp, Hugh. It's not only what lies beyond these walls that we need to search out.'

'You look where you must. If we have a fight ahead of us we need to know where della Scala's army is encamped.'

Henry fell silent. He nodded. The man-at-arms was right to correct him. The soldiers guarding the walls watched but never challenged them. They had seen them being brought into the *castello* by Lord Cansignorio.

Henry and Gifford reached the far corner where they could see the river's reflection curving to the north-east. The city lay predominately behind them but the city walls followed the river and then across onto the far bank into the countryside. On the far hills two more castles braced the walls before they curved back east and south. It was not just the castle that was fortified, Verona city and the countryside beyond was blockaded by walls. Della Scala must have a garrison of thousands to man so many walls.

Gifford pointed to an open area that lay to the north of where Blackstone's men were encamped. The hillside glittered with firelight. 'Our men are in an enclave. Those are della Scala's skinners. If he takes it in his head to encircle them all he has to do is close the gap behind them,' he said. 'Let's hope Sir Thomas has a plan.'

'He always does,' said Henry. But his confidence faltered at the sobering sight of so many armed men that close to their own. He slapped Gifford on the shoulder and pushed away the doubt. 'Come on. We report back and then we look for the woman I came to find.'

By the time they returned to the stables the others had delivered their report. The city nestled close to the walls on the opposite side of the river. Farmland and settlements stretched beyond as far as could be seen until they reached the extended city walls in the distance. Henry told Killbere what they had seen.

'Then we are well and truly surrounded and by the sound of it the only chance to escape is the way we rode in. All right. Now we attend to ourselves. John, get me out of this mail. My skin crawls in this heat.'

'Sir Gilbert, should we not try to find out as much as we can about what lies within the walls now that we know what's out there?'

John Jacob was helping Killbere off with his mail, so the voice from the bent-over knight was strained. 'God's tears, John – pull, man, pull.' The mail came free. Blackstone's squire laid it across Killbere's saddle. Killbere sat on the stool next to where his saddle rested. 'Will you not give a moment's respite to your hunger for this woman? Especially when we have to be fed?'

Henry had the sense not to pursue the matter. He had already decided he would explore as much as he could. 'Then Gifford and I will go to the kitchens, Sir Gilbert.'

'Good. Terrel, go with them. Bring a large pot of hot food so we don't have to ask for more. And bowls. And bread, and whatever meat is lying unclaimed on a spit. Thieve it if necessary. My teeth need something to chew on. Mallin, put your arse on that stool and stay with the mules. We'll organize a night's guard rotation when Sir Thomas returns.'

'Should we not unload them?' said the old horsemaster.

'If you've the strength, be my guest. No, they stay until we are told otherwise by Sir Thomas, but check them for any chafing from those caskets on top of their blankets.' He looked at Henry and the others as if to ask what they were waiting for. They went into the vast courtyard.

When out of earshot, Henry instructed the two men. 'Terrel, go into the kitchens and secure us food. Remember, Sir Thomas has yet to eat so a good enough amount for us all. Ask what you can of any woman held here or why there's a papal legation within the walls.'

'They're not going to tell me anything about that,' Terrel moaned. 'They'll raise a hand to me for being so damned nosey and the next thing you know, I'll have a knife in my hand and there's blood on the floor and I'm the one to be hanged.'

'Then curb your temper,' Gifford said. 'What Master Henry

asks is for nothing more than a guest of della Scala asking a simple question. How often does a common man get to see a papal legation? It's natural to ask.'

Defeated, Terrel shrugged. Gifford gestured him away. 'We should never have brought him out of France, Master Henry. He's weak. No spine.'

'He's proven himself so far. We must make allowances.'

'And hope he can manage to get us hot food without causing trouble. And us? What do you have in mind? I'm wary of what you're planning.'

Gifford strode alongside Henry as they walked around the perimeter, staying in the soft glow of wall lanterns. 'If there's a woman being held here, where would they put her?'

'The dungeon?'

Henry shook his head and pulled Gifford into the shadows. 'No. If the Church is here, then I'll wager she is the reason. Della Scala has a reputation for being as much of a tyrant as the Visconti, but he is also a devout man and would bend the knee to any Church edict, so although she is held against her will, she will not be harmed. No, she's up there somewhere,' he said, pointing to the opposite wing of the castle. A few lights burned in the lower windows but only one light showed from a single window on opposite sides of the building, leaving darkness in the other rooms between them. Above those darkened windows, on the top floor, only one window cast light into the night. 'Who is going to be isolated in those quarters?'

Gifford sighed. 'A bastard son? A mad wife? A mistress? A rabid dog fed on pilgrims? I am no diviner, but you're suggesting that's where the girl might be.'

'Yes. Girl or woman. That we have yet to determine.'

'And to determine that, I suggest we wait until the court convenes, and she is brought out for all to see. If, in fact, she is within the castle walls. For all anybody knows the ecclesiastical court is here for a different, unrelated reason.'

Henry laid a hand on his shoulder. 'Hugh, you lack imagination and a belief in fate.'

'Fate is a fickle bitch. She will entice a man towards her and then turn into a wolf and tear his flesh and before I sink my teeth into the nearest warm body...' He stared knowingly at Henry. '... we should eat.'

Henry accepted Hugh's suggestion and turned back towards the kitchen. And then he stopped, causing Gifford to curse under his breath as he bumped into Henry's back.

'There,' whispered Henry. He nodded towards a woman servant carrying a pot of food covered with a cloth. 'Men serve food. Women serve their mistress. I'll wager she's taking food to Elena.'

Hugh grabbed Henry's shoulder as he stepped out of the shadows, ready to follow the woman across the open expanse of the vast yard.

'No, Master Henry, we cannot do this.'

Henry snatched free. 'Go to the kitchens, help Terrel carry the food back to the stables, tell them I've gone to the latrines.' With that, he strode after the woman, who'd reached the far side of the yard and entered the darkened wing of the castle.

Gifford swallowed his irritation. For a moment, he was undecided whether to follow his orders or the man he was committed to guarding. Cursing his own indecision, he hastened after Henry.

The entrance to that wing of the castle was lit by a flickering oil lamp, casting deep shadows up the stone steps. The entrance extended deeper into the building, devoid of any light. Henry hesitated as he listened to the woman's footsteps scuffing the stairs ahead. When they stopped, he heard muted voices. A man's heavier timbre and the woman's higher register. They were on the upper floors, so he couldn't make out what they were saying. He was concentrating so much he didn't hear Gifford step into the entrance hall behind him. Startled, he twisted, hand reaching for his knife. Gifford's arm wrapped around his chest, pulling him against the wall.

'Easy,' he whispered. 'There's a man on the first floor. He stepped to the darkened window when I crossed the yard.'

Henry exhaled the tension in his chest and pointed up the stairs, meaning Gifford to listen. The voices continued for a few seconds more and then fell silent.

'There's another higher up,' said Henry.

'Perhaps the woman was taking food to him?' Gifford whispered.

It was a reasonable consideration. Henry's doubt was plain to see, even in the poor light. 'Would she stay up there if that's the case?'

Gifford shrugged. 'That depends what they plan after he's eaten.'

Again, Henry considered the possibility of a guard having a woman stay with him. He shook his head. 'Della Scala would never allow whores here. This is his home. And there would be no women servants taking them food. Besides, the woman was too well-dressed. No. She's up there. I'm convinced of it. But how do we get past the guard you saw on the next floor?'

Before Gifford could think of an answer, they heard the scuff of boots descending. With their backs against the wall, they slipped out into the darkness offered by the castle walls. Quickening their pace, they made for the stables.

Henry's mood surged with excitement. Now all he had to do was get past the guards who were on duty on the first landing and perhaps the one above. The obstacle they presented did not dampen his spirits.

He would find a way to reach Elena, the woman he had promised to save.

CHAPTER SIXTY-ONE

Henry and Gifford returned to the stables. Blackstone sat with Killbere, John Jacob and Mallin in a semi-circle as Terrel ladled pottage into wooden bowls. No sooner was it in the bowl than Killbere stirred the offering and spooned hot food into his mouth. He churned it in his mouth, grunting from its heat, drawing in air to cool it.

'Gilbert, you send fire past your throat into your belly when a moment's restraint would allow you to taste it.'

Killbere swallowed and blew on the bowl. 'Thomas, I have endured years of eating Will Longdon's offerings. Taste does not come into it.'

John Jacob had chosen his first spoonful carefully. 'Sir Gilbert, there is wild boar meat in here and it is seasoned with herbs. It's good.'

Killbere fished around his bowl. 'Terrel, you deny me the pleasure. There's no meat in here.'

Terrel, who remained standing with the ladle and pot shrugged. 'I show no favour, Sir Gilbert. It must have sunk to the bottom.'

'Then scoop deeper, man.'

'And for us,' said Henry as he and Gifford pulled up a stool each and grabbed a wooden bowl and spoon.

Terrel served the newcomers first as Killbere looked on.

'Am I not to be considered?' he moaned.

'Sir Gilbert, I wanted to make sure Master Henry and Gifford had a serving.'

'And yourself,' said Blackstone. 'Don't forget to fill your own bowl, Terrel.'

'Thank you, Sir Thomas.'

Terrel did as Blackstone suggested and then scooped the last of the pottage from the pot and tipped it into Killbere's bowl.

Killbere stared at the offering. 'I see none of the meat John spoke of.'

Terrel winced and shrugged. 'It's finished.'

Blackstone smiled at Killbere's disbelief and spooned some pieces of meat from his own bowl into Killbere's. 'Gilbert, we cannot have you bereft. There's enough for us all.'

The offering quietened Killbere's discontent. The men shared a loaf of bread, pleased to break the long fast since their last meal. Blackstone broke the silence.

'I am to show della Scala the gold tomorrow.'

John Jacob glanced at those who sat with them and who were not privy to the truth of what lay in the chests. 'So, then he knows what we carry.'

'Did we ever doubt it?' said Killbere.

John Jacob's spoon hovered between the bowl and his lips. 'And when he opens the chests?' It was an open-ended question.

'I'll open only one,' said Blackstone, following the same cautious line as his squire. 'The gold is another issue that might draw him on the Prince's death, but as yet I don't know how. I still think he had a hand in it. The message sent from France that Montferrat found, and what Henry was told by the assassin at the monastery, point a finger in his direction.'

'Even so, Sir Thomas, that's scant proof,' said John Jacob.

'Right enough, John. I'm not yet ready to challenge him about his involvement, but if Henry's wild goose chase for the girl proves to be a part of it then we might force his hand. Good fortune might be on our side with the papal legation being here. Perhaps I can challenge him to swear an oath in front of them that he had no part in or knowledge of the Prince's death. He would not condemn his soul by lying in front of them. And if he tries to talk his way out of it, then he's as good as admitting his guilt.'

'Aye, but you need spokes in a wheel to make it turn,' said Killbere, wiping up the last residue of the pottage with a piece of bread. 'We need evidence of the girl's association with the assassin and then to link that to della Scala. There mustn't be any doubt if we are to use the Church against him.'

'If the girl even exists,' said John Jacob.

Henry glanced at Gifford. It was time to tell his father where he thought the girl might be. Even though he still had no proof. But before he could speak, Terrel belched, his attention on the food in his bowl, and apparently without thinking said matter-of-factly: 'The girl's here all right. They held her in another castle up on the lake at Torri del Benaco. It's where della Scala has a lot of his administration. She was there for months. They brought her here ten days ago while they were waiting for the Cardinal to arrive. She's up in a room at the top of the west wing. Got a woman servant with her.'

He pushed his face into the bowl to lick any last morsel clinging to the sides, not yet conscious that everyone else was hanging on to his words. He wiped a sleeve across his face. 'It's a land claim. They had to wait until she was of age.' He realized the others were staring at him. He shrugged. 'I thought that's what you wanted to know,' he said, looking from one to the other.

'And who told you all this?' said Blackstone.

'Servants. They gossip. And having the Church here to give their judgement, that's all they can talk about.'

Blackstone looked at Henry. 'Then your quest has proved successful.'

'It will be successful when I fulfil my promise to save and protect her.'

'Well, you are not to challenge the Lord of Verona, do you understand?'

'I do, lord.'

Blackstone's glare reinforced his command. He addressed the others. 'Events are unfolding, and as they do, it will become clear how we should pursue this matter.'

'He has us caged, Thomas,' said Killbere. 'Challenging him is one matter. Drawing him outside these walls to fight is another.'

Blackstone didn't answer for a moment. 'Then we shall have to think of a way of provoking him.'

CHAPTER SIXTY-TWO

The castle servants were already going about their duties when Henry rolled clear of his blankets, eager to find a way of reaching Elena, the mysterious woman who had drawn him across northern Italy since that fateful day on the Mont Cenis Pass.

On the far side of the Corte d'Armi, a swarm of men were erecting a broad canopy as other servants constructed two levels of platforms. Chairs and benches were already being brought into the yard. Henry realized that this was where the court would be held. And if there was this amount of activity, then it meant the papal legate would sit today and hear Cansignorio della Scala's case against the woman Henry had yet to meet. As a papal flag was erected at each end of the canopy, Henry saw the servant woman crossing the yard carrying a wooden bucket in each hand. Each bucket had a lid and he guessed they would hold hot water for the woman facing trial to bathe.

Henry quickened his pace so that he could draw alongside her. She cast a wary look at him.

'What?' she snapped.

'I want to help.'

'Does it look as though I need help? Get out of my way. Let a woman do her work.'

He kept pace with her. 'I want to help the Lady Elena.'

She scoffed. 'And what use would a young man like you be? She needs no suitor; hot water to bathe is what she needs. Stop bothering me.'

'I am a lawyer,' he said, exaggerating his status.

'She needs no snake-tongued lawyer. She stands up for herself.'

'But an ecclesiastical court requires a knowledge of canon law.'

'Ha! Church or noblemen, they have their own laws to suit themselves. Speaking the truth will serve my mistress well enough.'

'And will she be able to speak that truth in Latin? Because that is the language of the court.'

The servant hesitated, but only for a moment. 'When a woman has to defend herself she will speak from the heart and they will listen. They can think in Latin while she speaks plainly.'

Henry was losing what looked to be the best chance he might have to reach Elena. 'Signor Salvarini sent me.'

The servant stopped in her tracks. Her face creased with concern. Her voice lowered. 'Do not seek to reach my mistress with false claims.'

Henry lowered his voice and held her gaze. 'I swear it's true.'

She turned her face away for a moment, as if deciding whether to believe what the young stranger had told her. She stared up at the top room where her mistress would be waiting. She became more conciliatory. 'Very well. If you attempt any move to harm her, I will kill you and go to the scaffold for my sin. Do not think because I am a woman that I would not do it. And if I fail, then my mistress will pierce your heart with her blade. Understood?'

Henry nodded. He would not admit to the servant that her mistress had already pierced his heart with longing.

She lowered the buckets. 'Then make yourself useful. The stairs are steep.' She gathered her skirts and walked off. Henry lifted the buckets and followed.

She was right. The stairs were steep and confirmed that the servant woman was as sturdy as she looked, and he was in no doubt that she could carry out her threat. They reached the first landing. A garrison soldier sat on a stool. He stood when he saw them turn up the half-landing.

'Who's he?'

'Never you mind,' she told him. 'I needed help. You think a woman my age can climb these stairs every day without help once in a while?'

'No one comes up here without permission,' the guard insisted.

The servant faltered. Her brash attempt to get past the guard had failed. Henry was four steps behind her, carrying the buckets. He reached the landing. 'This damned woman should be whipped,' he said, his voice sharp with authority. He put the buckets down and faced the guard. 'She pleads injury, yet she climbs these stairs like a mountain goat.'

The guard looked uncertain, but was having none of it. 'And who are you?'

'I am the woman's lawyer. The one you guard.'

'I know nothing of this.'

'Does Lord della Scala tell a common soldier what he desires? The woman's case is to be heard today, is it not?' he said, guessing the activity in the yard meant it was.

'So what?' said the guard.

'The papal legation insists the woman should have a voice before the court. I am that voice.' Henry slapped his jupon as if dusting himself off. 'Now, if Lord Cansignorio is to have matters go his way, he will do as the Church asks. If you wish to question your master, then I will wait here. Though I doubt you will be returning anytime soon.'

He stared down the guard, who hesitated. And then nodded. He stepped back to let them pass.

'A wise decision. I will make sure your good conduct is reported to your captain.'

The compliment flattered the lowly soldier. 'Thank you, signore.'

Henry gestured for the servant woman to carry on up the next flight of steps. He gave the guard a questioning look. The guard didn't understand.

'I am a lawyer, not this woman's servant.'

Without waiting for an answer, he turned onto the stairs, leaving the guard to heft the buckets and follow. At the top landing, another guard stepped forward and before he challenged the woman and Henry, his fellow soldier called out. 'Let them pass. He's to speak for the woman. Lord Cansignorio's orders.'

The guard retreated and let the woman and Henry go past him to the only door on the top landing. The woman was astute enough to open the door and then relieve the guard of the water buckets. Henry stepped inside after her and closed the door.

'Wait,' said the servant and disappeared with the water into another room. Where Henry waited was spacious. A rush flooring laid over wood. A fireplace and a supply of wood. The single window facing the yard was the one he had looked up at the night before. On the opposite wall was a similar window. He looked down onto the river and the three-arch bridge to one side. Across the river, he saw movement in the trees that crept down towards the river's stone beach. His eyesight was sharp enough to see that his father's men had prepared a defensive position. He was barely able to resist the temptation to open the window and call out to Meulon, who strode across the front line of defence to where the archers were stationed, but the moment was snatched away. He spun around at the sound of someone entering the room. It could be only one woman, shadowed by her servant, who stepped into the room.

Elena.

CHAPTER SIXTY-THREE

Henry stared at the young woman facing him. She was not yet fully dressed, her servant having summoned her to meet the man requesting an audience. The no-nonsense servant hovered a few paces behind her. Both women glared at the unbidden visitor. Henry had not averted his gaze. The mystery of the woman he sought, once an illusion, was now someone different from he had imagined. Yet not a disappointment.

She wore a chemise, and for propriety a loose gown to cover it. Her auburn hair was not yet braided and hung loose to her shoulders. There was a flash of defiance in her green eyes as she stared at Henry. Sharp and observant. Yet there was a hint of concern at his presence. Her skin was fairer than that of her servant. A trait Henry knew was not unusual among northern Italians.

'Who are you?' she said.

For a second, he hesitated. Should he remain disguised by his mother's name or declare his true identity? 'I am Henry de Sainteny. And I am here to serve you.'

'Sainteny?' The word was a whisper. As if trying to remember whether she knew of his name. 'You say a man called Salvarini sent you?'

'He did, my lady.'

'With a message?'

'Yes. That you were being held and that you needed protection.'

'And he told you of the predicament I face?'

'No, that I learnt from a lady in Milan.' He saw the glint of alarm in her eyes. 'She is a woman of nobility that I trust, as she favours me with hers. She told me you were being held at Lake Garda.'

'I was. And then they brought me here to face the papal legate and the man who wishes to steal my inheritance. She hesitated. 'I am abandoned to my defence. How are you able to help me?'

'My lady, I am not a lawyer who has practised in any court. I am an Englishman who studied at Oxford University and I was going to study law at Bologna, which is renowned for its legal teaching. I cannot profess to be anything more than a Latin student who knows Roman law. And hope that what little I know might benefit your cause.'

She listened attentively and then settled into a small half-curved chair. She draped her gown across her legs. The servant woman stayed where she was. Within striking range, thought Henry, should he prove to be a threat.

'I am to be paraded before a cardinal and officers of his court. Noblemen will be there as witness. The Church has an interest in my lands being seized. Cansignorio della Scala supports the Pope, and the Pope likes to bargain for territory. It is called a papal hearing but it is a trial. I am being judged as to my ability to control my inheritance.' She glanced at the river through the window. Freedom denied. 'And for the lands to be seized I am to be married off to a man old enough to be my grandfather.'

The servant woman couldn't restrain her outburst. 'A man of cruel habits whose previous two wives sit at the feet of Our Lord'—she crossed herself—'released from a vicious monster. Thankful, I'll wager, that the pestilence took them.'

Elena raised a hand in gentle rebuke. The servant bowed her head.

'Della Scala gains another ally by offering me. And the Lord of Verona also gets my inheritance. You see, Master de Sainteny, I have already lost my case before it has begun. What use would I have of your services, no matter how noble your intention in offering them?'

Henry's mind raced. Salvarini had used his desire to find the beautiful woman he thought existed and had sent him to protect this woman. What kind of protection could he have intended? Salvarini did not know that Henry had studied Latin and Roman law, so he must have meant for him to fight for her.

'Then I will fight for you. I will be your champion,' said Henry.

She smiled. Was his naivety so obvious?

However, Elena didn't mock him. 'The Church does not permit duels. You should know that, Master Scholar.'

'Then we must challenge them in court. It's the only way. Even if you believe you cannot win. What is the best outcome you could wish for?'

Henry's suggestion was one she had never considered. He saw her flicker of hope.

'Freedom. I would rather be poor than enter into a marriage with a man I abhor, even if it means my inheritance being stolen.'

'Then if nothing else, my lady, I will secure that for you.'

Elena looked at the serving woman. 'If Master de Sainteny gives me that priceless gift, then we are both cast out into the world, Morena.'

The admission of the servant's name enhanced Henry's sense of achievement. It was a step closer to the young woman trusting him. The servant nodded fervently at the prospect of her young mistress's freedom. 'We will find a way to live, signora. No matter what.'

'Then I accept your offer,' said Elena. She stood and extended her hand. Henry bowed and kissed it.

'There is a part of this story I do not understand,' said Henry.

'Della Scala sent away a man sworn to protect you.' He chose not to mention that Salvarini's mission was to kill a prince.

'If he hadn't gone – for whatever reason Cansignorio demanded of him – I would have been killed.'

So, Henry thought, she didn't know why Salvarini had been sent north to intercept the Prince.

'He went to save my life. The bargain was struck. He was already ailing. There was nothing else he could do. And with you being here, that tells me he is dead.'

'Yes, my lady. He is.'

'Were you there? Do you know how he died?'

Henry remembered every moment of that fateful encounter. 'He died... he died saving an English prince,' he said. In a manner of speaking that was true. The old man's moral aversion to committing murder had caused him to hesitate. He had sacrificed himself. 'And he died in my arms.'

Elena's hand rested on her lips. Morena, her servant, placed her hands on her mistress's shoulders.

Henry dipped his head. 'He was as loyal a servant as anyone could hope for. His dying breath was that he had failed to protect you and urged me to seek you out so that I might. Such a guardian, my lady, is a rare man.'

'My guardian since birth,' she said with a rueful smile. 'When my mother died, bringing me into this world.'

'Then his memory will be honoured,' Henry said.

She nodded and gathered her robe around her. 'It always was,' she said. 'My father was a kind and generous man.'

Like a condemned spirit looming from the grave, history repeated itself. Blackstone had unknowingly killed Christiana's father when he first went into battle as a sixteen-year-old archer. Henry felt the same deathly chill embrace him. Not for one moment in his obsession with finding the woman he pursued had he thought of Salvarini being anything more than a loyal servant.

Now the knowledge he had killed her father clawed his heart.

CHAPTER SIXTY-FOUR

Blackstone and Killbere hunched over a wash bucket, sluicing their faces, using the exercise to watch the activity in the yard. Della Scala was nowhere to be seen, but the fevered activity of the servants setting up the dais and canopy signalled that the hearing against the woman would take place that day.

Killbere nudged Blackstone as he rubbed a drying cloth over his face. 'What's wrong with Henry? He looks like someone kicked him in the balls.'

They watched as Henry made his way towards them, head down, scowling. When he looked up and saw his father and Killbere watching him, he veered away and went into the stables through another entrance.

'God's tears, Thomas, I'll wager the lad's found the woman, and she's the face of an upturned bucket and the body of a toad. He was thinking he was going to find some damned fairy-tale princess.'

'Whatever the reason, he'd better snap out of it,' said Blackstone. 'He's to translate for us what's going on when the whole thing starts.'

Killbere sluiced away the bucket of water. 'Thomas, how does this play out? How do we goad this bastard to fight us?

We can't do it here. We'd be cut down before we made ten yards against him.'

Blackstone pulled his fingers through his long hair and reached for his jupon. 'We use the trial. There'll be noblemen in those stands to act as witness to the Church's decision.'

'The woman has no prospect of keeping her lands,' Killbere said, pulling his shirt over his head. 'I don't see how this damned entertainment for della Scala, because that's what it is, aids us.'

'The trial holds their attention. Once the verdict is given, then I will make my claim against della Scala. We will stir the hornet's nest and see what happens.'

'Us getting thrown into a dungeon and worse is what'll happen.'

Blackstone saw a captain of the guard approaching with his men. 'No, Gilbert, we'll use the occasion to our advantage. But here they come for the gold. Let's hope I can bluff our way through this.'

The guard commander stopped a few paces away from Blackstone. He dipped his head, acknowledging Blackstone's rank. 'Sir Thomas, my Lord della Scala requests you have the gold brought to him.'

'Of course,' said Blackstone. He turned aside to Killbere. 'Find Henry and see what ails him.' He gestured to the guard commander and led him into the stable where the mules still carried the caskets. The beasts of burden were unperturbed by the weight they still bore and munched on the feed nets. Mallin and Terrel stepped aside from the stall which they had been tasked to watch. Blackstone pointed to the one chest he hoped della Scala would not inspect too closely.

'It takes four men to lift each chest,' he told the guard commander, who had only six men with him. 'One chest will satisfy Lord Cansignorio. Use those rods on the mules and put them through the iron hoops.'

He stood back as the men were told to do as Blackstone instructed. The four garrison soldiers struggled to lift the weight off the back of the mule. Blackstone nodded to Terrel to lend a hand. Mallin went forward and placed a calming hand on the mule's face and muzzle as it shuddered from the men's clumsy efforts. The chest was lowered and the four men assigned to carry it spat on their hands, bent their backs and lifted as one.

The guard commander held out his hand. 'And you have the key? Sir Thomas?'

'I do,' said Blackstone. 'And I shall keep it. I'll accompany you and open the chest for inspection.'

That was not what the guard commander's orders had been, but who was he to challenge the scar-faced English knight? 'Very well.'

He led the men carrying the chest across the courtyard. Blackstone patted the key tied around his neck and tucked beneath his shirt. A man's greed would soon determine whether or not his bluff would work.

Cansignorio della Scala stood arms outstretched in the great hall as two valets dressed him, fussing over the decorated tunic, one moving to his front to fasten the ties. The della Scala blazon decorated the long sleeves alongside other designs.

'Down there!' he commanded the men carrying the casket. Della Scala glanced from his captain to Blackstone. 'Who has the key?'

'I do, my lord,' said Blackstone.

Della Scala did not rebuke his captain. He nodded. The men bowed and left. He offered no greeting to Blackstone, who had dipped his head respectfully. Better not to antagonize the Lord of Verona before it was necessary. Blackstone acknowledged the superiority in rank of the Veronese lord, who glanced his way and then turned his attention to the manner of his dressing. Unconcerned, Blackstone waited, hiding his bemusement at the show being presented to him.

On the broad chestnut table to one side lay della Scala's

sword and bejewelled scabbard, almost matched in its finery by the sheathed dagger. The trial today would be as much a ceremony as a hearing, and those attending would wear their finest clothes. Two more valets stood to one side, holding della Scala's mantle to be worn over his tunic. Once the tunic was arranged, the servants attached the sword belt and dagger.

Della Scala shrugged and tested the fitting. He nodded. The servants stepped behind him and lifted the mantle onto his shoulders. The fabric – scarlet and dark blue velvet, with intricate patterns stitched in gold thread – declared della Scala's wealth and status. A sable trim adorned the mantle's edge.

A nod of his head told the valets he was satisfied. They retreated.

'Blackstone, why only one chest? I wanted to see it all.'

'My lord, one chest is much the same as the other. There were not enough men to carry the rest. The Lord of Verona is no stranger to gold.'

'Don't flatter me, Blackstone. Open it. I want to see the Visconti gold glitter under my roof.'

Blackstone undid his jupon and loosened the ties on his shirt. Della Scala had made his intention clear. He wanted the Visconti gold for himself.

Della Scala waved a finger as Blackstone pulled free the key. 'You bear the cross and something other. What is that? Pagan? It would not sit well with me or the papal legate if he knew I housed a heretic.'

'It's Arianrhod, the Goddess of the Silver Wheel. She is an archer's token.'

Della Scala grunted. 'Ah, I had forgotten you were once more common than you are now, Sir Thomas. But at least you wear the cross. Very well, keep it hidden and no more will be said.' He made an impatient gesture for the chest to be opened.

'My lord,' said Blackstone, offering the key to the lock without inserting it. 'Milanese locksmiths are renowned for their skill. The teeth of the key must align, but then there can be no hurry. The lock must embrace the key.'

Della Scala frowned. 'There is this one key for all the chests?'

'Only one,' said Blackstone.

Della Scala nodded and waited expectantly as Blackstone inserted the key and made a show of taking time for the lock and the key to sit correctly. 'There must be no hurry,' said Blackstone, thinking ahead. He knew Della Scala would seize the gold by one means or another once the trial was over – Blackstone had no doubt that there would be some excuse offered. But when he left the *castello*, he wanted Della Scala to take as much time as possible before resorting to his blacksmith smashing the locks. Once the subterfuge was discovered and Cansignorio's overwhelming force gave chase, he and his men needed to have covered as much distance as possible.

The key clicked. The lock turned. Blackstone saw della Scala's eyes widen with expectation. Blackstone lifted the lid, checking that the coins sacrificed for the ploy had not shifted or exposed the scrap metal below. It looked as if the chest was full to the brim with gold florins. The raised lid obscured the sight from della Scala, who stepped around. He laid a hand on top of the coins. Blackstone hoped he did not dig down to clasp a handful. Cansignorio's fingers curled into a claw and scraped a few pieces from the surface. His eyes never left the bed of gold. The coins tinkled from his fingers as he let them fall back to join the others.

Blackstone eased down the lid, locked the chest and replaced the key around his neck.

Della Scala's throat had tightened; his voice's timbre lowered. 'Two hundred thousand in four chests,' he said. It was not a question but a confirmation to himself that the Visconti gold was now held in his castle walls. He saw Blackstone tuck the key away. He was shrewd enough not to demand it.

'We must discuss this matter, Sir Thomas,' he said, his voice more conciliatory.

'Of course, my lord. Shall we leave this chest here?'

'Yes, yes, leave it here. It will remain where it is until we meet again after the papal hearing. It is safe here. So heavy no one man can lift it. And the other three chests?'

'Guarded by my men.'

'Good. Yes, as it should be,' said della Scala, clearly subduing his desire to have it all brought to the great hall, his longing for the wealth barely suppressed.

Blackstone took a couple of paces back and bowed. Then he faced della Scala. 'It is my King's gold,' he said simply. 'I mean for it to reach him.'

'I would expect nothing less.'

The two men held each other's gaze a moment longer.

'By your leave, my lord?' said Blackstone.

Della Scala nodded his approval for Blackstone to leave. As Blackstone turned, he saw the Lord of Verona place a possessive hand on the chest's lid.

Blackstone knew fate was racing towards him and his men. Whom would it favour? If Blackstone's plan failed, their heads would be on a spike by nightfall and his men surrounded and cut down.

It now depended on who drew first blood.

CHAPTER SIXTY-FIVE

John Jacob and Gifford walked to where Killbere waited. The veteran knight sat on a stool outside the stables, watching the final preparations for the hearing as he peeled a fig and sucked its pulp. A breeze had picked up along the river, teasing the heavy papal flags bearing the crossed keys of St Peter. Six tables and benches were arranged in front of the raised dais, with three more rows of benches under the canopy behind it. That's where the invited noblemen would be sitting. In front of them would be the papal legate. Clerks would sit below, recording proceedings in Latin to ensure adherence to canon law. Much good it would do for scholars in the future, Killbere thought, spitting out a seed, the truth would be something different. The case would be manipulated. The rich bastards would have the best legal minds. And the Church would have its snout in the trough as well. Killbere tossed the fig skin away and punctuated his thoughts with a satisfying fart.

'Well?' he asked John Jacob, whom he had sent to find Henry.

John Jacob helped himself to one of the figs in the basket next to Killbere. He felt its firmness and put his nose to it. 'He won't say what ails him.'

'John, give him a damned cuff around the ear. When times

were hard, you were his surrogate father. He needs to understand that he's not a mewling infant.'

'I do that, Sir Gilbert, and he'd as soon strike me back. His skin is brittle. It bleeds easily.' He sat on the nearby stool.

'Hugh, you're his man. You must know something.'

Gifford leaned against the stable wall and accepted a fig from John Jacob. 'Sir Gilbert, he will not speak to me either. He's a man struck dumb.'

'It has to be the woman,' said Killbere. 'Have you seen her?'

'I have not. He went off this morning and found a way into her chambers.'

Killbere picked his teeth free of a lodged pip. 'Merciful Christ, do you think he bedded her? If she is a woman of vigour and he couldn't perform, that can cast a man into the abyss.'

John Jacob gave a questioning look his way.

'Not that I have ever experienced such a blight, but it's commonly known among physicians and such.'

Gifford shook his head. 'If there was sex to be had, his grin would be breaking his face. I knew the lad at Oxford. He could not satisfy his lust. Perhaps he made advances, and she rebuffed him.'

'Aye, I've heard that can shrink a man's cock and close his heart,' Killbere admitted.

'Not that any woman has ever rebuffed you though?' John Jacob said, grinning.

'I admit I have been obliged to increase the payment for a desirable whore once in a while, John. A business transaction does not have the same death knell as a lover impassioned with desire, and if young Henry had his heart set on this woman, then I'll wager she has spurned him. Aye, that will be it.'

John Jacob stood when he saw Blackstone approaching. 'It's late in the day for Sir Thomas to hear about his son's malaise. The hearing begins soon enough, and he needs Henry to translate so he can plan his next move.'

'Thomas? Did you show della Scala the gold?' said Killbere.

'I did. And he lusts for it.' He looked at the dais and canopy. 'The hearing will start soon. We must have the horses saddled. If my plan is to work, then we will be back with the men before nightfall.'

'And what plan is that, Thomas?' said Killbere.

'Once we hear the woman's case, then I will accuse della Scala of sending an assassin to stop the Prince from reaching Italy.'

The gathered men looked stunned. John Jacob saw the reality of it. 'Then he'll challenge you to a duel.'

'And the Church will never permit it,' said Killbere.

'I'm counting on della Scala's pride to convince them to allow it.'

'And if you kill him, Sir Thomas?' said John Jacob.

'That will come later. If he appeals and convinces the papal legate that he has the right to defend his name, then it will be a duel to first blood or the first to yield. After that, when we're gone from here, he'll give chase.'

'A half-decent plan, Thomas,' said Killbere. 'Those attending will bear witness no harm can be inflicted on you once the duel is over. But what if he doesn't confess?'

'No matter. I'll wager every gold florin gifted to our Prince that della Scala and the Church will want to get their hands on what they think lies in those chests. And when they eventually open them, della Scala will not be able to keep his rage in check. Humiliation and greed. They are essential to the outcome we seek.'

'Thomas, he's a sturdy man with a fearsome reputation. And that leg of yours is not yet fully healed.'

'Then I'll have to make an allowance for it, Gilbert. This is the way to goad this bastard out from behind these walls.'

'Sir Thomas,' said Gifford, 'does the woman play any part in this?'

'Do we believe she will escape judgement against her?' said Blackstone. 'We are here for the man behind the assassination attempt. I suspect the girl's fate is already written. But if she is abandoned because of the ruling then we will take her with us. Once Henry translates the proceedings, we'll understand her fate.'

None of the men had spoken about Henry. An awkward glance passed between them.

'Thomas, some hidden hand has struck Henry dumb. We don't know what. Neither Gifford nor John can get a word from him.'

'He's sitting in a stall, head in his hands,' said John Jacob.

'What ails him?' Blackstone looked at the basket of figs. 'Too many of them can purge a man.'

'It's nothing he's eaten, Sir Thomas,' said Gifford. 'It's something to do with the woman.'

Blackstone, his patience stretched, gritted his teeth. He closed his eyes for a moment, then took a breath. 'I need his skill with the language. If he's to be no use to me, I'll send him back to the men. What in God's name has the woman done to him?'

The men's silence compounded his frustration. A church bell rang in the city. 'Time is pressing,' he said. 'Make yourselves and the horses ready. With or without his help, we'll be gone from this place by nightfall. Where is he?'

Blackstone found Henry in an empty stall, squatting with his back against the wooden divide, head in his hands.

'Stand up,' said a stern-voiced Blackstone.

Henry glanced up with a grief-stricken face and pushed himself upright. 'My lord,' he said.

'We are alone, Henry.' Giving Henry permission to address him as his father. 'What is this?'

'I saw Elena. She's a girl. Sixteen years old and vulnerable. She has no chance against della Scala's lawyers. I said I would represent her.'

Blackstone stared at his son. His self-willed behaviour had now placed him in front of the papal legate and della Scala's lawyer. 'Because her dilemma touched your heart, but your mind lagged behind it.'

Henry was defiant enough to face his father without flinching. 'Would you have abandoned my mother if you stood where I stand now?'

'I rescued your mother and fought a war. I damned near died. She nursed me. The bond between your mother and me was more than a random meeting, unlike your pursuit of a ghostly woman. She can have no meaning for you.' He paused. 'All right. Your heart is in the right place. Now, have Gifford brush your clothing and attend to your appearance. If you have committed to her, then you will see it through. I had hoped you would translate the proceedings. Now you force me to sit in ignorance like a deaf man. It is what it is.' He studied his son. Blackstone's acceptance of the situation had not lifted his mood. 'What in God's name ails you? There's a battle to be fought with words, and you are the woman's champion. Where's your courage? This is no time for regret.'

'I killed her father.'

'What?'

'I thought Salvarini might have been a man who served her family. But he was her father who sacrificed himself for her. He fooled me and found a way to send me to her. To save her.'

Blackstone's memory never let him forget. It haunted him. A fateful day twenty-two years before when an old knight challenged the invading English and his arrow struck down a courageous man. He reached out and gripped Henry's shoulders. 'Look at me, Henry. You must endure this.'

'I don't know how. I remember the breach it caused between you and my mother when she learnt the truth.'

'There are times when we should bury the truth. Bury it deep and cover it with river stones so that it can never be dug up. If this woman has touched your heart, then so be it. Your duty now is to live up to your promise. Defend her. After that, well, none of us know what the future holds. But do not make the same mistake as I did. One can never forgive that pain, no matter how deeply feelings might run. Understand me?'

'I do, Father.'

'This is your burden. No one else's. But you must take solace from that man's death. He held back from killing the Prince knowing he was going to die by your hand. Salvarini allowed that to happen so he could send you here. Everything he did, he did for his daughter. Accept that. He died by your hand and his desire. There is no blame.'

Blackstone pulled his son to him. The embrace was brief. Given with love and strength. And then relinquished. 'You are my son. Now you will honour me and her father. When the hearing is done, I'll turn to you for help so that my plan will succeed. I need you, Henry. Focus your mind and put your grieving heart to rest.'

Blackstone's words and embrace shook away the melancholy that gripped him.

Henry nodded. 'Send Gifford to me. I must be ready.'

CHAPTER SIXTY-SIX

Blackstone and the others stayed at the entrance to the stables as they watched Henry stride across the yard to the entrance of the girl's apartment, where he would wait to accompany her. He looked more presentable than when Blackstone had spoken to him, but he was clearly a commoner, his dress plain when compared to the richness of della Scala's attire and of those noblemen who were already seated beneath the canopy. Four liveried guards were waiting to escort the subject of the hearing to where the full ceremonial panoply of the papal legates waited. The Cardinal had not yet arrived. The clerks sat waiting at their writing desks, each with sharpened quills and parchment.

Cansignorio della Scala sat next to his lawyer, and a table bearing documents. They faced the court under a small canopy to shield them from the day's heat. Ten paces to one side was a low curved chair in the shade of a similar canopy. Elena Salvarini was to be the centre of attention sitting in front of the papal legate. There was no table. No documents. Whatever Henry Blackstone was going to say had to be recalled from his time studying at Oxford.

A murmur rippled through the crowd as Elena came out of the building. Her dress was modest, but elegant. Its dark green silk shimmered. Her braided hair was tied with two silk ribbons. Henry thought she was beautiful. His uncertainty of not knowing how to approach her when he had met her earlier had been replaced by the self-confidence that had served him well at Oxford. Elena dipped her head to acknowledge his presence. Her smile warmed him.

'Master Henry, let us face my tormentor with dignity. I would be grateful if you would escort me.'

'My lady,' said Henry, forcing aside the burden that her father had died by his hand and more clearheaded than he remembered being for some time. She laid her arm on his, and with the other, touched the simple gold necklace at her throat which Henry guessed was an heirloom inherited from her late mother. As they walked without haste towards the dais, the four guards kept pace, five strides ahead and at the rear. Once they reached the small canopy over her chair, she sat, her back straight, hands folded in her lap. Henry stepped to one side and waited. He glanced to where della Scala stared at him and then had a whispered conversation with his lawyer. Henry restrained the smile that tried to break out. He had scored the first minor victory over the Lord of Verona, who had not known Elena was to be represented.

Those attending the hearing stood and bowed as Cardinal Guido Alberti da Viterbo, the papal legate, was escorted to take his place. The tall, angular man with sharp features showed his authority in his bearing. He wore a scarlet cassock with a matching mozzetta, a short cape, across his shoulders. As he bent to settle into the ornate and gilded chair, his hand steadied the large gold cross adorned with pearls and rubies hanging from its chain, pressing it against the white vestment over his cassock.

Henry noticed the size of the ring on his finger. The Church was there in all its glory, wealth and power. His mouth dried. He swallowed, forcing spittle to ease his throat. He would have to make the first move because as the Cardinal sat and an attendant straightened his biretta, the cleric's eyes had not left Henry. They pierced him with a frightening intensity. Henry knew this was his first challenge: to meet that gaze and not to flinch. A memory flashed into his mind: when the warden had summoned him to the office at Merton College. Master William Durant had challenged him then as well. Accused him of not attending to his studies. The questioning was in Latin, as was the rule. This Cardinal was no William Durant whose niece Henry was bedding. This man had such authority that even Cansignorio della Scala would yield before it.

The Cardinal nodded, struck the gavel once on the gavel's block to signify the hearing was in session.

Della Scala's lawyer took a step forward to begin his defence of his client but Henry beat him to it. He bowed and addressed the Cardinal in Latin, his voice carrying across the vast yard.

'*Reverendissime legate, illustrissime domine Cansignorio, adsum pro hac iuvene domina.*'

The murmur from the gathered noblemen fell silent. Henry waited. The Cardinal stared at him.

At the stable Blackstone and the others squatted on their stools watching the spectacle unfold.

'Damned if we're to know what in God's name is being said, Thomas,' said Killbere.

'Henry has to find a way for the girl to understand. Until then, like her, we sit in ignorance.'

'He paid respects to the Cardinal and honoured della Scala. Said he was speaking for the woman,' Mallin said nonchalantly.

John Jacob nearly fell off his stool as he twisted around to look at the old man.

'You understand what's going on?' said Blackstone.

'I do.'

'What?' Blackstone asked. 'How?'

Mallin shrugged. 'I was a foundling. Spent twelve years being raised by Franciscans. Latin was their common tongue. Taught me all I know about looking after horses. I ran from the place when I had the legs to carry me.'

'Then why didn't you speak up before?' said Blackstone.

'You never asked. There was no need.'

The men's surprise settled.

'Well, now there's a need. You'll tell us what happens.'

After Henry had addressed the Cardinal and flattered della Scala, his lawyer stepped forward to object that the Englishman was not even a notary and had no standing in the hearing.

Henry's knowledge of the language was as effortless as that of his native tongue. He was about to respond to the criticism when the Cardinal raised a hand to cut della Scala's lawyer short.

'I determine who stands here.' He faced Henry. 'Who are you?'

'I am Henry de Sainteny.'

'How is it you speak and understand Latin?'

Henry answered carefully, explaining he had studied rhetoric, Latin and Roman law at Oxford. The Cardinal nodded his understanding. The place of learning had a reputation as esteemed as that of Paris and Bologna.

'And what can you know of what is being considered here?'

'This case is not one of land alone, but of a young woman's inheritance threatened by coercion and greed. In the eyes of both divine and human law, her rights are inviolable.'

The Cardinal sighed. He turned to della Scala's lawyer. 'So, we have a scholar who understands the principles of justice. I hope you have rehearsed your arguments, Maestro Bernini. Present your petition to us.'

Della Scala's lawyer took a step forward and bowed his head.

Elena touched Henry's arm. 'Are they going to allow you to speak for me?' she said in a low voice.

Henry glanced down and nodded. He gave a reassuring smile, which she returned. It fed his confidence. He turned back to concentrate on what the opposing lawyer was saying.

'My Lord della Scala does not act out of selfishness. The late nobleman's death has left his lands without a strong ruler. In the best interests of the region, he would control half lest they fall into disrepair or lawlessness under one so young and inexperienced. He then proposes the girl's marriage to a nobleman known and respected by Lord Cansignorio, so that the rest of the lands remain secure. Our feudal system states plainly that an experienced lord should control such lands.' He nodded towards Elena. 'Not a girl who has not yet come of age.'

The Cardinal clearly expected Henry to offer a counter-argument. He nodded at Henry, who felt that the Cardinal might favour him as he had already touched on divine rather than feudal law. However, they would put aside divine law when considering the practicality of a lord's domain and its security. His mind searched back for one of the many lectures he had attended rather than go drinking in the Bear Inn in Oxford with Gifford. If the students could not compose an intelligent argument using Roman law, the tutors did not show any leniency. Ridicule was their weapon of choice. One of the key textbooks he had studied was that of a twelfth-century monk, Gratian from Bologna, known as the 'Father of Canon Law', and his standard legal text book was required reading.

'Gratian's *Decretum*'s principles assert the necessity of upholding rightful inheritance that supersedes any claims of political expediency. The lands in question have been in her family for generations.'

Henry was struggling to find the finer points of law that an experienced lawyer would present. But whatever had been drummed into him during those lectures started to surface in Henry's mind. '*Corpus Juris Civilis*. Justice demands we grant each their due. This young woman's due *is* her rightful inheritance. It is not to be forced into an unwanted marriage to expand another man's power.'

Della Scala's lawyer smiled and picked up the tied pages from his desk. 'The welfare of the people is the supreme law! This alliance and the control of her land are not just for her benefit but for all who dwell on those lands. These rights must be guarded.' He extended the pages as if offering them as evidence. 'As Ulpian reminds us in his *Digest*.'

Henry remained silent. He was concentrating hard on how to counter one legitimate and respected jurist's reasoning against another. But what other? An anxious Elena looked up, sensing his uncertainty. He forced a smile. The Cardinal leaned forward, questioning whether he would continue. Henry raised a hand to acknowledge the unspoken question. He nodded. Took another moment and then faced the Cardinal.

'Tradition might exclude women from inheritance without a male heir,' he said, pacing his argument, trying to put the emphasis in the correct order. 'But who will guard the guards? The desire to seize these lands and a proposed marriage alliance is just that. Seizure. Absorption. To extend Lord Cansignorio's domains. Evolved interpretations of jurisprudence have set precedents to allow female inheritance. Such precedents establish Donna Elena's right to her lands.' He took a breath. He concentrated on those days when scholars argued canon law back and forth in the lecture hall. And then he had it. 'Most revered legate, I refer you to Pope Gregory IX's decrees that state the Church's roles in protecting the rights of widows and orphans. Donna Elena is orphaned. The principle of protecting the vulnerable applies in this matter. The Holy Mother Church has always stood by this. Donna Elena now stands as a lamb in the path of a wolf.'

It was a suitable response, and it showed on Cardinal da Viterbo's face.

Maestro Bernini glanced with undisguised menace at Henry. He made a dramatic gesture embracing della Scala, Henry and

Elena. 'We are here to examine the goodwill of Lord Cansignorio della Scala, Lord of Verona who, by governing the lands in question and by making the proposal of an arranged marriage, protects Donna Elena Salvarini and all of those who live and work on those lands.'

The Cardinal tapped his finger on the arm of his chair. 'You have offered that argument before. If a decision is to be made, it must be reached before I go to my prayers. Get on with it, Maestro Bernini, or we shall die as sinners unconfessed in our old age.'

The gathered noblemen were amused and their tittering agreement humiliated Bernini. He swallowed his pride. 'Most wise legate, I apologize. My opponent speaks of evolved interpretations. They are that and nothing more. Interpretations. A reasoning. Not law. Feudal alliances are beneficial and necessary. The great Bartolus of Sassoferrato teaches us that law must adapt to the needs of the time. Our time calls for unity and strength. The marriage proposal and the control of these lands by Lord Cansignorio ensures peace and prosperity for all involved.'

He gave a studied look at Henry. 'And the principle of "what touches all should be approved by all" supports our case. The security of these lands affects not just this young woman, but the entire region.'

Mallin was leaning forward, chewing a piece of straw, listening intently. He chuckled to himself and turned to the others, deaf to what was going on without his help.

'Better than any travelling jester and juggling troupe, this is.'

'Walter, I'll put you under my horse's hooves if you don't tell us more of what's happening.'

'Oh, aye, Sir Thomas, forgive me. It's a circus out there. Young Master Henry, my word, who'd have thought he knew so much?'

'I would,' said Gifford.

Mallin sighed with pleasure. 'The lad's given them things to think about right enough. I don't know the stuff he's talking about, Pope Gregory this and Corpus something or other, but he's spat in their face he has.' He pulled the straw from his mouth and pointed it towards the hearing. 'That boy of yours, Sir Thomas, he's a fine mind on him and a quick tongue.'

'Then he's winning?' said Blackstone.

'Winning? My word, no. The other lawyer's just put a sheaf of arrows through his argument.'

The Cardinal looked at Henry. 'Maestro Bernini offers a valid consideration, Master de Sainteny. This matter is narrow in its scope and now we must draw together final thoughts. Do you understand? Do you have more to say?'

'I do, most reverend Cardinal.' He faltered. 'A moment?'

The Cardinal nodded. 'Do not try my patience or that of Lord Cansignorio. The words you choose to follow Maestro Bernini's argument must lead us towards a conclusion.'

Henry was stuck. He had so far kept panic at bay. Now his chest tightened, and he wished he had spent less time whoring and drinking in Oxford and more time with an open book and an even more inquisitive mind. He drew a breath. He told himself that in his young life he had fought with knife and blade and killed in the name of self-defence. Now he had to go in for the kill and save Elena. How much longer did he have? And if he could not stop della Scala from winning the case and seizing Elena's land then he must stop her being forced into marriage.

'Very well. Indeed, Bartolus teaches us that law must adapt but not at the cost of its fundamental principles. The security Maestro Bernini offers is illusory if it comes at the price of justice. Forcing this alliance of marriage would violate the principal of *voluntas* – willingness – which is essential in both Roman law and Church doctrine regarding marriage. A coerced union serves neither justice nor the stability it purports to create.'

The Cardinal waited for Bernini as he bent and listened to what della Scala was whispering in his ear. The lawyer straightened and addressed the Cardinal. 'Not coercion but opportunity – one that many would eagerly embrace.' He picked up a faded document from the sheaf of papers on the table. 'Reverend Cardinal, I draw your attention to the case of Agnese di Castelbarco versus the Este family, adjudicated in Ferrara in 1352. The Pope's representative, Cardinal Luzzago, ruled that strategic marriage alliances take precedence over female inheritance when securing the region is at stake. Furthermore, the Statuti di Verona grants the Lord of Verona authority to intervene in matters of inheritance that affect the city's defences. The Scaligeri have maintained peace in this region through a careful system of alliances. And in these troubled times, Lord Cansignorio allies himself with the Pope against the Church's enemies.' He paused for effect. 'Thanks in part to these alliances.'

Henry knew he had lost the prime case.

Mallin sighed, cleared his chest and spat phlegm into the dirt. 'Ah, there you have it.'

The others waited expectantly.

'Meaning what?' said Killbere.

'I'll say this, he doesn't back down does Master Henry. I remember when we travelled across from France and he was—'

'Mallin. What is happening?' insisted Blackstone.

'Well... far as I can make out Cansignorio's lawyer just skewered him on a spit. Shame that. He was doing so well.'

'God's tears, Mallin. Is it over or not? And if it is what is the verdict?' said Killbere.

Mallin shrugged. 'Oh, we haven't got to that yet, Sir Gilbert. No, no, they've more words to spout. Della Scala's got the land tied up, I reckon. Borders and security and alliances and the safety of his domains. There's no way the Cardinal's going to risk the girl keeping the land.'

'Then what's left of this business?' said John Jacob.

Mallin squinted towards the dais. 'The girl's fate.'

Killbere sounded content. 'And that's no business of ours, Thomas.'

He looked at Blackstone who met his glance with a worried expression. 'I hope not.'

Henry stood next to Elena and without thinking, put a protective hand on her shoulder. She looked up at him. Did she sense the verdict would go against her? If so, she showed no sign of it. Her hand covered his.

'You may offer a closing statement, Master de Sainteny,' said the Cardinal. Henry detected a note of sympathy in his voice.

'With the utmost respect, reverend Cardinal, may I remind you of the maxim: "Let justice be done though the heavens fall." Regardless of political pressure or promises of protection, we must uphold the law. I implore the wisdom of the Church to fulfil the duty of the righteous and defend a woman who is orphaned and without a champion. May the Church be that champion.'

The Cardinal leaned left and right to each of the men who sat either side of him, canon lawyers there to consult and advise. It took several minutes. Apart from the cawing of crows in the forest across the river, there was silence. Then the Cardinal nodded as each of the men finished their advice.

Cardinal Guido Alberti da Viterbo addressed della Scala's lawyer and Henry. His expressive gestures followed his summation.

'On the one hand, this has been a simple case to adjudicate. On the other, the Holy Mother Church has a duty to protect the vulnerable as eloquently stated by this Oxford scholar.' He pointed to Henry. 'Master de Sainteny, I would urge you to attend Bologna University and complete your studies. You have the makings of a lawyer.' He smiled. 'A good one.'

Settling back, he sighed and finally took the time to sip the glass of red wine that had been untouched throughout the hearing. He nodded, as if he was considering his judgement on the matter. The Cardinal looked at Henry. 'Does she understand?'

'She does not understand Latin, most reverend Cardinal.'

'Then you will translate as I give my verdict. Make sure your words reflect mine.' He waited as Henry told Elena his instructions. She nodded.

'Very well. It is correct that the age of majority for marriage is twelve to fourteen years, but with inheritance of property and the responsibility of owning and running the land and securing the safety and future of those who work on it then that majority is eighteen years. My judgement is as follows. Lord Cansignorio della Scala may take over the Salvarini domain and secure its safety. The Church is well aware that these are troubled times.'

Elena dropped her head; Henry glanced at her. She lifted it and stoically stared ahead.

The Cardinal indicated her. 'Donna Elena,' he said, 'once you are eighteen years old, you have the right to appeal this judgement. If the ecclesiastical court finds in your favour, they will return your father's property and land to you.'

Della Scala prodded his lawyer, who stepped forward, hand raised, begging to speak.

'No, Bernini, you cannot question my judgement.' He looked at Elena. 'Donna Elena. You are to be placed for your safety and welfare in a convent until you are of age to appeal. Or you may find a guardian until that time.'

Henry explained the judgement. Elena's shock was apparent.

'A convent?' she whispered to Henry.

'Yes.'

She palmed away the single tear from her cheek. She crossed

herself. 'Mother of Christ, please help me,' she whispered to no one other than the image of the Virgin Mary in her mind's eye. A shiver went through her.

The Cardinal spoke to the clerks, writing his judgement, assuring himself that everything had been noted correctly.

Henry interrupted his conversation. 'Most reverend legate, may I speak? And as before may that be so that Donna Elena understands what it is I say?'

'There is no challenge. I have made my judgement.'

'I do not challenge it. I applaud it.'

The Cardinal turned his attention from his clerks and stared intently at the upstart scholar who had broken his train of thought by stating the opposite of what he had expected.

'Then speak so that she may understand. But even though you no longer address me in Latin, your statement will still be written for the record.' He nodded and gestured for Henry to continue.

Henry placed a hand briefly on Elena's shoulder. She looked up at him.

He took a step forward, intending for the papal legate to see him as clearly as possible so that his words would not come across as flippant. He first addressed the papal representative in Latin, enforcing his show of respect for the Cardinal and his court before continuing in the common tongue understood by everyone present.

'*Sapientissime legate*, most wise legate, your judgement is profound. It offers protection for those dependent on the land in question, the security of Lord Cansignorio's domains and the guiding hand of the Holy Mother Church to a vulnerable girl.' He took a breath. All present were hanging on to every word he spoke. It was exactly what Henry wanted. 'I beg your permission to act on Donna Elena Salvarini's behalf when that time comes.' A beat. Another step forward. 'And until that time, to act as her guardian.'

There was an audible gasp from the gathered noblemen.

The Cardinal pushed back into his chair. The clerks raised their heads from their verbatim record keeping.

Elena sat bolt upright.

A murmur rippled through the crowd.

The Cardinal leaned forward and stabbed a finger at Henry. 'You are an audacious man, Henry de Sainteny. Who are you? Why would I grant a vulnerable child into your care?'

'Because I can protect her.'

The Cardinal could barely believe the suggestion being made. 'A poverty-stricken swordsman who had the good fortune to attend Oxford? Little more than an educated vagabond? You have no standing. No wealth. No patron.'

'My patron is Edward, King of England.'

The Cardinal's jaw opened and closed. The noblemen drew a collective gasp.

'The King paid for my education. At his request, I am afforded a man-at-arms to serve me. I have lived in the Florentine Bardi banker's residence in Avignon, not a street away from where his Holiness the Pope resides. The King, the Pope and the Bardi favour my father.'

'Your father? I don't know of any de Sainteny.'

'I use my mother's name so that I do not draw attention to myself. My father is a guest of Lord Cansignorio. He's here. Within these walls. My father is the King's Master of War. I am Henry Blackstone.'

It was more than a gasp from the crowd of noblemen. It bordered on a roar of disbelief. The Cardinal hammered his gavel. He looked for confirmation to the surprised della Scala, who nodded dumbly.

The restless crowd settled into silence as the Cardinal stood. His advisers hovered. He looked at Elena. 'Does the girl agree?'

Elena stood. 'I do. I accept the offer.'

The Cardinal pulled his robes around him.

'Then let it be so recorded.'

The gavel slammed down, sealing Henry's fate.

CHAPTER SIXTY-SEVEN

Henry returned to the stables to find Blackstone waiting for him. The men were nowhere in sight. That, and the furious look on Blackstone's face, meant only one thing.

'What in the name of all that's holy have you done?' Blackstone demanded. 'Have you lost your mind? We sit in the heart of the domain of a man we believe had the Prince killed and you agree to be a girl's guardian?'

Henry stood his ground and faced Blackstone. 'I killed her father.'

'He had to be killed! It was not your responsibility to take on the burden of his daughter. Two hundred yards away beyond the main gate, hundreds of skinners are waiting for the order to attack us. He wants the gold. I have to fight him! And when that's done, we ride for our lives. And you bring a woman into a battle that we cannot avoid. Does that make sense? She was safe in a convent, and now her life is at risk.'

'And she has a servant as well,' Henry said, wincing at the confession.

Blackstone looked away from his son. Disbelief helped cool his temper. His voice softened with regret. 'It was my wish for you to stand by my side as I confront della Scala. Your learning was necessary for me to approach the Cardinal. I told you this. And you've turned your back. Damn you, Henry. The world does not revolve around you and your boyhood romances. You're a grown man. It's time for you to act like one.'

Henry's anger flared. 'I've stood my ground before now. In an effort to save the Prince. Every request you made of me, I have fulfilled. It's never enough.'

'You chased a phantom. You went on a damned quest like a hunting dog with its nose to the ground. Never looking up. Not once seeing the danger every man who serves with me places himself in. You dream of the impossible.'

'At least I have a dream. Your only wish is to die a glorious death on the battlefield.'

Blackstone did not rise to the accusation. 'You're a fool, boy. I serve the King. That is my only wish. And that means facing those who threaten harm to his cause and to his family.'

Henry lowered his gaze. Yet again, his temper had got the better of him. And he regretted insulting his father.

'I'm sorry, my lord. I have no wish to disappoint you.'

They fell silent.

'I need you gone from here,' said Blackstone. 'Gifford will escort you back to the men outside. We must ready ourselves for a fight and you will not be a part of it.'

'I can still speak on your behalf to the Cardinal.'

'No. You've told the Lord of Verona and every enemy in earshot who you are. You add to the problem. You weaken my cause. He will see you as a pawn to be played. You're vulnerable now, Henry. It's your duty to stay alive and protect the woman.'

Blackstone walked away, leaving his crestfallen son.

Then he turned back. 'And her servant.'

Gifford was saddling his horse when Henry appeared. He gave his charge a quick look. Henry shrugged.

'In the shit pit again, Master Henry.'

'I'm getting used to its stench, Hugh.'

Gifford tidied his reins. 'Aye, well, I'm finding it takes longer to wash the stench off me. When you jump in feet first, I'm the one getting more than his boots caked in shit.'

'You can leave anytime you like.'

'No, I cannot, and you know damned well that's true. Now I'm supposed to wet-nurse two women? One a child herself. How am I to do that?'

'You're forgetting that I am guardian to Donna Elena.'

'And I to you.'

'If you doubt I can protect her, then speak to my father and join the men. I'll manage.'

'You can't manage changing your braies without getting both legs in the same opening.'

'Damn it, Hugh, don't chastise me today of all days. My father has banished me with the women to the rear if there's a fight.'

Gifford patted his horse. Bridle, saddle, girth strap and bedroll were as they should be. 'Your mount is ready. I'm to go down the stable and get your lady's horse. We leave by the bridge gate when they're ready. Sir Thomas wants us gone from this place. Best go and bring those you're responsible for.'

Gifford made his way down the length of the stable. Henry looked this way, and that, and saw no sign of the men. He decided that was a good thing under the circumstance. He stepped around Gifford's horse and checked his own. There was no need. Gifford had attended to it. It was time to get the young Italian noblewoman and her servant. He felt a tinge of regret. Not at the killing in the monastery or the wild chase that had made him look a fool, but the unthinking act of offering to be the girl's guardian. His life was now bound up with hers. She was the reason he couldn't stand with the men when danger struck. He had sacrificed that camaraderie.

Stepping out into the courtyard, he saw the noblemen, still gathered at the end of the Corte d'Armi where he had last seen them. The Cardinal and della Scala were in discussion with a handful of the noblemen as the others clustered in their own small groups. Della Scala extended an arm, indicating the Cardinal should go ahead of him, and then followed at a respectful stride behind him. The noblemen joined on in a ragged procession as they walked towards the great hall. Henry was halfway across the vast yard when della Scala summoned a man-at-arms to him, who had appeared through one of the small gates leading from the outside. He was taller than della Scala, likely a captain of some sort. The man-at-arms listened respectfully to what was being said to him. It seemed that the Cardinal agreed. Turning away, the man-at-arms made his way towards one of the buildings.

By then, Henry had reached the entrance hall and stairs that led to Elena's quarters. He stepped up the stairs slowly. Henry could not avoid the inevitable responsibility he had agreed to, but he delayed it for a few moments more by climbing the stairs with an unhurried pace. He faltered. And then stopped. What was it that had drawn his attention to the man-at-arms?

Abandoning the stairs, he went back into the courtyard. The dais remained. The clerks' tables were being removed. No one appeared to be in a hurry to take down the banners and canopy. He saw his father and Killbere with the men gathered at the stable entrance. They were looking his way. Not at him. Past him. He turned. The man-at-arms was leading a dozen soldiers towards the stables. Henry was nearer than the body of men being led across the yard and without knowing why, he strode back to his father's waiting men. Was there to be a fight? Even so, he told himself, a dozen men against his father and Gilbert with John Jacob, Gifford, Mallin and Terrel would stand little chance of success.

He reached his father.

'Henry? You're supposed to be getting the woman and her servant.'

Henry looked at the men spread out by the stable door. They

weren't watching Henry; their eyes followed the approaching soldiers.

'I thought there might be trouble.'

'No,' said Blackstone. 'Not yet. They're coming for the gold. Della Scala has the Cardinal's permission to take it into safekeeping.' He touched Henry's arm. 'Stay back and do nothing. They can have it.'

Henry had no time to question Blackstone. He stepped into the gloomy stables, out of the way.

Killbere's hands rested on his sword's pommel. He spat. The contempt in his voice was as thick as the spittle. 'Dumb, stupid bastards. They come with men to carry the gold. A village idiot would have led the mules across the yard and unloaded them there.'

He watched as Blackstone stood back and pointed at the mules still bearing the heavy chests. Mallin and Terrel stood at each of the beast's head, soothing them as the men packed into the stall and fumbled the iron poles into the caskets.

Blackstone and Killbere stepped inside to watch the awkward wrestling of the chests. The man-at-arms who led the soldiers stood half in, half out of the stable, framed by the entrance. Henry was a dozen steps away from him, concealed by the dim light. The man-at-arms snorted and spat and then wiped an arm across his nose. Wiped it with his right arm. A shadowy movement that triggered Henry's memory. His thoughts flashed back to the Prince's quarters when the assassin attacked him. An image emerged. Slowed down by time, blurred. Choking. Held around the throat. Gasping, struggling to fight free from the assassin's strength. The stench of the man's sweat. He had grappled the man's wrist before the man's left hand swung the cosh that nearly felled him. His *left* hand – because Henry was holding the right wrist of a hand missing the middle two fingers.

Like the man who had wiped his sleeve across his nose with his right hand.

Henry's breath snatched. He turned away as the man

looked in his direction, drawn by the quick intake of breath from the shadows. Gifford was half blocking him. The man-at-arms switched his attention back to the clumsy attempts of the soldiers, berating their efforts. Once they'd lifted the chests free, he turned his back to Henry and instructed them to carry the chests across to the great hall where Lord Cansignorio was waiting.

Blackstone had looked beyond the man when he saw Gifford pivot around, alerted by Henry's gasp. Gifford heard Blackstone tell the man-at-arms he would follow and deliver the key to the chests to Lord Cansignorio. The man nodded, muttered a word of thanks and led his men away. It would be slow progress across the yard, no matter how often the man-at-arms cursed the men as they bent under the chests' weight.

'Master Henry?' said Gifford as Henry brushed past him.

Henry kept back from the entrance. 'My lord,' he said, addressing Blackstone. 'That man is the Prince's assassin.'

All eyes locked on Henry.

'The man-at-arms?' said Killbere.

'Yes. The man I fought was left-handed. He couldn't grasp a weapon with his right because he had two fingers missing. The same as him,' he said, gesturing to the man leading the others across the yard.

'Without doubt?' said Blackstone.

'I grasped that same hand in my own. It's him. He poisoned the Prince.'

Fingers curled around sword grips. Blackstone raised a hand. The men were edgy. Ready to fight. 'Not now,' he told them.

He beckoned Henry to him as he kept an eye on the men's slow progress across the yard. 'Was that man sitting with the nobles when you defended the girl?'

'No. I was over there at the entrance when I saw him come from outside the walls through a postern gate. Della Scala beckoned him and then he went to get men and make his way here.'

'So he hasn't seen you since you've been here?'

'No.'

Blackstone paused as he thought of a way through the danger that would arise as soon as the killer recognized Henry.

'All right. Get back across the yard before he reaches the great hall. Bring down the women. Gifford, go with him. Step out of that entrance when he is close enough to recognize you. Show surprise but turn your head away as if you have just recognized him. That is not the time for confrontation. Then you make haste for here. He has a duty to della Scala to deliver the gold. He'll look for you later. We'll deal with that then. Terrel and Mallin will have the horses ready.'

He turned to Killbere. 'Gilbert, take everyone out with you except John.'

'Leave you two alone?' said Killbere. 'They'll cut you down if you challenge della Scala.'

'Not with the Cardinal here. You must pull the men back beyond the river that blocks their flanks. There'll be another bridge upstream and if della Scala attacks, he'll have men pouring across it to cut us off.'

Killbere saw the truth of the situation. He nodded.

Blackstone laid a hand on Henry's shoulder. 'Get the women. Let him see you and then get back here to Sir Gilbert. And then there is one more thing you must do for me.'

Henry and Gifford angled away from the slow-moving men. They raced up the stairs, pushed open the door to Elena's quarters. Henry calmed the two women's alarm at the sudden intrusion, raising a hand and offering urgent assurance.

'We must go. Now. Whatever you have packed is enough. This is Gifford. He will help you.'

Henry's urgency demanded Elena made no complaint. She stood and pulled on a fitted tunic over her dress as Morena closed the bag and settled a smaller one on a strap across her body. Gifford stepped forward and lifted the satchel as Henry peered down from the window to the courtyard and the men bearing the chests of gold.

'You can both ride? There's no cart.'

They nodded.

'Follow me.'

When he reached the bottom of the stairs, he held them back as he peered around the entrance. He turned to Elena. 'We're making for the stables. The horses are ready. Ignore the men who are crossing the yard. Do not look at them. Keep your gaze on the men waiting with the horses at the stables.'

They nodded their understanding.

Henry took a breath and stepped into the open.

Ten strides away, the man-at-arms was surprised by Henry's sudden appearance. He glared at the man he had last seen in Prince Lionel's quarters. His hand went to his knife but didn't draw it. Henry had averted his eyes. Had he been recognized? The man-at-arms was helpless. A sudden fear gripped him. If he told della Scala that he had been identified what chance would he have of survival? And he couldn't kill the only witness to his crime in broad daylight. By the time the thought of doing so had formed, Henry, Elena, Morena and Gifford were beyond him. With a nervous glance over his shoulder at the retreating eyewitness, he ushered his men into the great hall's entrance.

Whoever he was he had to be killed.

CHAPTER SIXTY-EIGHT

Killbere led everyone except Blackstone and John Jacob on an unhurried walk to the gate that opened onto the bridge and where Blackstone's men were camped on the river's far bank. Once those heavy gates slammed behind them, there could be no rescue if Blackstone's plan failed. He and John Jacob would face a lonely death in a desperate fight inside the walls.

Killbere took a final glance as Blackstone and John Jacob went into the great hall. For all he knew, that might be the last sight he had of them.

The great hall's doors closed behind Blackstone and his squire with a sullen, echoing thud. John Jacob remained a few paces behind Blackstone, ready to fight their way clear if events turned against them. The two men faced the might of Verona's nobility and the papal legate. A dangerous moment loomed in the next few minutes: Blackstone intended to accuse Cansignorio della Scala, Lord of Verona, ally of the papal forces, of being involved in the assassination of the English King's son, Prince Lionel. He was gambling on there being no direct attack on them because of the Cardinal's presence.

Della Scala sat at a long table with Cardinal Guido Alberti da Viterbo at his side. A clerk hovered at their shoulders and passed a parchment between the two for signing and then for their seals to be placed at the foot of the document, the official papal adjudication on the matter between Donna Elena Salvarini and Cansignorio della Scala. Two matching tables stood one on either side of della Scala's where the Veronese noblemen were seated. The rich hues of their garments, the guards in the background, the papal and Scaligeri banners added to the solemnity of the scene. Blackstone stood between the two rows of noblemen and waited for his presence to be acknowledged.

The clerk went to the top of each table, offering an inkwell and quill to each nobleman to sign as a witness. Della Scala and the Cardinal waited, both men watching Blackstone. Despite his status as the King of England's Master of War, to them he was nothing more than a fighting man without a noble title. As the document made its way around the table, the scratching of quill on parchment was the only sound. Della Scala turned and whispered something to the Cardinal, who nodded. Blackstone noticed that his eyes focused on the chests placed on the floor to one side of the hall. Standing by them was the man Henry had identified as the assassin.

The noblemen finished witnessing the document. Once Cardinal da Viterbo was satisfied, the clerks withdrew. All eyes were on Blackstone.

'Sir Thomas. You grace us with your presence,' said della Scala without any hint of sarcasm. There was no need to belittle Blackstone. Della Scala had full authority over the two men who stood before the gathered nobles.

'I am no Latin scholar like my son, reverend Cardinal,' said Blackstone, ignoring della Scala. 'And I would ask that you allow me to address you in the language understood by everyone here.' The slight against the Lord of Verona was immediately obvious. Della Scala's face showed it and so did the murmuring of discontent from the gathered noblemen.

The diplomatic Cardinal said, 'Sir Thomas, I am not your host here.'

'But you have an authority that he does not and what I have to say needs the power of the Church to condemn Cansignorio della Scala for his involvement in the assassination of Prince Lionel of Antwerp.'

Blackstone's defiant accusation caused an uproar. Guards looked at each other uncertainly; the noblemen were on their feet. Blackstone strode forward until he was ten paces from the two most powerful men in the room. Their shock at the accusation had rendered them speechless. Blackstone spoke directly to the Cardinal.

'Reverend Cardinal, let me speak. The Church needs to hear what has happened.'

Cardinal da Viterbo got to his feet at Blackstone's direct appeal. He raised a calming hand, gesturing the baying noblemen to quieten. Della Scala remained seated, fists clenched, face flushed.

'This is the most serious of accusations and I will hear it.' The Cardinal sat down, his hands folded. Attentive. Eyes on Blackstone. Searching for any sign of half-truths and lies.

The room quietened. Now everyone wanted to hear the accusation.

Blackstone faced the Cardinal. 'Before Prince Lionel of Antwerp, Duke of Clarence, travelled through the Mont Cenis Pass, I killed mercenaries recruited by the Lord of Verona. Soon afterwards, a man called Salvarini made an attempt on the Prince's life in the Mont Cenis monastery.

The mention of Elena's family name caused a murmur, and a raised eyebrow from the Cardinal.

'Salvarini's attempt to kill the Prince was witnessed and stopped. During that attempt it was obvious the man hesitated. Was it his conscience that made him falter? With his dying breath, he asked the man who had saved the Prince to seek his daughter. And to save her. I believe that girl was Donna Elena

Salvarini, the young woman whose land Cansignorio della Scala coveted. My son Henry Blackstone was the man he appealed to.'

The events of the day were still vivid in everyone's memory. The papal hearing, the skill of the young Latin scholar. Some noblemen cast concerned glances at della Scala.

'I and my men travelled ahead of the Prince. The Duke of Montferrat had intercepted a message from someone in authority in Paris to an unnamed Italian lord beyond Milan, warning him I was in Italy. I now believe that man, in the pay of France, to be della Scala.'

Blackstone placed the folded document in front of the Cardinal.

'There is no person named here,' said the Cardinal after reading it. 'I do not accept this as admissible evidence of Lord Cansignorio's involvement. And why would he wish to see the Prince dead? The English King and Lord Cansignorio side with the Pope against Bernabò Visconti.'

'With the Prince dead, everyone would obviously point the finger of guilt at the Visconti. It would break the alliance between the Visconti and the English Crown.'

'Then it is Bernabò who killed your Prince,' said della Scala. 'He would want that alliance stopped so that his brother did not gain more power.'

The noblemen agreed. Blackstone ignored them.

'*Condottieri* attacked my men who were encamped outside Milan's walls. Men that Bernabò Visconti had never used before. When the attack failed and their bodies searched, their purses were heavy with Veronese-minted coin. At Piacenza more *condottieri* attacked me. In their leader's possession was a valuable reliquary from the Basilica di San Zeno Maggiore. I believe this was gifted to him by the Lord of Verona. As part of his payment.' He tugged it from beneath his tunic and placed it, along with the silk scarf it was wrapped in, on the table in front of the Cardinal.

The Cardinal leaned forward. 'Sir Thomas, this is

circumstantial evidence. Stolen by a mercenary. I urge you to withdraw the accusation.'

Blackstone then put the folded paper of safe passage on the table. 'A safe-conduct pass signed by della Scala with his seal and found on the same *condottiere*.'

The evidence might have been circumstantial, but it was mounting in Blackstone's favour, as the worried lines on the Cardinal's face revealed. His eyes raised from the safe conduct and he searched Blackstone's face.

'He wants the gold,' said Blackstone. 'It's that simple. He gets the gold, and I suspect he has an arrangement with Bernabò Visconti to deliver me to him. It is treachery at every turn.'

Della Scala appealed to the wavering Cardinal. 'Reverend Cardinal. This is nonsense. There is no direct witness to any of this. Only Blackstone's word against mine.'

Blackstone glanced back at John Jacob, a signal for him to come forward. John Jacob took a folded letter from his gambeson and handed it to Blackstone. He returned to stand ready at the door. Blackstone placed the letter in front of the Cardinal.

'This is written in Latin so that you will know it comes from a learned hand, someone you might trust. It describes the assassin. My son wrote and swore it to you as a deposition. It was he who grappled with the Prince's killer. A man who has two fingers missing on his right hand.'

The noblemen knew who that was. They looked at the man-at-arms standing by the gold chests. He was brazen enough to stare down those who glared at him. A killer without remorse in the pay of a tyrant.

'Who is this man?' said the Cardinal.

'Mastino Gambetti. A trusted man in my service.'

The Cardinal beckoned him forward. The killer took barely two steps to comply.

'Your hand,' said the Cardinal.

Gambetti exposed the hand with the missing fingers.

'What do you have to say about Sir Thomas Blackstone's accusation?'

'He's wrong. I've never been to Alba.'

There was a brief moment of realization among the men. The Cardinal darted a look at Blackstone.

'I never mentioned where the Prince was slain,' said Blackstone.

Della Scala jumped in. 'That news travelled. I knew of it. And so did my men. None of this is evidence!'

The Cardinal was conflicted. Regardless of what was presented to him, every scrap of evidence might have been hearsay or manipulated. Even Henry's letter might have been part of a ploy by Blackstone to discredit and dishonour Cansignorio della Scala in the eyes of the Church.

And della Scala knew it.

'He has nothing. He is nothing more than a *condottiere* himself. Ask him why he kept the gold. He wishes to smear me and convince you to let him take it with him.'

'No. You can have the gold,' said Blackstone. 'My Prince's memory is better served without it. I accuse you of murder.'

The offer to let the Scaligeri family keep the gold made Blackstone's accusation more pointed.

The Cardinal faced della Scala. 'What reason could Sir Thomas have to make this accusation if it did not bear an element of truth? And your man there? He is disfigured as Master Blackstone has testified. I find the evidence compelling, Lord Cansignorio.' He hesitated. 'But...'

His glance at the gold chests revealed his own desire to take a share of the gold for the Church. That or for himself, Blackstone guessed. A lust for gold corrupted the best of men. Blackstone's instincts told him the Cardinal and della Scala had already agreed to share what they thought to be two hundred thousand gold florins.

'But it is still inconclusive,' said the Cardinal.

If Blackstone had caused enough doubt, and given sufficient insult, then della Scala should play into his hands. Which he did.

'I demand satisfaction against this vile accusation. I will fight him.'

The Cardinal shook his head. 'No! There can be no duel. The Church forbids it. That cannot be sanctioned.'

Blackstone gave a final taunt to della Scala. He smiled at him.

Della Scala slammed his fist on the table. 'A contest! If not to the death, then the first man to yield loses – or the first to draw blood triumphs.'

The overwhelming support from the baying noblemen forced the Cardinal to back down.

The Cardinal nodded his agreement. 'So be it. First to yield or first blood.'

CHAPTER SIXTY-NINE

In the vast arena of the Corte d'Armi the dais and seats filled once again with the noblemen. And, as before, the Cardinal's chair took precedence. His advisers sat on either side. This time, there was only one clerk to record the outcome of the contest. This was no ordinary challenge. The Lord of Verona, a man renowned for his adherence to the rites of the Church, a patron of the arts, a ruler who had brought beauty to his city and created a legacy that strengthened Verona's cultural and political status. Challenged by a scar-faced Englishman without title other than being chosen by an English king to wage war. Thomas Blackstone looked vulnerable. He limped from old wounds. A weaker man, unlikely to last any time against the bull-necked Cansignorio. Piety and largesse were a thin veil of respectability covering the ruthlessness that lay within the man who had orchestrated the murder of his own brother to gain power.

Della Scala stood, feet braced, wearing mail, his feather-crowned open-face bascinet exposing an expression described later as that of a ravening wolf. Eager to pounce. He bore his emblazoned shield, a bejewelled-handled sword, and a more common unadorned flanged mace in his belt.

John Jacob had bound Blackstone's troublesome thigh before helping him into his mail. His open-face helm, dented from so many close-quarter battles, was plain, unlike his opponent's. He carried his shield with its distinctive blazon, but to the eye of the beholder, Thomas Blackstone gave the appearance of an ill-equipped man-at-arms whose battered shield and unadorned surcoat stood poorly against the might of a regional lord.

Blackstone gripped Wolf Sword and glanced up at the ramparts and walkways. Garrison soldiers gazed down from their positions, eager to see the Englishman humiliated and forced to recant. The sight gave Blackstone a moment's satisfaction. If they were looking into the courtyard and not across the countryside, they would not be watching Killbere moving out the men, abandoning the position that could have had them trapped.

There was no signal to begin. Della Scala, seeing Blackstone turn his attention to the high walls, strode forward. Blackstone wasn't taken by surprise. He wanted his opponent to take the initiative. Driving himself forward, sword raised, his shield smothering his body, della Scala struck Blackstone like a battering ram. Shields clashed. Blackstone allowed the force of the impact to make him give way to one side. Momentum carried della Scala off balance. Blackstone pivoted and slammed the flat of Wolf Sword's blade across the back of della Scala's helm. The honed steel blade's strike rang like a bell. Della Scala nearly fell forward. Noblemen gasped at the Englishman's rapid change of direction. Blackstone smiled at the Lord of Verona, who bellowed with rage. Blackstone's taunt wounded his pride as deeply as drawing blood. But Della Scala checked himself; training and restraint made him focus. Timing and control were everything. Ramming Blackstone with his shield had proved fruitless, despite his bulk and strength. Blackstone was light on his feet even though he favoured his injured leg. Della Scala abandoned his shield and gripped the flanged mace. He waited for Blackstone to follow his lead. He didn't.

'We fight without shields!' he demanded.

'No,' said Blackstone. 'Not yet.' He taunted della Scala again with a smile.

Della Scala turned to the Cardinal, noticing as he did that some of his noblemen had to suppress their own expressions of amusement. 'Reverend Cardinal. He does not fight like a knight.'

The Cardinal nodded in agreement. 'There are no rules, Lord Cansignorio, other than not fighting to the death. How Sir Thomas fights is his decision.'

'You dishonour me!' della Scala told Blackstone.

'I honour those who deserve honour,' Blackstone replied.

Blackstone saw the change in the man. Gone was the hot-headed, self-indulgent lord of the region. In his place was a calculating tyrant, falling back on years of swordsmanship, now intent on forcing Blackstone onto the defensive.

Della Scala struck repeatedly, smashing the mace into Blackstone's shield, followed by what would have been lethal sword blows, their deadliness apparent in the gasps of the crowd. The Cardinal was half out of his seat at one point. Blackstone and della Scala were a yard apart. The grunting Cansignorio hammered to break down Blackstone's defence. Blackstone absorbed the blows. His stocky opponent was gasping with effort. The wave breaking on the rock was foundering.

As della Scala feinted and swept his sword high and down, looking to angle it onto Blackstone's neck, Blackstone danced back three paces. It was so quick della Scala almost lost his footing again as the force of his blow cut into the space where a second before Blackstone stood.

It was time for Blackstone to unencumber himself. The mis-strike gave him time to drop his shield, snatch the mace from his belt and move back into position, ready to hammer the mace onto della Scala's shoulder. A blow that would have numbed his arm, forcing him to lose the grip on his sword. He was too slow. His leg gave way. With a nimble sidestep, della Scala swept his blade low and fast. Had his wrist turned in time, the honed edge of the blade would have cut deeply into Blackstone's ailing leg. The force behind the flat of the blade striking Blackstone's old wound made it flare in pain. A branding iron of searing heat. He stumbled, regained his balance in time to block della Scala's high guard strike, held with both hands on the sword's grip as he abandoned the mace. It was an attempt to maim Blackstone which could have been lethal. Blackstone caught the glistening blade on his crossguard, twisted it away, forcing della Scala to drop his arms. In that instant Blackstone trusted his failing leg to take his weight and kicked della Scala firmly between the legs.

Della Scala folded. He gagged, hands over his crotch. Then he tried to clamber to his feet. Blackstone kicked him in the chest. Della Scala sprawled. The crowd bellowed. Blackstone stood over him.

Della Scala gasped for breath. 'You fight like a street dog.'

'So I am told,' said Blackstone without showing the pain from the deep-seated fire in his leg. He pressed a boot on della Scala's stomach, straddled the man with the other, forcing his weight onto his sword arm. Della Scala was pinned.

'Yield,' said Blackstone.

Della Scala spittle smeared his beard. He shook his head. 'You will be dead the moment you leave this place,' he said.

'Yield,' Blackstone said again.

'I will not!' he hissed.

'First blood it is, then,' said Blackstone, drawing Wolf Sword's point down the side of della Scala's face.

The Lord of Verona winced from the hairline cut. Blackstone stepped away. Della Scala squirmed back, a hand to his face, looked at the blood, and then staggered to his feet.

Blackstone addressed the Cardinal. 'Now send me Mastino Gambetti so that I can deal with the man who killed my Prince.'

Della Scala pulled free his gauntlets and wiped a hand across his bloody, snot-laden face. 'He's gone. I don't know where,' della Scala lied.

The Cardinal stood and gazed down at Blackstone. 'Sir Thomas, what has occurred here today has been noted. The matter is closed.'

Blackstone dipped his head respectfully. 'Reverend Cardinal, I ask for a token of my victory here today.'

'A token?'

'One chest of gold. I entrust the rest to you and Lord Cansignorio.'

Cardinal Guido Alberti da Viterbo glanced at the dishevelled Cansignorio. The Lord of Verona had lost. Better to have the whole matter settled here and now. It was obvious to the papal legate that everyone had a taste for gold.

'Very well. One chest.'

PART EIGHT

La Battaglia del Dosso dell'Aquila

THE BATTLE AT EAGLE'S RIDGE

CHAPTER SEVENTY

Blackstone and John Jacob wasted no time in leaving Castello degli Scaligeri. Ignoring the persistent throb of pain in his leg, Blackstone led the way through the gates onto the bridge. John Jacob hauled a mule behind him carrying the only chest that contained any gold.

They spurred their horses as the gates slammed closed behind them. A crossbow bolt narrowly missed John Jacob, its iron bodkin point sparking against the bridge's parapets. A flurry of missiles followed. One struck the yoke on the mule that carried the gold chest. The crossbowmen shooting from the high walls could not gauge the angle. Blackstone heeled the bastard horse. Its uneven gait helped throw off the aim of those trying to kill him. When they were halfway across, men ran from concealment in the forest towards the sloping stone beach.

Blackstone and John Jacob heard Will Longdon's command over the clattering of hooves.

'Loose!'

Those crossbowmen who had dared to lean out to aim at the escaping horsemen fell screaming. Bodies bounced against the wall and thudded onto the riverbank. Some crossbowmen slumped in the gap between the battlements. Their comrades backed away. As Blackstone and John Jacob reached the far bank, Longdon's archers turned and ran back into cover with Blackstone.

'Sir Gilbert said you might need some help,' he grinned.

'Your horses?'

'Back here. Sir Gilbert's taken everyone else.'

One of Renfred's German scouts, Becker, rode up, trailing Longdon's horse. Mounted archers surged from the trees. 'Follow me, Sir Thomas. Renfred sent me to take you to Sir Gilbert!'

No pursuit came from della Scala's castle. The dishonoured Lord of Verona would strike with the full force of his mercenary army when he was ready. If luck was on Blackstone's side, they would put enough distance between him and della Scala's killers as they rode south towards Bologna. So far, everything had gone as he planned.

Fortune deserted him twenty miles away.

Becker led the archers and Blackstone south across open flatlands of drainage ditches and marshland. Earthen banks buffeted streams swallowed by reed beds. An ancient Roman road cut through the plain and dense low-lying forests. Clusters of willow and alder screened some of the slow-moving waterways. The open ground stretched to the horizon, broken by distant clumps of forests, their treetops spiking into the sky. As did the pennons and flags from the dark outline of gathered men miles away, smudged colours unmoving.

'Bernabò Visconti,' said Becker. 'He holds the way south. Sir Gilbert thought we could not fight our way through, so he stopped here.' He led Blackstone to where Killbere and the men were busy preparing a defensive position around the remains of a derelict farmstead. The low walls and shells of buildings would afford some protection from attack. Rocks and boulders littered the forest floor behind the old farm. Mallin and Terrel came forward to take Blackstone and John Jacob's horse and lead them and the pack mule into the trees.

Killbere slumped onto a boulder and wiped the sweat from his face. 'Thomas, they didn't kill you then?' He laughed. 'Did you kick della Scala's arse?'

'Thrashed him,' said John Jacob. 'And convinced the Cardinal to let us take one chest of gold in payment for Sir Thomas's efforts.'

Killbere threw back his head and guffawed. 'I would have cast that gold into the river had I been able to see that, Thomas. You're limping.'

'Aye. It'll pass though. He caught me with a blow and the leg took some strain, but it serves me well enough.'

Killbere swept a hand across the horizon. 'We found our way south blocked by those bastards on the skyline. It's Bernabò all right. Renfred and his lads rode ahead and confirmed it. We'd be hard-pressed to take them on out there. They hold the road that's the main stretch of dry ground and we can't get behind them because of this godforsaken wetland on either side. This was the best place I could find.'

Blackstone's eyes scanned the horizon beyond the reed beds. 'When they come they'll move along that road and then plunge into the shallows and come straight at us.'

Killbere looked back to where Blackstone had approached on the track around the headland. 'That track that brought you from Verona. It bleeds off into the marshes on a raised causeway and connects to the road Bernabò holds. He would most likely breach the causeway as it nudges up to the track and come at our flank.'

'Or leave it to della Scala to get around the headland, past our defences and use the causeway the same way,' said Blackstone.

'Aye, we'll have Meulon and his lads defend the track you came in by, which leaves us to face the frontal onslaught.'

Killbere got to his feet and pointed to a bedraggled-looking man, a hand-woven straw hat slouched onto the back of his head, who squatted next to a fire slicing meat from a small pig on a spit. 'He's a local fisherman. The dialect here is difficult to follow but I think I understood him. This place used to be a pig farm, but the pigs escaped over time to forage in the woods. Fishermen come and trap them for fresh meat. I had Halfpenny shoot a dozen for the lads. No man should die on an empty stomach.'

'Then let's hope our enemy is well fed,' said Blackstone, sharing Killbere's smile of anticipation of hot food and a hard fight.' He scanned the landscape again. 'The only way south is through Bernabò?'

'Aye, unless we can fit a hundred men and horses on punts.'

'And Bernabò has made no sign of attacking?'

'No, and I don't know why, unless he's been chased east by the Pope's forces. Despenser should be with them by now.'

'Instinct tells me it's because he has a pact with della Scala.'

Killbere's face broke into a wide grin. 'Ha! So the bastard thinks he's got the gold, and you were part of the bargain.'

'I think so.' Blackstone pulled the key for the chest from around his neck and handed it to John Jacob. 'John, find some strong sacking. Use it for the gold in the chest and secure it in saddlebags.'

As John Jacob strode towards the horses, Killbere's mood became more solemn. 'Thomas, we can hold them off from here. These old ruins offer cover, and the stony ground on our flanks goes down to reed beds.' He pointed to the rising hillside forest behind them. 'There's a track around the base of the trees that ends where those alder are. Unless they are blessed by the Almighty, they won't be walking on water to outflank us there. The water cuts off the track. And there's marshland to the rear.'

Blackstone nodded towards the fisherman who was wiping his greasy fingers on his grubby linen tunic. 'Where does he live?'

'Fishing village a couple of miles from here. Can't see it because of the forest. Says they live off reed cutting and fishing. They sell to another village down the old Roman road who are on dry land so they grow crops. The villagers barter and exchange. And that's the route Bernabò has blocked.' Killbere looked at Blackstone as the two thought the same thing. 'Maybe he'll be more friendly to us than the Visconti bastard, especially if Bernabò is stopping the fishermen from selling their catch.'

'Do we know where we are?'

A distant high-pitched screech carried across the wetlands. 'You see him?'

Blackstone shielded his eyes. He searched the sky and saw a raptor with a wriggling fish in its talons.

'Fisherman says it's a place called Dosso dell'Aquila,' said Killbere.

'Eagle's Ridge. Then we must do what the eagles do and get lookouts up into a couple of trees. Don't let him leave yet. I'll speak to him later.'

'We've never fought a battle in wetlands, Thomas.'

'Then we must learn to use it to our advantage. You chose the best place for a fight, my friend. They must come to us, and we'll greet them with blade and arrow. Della Scala will know this place. Where's Henry and the woman?'

'Up in a ruined pig pen in the forest. I thought it best to keep them away from where there's going to be fighting.'

'Good. Keep the men busy. We need every obstacle we can if they come straight at us. If I were Bernabò, I'd use those crossbowmen we saw at the olive grove on our way to Verona to buy time for men on foot behind them. And then...' He stared at the way he had entered the ruined compound. 'Della Scala would send his skinners on horseback and breach our flank. He won't care how many he'll lose. They'll overpower us just by their numbers.'

'Lucky for us Bernabò isn't you. He's a fighter right enough, but he's a rich, indulged bastard who likes his comfort. We might be able to wait him out.' Killbere shrugged. He knew Bernabò would not wait forever before attacking. And Blackstone was right; della Scala wouldn't hesitate to sacrifice as many men as it took to reach him. Especially now, after his humiliation. And once he broke open those chests, the humiliation would sting even more, knowing he had been fooled. 'How long do you think we have if della Scala's joining the fight?'

'Tomorrow morning. No later. We've much to do.'

CHAPTER SEVENTY-ONE

Blackstone clambered across the stony ground to where Henry had taken the young woman he had defended. He and Gifford had built up the wall of the ruined pig enclosure to chest height. Tucked into the corner were Elena and her servant, who was stirring a pot over a slow-burning fire.

Gifford saw Blackstone first. 'Sir Thomas,' he said eagerly, realizing his presence meant he had bested della Scala.

'Gifford. A good day's work, by the look of it.'

Elena and Morena saw the figure looming over the wall and got to their feet to acknowledge him. Blackstone studied the young woman for a moment. 'Donna Elena, your circumstances are not what you wished, I know that, but you are safer here than you would be with Lord Cansignorio.'

'I'm content, Sir Thomas. Master Henry has done more for us than many others would consider doing.'

'I urge you to stay here. An assault is coming at us and it will be hard and fast. Better you should know what lies ahead.'

'I'm not afraid.'

The defiant tilt of her chin stabbed Blackstone's heart. It was Christiana, standing boldly proud in the face of danger. Where did such women get their courage from? he asked himself. But then the urgency of their situation swept aside the instant of sadness from the memory of his dead wife. 'Arm yourself when the time comes. My son will give you a fighting axe and knife. If we are overrun...' He hesitated, not wanting to bring the horror of rape into her thoughts.

'I know what will happen,' she said. 'We will face them when the time comes. They'll have cause to regret it before we're taken.'

Blackstone was damned sure there would be two she-wolves with their backs against the wall. 'Henry. Gifford.' He beckoned, and turned his back and walked a few strides from the enclosure. Henry and Gifford followed and waited.

'They'll attack on two fronts. We must split our force and face them. It's inevitable that if they break our line, they will reach you. Remember this. Della Scala will kill the girl. That way, he will keep her lands. The Prince's assassin's name is Mastino Gambetti. He will look for you because you are the sole witness to his act. You – more than me, or anyone else here – you're the ones they want dead. Hold your ground and don't let yourself be drawn to come to us, no matter how bad it looks or sounds. The cries of battle call men eager to fight like moths to the flame, but it serves no purpose to abandon this place. Understand?'

Henry and Gifford nodded.

'We have until tomorrow. Be ready.' He gave Henry an encouraging smile. Despite his son's courage, the impending conflict caused doubt to crease his face. Blackstone resisted the urge to embrace his son. To do so in front of Gifford and the women would diminish him.

'God bless you both and those you protect.'

'And you, my lord,' they said.

Blackstone turned back down the hill, using slender alder trunks on his descent to ease the weight on his leg. Father and son had shared moments of conflict. A headstrong son, not yet past the exuberance of youth, and a father seasoned in warfare.

There was always going to be argument. He hoped they would both live through the following day so that they could journey towards a better understanding.

Blackstone and Killbere sat hunched with the fisherman. His belly full, he was ready to leave for his village. Blackstone had asked Killbere to gather a purse of the Veronese-minted coin taken from the dead mercenaries when Killbere was attacked outside the walls of Milan. Blackstone had persuaded the fisherman to supply what he needed. He'd offered one purse of coins and promised another for every boat that returned with what Blackstone had asked for. Sated from the cooked pig and the weight of the purse, the fisherman poled his boat with as much haste as he could muster. He had to bring back what Blackstone needed long before dark.

'That's shallow water, Gilbert,' said Blackstone, watching the reed beds a hundred yards away sway in the breeze. 'Wind's picking up from over there,' he said. 'Across our left flank. If it's shallow enough it could be a route for us to be attacked. We bring them to us there and we have an advantage. Horses move slowly in water.' He stood up, caught Will Longdon's eye and beckoned him over. 'Come on, let's get our feet wet.'

The three men stripped down to shirt and hose and waded out into the wetland. When they reached the reed bed, they were chest-deep in slow-moving cold water. Blackstone's leg complained at first but then the chill water eased the pain. They pushed through the bulrushes until they reached a low earth embankment, baked iron-hard by the sun, which kept the water at bay. Beyond them, the soggy terrain underfoot soon gave way to firmer ground.

'How close would Bernabò bring his crossbowmen?' said Blackstone. 'Where are we now? Two hundred yards from shore?'

'More,' said Longdon. 'My balls have been aching for at least eighty yards. I'd say we're two hundred and thirty, maybe fifty, depending where we take the point from back there.'

Killbere grimaced. 'I fear we'll both be eunuchs if we stand here much longer. My vitals are shrinking. What purpose is there for this?'

'Bernabò has no crossbowmen of his own. These will be contracted Genoese. They'll not want to get close enough for Will's archers to kill them even with every man having a pavisier to shield them while they reload.' Genoese bowmen were famed for their efficient drills: load the quarrel, step aside from their protective shield, shoot as one at the command, and then retreat into cover again.

'If they want to kill us, they'll need to be at a hundred and fifty yards. To have better protection from our bowmen they'll go no farther than here,' said Longdon. 'I'd rather not waste our arrows on them. We won't kill enough of them. Better we save what we have for when the other bastards come at us on horseback.'

'That's what I thought,' said Blackstone. 'Bernabò and della Scala have five or six hundred men between them. We'll kill these crossbowmen from here.'

'I can't put my lads this close, Thomas. I can't risk losing them or their arrows.'

'Not you, Will, me and twenty of the men. We'll wait in hiding and kill as many as we can where they stand.'

Killbere grunted. 'Makes sense. But you'll need a hand for your sword and the other to keep your cock from dropping off.'

The fisherman returned as evening mist settled across the wetlands and helped to obscure his arrival. Blackstone's men had toiled all day to create a hazardous approach for any attack. Low walls had been reinforced. Narrow pits were dug to break men's ankles and to cast horses down if they got too close to the defenders. Meulon and his men had dragged fallen branches across the only way in from their right flank, the way that Blackstone had used from Verona. Blackstone's men stopped their efforts when they saw the fisherman bring his punt ashore. A dozen or more fishermen followed him. Bundles of reeds and rushes were stacked on all the punts.

'Unload those boats,' said Blackstone.

The bundles were several feet long, bound with hemp ropes. It needed two men to carry the weight of each bundle. As soon as the fishermen had delivered what Blackstone had asked for, he paid them with the Veronese coin. The men poled their flat-bottom punts back the way they came, but Blackstone asked the lone fisherman to wait.

'The men beyond the marsh are not Cansignorio's men,' Blackstone told him. 'They are the Lord of Milan's, but Lord Cansignorio is coming to join him. If they break through here, they'll know where these bundles of reeds came from. You have placed your village in danger.'

The wiry fisherman shook his head. 'You held me as hostage and threatened to burn our village down.'

Blackstone smiled at the quick response. 'I have nothing more to offer you, but I would ask you for one last thing.'

The fisherman watched as Blackstone's men hauled the reed bundles to where they could best be used as barriers. 'You have paid us well, lord. We have everything we need now for when winter comes across the mountains. What is it you want?'

'Take me close to those men who want me dead so I can see how many there are.'

The fisherman scratched his leathered face as he stared out across the marshes. 'I have no reason to take that risk,' he said.

'No, you don't.'

'He's the Lord of Milan, you say?'

'Bernabò Visconti,' said Blackstone.

The fisherman shrugged. 'I have never seen a lord of Milan.'

★

463

The mist clung to Blackstone's gambeson and hair. It had settled more heavily than he had anticipated, but despite not being able to see more than a few yards ahead, the fisherman poled his boat without concern. He knew every side stream and reed bed. When the punt pushed aside the bulrushes into clear water, the shimmering lights from Bernabò's camp torches burned halos in the mist. The fisherman shipped his pole and squatted down. The water's momentum eased them closer. As they nudged into a dense reed bed, the boat came to a stop. Blackstone heard voices. Muffled by reeds and mist, they merged into a hum. The fisherman hissed to attract Blackstone's attention and pointed forward. He tugged on a handful of reeds and brought the boat closer to the sounds of men. Without warning, Blackstone was staring at a pavilion thirty yards away, encircled with burning torches. It was visible even through the shroud of haze. Bernabò Visconti sat at a table being served food. A group of men stood in a half-circle around him. He recognized Marchesi, who had alerted him to the imminent attack on his men outside Milan. The others looked like *condottieri*.

Blackstone was intent on trying to hear what orders were being given when the fisherman yanked the punt back deeper into the reeds. A guard had strolled into view on the bank between the water and Bernabò's pavilion and was gazing out across the marshland.

Blackstone and the fisherman lay flat. The boat creaked. The current was pushing them towards the sentry. Bernabò raised his voice, berating a *condottiere*, making the guard turn. The fisherman took his chance and hauled the punt away by pulling on handfuls of bulrushes. By the time the man turned back to study the wetland, they were out of sight.

The fisherman stood and poled away from glimmers of torchlight, ghosting through the reed beds between the boat and the shore. The lights and the hum of voices continued until Blackstone urged the fisherman to take him closer to the low earthworks, where more lights disappeared into the evening mist. The fisherman held back and shook his head. Blackstone calmed him with the open palm of his hand and, for the second time that day, slipped into the cold water. Twenty yards later, he slithered over the low embankment. There was no one close enough to see him. He risked standing. As far as he could see, the firefly pinpoints of lights scattered into the distance. This was a vast camp. It looked as though Bernabò had brought even more men with him than Blackstone had encountered days before. He swam back to the waiting boat. The fisherman backpoled the punt away and then turned it for Dosso dell'Aquila.

'How long after sunrise will the mist take to clear?'

The fisherman angled his hand upwards. 'When the sun is here, it will lift.' He wrapped an arm around the pole and slapped his two hands together. 'And then it will be gone.'

Blackstone expected Bernabò would move his Genoese crossbowmen forward soon after sunrise and let the mist disguise them and muffle any sound they made.

And then Cansignorio would strike from the direction of Verona, and Bernabò would follow his crossbowmen with a direct assault in a pincer attack. Blackstone was eager to return to Killbere and the men. There was still work to be done to slow the attack.

A purple sky tinged what remained of the day's light.

As the night's ghostly shroud embraced him, Blackstone knew the cold waters would soon become a fighting men's graveyard.

CHAPTER SEVENTY-TWO

Blackstone's men worked into the night. The heavy bundles of bound reeds were stacked and placed in strategic positions to slow their enemy's progress. They shared cooking duties and while one man ate, the other laboured on. Blackstone insisted they were to eat well that night, for the following day would be long and arduous. The tantalizing smell of cooked pork wafted across the silk-laden waters towards their enemy in the mist. Bernabò's men probably had little else to eat besides salted fish and pottage. Any means of tormenting the enemy had value.

Three campfires were lit for every one of Blackstone's men and spread across the bowsprit of land known as Eagle's Ridge. There was enough dried kindling and fallen wood to ensure the enemy would see the flames through the murky darkness. The fires served more than one purpose. The smoke kept the biting swamp insects at bay. They used one fire for cooking and the others to help create the illusion that Blackstone had more men than he did. If Bernabò could be made to believe that Blackstone had gathered more men than were known to him in Milan, he would spread his forces more widely when they attacked. If they saw the scattered campfires on Blackstone's flank, they could not know the waterlogged land that lay there.

This illusion would entice horsemen to where man and mount would be at the mercy of Blackstone's archers.

Mallin and Terrel went among the horses, checking that they were hobbled with quick-release knots. If the time came for a final desperate counter-attack the men needed time on their side.

'We should stay where we are,' said Terrel, holding the torch so that Mallin could double-check the fastenings. 'In case we need to help get these horses loose.'

Mallin went to the next horse, staying bent, using the light to see his work remained intact. 'You haven't heard, have you?' he said, moving along the line.

'What?'

'We're to be down on the waterline to light those stacked reeds and then fight in the centre with Sir Gilbert. Smoke will help like before.'

'What? We'll be cut off.'

'Aye, well, we'd better learn to be fleet of foot.'

'Listen, you old bastard, I'm not dragging you to the battle line. You're on your own.'

Mallin raised his head. 'Always have been, lad.' He gave a knowing look at Terrel. 'Except for when some village idiot tossed a gold florin and saved my life.'

Terrel grimaced. 'That's the trouble with village idiots. They don't know when they're well off.' He followed Mallin to the next horse on the rope line. 'But I'm not carrying your sorry old arse back to Killbere. Know that.'

Mallin nodded. 'I know. Now put your light where I can see what I'm doing.'

Before the men retired for what few hours of sleep remained, Blackstone briefed his captains. They gathered around the model he had made using sticks and stones to show their positions and how they would fight.

'I need twenty men with me ready to move into the water

when Bernabò sends his bowmen forward. We strip down. Axe and knife. We go ashore, we kill, we retreat. Meulon, Renfred, Aicart, John, choose men from your command.'

'Do you want Brun? He's strong enough to charge down two men at a time,' said Meulon.

'No, keep him with you. You and your men guard the approach from the right where della Scala will attack us. He'll use the same road we did to get here. Get in among them and bring down horse and man.'

Meulon nodded. Once they wounded the horses with their spears and halberds, they would use war hammer and blade in close combat. A man of Brun's size and strength, which matched Meulon's, would rapidly inflict injury and death. 'We've stacked enough of those reed bundles to block their route. Once they try and push the horses over them, we'll attack.'

Blackstone looked at the added defences the men had created by laying reed bundles one behind the other with a gap in between, directly in the path from where Bernabò would launch his attack from the firm ground. These repeated, exhausting obstacles would slow both men on foot and those mounted. And where he hoped to draw in Bernabò's horsemen, the driest of bulrush and reed bundles were ready to be lit. The wettest reeds topmost. Their smoke would smother Bernabò's attackers.

Blackstone pointed out where he wanted his archers. 'Will, you put Jack Halfpenny on that left flank. If luck is with us, then some of Bernabò's horsemen will founder there. Jack's lads must kill as many as they can. Then he comes back here to the centre with you.'

'And how will you strike fast enough against those crossbowmen and their shield carriers?' Longdon said.

'Neither side can shoot while the mist is down. Have one of your lads high enough in one of those trees. We'll be in the water waiting. The fisherman said the mist will lift quickly. The moment it begins to rise, your lads have their arrows nocked, and whoever's up that tree tells you when to shoot. Once you strike them, we'll go in. It will be fast,' said Blackstone, searching his captains' faces, 'so everyone must be ready.'

'And how do you get back before Bernabò's men get to you? They won't be far behind their bowmen. Run straight for us. We'll cover you.' said Longdon.

'No. The horsemen will run us down even with you and the lads shooting. We'll come back the way we went in. If they come into the water Halfpenny can use his men on the flank. That gives us a chance and saves your arrows for the main assault.'

'What about Henry and the woman?' said John Jacob.

'He stays where he is with Gifford. They're far enough back from where we make our stand. You, me and Sir Gilbert hold the centre. We must watch for any breakthrough on the flanks. We turn and fight where we're needed, but we must hold the centre. That's where Bernabò will throw the weight of his attack.'

He gave each man a questioning look. They nodded. They knew what they were expected to do.

CHAPTER SEVENTY-THREE

Blackstone's skin prickled from the cold. The first streaks of pink were creeping through sky and mist. With enough warmth, the mist would rise and the killing would start. He looked at the men who flanked him. Bezián was at his right hand, Becker on his left. Like him, they were waist-deep, moving closer through the fog-laden reed bed. When the water reached his chest, he knew he was close to the earthworks that buttressed the water from dry land. He and his men each gripped a short-handled battleaxe. The vicious spike behind the blade could puncture mail, pierce helmet and skull and drag a man down to be hacked to death with the axe blade. Once ashore, they would pull honed steel knives from their belts to cut a swathe through their unsuspecting enemy.

Ignoring the water's creeping cold, they nudged below the head-high earth bank. Calming their breathing, they listened. Shuffling, heavy-footed men were approaching, crossbowmen with their pavisiers carrying their long rectangular shields. Blackstone hoped Will Longdon's opinion had been correct, that the Genoese crossbowmen had no intention of getting any closer than necessary to English longbowmen. Blackstone dared to peer over the edge.

The Genoese captains had indeed halted their crossbowmen and pavisiers where Longdon had expected. Blackstone offered silent thanks to his veteran archer. The Genoese blazon of a silver cross against a red background was stark and distinctive enough to be seen from a distance. It would make it easier for Longdon's archers to deliver a lethal shower on them. The Genoese crossbowmen were muttering among themselves as they sheltered behind tall wooden shields covered in leather and bearing the same red and silver blazon. Blackstone waited. Mist began shifting up the length of the reeds: a fine silk veil being carefully lifted, revealing more of the reed beds and the crossbowmen. The mist clung to their shields. Then the men's shoulders. Now Blackstone said to himself: *Come on, Will.* He glanced left and right. All eyes were on him. The moment he hauled himself onto firm ground, the men would be with him. Crossbowmen glanced up. The mist was now above their heads. Captains called for their men to be ready. They stepped beyond the shields, their crossbow bolts in place.

Dammit, Will. We need them in the open.

Blackstone heard a faint command from Eagle's Ridge. 'Draw! Loose!'

With their arrows already nocked, all Will Longdon's archers needed to do was bend their backs and send a terrifying hail of death into their targets. Blackstone felt the air shudder.

The Genoese realized what was about to befall them. Panic and then screams from the strike of yard-long iron-tipped arrow shafts piercing muscle and bone. Blackstone hauled himself onto dry land and ran the thirty yards to where the bowmen were trying to regroup. Some had fled behind the shields; others brought their crossbows to bear on their unseen enemy. Captains bellowed their orders. Too late. It was chaos. Blackstone and twenty men roared their defiance and slammed into the bewildered Genoese. Blackstone's impetus carried him past three men. Bezián slashed left and right, then hauled a pavisier away from his shield and hacked him to death. The crossbowman he would have protected lay dead, pierced by an arrow in his throat.

Blackstone was surrounded. He had killed four men in as many strides. He pivoted as a blow swept past his head. A brave Genoese captain had stood his ground, trying to help a wounded man. Blackstone's leg gave way. He was off balance, axe raised to take the sword strike. Becker shielded him from two other men. One drew his sword, while the other lunged with a quarrel, attempting to stab Blackstone. Bezián barged Blackstone aside and positioned himself between him and the Genoese captain, shielding Blackstone from the attack. Becker struck his axe into one man's leg, and slashed his knife across the throat of the other.

With a rapid blow, Bezián struck his spike into the Genoese captain's shoulder. His sword dropped. He sagged in agony. Bezián ripped free the spike and turned the axe blade in a fluid, almost graceful arc, striking the man's throat. He was dead before his body struck the ground.

Blackstone had spearheaded the strike into the packed crossbowmen. He dare not go any further: his men would be overwhelmed. Surrounded by screams of pain and panic, he saw the bloodletting behind him. Four of his men were down, wounded. The few minutes' carnage showed over thirty dead enemy. Others maimed, destined to die, crawled away with pitiful cries. There was to be no pity given this day.

'Back!' Blackstone yelled. In the distance, he saw the Visconti horsemen gathering.

The men plunged into the water, hauling their wounded comrades with them. The ground shuddered. Bernabò had sent the first wave of horsemen after them. Blackstone and the men were halfway to the shore when the riders plunged their horses into the water. Waist-deep for men, it barely covered the horse's legs. Blackstone and the men turned. The reed beds funnelled the horsemen so that they rode only two abreast. Blackstone reached for the reins of the first horse and let his body weight haul down its head. Bezián ignored the tumbling beast as it fell sideways, pinning the rider. No need for a blade to kill him. Bezián knelt on his head and drowned him.

Becker and three others stabbed and slashed the next horse. It reared; the rider fell into the path of the panicked horses behind him. They trampled him as their riders tried to rein them away towards the shore. The two downed horses served their purpose. As Bernabò's riders lunged through the water, Halfpenny's men loosed their arrows into them. The water turned crimson. The line of attack was now blocked by dead horses and men. Those at the rear turned their mounts and clambered across the earthworks onto dry land. They had no choice but to strike for the defenders behind their barricades. Not to do so would have roused Bernabò's wrath. The Lord of Milan saw the failed attempt and unleashed so many more horsemen that they had to jostle for position, stirrup to stirrup, down the stretch of dry land.

Blackstone and the others raced ashore, the cold forgotten, the heat of battle already coursing through them, pumping warmth and raw energy into muscles.

Blackstone yelled, 'Now!'

As the men in the water ran back to their captains, Mallin and Terrel plunged their ready lit torches into the bundles of stacked reeds on the water's edge. The flames caught. Bulrushes crackled and flared. Smoke swirled, found the breeze and soared towards the attacking horsemen, who were now hurtling through the surviving Genoese bowmen, forcing them to plunge into the water to escape being trampled.

Aicart and the Gascons held the centre with Killbere and John Jacob, who tossed Blackstone's scabbard to him. The deafening noise of a cavalry charge added to the thudding weight of the horses causing the water's edge to ripple. Meulon and his men waited on the right flank to block the narrow route. Blackstone drew Wolf Sword, saw the big man look his way and then stay where he was, ignoring the instinct to bring his men to help.

He would soon have his own assault to deal with. And then the horsemen rode into the smoke. Will Longdon's archers waited. Bernabò's mercenaries emerged into a killing zone. They didn't hear the centenar's command over the horses' exertions and the thudding from their hooves. By the time they reached 150 yards from the men standing ready behind their defences, it was too late. The first three ranks were cut down. Horses tumbled. Bones broke. Men who were not already dead from being pierced by an arrow were crushed. The riders behind steered their horses into the water where they splashed and surged, trying to find their footing. Riders fell from the saddle; a boot caught in a stirrup dragged them until drowned. Men bellowed commands, cursed their mounts, raked them with spurs, sawed the bit until the horses' mouths bled. And then they too died as Halfpenny's archers on the flanks lowered their bows, aimed and shot into the mêlée. The slaughter's intensity had not stopped the next wave of horsemen, forcing their mounts through the dead and dying on the firm ground. Their enemy was now a hundred yards ahead of them. So few of them, they thought. The English had no chance.

Mallin and Terrel had run for Killbere's position after lighting the reeds. Mallin was slow; Terrel ran ahead for his life. And then he fell. Hard. Wind thumped out of him. Mallin reached him, bent to drag him onto his feet. A rogue horseman who had escaped Halfpenny's archers bore down on them, sword raised. Mallin fumbled for his own sword, but the horse was closing. He could see the man snarling behind his beard. The rider lifted himself in the saddle, brought his arm down in a sweeping arc for the death blow. Mallin froze. There was nothing to be done except die.

The man was flung back as Halfpenny's well-aimed arrow struck him in the chest. The weight of his body falling made the horse veer away. Mallin looked to where the miracle had come from. A hundred yards behind him, Halfpenny was moving his men closer towards the centre's flank. No gesture or acknowledgement made. None needed. Mallin hauled a dazed Terrel to his feet.

Blackstone stood at the centre of the defenders, John Jacob to his right, Killbere on his left. The surviving horsemen had reached the first obstacles of the reed bundles. Horses attempted to jump them, but the way the bundles had been placed caused them to falter or straddle the hurdles, resulting in riders falling to Longdon's archers. And then some broke through.

Blackstone's men worked together. Strike the horse, or yank the reins, or slash its neck: whatever it took to wound the beast or throw it from its stride so that another could ram a blade into the rider's groin or drive it deeper into his belly. Along the defensive line Blackstone's men were being punished by the sheer weight of horsemen that had found gaps and ridden through.

Killbere swung his chained mace, its spikes aimed to strike the rider in the face. Blackstone was on the other side of the horse and as the rider attempted to curl the chain around his sword blade, his raised arm exposed an armpit where Blackstone rammed Wolf Sword's hardened steel.

Bezián hauled another horseman onto the ground. His mount broke free and careered into other wide-eyed horses. Bezián struck the man twice with his battleaxe, turned in time to avoid being charged down by a huge black beast of a horse whose momentum took it past the Gascon and whose size made it a formidable opponent. Renfred's men jumped on top of a stacked bundle of reeds. The beast faltered when it couldn't get past the obstacle. The rider slashed left and right, his shield high on the one side of his body. Becker grabbed the shield and yanked hard, letting his body drop below the reed bundle. The rider kept a tight grip on his reins, but Becker's weight pulled him half out of the saddle, exposing his neck and head. Renfred hacked his blade down, severing the man's collarbone. He screamed. The horse rolled. Renfred's men danced clear.

Meulon held his men back. The fighting was raging less than

sixty yards from where he guarded the road. Blackstone's men were in a curved defensive line. The horsemen were desperately trying to navigate around obstacles and evade Blackstone's men, but they were relentlessly pushed back. Behind Blackstone's centre, Will Longdon's archers were twenty yards back up the rising ground, their arrows flying across the defenders' heads, punishing the enemy horses and riders.

Meulon saw Aicart, the Gascon captain, go down, buffeted by a horse. Bezián leapt and grabbed the rider, but was swept aside with a mace. Dazed and injured, both men rolled free of the horse's hooves. The horse went past them; two more horsemen followed behind it to trample and kill the fallen men. John Jacob hurled his axe at the first rider, catching his shield. The man raised it. Killbere had abandoned his own shield and rammed his sword into the horse's neck. It reared. The second horseman barged John Jacob aside. Blackstone's men were going down under the weight of the attack.

'Meulon! They're here!' cried Brun as della Scala's horsemen tried to force their way around the bend between the water and rising ground, slowed by the reed obstacles in their path. The last glimpse Meulon had of Blackstone was of him slashing at a rider and then being caught between that horse and the next.

Blackstone went down.

Meulon's men jumped in front of the startled horses trying to mount the defences as yet more horses pressed from the other side. A forest of spears and halberds met the cursing horsemen. Meulon's agile men scurried beneath the spear shafts to gut beasts. Halberds hooked men from their saddles. Other men crouching waited to stab to death any rider who was able to get to his feet. Wounded men had no chance beneath the panicked horse's hooves. The weight of the horses forced those attackers at the front to sacrifice themselves, but the animals rolled clear in their death throes, pushing aside the defences and allowing others to break through.

Meulon and his frontline men fell back twenty yards. They

had laid rocks and boulders on the path along with torn-down limbs of trees. The horses shied. Some went into the water. Others tried dancing over the obstacles. Every mount that got through the gap caused their riders difficulties in trying to control them. Meulon's men attacked. Spears rammed into horses that reared or toppled, men on the ground trying to get to their feet were hacked to death. Della Scala's mercenaries came on. Meulon fell back again, drawing the horsemen in until they were level with the hillside. Brun and Meulon hefted the weight of tied reeds, several feet long, and threw it into the horses' path. A dozen men followed behind and did the same. Three of Meulon's men fell beneath savage, desperate sword thrusts. They were being pushed back.

Meulon's face streamed with blood from a blow he didn't remember receiving. He wiped the blood from his eyes. They couldn't hold much longer. They were desperate.

'Will!' Meulon's lungs bellowed. His desperation rising above the cacophony.

They fought as they retreated step by step, the horses being slowed, some being killed, yet more rearing in fear, others bolting into the shallows and then deeper water.

Meulon turned. Will Longdon had split his archers and raced in their direction. Still behind the main defensive line they hurriedly nocked their bows and ten archers shot twice into the crowded horsemen. Meulon almost ducked as the arrows whispered over his head. Two rows of horsemen died. Horses went down. The way was blocked. Meulon pressed forward on the offensive, yelling for his men to attack. Without hesitation, they followed.

A collective cry urged them on: *No mercy!*

Death's momentum continued.

Will Longdon turned back. Blackstone had disappeared from view. Killbere was alone with a handful of men scattered around him. The archers showered a storm of rhythmic terror on the main attack. With his archers shooting from the centre and Halfpenny's from the flank, so many of Bernabò's men died before they could reach the defences. But enough did. Longdon saw a bloodstained Blackstone rise from the dead. Then Blackstone was at Killbere's side, who remained where he stood, letting the enemy come to him. Bezián was on his feet. Not Aicart, the courageous Gascon captain. He couldn't be seen. Nor John Jacob. Longdon glanced to where Mallin and Terrel were standing behind a wall, hurling rocks in desperation at the horsemen unable to breach their defence. And then Longdon's heart almost seized. Jack Halfpenny and one of his archers were wading out into the water to snatch arrows from the dead and dying. They had nothing more to shoot and if Bernabò's men realized that, they would come in hard across the water and outflank Blackstone.

The two archers yanked arrows from corpses, wading deeper and deeper in the bloodied water until they were too close to the earthwork bank where a horseman held back by the logjammed riders in front of him saw them. Heeling his mount, he yanked the reins and plunged his horse into the water. Longdon saw Halfpenny make a sweeping gesture to the man with him, telling him to escape and take the armful of arrows back. Halfpenny, refusing to release the arrows he had collected, tucked them under one arm and drew his sword with the other. Later, Longdon would swear he could hear the clang of the sword strike against Halfpenny's helmet from where he stood. Halfpenny's body fell into the reed bed. Now the horseman, with a clear run at the shore, urged his horse forward. Longdon thought the carnage in front of him had distracted the rider. Levelling his bow with the rest of the men he loosed into the marauding horsemen that were urging their horses ashore. When he looked again, John Jacob had appeared and slammed his battleaxe into the lone horseman, using its spike to pull him down. The rider fell, gasping for air as he swallowed water. Another axe blow killed him.

Longdon saw the battle shift against them. They were down

to three arrow shafts each. They would kill those breaching the lower walls and then cast aside their bows and join the men below.

'With me!' he yelled.

CHAPTER SEVENTY-FOUR

Henry Blackstone could barely restrain his desire to go to the bottom of the hill and join his father. The battle noise rose. Glimpses of men through the trees against the shimmering water told him the fight was desperate. Nothing was clear, but he witnessed enough death as shadows fell into light and then swarms of men and horses clashed. Regret heaped upon regret for having promised to be Elena Salvarini's guardian. Anxiety creased his features.

'Hold fast,' said a calming voice at his side, knowing what thoughts taunted the younger man.

'Hugh, we should go down there.'

'No,' said Gifford. 'We should not. Sir Thomas is depending on you. On us. To protect these women. That was your pledge. Meet it. That fight might come to us if they breach the defences.'

Henry looked at Elena and her servant huddled in the corner of the stone pen. Two stout branches criss-crossed the entrance. Both women held a short-handled battleaxe. Morena gripped hers as a supplicant might clutch a church cross against her chest to ward off evil spirits. Fear creased their faces, but Elena's back was straight and she had ripped away a layer of her dress so that she could move more easily. For a second, Henry felt as though the look she gave was to comfort him. That she was there to protect him. He nodded, receiving a slender smile in return. One that might be of sadness at what was soon to be inflicted on them.

'We hold,' he said to Gifford. 'You're right. I must do as I pledged. I'm sorry you're bound to it as well.'

Gifford sighed. 'Aye, but if there's a next time, Henry, don't make promises that might be impossible to keep.'

A shaft of sunlight beamed through the trees. Time had passed and still the fight ebbed and flowed. Bernabò's hundreds of horsemen might have worked on an open battlefield, but confined to the strip of land they were proving as much an obstacle to get past as Blackstone's determined defence.

Henry closed his eyes. The sounds below assaulted his mind with a hundred images. Somewhere behind him, he heard pigs squeal. He spun around. Gifford had heard them as well. Shadows were plunging downhill through the trees. Five, no, six men running had found a way over the ridge behind them. Sword in hand. Led by Mastino Gambetti. Determined to kill the only witness to his crime.

The women saw their guardians raise their shields and then the reason why.

Henry and Gifford went forward ten yards and covered the approach to the women's pen. Five strides apart, they readied their swords at the high guard. Gambetti's momentum struck Henry, knocking him sideways, but the weight of his shield counterbalanced him. From being on one knee he was back on his feet when Gambetti, using the walls to stop himself, slowed his own uncontrolled descent downhill. In their haste to attack, their speed proved to be a mistake. Gifford sidestepped one man, half turned and struck the man's thigh with a blow that, aided by the man's descent, severed his leg save for one strip of muscle and skin.

Gambetti turned to see Henry trading blows with one of his men. He bent forward into the hill and drove himself forward, ready to strike Henry from behind.

'Master Henry!' Elena cried.

Gambetti spat the phlegm of exertion from his throat and attacked. Henry rammed his shield against Gambetti's man, who thrust his sword through it, narrowly missing Henry's ribs. He released his arm from the shield's restraint, letting its weight snare the sword, then struck the man's unprotected arm. A vicious blow. Blood spurted from a severed artery. The man staggered back and sagged onto his knees. Gifford tried to get between Henry and Gambetti but could not fight past another man who held the higher ground and struck repeated blows, grunting with effort, forcing Gifford to fight back.

'No!' Gambetti shouted as one of the other men joined the attack on Henry. 'He's mine! Kill the girl!'

As Gifford fought the determined swordsman stopping him from going to Henry's aide, he shouted to the women. 'Defend yourselves!'

His concern was unnecessary. Elena gripped the battleaxe as Gambetti's man stepped awkwardly across the threshold. Morena hurled a sharp-edged rock at him. He raised his hand. Elena held the axe in both hands, spike down, and rammed it into his head. He fell forward into the pen, slumped over the crossed branches, the falling body pulling free the axe shaft from her grip. She backed away, shocked for a moment by the man's death and the gruesome manner of it.

The last man's steel blade sparked against the stone wall as he stretched to reach Morena. She backed away, threatening him with the axe but unable to reach him over the height of the wall. As Gambetti fought Henry and Gifford was still occupied with his man, the attacker took his chance and clambered onto the wall. Two women, one nervously holding an axe, pressing a protective arm around a girl, urging her to get behind her, didn't offer any threat.

Morena lunged. Brought the axe down. And missed. The shuddering blow against the stone wall shook her grip free. Their assailant backhanded her. She sprawled unconscious. The man dared a glance at Gambetti trading blows with the man he'd come to kill. That man's companion had moved downhill; sword strikes slammed against shields as neither he nor della Scala's man could get the better of the other.

That was good. Now he had the girl to himself. He reached for her. Grabbed the top of her dress and pulled her to him. She raised her hands to protect herself. He slapped her. Enough to teach her a lesson without stunning her. He plunged his mouth into her neck and tasted the sweet fragrance of a woman whose skin smelled nothing like the whores in Verona. Elena released an arm from his embrace and tried to reach his face. He snatched it away, settling his foul mouth on hers.

His lust blinded him to the girl's other hand. She pulled free the dagger from his belt and stuck it into his exposed neck. He jerked away. Hand to the wound. Eyes wide with disbelief. Two staggered steps back and then rage took over. He reached for her. She was on her knees. He cursed, spitting blood, and then saw the spiked axe veer upwards into his forehead.

Blood-soaked, Elena scrambled for Morena. She was alive. She cradled the loyal woman to her and prayed that Henry Blackstone could kill whoever was trying to kill them.

Henry couldn't reach Elena during her struggle. He was younger than Gambetti, but the man was taller, and a proven fighter. Henry had the advantage of being on higher ground, which gave his sword strokes added heft and which forced della Scala's assassin to stand upright, almost back on his heels instead of bending into the rising ground to defend himself. It also made Henry vulnerable. He swung his sword down; Gambetti bent his knees, absorbed the blow, pivoted to one side. Henry's momentum carried on the downward strike. If Gambetti had been able to hold an axe or knife in his maimed hand, he would have killed him. As it was, Gambetti's bent arm slammed his sword's pommel into Henry's shoulder. Pain numbed his arm. His right hand gripped his sword and he willed his left to ignore the pain. There was no time to stand still. He swept his blade low and fast, its point slicing across Gambetti's thigh: a tear across the muscle that barely made the killer falter. Henry was now below the taller man, who struck with force and speed, bearing down on him. Henry backtracked, felt a rock behind his heel, almost tripped but pressed his foot against it and used it to propel himself forward. His blade caught Gambetti's crossguard. Henry twisted, forcing Gambetti's sword down. Blackstone's training in close-quarter fighting skills loomed large in his memory. His numb arm didn't fail him. He snatched at Gambetti's sword belt, pulled him down and headbutted him. The assassin's nose flattened. Blood spurted. His beard clogged with snot and gore. Eyes wide from the pain, he parried Henry's following sword strike, twisted the blade and jabbed, attempting to eviscerate him. The blade skidded off Henry's honed steel, missed the vital stomach target, but pierced his side. He bent into the pain and Gambetti struck him with such force Henry fell back. He slammed into the ground. Pain swallowed him from the impact. He fought it but couldn't lift his head.

Gambetti spat blood and stalked to where his opponent had fallen. Sword raised. In for the kill. A hefty stone struck him in the face. The sharp-edged rock split his cheek and closed his eye. Elena picked up another and hurled it. He half turned away. The rock caught his shoulder. He stepped over Henry's body and took the several strides towards the defiant Elena. He hauled the dead body from the entrance and stepped inside. Defenceless, she backed away. As he snatched her hair, forced her down and lifted his sword to plunge into her neck, she cried out. He choked. His back arched. Henry's sword strike was so powerful the blade rammed through Gambetti's back and out of his chest. Henry grabbed the falling man and hauled him away from Elena. The last thing Prince Lionel's assassin saw was Henry Blackstone staring down at him.

Henry staggered to Elena. She sobbed a breath, releasing the tension. Henry embraced her, pressing his lips into her hair. She touched his face.

'You're hurt.'

He nodded and took away a bloodstained hand from his wound. She picked up the torn strips from her dress and pressed it into his side. He covered her hand with his own. She looked as though she had been in a fight. He smiled, pulled a strand of hair from her face.

'Is she alive?' he asked, looking at Morena lying on the ground.

'Yes.'

Henry looked around him. No other men appeared to be coming through the forest. The sound of fighting still raged below. 'Attend to her. I must find Hugh.'

He found Gifford thirty yards downhill. The man-at-arms lay in a deathly embrace with the man he had fought. His body smothered the man beneath him. Both men were jammed tight against a tree trunk where they had tumbled in their desperate fight to the death, neither man yielding. The dead man's arm embraced Gifford, his fist protruding from beneath the man-at-arm's body, still gripping the dagger he had plunged into the back of his shoulder. Henry eased down next to the man who been his guardian and friend and served the King so loyally. Gifford's knife was deep into the man's neck.

He smoothed the hair from Gifford's face and saw the cut and bruising from where his head had struck the tree trunk in that final plunge. He laid a hand on his back.

'I'm sorry, my friend. God bless you.'

Ignoring the pain and defying the urge he still felt to go down to where the battle still raged, he stood to make his way back to Elena. Gifford groaned.

Henry dropped to his knees and eased his head to one side. Death had not claimed him. The strike against the tree had rendered him unconscious.

'Hugh! Thank God. I thought you dead.'

Gifford's eyes opened. For a moment, he was bewildered. He nodded. 'So did I.' He winced.

'You're wounded. We need to get that knife out of your shoulder.'

Gifford nodded. 'Help me up.'

Henry got Gifford to his feet. 'My knife,' he said, pointing at the blade embedded in the dead man.

Henry yanked it free. Gifford wiped the blade on his sleeve. 'If that's how you free a knife, I'll let the women attend to mine.'

The two wounded men, supporting each other, made their slow way back to where Elena waited.

CHAPTER SEVENTY-FIVE

Dead horses and their riders lay scattered across Blackstone's line of defence. Cries of pain from dying men; horses whinnied in their death throes. Yet Bernabò's horsemen could see there were so few defenders on their feet that they surely couldn't fail to destroy the last of Blackstone's men.

Meulon and his men still defended the gap in the road, denying della Scala's mercenaries the breakthrough they needed to cut into Blackstone's flank. Every man was forced back, again and again. But still they held.

Blackstone stood with Killbere. A carpet of bodies lay at their feet and down to the water's edge. The obstacles they had laid had bought them time and helped them fight off every wave of attack. But now those defences were little more than a man with a sword.

Every man left alive was wounded. Renfred and Becker had survived but the scout looked as though he might not live through the day given his wounds. Who among them might? Blackstone thought. John Jacob supported a wounded leg on a broken spear shaft. Blood soaked Killbere's gambeson. His own and that of the men he had killed.

There was a lull as Bernabò's horsemen gathered on the dry

strip of land. Whether they attacked through the shallows or where Blackstone and his survivors stood would make little difference. There were so many corpses that they would need to give their mounts free rein to find their own way through the carnage. The stench of death struck fear into the beasts and drove them on.

A surge of twenty horsemen came at pace across the dry ground. Was this a final desperate push to kill the survivors? No one knew how many more charges would come.

Bezián stood close by with the surviving Gascons. Will Longdon, long since without arrows, had gathered his and Halfpenny's archers to stand and fight with sword and buckler.

Blackstone looked at the grim, determined men around him.

'Let them come,' he said. 'They'll be scattered as they try to get past those carcasses. Will! Break left and strike at their flank. Bezián! You and the others with me when I move.'

He placed a hand on Killbere's shoulder. 'I'll leave you here to hold the centre.'

Both men were weary from the constant assault. 'Thomas. I see no benefit in exerting myself any more than I must. I shall do as you say and hold the centre.'

Blackstone nodded to his squire, John Jacob. 'Stay with Sir Gilbert, John. Kill those who get past me. There's no one else behind us.'

He cupped his hands and bellowed. 'Meulon! Hold now! Hold!' The throat-cutter had to keep della Scala's men from breaking through.

The big man turned and raised a hand. Blackstone saw they were being hard-pressed.

John Jacob crossed himself. The horses were fifty yards away and closing. Blackstone brought Arianrhod, the Silver Wheel Goddess, to his lips.

'We'll need her help this hour,' said Will Longdon, doing the same with his own protective talisman.

Killbere looked at Longdon. 'I have never found it wise to

trust a woman.' He smiled at the veteran archer. 'But ask her to watch over us all.'

'Now!' said Blackstone and ran forward to get among the horsemen twenty yards away, who had slowed trying to get past the fallen horses. A swarm of armed men followed him, driving their bodies for a last effort. Ignoring exhaustion. Dry-mouthed. Barely able to bellow defiance.

They slashed at rider's legs. Swarmed around horses. Stabbed into their bellies and necks. Hauled men down on the ground and slaughtered them. Men lost their minds in the frenzy of killing and descended into the final horror that took them beyond anything they had experienced before.

Blackstone thrust Wolf Sword into vulnerable riders, ramming the honed blade into groin and belly. Slamming his battleaxe into lower limbs. Ignoring cries. Knowing men around him were hauling those he had wounded down to die.

The stench of horse sweat and men's bodies spilling their innards clung to him like the miasma of acrid smoke from the smouldering reeds. A horse barged him. A mace swung against his helm. He fell to one side and rolled between another horse's hooves. His head rang. For a second he thought he heard trumpets in the distance. Clambering to his feet he readied himself to attack the nearest horseman, but the rider yanked his horse's reins, spurred its bloodied flanks and rode back the way he had come towards Bernabò's headquarters. The sound of the trumpet's recall was now sharp as it floated across the wetlands. Blackstone looked around. His scattered men stood watching the few surviving horsemen retreating.

Eleven of Bernabò's horsemen in that last attack had survived and cantered back.

'Recall!' shouted Bezián. 'They're regrouping.'

Blackstone saw Meulon's men standing unchallenged for the first time as della Scala's men too turned back their horses. There was no time to waste. He strode back to Killbere and the others. There were too few of them left to withstand a concerted attack by Bernabò and della Scala's men. Holding a flank served no purpose now. They must gather and hold the centre and fight their way from the shore up the hill towards the ridge.

'Meulon!' he bellowed. The throat-cutter saw Blackstone's gesture to join him. A handful of his men had survived.

Blackstone reached Killbere and John Jacob, who stood where he had left them. Only three enemy horsemen had broken through. Will Longdon brought his men in from the shallows. Longdon and another archer supported Jack Halfpenny's body.

'Went into the reed bed. Reckon that saved him from drowning.' He broke into a wide grin. 'The slow-moving fool got himself knocked senseless.'

The men murmured their pleasure when they saw the ventenar was still alive.

'Will, take him into the ruined house. Do what you can for him. Then come back into the line,' Blackstone said.

Meulon joined the group of desperate men.

'So few, Meulon,' said Killbere.

'Aye, Sir Gilbert. They came hard at us.'

Mallin and Terrel had fought with Killbere. Blood matted Terrel's scalp. The old man looked even older than he had before the battle. He grinned through his blood-flecked beard. 'They never got into the trees and our horses, Sir Thomas. Not one horse lost.'

The trumpets sounded again. More distant. It felt eerily quiet. Water lapped. A fish eagle screeched. A low moan of a dying man persisted.

Blackstone looked at his bedraggled survivors. What was left of them. Aicart the courageous Gascon captain was dead. Renfred lay wounded, unable to stand. Becker stood with Renfred's men to shield their captain.

'We'll not stop their next charge. If Bernabò called his men back, they're regrouping in force. We'll move behind the low walls and the ruined house,' Blackstone said.

They trudged back from the water's edge. Arms weary, sweat and blood caked into the grime of their skin.

'Terrel, see that my son and Gifford and the women are unharmed. Tell them they should try and seek a way out of here.'

Terrel nodded. He turned. Mallin grabbed his arm. He lowered his voice. 'You go with them, lad.'

Terrel checked to see he wouldn't be overheard.

'That was my plan.'

Mallin smiled. 'I thought as much.'

Terrel looked as though he was about to say something. A flicker of regret in his expression but he turned for the wooded hill.

John Jacob found a wineskin and passed it to Blackstone.

'You and Gilbert first, John.' Blackstone walked along the ragged line of men. 'Drink what you can. And if they don't come soon, rest. Look to your wounds.'

The men waited. Flies were gathering on the dead.

Bezián stared into the distance. The horizon had changed. It bristled. A vague smudged line across the dry ground. 'Bastards are here, Sir Thomas.'

Killbere followed his gaze. 'It looks as though they mean to end it,' he said. 'We must have upset them.'

'Was it something you said, Gilbert?' Blackstone asked.

The men laughed.

'Fuck them,' said Blackstone.

'Fuck them,' the weary men chorused.

Blackstone took a stride forward. He would be the first to face the charge. The first to die. 'Let's send them to the devil.'

Several hundred men rode at an unhurried trot down the strip of land that served as the road south and where the main assault had come from. It had been churned by horsemen before them. These men, unchallenged by the previous fighting, had been eager to engage and kill. Two of them rode ahead of the main body, exercising caution, knowing that if archers were on the shore a flight of arrows would cut them down. They edged around what remained of the Genoese bowmen. Revealed before them was a field of death. Arrows forested the ground. Men lay curled from an agonizing death. Horses stared wide-eyed, lips drawn back in a rictus grin from the pain inflicted before they too perished. Bodies floated to one side in the water. Crimson streaks spread across the lagoon surface, discolouring reed beds. Corpses lay on the bank below the forest, tightly packed, showing how severe the fighting had been.

Nothing lived.

And then men showed themselves on the shore. Defiant, shoulder to shoulder. Ready to die as they had done so many times before. One man stood in front of the rest.

The horsemen spurred their mounts towards them.

CHAPTER SEVENTY-SIX

'I'll be damned,' said Blackstone. He looked at the others. Grins broke out.

The two riders nudged their mounts through the dead.

'William! What in God's name are you doing here?'

William Ashford and Bullard dismounted and ran to embrace their friends. 'Sir Thomas. It's a long story, but one that ends with us being here.' He looked at the survivors. 'So few of you.'

'We've lost thirty men. Perhaps more. A hard fight.'

The sobering news tainted their joy at seeing those friends who had survived.

'The gold?' said Blackstone.

'In Florence. It's safe. We were met by the Tau knights outside Lucca. The Prince has what he needs for the war in France.'

Killbere leaned on his sword. 'Then our loss has been worth it.' He hawked and spat and looked at Blackstone with a smile that expressed something other than joy. 'As always, Thomas, our road is paved with the dead.'

The horsemen who had followed William Ashford and Bullard drew up fifty yards away. Two men rode forward.

'Oh, shit,' said Killbere. 'Are we to be lectured after our ordeal?'

Lord Edward Despenser reined in his horse. His visor was up, his face scowling.

'Lord Edward,' said Blackstone. 'It appears that you have completed your duties at Pavia. You buried Prince Lionel?'

Despenser let his eyes settle on the surrounding carnage. He was subdued, less aggressive than Blackstone had expected. 'He remains there until we return him to England. I left half the men and took the field and joined up with our friend here.'

Despenser's companion, who had held back, now leaned forward, a gentle hand laid on his horse's neck as it snaffled its bit. It pawed the ground. His blazon and shield showed a white cross on a black shield. *La furia 'd Diò.*

'Is it God's fury that brings you to us, or His divine providence?'

'I go where He takes me, Sir Thomas. I pursue Bernabò Visconti. The Lord of Milan sides with the devil. Perhaps it's the devil that led me to you.'

'One who recognizes his own,' said Despenser.

Blackstone stared hard at the man, who locked eyes with him. 'I know you. You're Gunther von Schwerin. You once pursued me. Years ago.'

'Six years past, Sir Thomas.'

'And then you sided with me. You were a Teutonic Knight.'

'As you see, I left my order. But I still wield my sword in the Lord's name.'

Despenser had listened patiently. 'Visconti took flight when he saw our approach,' he said, casting a last glance at the dead. 'God or the devil, Sir Thomas. One of them favours you.'

'We'll take whatever help we can, Lord Edward.'

Despenser gathered his reins. 'Von Schwerin has a barber surgeon with him. I have supplies. We'll attend to your wounded and let your men rest before we ride for Bologna. The road is clear.'

He turned the horse and gave a final, curt admonishment. 'William Ashford has since told me of your plan. You risked everything.'

'A common failing of mine,' said Blackstone.

Henry and Gifford, accompanied by Elena, Morena and Terrel, emerged from the forest. His father and the captains had gone to look for their fallen comrades as Blackstone's wounded men were being treated by the barber surgeon. Despenser had returned to the open ground and set up camp.

'Is that who I think it is?' Henry asked Killbere as Will Longdon was stitching a wound on the knight's thigh, shooing flies away and spilling wine into the wound to keep it clean.

Killbere grimaced. 'If my eyes were not watering because of this stunted-finger attempt to stitch me, I might know who you're looking at. God's tears! Will! Have a care.'

'Sir Gilbert,' said Longdon. 'This is only one of three wounds that needs attention. If you would prefer the barber surgeon to attend to you, I'll give way.'

'And take pleasure in knowing I would suffer even more at the hands of a stranger? Get on with it. Yes, it's him,' he said, turning to Henry, noticing for the first time his bloodied bandage across his side. 'Did Bernabò's men break through and reach you?'

'No. Della Scala's. Mastino Gambetti.'

'The assassin? You killed him?'

Henry nodded.

'I hope it was a long and painful death. Lord Despenser will want to hear of this. But you'll need Will to look at that,' he said, meaning Henry's wound.

Henry nodded. 'Later,' he said. 'Gifford needs attention first.'

Henry settled Gifford down with his back against the wall. 'Elena did a good job of packing your wound. Will Longdon will attend to you when he's finished with Sir Gilbert. I want to go and speak to that man over there.'

'You know him?'

'Six years ago, on the way to Avignon. He was a Teutonic Knight back then. I see his life has taken a different turn.'

'Just like mine when I was tasked to be with you.'

'And I'm grateful that they chose you.'

'Well, I would have argued my case had I known the trouble you cause.'

Henry smiled. 'You see, Hugh, it's better we don't know what the future holds.'

He left Gifford and walked towards Gunther von Schwerin, who was helping to lay out the dead.

Blackstone waded through the water with Meulon and Bezián a few strides either side of him as they searched for their fallen men. All three men were bloodstained from the hours of fighting, their wounds bound with makeshift bandages. Yet despite the heavy fighting, Blackstone's leg had not worsened.

He turned over a body floating face down. 'It's Girald. One of Aicart's men. Bezián, get him ashore.'

Bezián took hold of his fellow Gascon and eased him through the water.

Blackstone reached a dead horse. Its saddle was embellished with the Visconti emblem, a silver snake encircling a man. The rider who lay alongside the dead horse still had a boot caught in the stirrup. His chest was pierced by an arrow.

'One of Halfpenny's lads brought this one down,' said Meulon.

Blackstone bent into the water to raise the dead man's face. He felt a pang of regret as he cradled Marchesi's body.

'This man gave me warning of the skinners' attack on you outside Milan. Help me get him ashore. We must give him a Christian burial.'

Meulon and Blackstone got the Visconti captain free of the dead horse.

'He was a good man, fighting for a bad cause,' said Blackstone.

★

By nightfall, they had brought those who were to be buried onto the shoreline. The wetlands still carried bloated horses and slaughtered *condottieri* and Visconti soldiers. Blackstone's men, weary from the intensity of the battle, had washed off the filth from their efforts, stripped down and rested. Firelight and food offered comfort. The loss of so many friends subdued them, even as they recalled the battle and recounted their part in it. But they had won the day and had managed to survive. And that was every soldier's prayer.

Gunther von Schwerin sat with Edward Despenser in their camp as Blackstone related what had happened when Cansignorio had escorted them to his castle in Verona. The trial of the young woman Donna Elena Salvarini revealed a link that went back to the Mont Cenis monastery, where her father had been blackmailed into trying to kill Prince Lionel.

'You fought della Scala in a duel?' said Despenser. 'And were given permission to do so by a cardinal?'

'Della Scala's honour was put to the test. I bettered him, and he gave chase the moment we left Verona.'

'No matter how much evidence you offered to the papal legate, it remains circumstantial,' said Despenser. 'Even the assassin in Alba that Master Henry killed – which the King will hear about – even that cannot prove involvement from della Scala. It can be argued that a lord's man-at-arms could have acted alone.'

'Della Scala attacked from one flank, Bernabò the other. You must not think the two are enemies, no matter how it appears. Della Scala has switched sides. How long that arrangement lasts, no one knows. Cur dogs turn on each other over the next bone.'

Despenser had been Prince Lionel's second-in-command. A final report would be sent to the King of England that would relate all that Blackstone had achieved. 'Sir Thomas, once again, you prove many of us wrong. Prince Lionel trusted you. I, too, should have done so. I will return to Pavia and then take the Prince's body back to England.'

'Then you abandon the fight against Bernabò Visconti?' said von Schwerin.

'From everything Sir Thomas and his son have told me, he was not involved in the Prince's death. I have no just cause.'

'Then I'll take my men and chase after him again. Della Scala is another matter. If he declares for the Visconti, he becomes the Pope's enemy and mine. Until then, it is Bernabò I want.'

Despenser stood and looked across the stretch of open ground to where Blackstone's men camped. 'The stench of rotting corpses will be unbearable by noon tomorrow, Sir Thomas. You want to bury your men in a Christian graveyard but you're too few to withstand another attack while you look for one. I and my men will accompany you as far south as Bologna. We'll find a church along the way.'

Von Schwerin passed a wineskin to Blackstone. 'The Abbey of Santa Maria della Vangadizza is a day's ride south. It's beyond Scaligeri's control.'

'Is that agreeable?' Despenser asked Blackstone.

'It is,' said Blackstone.

'Then we start at first light.' Lord Edward Despenser stood. Despite their aching muscles and wounds Blackstone and Henry helped Killbere to his feet. They dipped their heads respectfully. The Knight of the Garter had invoked his authority.

Von Schwerin walked alongside Blackstone and the others towards their camp. 'La Battaglia del Dosso dell'Aquila will be remembered for a long time, Sir Thomas. Your victory here will be like a flail's scar on Visconti and della Scala's backs.'

'A man needs a good battle to be remembered by,' said Killbere. 'The Battle of Eagle's Ridge has a pleasing sound to the ear whatever language is used. Let's hope Despenser remembers to put it into his report.'

'Gunther, I've lost too many men. My plan is to go to Bologna and search for replacements among those who fight for any of the companies and find the best of them to join us. I would prefer it though if *you* would join us. I need another captain and a man I trust.'

'I'm honoured,' said von Schwerin.

'Every man who remembers your time with us those years back would follow you,' said Killbere.

Von Schwerin hesitated, remembering his own fatal moment of killing his best friend in Avignon to save that man's honour. 'Sir Thomas, even I have a stained past. And not something I'm proud of. A reason why I left my order and devoted myself to fighting the Pope's enemies. I fear you would recant your offer should the truth ever be revealed.'

'Then you'd be in good company,' said Blackstone. 'What man among us doesn't have a stain on his soul?'

Von Schwerin thought about it a moment longer. 'First I must serve the Pope and confront Bernabò Visconti.'

'I understand. But when that's done, seek me out,' said Blackstone.

The mist layered the killing ground the following day, just as it had done the day before the battle had begun. The corpses abandoned in the reed beds and shallow water reached out to them in grotesque supplication, as if trying to push aside the mourner's veil clinging to them.

Blackstone sat on the bastard horse, his men ready to follow, their friends' bodies wrapped in their blankets, strapped across their saddles. They waited as Despenser led his men towards them down the strip of ground along which Bernabò Visconti had sent his men to kill them.

Blackstone turned to Henry. The two women, Elena Salvarini and her servant, were several horses behind. 'Henry, I will be returning to England. There's a war coming with the French. We've secured the money the Prince needs to wage that war.'

His head half turned, indicating the women behind him. 'You know you cannot take her to France. She's a noblewoman and asking her to go into exile in a foreign land soon to be scorched with war until she is old enough to reclaim her lands is an unfair proposition. You are her guardian.' He paused, watched Despenser's slow approach, buying himself time to finalize his thoughts. 'How will you support her?'

'I'm not sure yet, lord. I'll find a way.'

'Then, until you decide, this is what you will do. You will take her to Florence and be under the protection of Father Torellini and the Bardi family. You will earn an honest living by teaching and acting as a notary. She is not a common woman and will require some comforts.'

'Donna Elena will manage whatever comes her way,' said Henry, and then added with a knowing determination in his voice, 'She's as strong and brave as my mother.'

Blackstone nodded; of that he had no doubt from what he had learnt about the fight in the forest. 'Even so. She must be protected. That is your sworn duty. Understand?'

'I do.'

'Good. Then that's settled.' He addressed Gifford. 'I need accomplished men-at-arms. Join us and return to France.'

Gifford's arm was in a sling. He fussed over it for a moment. He looked at Blackstone's son. 'I'm sorry, Sir Thomas, but only the King can relieve me of my duty. It's a cross I shall bear with as much goodwill as I can muster.'

Henry's pleasure at his continued companionship was obvious. Gifford shrugged. The two were fated to be together. Blackstone saw the look of mutual respect that passed between them.

'Then you have my gratitude, Hugh Gifford. And I wish you well.'

Despenser's men reached where the strip of land touched the shore. He reined in his horse. The massed men behind him waited.

'Lord, am I to continue using my mother's name, as proud as I am to bear it?' said Henry.

'That's up to you.'

'Then with your permission, I would like to be known as Henry Blackstone.'

Blackstone's gaze lingered on his son. He had been tested and had not failed. And his wayward tendencies would be reined in by his commitment to Elena and with Gifford at his side.

'Then that is how you shall be known,' said Blackstone.

Killbere spat to one side. 'God's tears. About time.'

Blackstone gathered his reins. Since leaving France a trail of death lay in his wake. Bernabò Visconti and a new enemy, Cansignorio della Scala, had forged an alliance against him. A third of his men lay dead; every survivor bore wounds. It was time to bury their friends and a time to heal.

Lord Edward Despenser yielded the road ahead to Blackstone, honouring him so that he might lead the men.

Blackstone heeled the bastard horse forward.

He didn't look back.

AUTHOR'S NOTES

While Prince Lionel of Antwerp is often referred to by historians as the 'second son' of King Edward III of England, he is in fact the third son in terms of birth order among Edward's sons. Edward's second son, William of Hatfield, died in infancy.

When he travelled through Paris on his way to marry Violante Visconti, the widower was accompanied by Lord Edward Despenser, Knight of the Garter, and several hundred in his retinue, as well as Amadeus VI, Count of Savoy, who had returned from crusade against the Ottomans in time to join Prince Lionel in Paris. The marriage feast in Verona is recorded in history because of the extravagance of food served and the lavish gifts given to the Prince. Both served as a showcase for Galeazzo Visconti's enormous wealth.

When the Prince died in Alba Edward Despenser briefly thought that the Visconti had poisoned him, despite the loss of political influence that would have caused Galeazzo. Edward Despenser blamed Bernabò Visconti and joined the papal forces against him. Later, it was believed that his death was due to the excess of food he had consumed at the wedding's lavish feast.

Cansignorio della Scala ruled Verona and its surrounding

territories from 1359 to 1375. During his reign, he sought to maintain a balance of power between the neighbouring states and to protect Verona's interests. In the conflict between the Papal States and Bernabò Visconti in 1368, Cansignorio della Scala initially sided with the Pope's forces. Pope Urban V had formed an alliance against the Visconti, who were seen as a threat to the Papal States and other regional powers. However, Cansignorio's alliance with the Pope was short-lived. In *Rage of Swords* I foreshadowed Cansignorio's shift in allegiance by a year as I thought it reasonable that such a switch was already being considered. In 1369 he formed an alliance with Bernabò Visconti. This change of sides was likely motivated by the Scaligeri's long-standing rivalry with the Carraresi family of Padua, who were allied with the Papal States. This alliance with the Visconti helped to secure the Scaligeri's position and protect their territories from the Carraresi and other potential threats. However, it also put them at odds with the Papal States and their allies. I thought it served the story knowing that during the conflict between the Papal States and Bernabò Visconti in 1368–9, Cansignorio della Scala initially sided with the Pope's forces but later shifted his allegiance to form an alliance with the Visconti.

In the book I briefly mention the Marquis de Montferrat's son, Secondotto, when Blackstone arrives at Chivasso to provide a glimpse of the cruel eight-year-old child whose behaviour was considered extreme even in medieval days, and by those who knew him. As he grew older it is claimed by one historian that he liked to strangle boy servants. It was this monstrous child that poor Violante married nine years after Prince Lionel's death.

Prince Lionel of Antwerp, Duke of Clarence, was initially embalmed and buried in Pavia at Chiesa di San Pietro in Ciel d'Oro and later taken home to England to be buried at Clare Priory, Suffolk.

ACKNOWLEDGEMENTS

I AM always pleased to hear from my readers – both those new to Thomas Blackstone's journey and those who have been with him since the first book, *Master of War*. Do drop me a line on the various social media sites: I always like to hear from you and your ongoing support is appreciated. If you have any thoughts on your reading experience an author always welcomes a review on sites such as Amazon and Goodreads.

My heartfelt thanks to my amazing agent Isobel Dixon and everyone at Blake Friedmann Literary Agency. I am ever grateful for the attention to detail, patience and professionalism of my editor Richenda Todd. Ian McLean has once again done a wonderful job of going over the final manuscript, seeking out anything amiss. It's been a wonderful journey with Nic Cheetham and all of those who work so diligently at Head of Zeus/Bloomsbury Books, whose enthusiasm for Thomas Blackstone keep the *Master of War* series' momentum going forward. Many thanks also to Iris Homann and everyone at Rowohlt, my German publisher, who do a wonderful job producing the *Master of War* series and bringing the books to such an enthusiastic German readership with their excellent team.

Finally, but not least, a huge thank you to my readers and to all those who follow Thomas Blackstone's adventures and wait patiently for the next book. I hope you enjoy *Rage of Swords* and that the wait was worth it.

David Gilman
Devonshire
2025

ABOUT THE AUTHOR

DAVID GILMAN has enjoyed many careers, including paratrooper, firefighter, and photographer. An award-winning author and screenwriter, he is the author of the critically acclaimed Master of War series of historical novels, and was shortlisted for the Wilbur Smith Adventure Writing Prize for *The Last Horseman*. He was longlisted for the same prize for *The Englishman*, the first book featuring ex-French Foreign Legionnaire Dan Raglan. David lives in Devon.

Follow David on @davidgilmanuk,
www.davidgilman.com, and on Facebook
at davidgilman.author